**Alison Roberts** is a New Zealander, currently lucky enough to be living in the south of France. She is also lucky enough to write for the Mills & Boon Medical Romance line. A primary school teacher in a former life, she is now a qualified paramedic. She loves to travel and dance, drink champagne, and spend time with her daughter and her friends.

# THE DOCTOR'S WIFE
# FOR KEEPS

## &

# TWIN SURPRISE
# FOR THE ITALIAN DOC

BY
ALISON ROBERTS

MILLS & BOON

Published in Great Britain 2018
by Mills & Boon, an imprint of HarperCollins*Publishers*
1 London Bridge Street, London, SE1 9GF

© 2018 Alison Roberts

ISBN: 978-0-263-93334-5

MIX
Paper from
responsible sources
FSC® C007454

This book is produced from independently certified FSC™ paper
to ensure responsible forest management.
For more information visit www.harpercollins.co.uk/green.

Printed and bound in Spain
by CPI, Barcelona

# THE DOCTOR'S WIFE
# FOR KEEPS

BY
ALISON ROBERTS

**MILLS & BOON**

For Sarah, Luke and Brendan,
with lots of love and very fond memories of our
adventures in the Czech Republic. xx

# PROLOGUE

'I THINK WE'RE LOST.'

Kate Saunders slowed the SUV she was driving to take another hairpin bend on this alpine road that seemed to be going on for ever and getting narrower as the tall forest pressed in on both sides. She glanced sideways at her companion—her best friend and flatmate, Georgia.

'Whose bright idea was it to enter this international medical rescue competition? Oh, yeah...*yours*...'

'It's an adventure.' Georgia was grinning. 'Admit it—you're loving it already.'

Kate snorted, tipping her head a little to ease the crick in her neck. 'Road trips always sound more fun than they actually are. It's a hell of a long way from Scotland to the back of beyond in the Czech Republic. I've never even heard of the town we're trying to find.'

'Rakovi. It's a ski resort. And this is the biggest competition of its kind in the world. I've been hearing about it for years—ever since I became a paramedic.'

'Well, I've never heard of it.'

'That's because you're a doctor and your lot aren't as adventurous.'

'Hmm...' There was some truth in that. Kate had

been focused on her career from the moment she'd been accepted for medical school at the age of twenty two. Georgia had helped her celebrate her thirty-fifth birthday a few months ago and her idea of a gift had been to enter her in this competition as a doctor/paramedic team. She had already booked accommodation in London and Germany to break up the travel and, probably thanks to the bottle of excellent champagne they were sharing, it had seemed like a brilliant idea at the time.

Now she wasn't so sure.

'Have we even got out of Poland yet?'

'Ages ago. It's not far now.'

'We don't want to be late for registration.'

'Don't stress. They've got a couple of hundred teams from about twenty different countries to process. If we're a bit late it'll just mean we don't have to queue for so long.'

Kate slowed again to cross a narrow bridge over a tumbling mountain stream. 'I can't believe we're competing in such a huge field.'

'It's broken up into categories, remember. There'll be paramedic teams with their ambulances from all over Europe. I can't wait till the end where everybody drives in convoy around all the local villages with their lights and sirens on. I've heard it's a memorable experience. Then there are the doctors and medical student teams and other combinations. I just hope there's enough like us to give us our own category, otherwise we'll be competing against teams that have up to four members.'

'I just hope I don't make an idiot of myself. I'm a paediatrician, Georgie. I work in a nice, safe hospital with any amount of resources and backup. You would have been better to pick an emergency specialist.'

'You do plenty of emergency work. And you've lived with me long enough to qualify as an honorary paramedic. You've even been out on the road with me a few times. You'll be brilliant and who cares if we don't win? We're here to have fun, remember? To have an adventure and meet lots of new people and...' Georgia's grin was decidedly mischievous now. 'We're both single and gorgeous. Have you thought about how many men there are going to be at this thing?'

'*Georgie...*' Kate shook her head. 'You never give up, do you? You've only just got over the last disaster and you're ready to do it again?'

'Oh, I have no intention of falling for someone. What's that saying? The best way to get over a man is to get under another one?'

Kate had to laugh. And she had to admire Georgia's resilience. At least she kept trying and Kate hadn't even done that for quite some time. It was so disheartening when a relationship failed to live up to expectations and the goalposts of true love and that dream family and children of her own got shifted a little further away yet again.

'Casual sex has never appealed to me.'

'Yeah...you're so old school, Kate. An ultimate romantic. You really believe that you're going to see 'the one' across a crowded room and it'll be love at first sight and a happy-ever-after with a few bluebirds fluttering over the carpet of rose petals and...'

'Oh, stop it,' Kate growled. Her friend's tone was teasing but, disturbingly, there was an element of truth in the scene. Not the bluebirds, of course. Or the rose petals.

But, yeah…she did believe that 'the one' was out there somewhere and that happy-ever-afters were quite possible for the lucky few. And who knew? It wasn't beyond the realms of possibility that *he* might be amongst this huge, random gathering of people with a common interest.

A flicker of excitement that had nothing to do with the adventure of competing lifted her spirits noticeably. And with that flicker came a rush of affection for her friend. Poor Georgia had been through the mill when it came to men so it was no wonder she was a little on the bitter side at the moment.

'Just be careful, hon. Okay?'

'Of course.'

Kate had seen that innocent look before. It meant that she was hiding something.

'You have given up on that hare-brained scheme you came up with after that bastard, Rick, walked out, haven't you?'

'I have no idea what you're talking about.'

'Oh, yes, you do. The one where you gave up on men completely and were going to have a baby all by yourself?' As much as Kate adored children, she couldn't imagine choosing to have a family on her own. The whole package was the goal and there was a proper order to do it in. You fell in love, got married and *then* had a baby. Georgia was only a year older than she was. They still had time…didn't they?

'Well, obviously I haven't given up on men *completely*. And I'm over Rick. He's ancient history—like

all the others. Ooh, look…a signpost. We're only fifteen kilometres away.'

That flicker of excitement ignited into a small but
steady flame. Kate hadn't given up on men completely
either and maybe fate, in the form of Georgia's determination, had pushed her in the direction of this competition for a reason.

'Halleluiah.' Kate grinned at her friend. 'The end
is in sight.'

'Nah…the *beginning* is in sight.' Georgia stretched
her arms above her head and gave a whoop. 'Bring it on.'

# CHAPTER ONE

No way…

It *couldn't* be…

'Come on, Kate. You can get your T-shirt later. We need to register and then find our room.'

A firm nudge made Kate turn her head and start moving again. 'Sorry… I thought I saw someone I knew.'

'Who?'

'Luke. Luke Anderson. An old friend. We went through med school together.'

'Hmm…' Georgia was scanning the queues in front of a line of desks. 'Can you see what's on that sign?'

'The desks are divided into alphabetic sections according to the country the team is representing. "S" is over there.' This time it was Kate leading the way. She approved of such disciplined organisation and it boded well for a smoothly run competition. The people behind the desks were looking weary. How many hundreds of people had they processed already? There was still a queue in front of the section that included 'S'.

Kate looked around at the sea of people, many of whom were in the uniforms of their ambulance organisation, with bright orange or red overalls and jackets.

It was noisy and she could hear languages she couldn't identify. A lot of people seemed to know each other very well and enthusiastic greetings added to the aura of controlled chaos. At least she had a few minutes to take it all in as they waited their turn.

'So…this Luke…' Georgia raised an eyebrow. 'Is he good looking?'

'I guess…' Kate tried to recapture that fleeting glance to decide whether it was possible she had really seen him. 'Very tall. Dark hair. Brown eyes.'

'Oh… I *love* brown eyes. My favourite.'

Kate's breath came out in a huff. They were both women in their mid-thirties. Independent and successful. Were they really having a conversation that made them sound like boy-mad teenagers?

'I haven't seen him for five years. Since he got married.'

'Oh…' The tone was very different this time. Georgia's interest had evaporated.

For some reason that annoyed Kate. 'We were really good friends. We lost touch because his wife couldn't handle him having a female friend. I'd love to catch up. I don't even know what part of the world he's living in now. But he's a paediatric surgeon so it's pretty unlikely he'd come to something like this.'

'I'll bet he'd say the same thing if he thought he'd seen you.'

Kate couldn't argue with that. Not that there was any more time to even think about it because they'd reached the front of the queue. There were folders of documents to collect that included detailed instructions and maps. They received large identification numbers that they would have to wear pinned to their clothing at all times and coloured wristbands that were clipped on.

'These numbers go on your vehicle.' The official's English was excellent but heavily accented. 'These are your vouchers for meals and this is your room number. Go to the accommodation block and they will show you where to go. Don't forget the welcome ceremony and briefing at nineteen hundred hours. If you hurry, you should have time for a meal first.'

The ski resort sprawled over several levels on the steep hillside with a road that separated each level in a zigzag. A road that was jam packed with vehicles parked on both sides of it. The variety of colours was amazing. Red and white predominated but there were yellow and green emergency vehicles with various designs of reflective stripes and insignia. Amongst the dozens of ambulances and marked emergency Jeeps and SUVs—many of which were also decorated with flags and other accessories, Georgia's car looked small and plain. And it was parked far enough away to make it a mission to collect their bags.

'You've got a Scottish flag, haven't you?'

'Och, aye…' Georgia nodded. 'One for each front window. And a bagpipe-playing bear that we can attach to the front bumper. We can do that later, though. I'm *starving*…'

'I'll just put the vehicle number stickers on. It was one at the front and one at the back, wasn't it? Did they say which part of the windscreen it should go on?'

Georgia shook her head. 'Just make it visible. You can read the rules later.'

Kate frowned. 'I'll just put the front one on the dashboard for now. If we stick it in the wrong place, it might not come off.'

Georgia paused in her task of hauling their bags from the back to give Kate a loaded glance.

'You know, sometimes you make me feel like I'm out with my mother.'

'If it keeps you out of trouble then that's a good thing.'

'I'm a big girl, Kate. I *can* look after myself.' But Georgia was smiling now. 'It's a good thing you're here, though. We certainly won't get eliminated for breaking any rules. And, hey…how good is it that we've got our own category? There must be at least five other teams that have a doctor and one or two paramedics with them. Maybe one of them includes your friend.'

Kate pulled out the handle of her bag and started wheeling it down the road.

'Doubt it. It must have just been someone who looked a bit like him. I've seen a dozen tall men with dark hair since then.'

Because she'd been looking?

She was still looking, she realised as they lined up and presented their meal vouchers in exchange for a plate laden with stew and dumplings. There was a bar open in the dining area and many tables had people enjoying a beer or wine with their meals. So many tables. So many people.

She'd already decided Luke couldn't possibly be here so why was she scanning the room so carefully now?

'There's some space on that table.' Georgia led the way. 'Do you mind if we join you guys?'

'Please do.' The man's face lit up beneath sun-streaked blond hair as he looked at Georgia. 'I'm Dave. This is Ken and that's Sally, who's stuffing her face there.'

'You're from Australia, right?'

'No. New Zealand.' Dave sighed heavily. 'Everybody thinks our accent is the same but it really isn't.' He grinned at Georgia. 'No mistaking yours. You're Scottish.'

'I am. I like your uniforms. Are you paramedics?'

'Yeah… You guys?'

'I'm a paramedic. Kate's a doctor. Is this your first time here?'

'Sure is. Never seen anything like it.'

'Where are you based at home? City or country?'

'Auckland. Biggest city in the country. And up there in the top cities of the world to live in. You should come and visit sometime.'

'Oh? What's so great about Auckland?'

The conversation, as they swapped details about their home towns and talked about how little they knew of what was to happen tomorrow, was lively but Kate was only half listening.

Why was it so unsettling, she wondered, to be disappointed that she'd made a mistake? It wasn't as if Luke had ever been anything more than a friend.

On his side, anyway.

On her side, too, after she'd got over that silly crush. And it hadn't been that hard, had it?

Humiliating, maybe, when she'd felt invisible as anything more than a friend, but they had been very good friends and that was something special. Something that often lasted way longer than any romantic relationships. They'd studied together, competed fiercely to see could get better marks in exams and had supported each other in those first, nerve-racking encounters with real patients in real hospitals.

They'd kept in touch all through those early years of their careers after medical school, even though they'd ended up in different cities and she'd convinced herself that she was genuinely delighted when he'd fallen head over heels in love with the gorgeous Nadia—a nurse he'd met in his first year as a surgical registrar. She hadn't been the one for Luke but she'd cared enough about him to wish him complete happiness with the woman who'd been lucky enough to be chosen.

Okay, it had been more than a little hurtful when contact had ceased but she'd always hoped that, one day, when Nadia felt more secure, the friendship would somehow be rekindled. A hope that had been slowly evaporating over the years, however. She hadn't even thought about Luke for quite a long time. Until she'd thought she'd spotted him…

Maybe, when she got home, she'd find out where he was working these days. Drop him an email, even, and just say hi.

The plan was satisfying enough to enable her to put the distraction firmly to one side and tune in properly to the conversation around her. New Zealand was a place that had always fascinated her and she was keen to hear about what it was like to live and work there.

By the time she followed the others to get to the welcome ceremony and briefing, she had completely forgotten about Luke Anderson. It was taking more than enough concentration not to lose sight of Georgia or their new friends as they squeezed into a very crowded room.

'Excuse me…' She had to turn sideways to get past a group of medics wearing heavy coats with fluorescent stripes and rescue insignia. They were big men and maybe they hadn't heard her because one of them stepped back and pushed Kate into the person on the other side of the space she'd been trying to get through. She felt hands grip her arms as someone tried to prevent her falling.

'Oh, I'm so sorry.' Kate could feel her face reddening as she regained her balance.

'No problem. It's a bit of a squeeze in here, isn't it?'

Kate's jaw dropped as she lifted her head. She knew that voice *so* well…

'Oh, my God… *Kate?*'

A huge, dumb grin was spreading over her face but words had deserted her. Not that she needed them for a moment because Luke had enveloped her in a hug that was making it difficult to take a breath.

'Kate?'

The voice came from behind her and she turned as the tight hold loosened.

'Oh, thank goodness. I thought I'd lost you.'

'Georgie…this is my friend, Luke…'

Someone was tapping on a microphone, which triggered a screech of feedback that made people groan.

'Sorry about that but welcome, everybody… If we could have a bit of quiet, please?'

Kate shut up immediately but Luke didn't appear to have heard the request.

'What on earth are you doing here?'

'It was a birthday present,' she muttered. 'Long story…'

'*Shh,*' someone behind her hissed. 'We're trying to listen.'

Luke made an apologetic grimace but then winked at Kate.

'Later,' he mouthed, turning to peer over the heads of others to see who was speaking.

Kate started listening, too. After the welcome speech and a list of how many countries were participating, another speaker got up to share important information.

'Between eleven-thirty and midnight tonight, you will all receive your list of events. You will be given the GPS coordinates of the scenario and a start time. Please be there at least ten minutes before that time. If you are late, you will not be admitted and you will not be marked in that section of the competition.'

Georgia elbowed Kate. 'No chance of that happening,' she whispered. 'Not when I'm with you.'

The dig at her compulsion to follow directions to the letter failed to bother Kate. How could it when she was feeling so unexpectedly good?

She had Luke standing on her other side and, every so often, they glanced sideways—apparently at the exact same moment—to catch each other's gaze. And every time it happened, the feeling got stronger.

It was like going home. Or back to a beloved place, like where you'd had your summer holidays all through childhood. A feeling of something so familiar you could relax completely. Of something that had the promise of delivering the same good things it always had.

And, yes…there was something more.

A flicker of that initial crush, perhaps? A realisation that none of her own relationships had ever worked well enough because that flicker had never been fanned into something that had felt as meaningful as even her friendship with Luke had been?

'The rally covers a period of twenty-four hours and you will have both a daytime and a night-time section. There will be twelve tasks for you to complete but there will be breaks in your schedule during which you can take meals or have a rest.

Time to catch up properly with an old friend, perhaps? The feeling of anticipation took on a softer edge for Kate. A warm glow, even.

There were pictures on a big screen on the wall now. There was a map of the local area as an official explained how far they might have to travel to get to some of the scenarios and what local landmarks and hazards to watch out for.

Finally, there were reminders of the rules.

'The competition is held in English. All instructions will be in this language and your patients are fluent enough to answer any relevant questions. The officials grading your performance will also be doing this in English and teams will be marked down for communication in any other language.'

Kate caught Luke's eye again. Surely that gave them a distinct advantage over many of the teams here? For the first time, she could feel a kick of a desire to do well. To win, even?

Maybe that was down to the gleam she'd caught in

Luke's gaze. They'd always set out to see who could better the other. And then they would always celebrate the winner without any suggestion of animosity. With a dollop of pride, even...

'And while we're on the subject of communication,' the official continued, 'it is forbidden for any team to discuss the scenarios with other teams until the competition is finished so please be careful. Anyone found to be using information they have received in advance will be eliminated.'

'What section are you in?' she asked as soon as the formalities were over. 'All doctors? Doctors and med students?'

'Doctor/paramedic.' Luke put his arm around the man standing beside him. 'This is Matteo Martini. Italian paramedic extraordinaire.'

'Ooh...' Georgia had moved closer. 'A martini? Yes, please... Extra-dry—with an olive.'

They all laughed. 'This is Georgie,' Kate said. 'My paramedic partner.'

She caught Luke's gaze again and this time the gleam took her right back to her student days. Standing in line outside an examination room with both of them knowing how hard they'd studied and both of them determined to be top of the class.

It had become a joke amongst their fellow students about whose turn it was to come first because they were such an equal match. There was never much of a gap between their marks.

'My turn, I think.' Kate grinned.

'I don't think so.' But then Luke frowned. 'Who got first last time? Good grief...it's so long ago, I can't even remember.'

'Finals,' Kate growled. 'And it was you.' She was scowling at him now. 'You don't need to look so smug about it.'

Luke adjusted his face. 'It was a long time ago.'

'Mmm.' Kate held his gaze. 'Too long.'

They were being herded out of the room now. A glance over her shoulder showed Kate that Georgia and Matteo were following so they went with the flow. It seemed that everybody was heading for the bar to wait until their scenario list and start times were handed out.

'So how *are* you?' Kate had to raise her voice to be heard over the babble of so many languages around them. 'I haven't seen you since your wedding.'

'I know. I'm sorry…' There was something in Luke's expression that suggested he was sorry for more than the lack of contact. 'Can I get you a drink?'

'Just a soda water,' Kate said. 'I need to keep a clear head for tomorrow.'

'Beer for me,' Matteo said. 'Georgie?'

The mischievous expression on Georgia's face made Kate suppress a sigh. It was clear she was enjoying the handsome Italian's company but surely she wasn't going to be obvious enough ask for a martini? The sigh came out as one of relief as Georgia spoke.

'White wine,' she said. 'Sparkling, if they've got it. I do love a bit of sparkle.'

Matteo raised an eyebrow. 'A taste for champagne, yes? Classy…' He went to help Luke carry the drinks while the girls found a place to sit down.

'You want me to take Matteo somewhere else?' Georgia asked. 'So that you and Luke can have some alone time?'

'Don't be daft.' The words came out sounding more

irritated than Kate had intended. 'We're friends. Or we were. It's so long since I've seen him that we're practically strangers now.'

She averted her gaze as she finished her sentence. It was so far from the truth. But she couldn't admit to Georgia how it made her feel to see Luke again. She hadn't quite got her own head around it yet.

It seemed that Luke had followed her example and got a non-alcoholic drink for himself as well. Clearly he wanted to be as competitive as possible tomorrow as well. Kate had to hide a smile as they touched glasses.

Game on…

'Cheers,' she said. 'I have to say, you're probably the last person I would have expected to run into here. Have you changed specialties and gone into emergency medicine?'

'No. I'm still a paediatric surgeon but I do specialise in trauma cases. It's Matt's fault I'm here.'

'Snap,' Kate told him. 'Georgia entered me as a birthday present. She said I needed some adventure in my life.'

'And do you?' There was a question in Luke's eyes that went far deeper than the amused query.

Was her life going the way she had planned it out so carefully? Was she happy?

She was saved having to find an answer by Georgia leaning closer. 'So how do you two boys know each other?'

'I did a stint in a hospital in Milan,' Luke told her. 'I got lost one day trying to find my apartment and this ambulance pulled up beside me. Matt was driving.'

'I'd seen him in the emergency department of the hospital,' Matteo put in. 'I'd stayed with a child I'd brought in who'd been hit by a car and Luke had been called for a surgical consultation.'

'He gave me a ride home,' Luke continued. 'And then he said he'd pick me up again after he finished his shift because he knew where the best beer in Milan was.'

'Italy,' Kate breathed. 'How exciting. Did Nadia love living there?'

Matteo was staring at Luke. 'Who's Nadia?'

'My ex-wife.'

'Ah…the cheating cow?'

'That's the one.'

It was Kate's turn to stare at Luke. 'Oh, my God… you and Nadia split up?'

Luke was eyeing Matteo's beer as if he was regretting his decision on drinks. 'Yep.'

'But…'

Everybody turned to stare at *her* and Kate bit her lip. 'Sorry,' she muttered. 'It's just that you guys were so in love…'

Luke snorted. 'Yeah…well, I won't be making that mistake again, believe *me*.'

'It kind of cures you,' Matteo offered. 'When the wife you love turns out to have been shagging every other man she met. I'm with Luke on this one. If someone cheated on me or lied to me like that, I would never let her name pass my lips again either.'

Kate wanted the floor to open up and swallow her. Poor Luke… And she'd made things worse by opening her big mouth and reminding him of something it was obvious he would rather forget. Good grief…he hadn't even told Matteo his wife's name? Just referred to her as 'the cheating cow'?

And something else was trying to push its way into her consciousness.

The fact that Luke was single again?

No. She was too old and wise to allow any seed to grow in that long-ago abandoned space. She'd been romantically invisible back then. Why would that have changed?

What needed to change was the subject. Fast.

'How long were you in Milan?'

'Two years. And then I won a consultancy position six months ago. In Edinburgh.'

'No *way*...'

Luke blinked. 'What's so surprising about that? Did you think I was going to stay a registrar for ever?'

Kate shook her head. 'It's not that. I'm a consultant too. In Glasgow.'

Luke laughed. 'You mean we've been living fifty miles from each other and we had to travel halfway across Europe to catch up?'

'Not even fifty miles. Georgia and I live in Brackenburn—halfway between Glasgow and Edinburgh. I work in the Eastern Infirmary in Glasgow and Georgie's a paramedic at a rescue base in Edinburgh.'

'Do you have helicopters?' Matteo asked Georgia.

'Yes. Two. I don't get to go up in them very often, though. Only when they're short of staff. You?'

'I've been a flight paramedic for eight years now. I love it...'

Kate and Luke weren't listening to the conversation between their partners. People around them were starting to move, which meant that the time for finding out exactly what tomorrow would bring was getting close.

But they were both sitting very still. So much had

happened in the years since they'd last seen each other. Kate wanted to know more and she was saddened by more than a hint of bitterness in Luke's tone when he'd confirmed that his marriage was over. How could that have happened to one of the nicest people she had ever known?

Maybe something of what she was thinking was showing in her face.

'What about you, Katy?' Luke asked quietly. 'You happily married now? Got a couple of kids at home? That was the plan, wasn't it?'

Kate dropped her gaze. There was something a little shameful about admitting that she had failed to achieve her most important personal goals. She didn't say anything, simply shaking her head as she reached for her glass to finish her drink.

'We'd better get going,' Matteo said. 'It's time...'

Kate stood up, more than happy to leave this conversation behind for the moment.

But Luke stayed where he was for a moment, staring up at Kate.

'It was your birthday in March,' he said.

'It always is.' Kate grinned. 'Two weeks after yours, in fact.'

'Yeah...so we both turned thirty-five.'

Was he trying to rub in the fact that she was still single? That parenthood was probably still years away? That she might get into her forties and get past the point where it might be even possible?

She could feel defensive hackles begin to rise. Maybe, thanks to his own unfortunate experience, Luke had changed from being the nicest person in the world.

But he was grinning. And he didn't have to say a

word for Kate to realise that he hadn't been trying to remind her that time was ticking on.

He was reminding her of something else. Something they'd agreed on after that legendary night of celebrating their final results as they'd graduated as fully fledged doctors. Something she hadn't thought about in at least five years.

Because it had become redundant the moment that Luke had got married.

Surely he didn't think it could be reinstated because he was single again?

No. Kate turned away with a dismissive shake of her head.

'The pact' was no longer in existence.

# CHAPTER TWO

'I THINK WE'RE HERE.'

Kate looked at the two-storeyed village house they were parked in front of. The door was shut and there was nobody to be seen trying to flag down medical assistance. She had programmed the satellite navigation system with all the GPS coordinates of their daytime tasks herself, however, so she was confident that no mistakes had been made.

'We've got ten minutes. We'll knock on the door at precisely seven forty-five. You might want to turn off the light.' The portable flashing light on the top of the SUV was plugged into the car's cigarette lighter. 'We don't want to flatten the battery while we're on scene.'

'Roger that.' Georgia pulled the plug from the socket. She smiled at Kate but then her face scrunched into a grimace. 'First scenario. You nervous?'

'I wish we had some idea of what we're going to. The name doesn't give us much of a clue, does it? "Sweetheart"?'

'Maybe it's got something to do with sugar. A diabetic emergency, maybe?'

'Good thinking.'

'Or…' Georgia wiggled her eyebrows. 'Maybe it's

a young couple who are madly in love and they were having morning sex in the shower and one of them has slipped over and hit their head on the side of the bath.'

Kate didn't want to think about people who were so crazy in love they couldn't keep their hands off each other. She'd never experienced that kind of love. Why was it that the balance always seemed to be tipped far too much in one direction? The people she fell in love with never felt the same way but if she was only mildly interested she could guarantee that the guy would fall head over heels for her and become suffocatingly attentive.

She checked her watch. 'Five minutes.'

'Do you think another team is still in there? Luke and Matteo, maybe?'

Kate didn't want to think about Luke, either. Not when thinking about the past could be a distraction. She had every intention of beating his team in this competition. It was her turn, after all. Payback for him getting better marks in finals.

He'd been so gracious about that, hadn't he? Toasting her with that excellent champagne he'd brought with him. The first bottle, that was. The second bottle had been a bad idea because it had culminated in concocting 'the pact' but the evening had been all about celebrating their graduation to start with. And each other's success.

*'I owe it all to you, Katy. If you hadn't been my study buddy and I hadn't been trying so hard to keep up with your brilliance for the last few years, I'd probably have been at the bottom of the class.'*

Not true, of course. Luke had one of the sharpest minds she'd ever had the pleasure of arguing with and, if she'd had the edge on remembering everything she learned, Luke had been better at the practical skills in those days. More confident, with surprisingly nimble fingers. It was no surprise that he had become a surgeon and Kate had no doubt that he was excelling in his field. Did those skills extend to an environment outside of an operating theatre? How much had Matteo taught him about front-line emergency procedures?

'Time?'

'Oh, help. It's seven forty-six.' How had *that* happened?

Both Kate and Georgia leapt from the vehicle, slamming the front doors to go around to the back and collect the well-stocked kits that Georgia's Edinburgh ambulance station had provided for them. She'd been distracted, Kate realised, by thinking about Luke.

It wasn't going to happen again.

'We're early.'

Luke grunted. Eight-fifteen was their start time for the scenario with the odd name of 'Sweetheart' but he'd been determined not to risk disqualification by being late at any of the tasks they'd been set for the day. Especially now, when he had the added incentive of competing with Kate.

Her turn to win?

He found himself smiling. Whatever the result, this competition had just become a lot more fun.

The smile faded, however, as he looked around them at the quiet street dotted with small, village houses. 'Doesn't look like much.' A bit disappointing, in fact. He'd expected to have something like a car versus pedestrian scenario for the coordinates in the middle of this small town. 'You sure we're in the right place?'

'*Sì. Assolutamente.*' Matteo pointed through the windscreen. 'That car parked over there is a competitor. It's got the numbers. And a light on the roof, like ours. And the flags are...'

'Scottish,' Luke murmured. There was only one team representing Scotland here and he knew who that was.

That smile was resurfacing. How astonishing had it been to run into Kate here, of all places in the world?

And how good had it been to see her again?

It made him realise that he'd been lonely ever since he'd taken up his new position in Edinburgh. He'd missed his mate, Matteo, who'd been so good for him during his time in Milan as he'd licked his wounds after escaping the disaster that his marriage had been. Focusing so completely on work in Edinburgh had left no time to try and make new friends, which was probably why he'd taken up Matteo's invitation to join him for this competition.

And while it had been great to catch up with his mate, seeing Kate again was on a whole new level. They had history—heart-warming history—that made her like family.

He hadn't thought about that 'pact' for years.

Not until last night, that was, when Kate's avoidance of answering his query about whether she was married with kids yet had reminded him of how much time had passed. Plenty of time to have achieved the 'plan'.

The plan they'd discussed that night after graduation, over that really great bottle of champagne.

'*Me? I'm going to start my stellar career and find*

*the woman of my dreams to share the glory. What about you, Katy?'*

*'Oh... I'm going to have a brilliant career, too. And I'm going to find the man of my dreams and get married and have a couple of the world's most gorgeous children...'*

And then they'd polished off that second bottle and things had become a whole lot more mushy. The 'plan' had morphed into the 'pact'.

*'You're my best mate, Katy. I love you to bits.'*

*'Love you, too, mate.'*

*'Tell you what...'*

*'What?'*

*'If we haven't found those dream people by the time we're...oh...say, thirty-five...let's marry each other.'*

*'Why would you want to marry me?'*

*'I might be desperate by then.'*

*'Cheers, mate.'*

*'Oh, come on...it was a joke.'*

*'Your idea of getting married is a joke.'*

*'No... I'm serious. Let's make a pact. If we're both still single when we're thirty-five, we'll marry each other. Okay?'*

She'd drained her glass of champagne, pushed her hair out of her eyes and given him a curiously intent stare. And then she'd done it. Agreed to the pact.

*'Okay. You're on.'*

*'So it's a pact? Signed and sealed?'*

*'It's a pact. But now I need to go to sleep.'*

Ancient memories but good ones.

Yes. It was extraordinarily good to see Kate again. Best of all, he had discovered that she lived close enough to his new home town that they would be able to see each other whenever they both had some free time.

Unless she had a boyfriend, of course. Thanks to Matteo's conversation with Georgia last night, he now knew that Kate wasn't married and that she was sharing a house with Georgia, but that didn't mean there wasn't someone else in the picture. Why wouldn't there be? Kate was gorgeous, with that impressive intelligence shining from those bright, blue eyes. And he liked that her hair was a bit longer these days. The blonde bob almost touched her shoulders and had a bit of a swing to it.

Not that it would be a problem if she had a significant other in her life. It could mean that Luke's circle of friends was about to expand, in fact. Maybe they could even double date. He and Matteo had had a lot of fun doing that in Milan. Nothing serious, mind you. Matteo might be dead keen to settle down and start a family of his own with the woman of his dreams but Luke had abandoned any such fairy-tale long ago. At about the same moment he'd learned that his marriage was a complete sham. As he'd remarked so bitterly to Kate, he had no intention of ever losing his head—or his heart—over a woman again.

Still…he wasn't getting any younger. It would be a shame to miss out completely and spend the rest of his life caring for other people's children…

The noise coming from the other side of the door was enough to make Kate and Georgia share a startled glance.

A party? At this time of the day?

Georgia pounded on the door. 'Ambulance,' she yelled.

There was no response, so she opened the door. They walked straight into a living room and there were at least half a dozen people, talking loudly enough to hear each other over the music. A bottle of vodka was being passed around and glasses clinked together. Nobody took the least bit of notice of the newcomers.

'Hello…' An earlier coin toss had decided that Kate was taking the lead role in this first scenario and she approached the nearest person. 'Did someone call for an ambulance?'

'Not me,' the young man replied. 'Hey…' He put his arm around a young woman. 'Let's dance…'

Kate blinked. This was nothing like she had expected. Where were the officials that would be judging their performance? Where was someone who looked remotely like a patient?

Georgia's eyes narrowed as she caught Kate's glance and she raised her voice loudly enough to be heard by everyone.

'*Oi…*'

The vodka carrier lowered the bottle. Heads turned in surprise.

'Someone called an ambulance,' Georgia said sternly. 'Who was it?'

'Oh…' There was a man sitting in the corner of the room, leaning on the wall. 'That was me. My girlfriend is upstairs. She's lying down because she has a bad stomach ache.'

'Anything else we should know?'

'No. I don't think so.' The man raised a glass as he smiled at them. 'Oh, she is pregnant. Is that important?'

Turning swiftly, they raced up a narrow set of stairs to find themselves in a bedroom and here it was. The scenario…

Two judges with clipboards were standing by. A young woman was sitting on a bed and she was holding a manikin of a newborn infant wrapped in a T-shirt.

'Check mum and get her history,' Kate told Georgia. 'I'll check the baby.'

The young mother didn't want to let go of her baby.

'How long ago was the baby born?'

'Only a minute…maybe two…'

'Have you heard it cry?'

'No. *No*… Please don't take my baby away…'

'It's okay,' Georgia told her. 'We just want to help you. Kate's a baby doctor.'

Kate moved the folds of the T-shirt to reveal the baby's face. The cord was wrapped tightly around the baby's neck.

'The baby is blue,' one of the judges said.

Kate scooped the manikin from the patient's arms. She turned to find that Georgia had stopped her examination of the mother for the moment. She'd laid a towel on the floor and had the kit opened, with the paediatric resuscitation gear that Kate would need within easy reach. A suction bulb, a tiny bag mask unit and tubes in case intubation was necessary.

'No significant haemorrhage from the mother,' Georgia told her. 'And she has a radial pulse.'

Kate nodded approvingly. 'Thanks.' If the mother had a radial pulse it indicated that her blood pressure was adequate and that meant they could both focus on saving the life of this baby.

She laid the baby on the towel and positioned its head to ensure the airway was clear.

'Can I feel a pulse?' Kate asked swiftly, her fingers now on the baby's neck.

'The pulse is thirty,' the judge said.

'Can I see or feel any movements of respiration?' Kate already knew what the answer was likely to be. This infant hadn't cried and its colour meant that it was receiving no more oxygen than the umbilical cord was hopefully still providing.

'The baby is not breathing,' the judge confirmed.

Kate gave five puffs of oxygen through the bag mask unit and then started CPR, which was needed even though there was a pulse to be felt. The heart rate was too slow and the baby wasn't breathing on its own yet.

She handed the bag mask to Georgia, who had positioned herself at the baby's head.

'Three to one?'

Georgia nodded. With only two fingers on the baby's chest, Kate kept her compressions gentle but swift. After every three compressions, she paused for a moment to allow Georgia to administer a puff of air. At the same time, she kept an eye on the mother, reassuring her that they were doing all they could and watching for any signs of a post-partum haemorrhage that they would need to manage.

Every thirty seconds, she checked what the baby's heart rate was. It crept up to forty and then sixty.

'The heart rate is now over eighty,' the judge informed them after a few minutes.

'Colour?'

'Getting pink.'

'Breathing?'

'Yes, she's breathing. She's crying now.' The judge was smiling. 'Well done.'

Kate put the baby back into its mother's arms and wrapped them both warmly. 'Keep her against your skin,' she said.

'Is she going to be all right?'

'She's going to be fine.' Kate smiled. 'Congratulations. You have a beautiful baby daughter.'

The young woman was a very good actor. Kate could swear she had tears of relief in her eyes as she thanked her rescuers and cuddled her newborn. The whole scenario had felt so real that Kate found she was having an emotional response of her own. One that she had had many times in her career—the sheer wonder of a new life being brought into the world and...

And envy of the mother who got to hold it and know it was her own?

Good grief. The baby was plastic and the whole scenario, however brilliantly acted, was not real. While this competition set out to test and even improve the skills of the participants, it was nothing more than a game. Kate needed to step back and not become so involved with the stories or she would be too exhausted to be a good partner for Georgia by the time the night tasks came along.

'That was awesome,' Georgia said, as soon as they shut the front door behind them again. '*You* were awesome. I think we smashed that one.'

'We certainly saved the baby. And the judges looked happy.' Kate checked her watch and then opened the back hatch of the car. 'We've only got ten minutes to locate our next task. We'd better get a move on.'

But Georgia had paused. She was waving. 'Look—there's Matteo and Luke in that car. They must be next.'

'I wonder how long it'll take before they figure out their patient isn't downstairs.' Kate felt a sudden urge to help Luke out. To give him a clue…

'It's no wonder it's against the rules to talk about the scenarios until it's all over.' Georgia slung her kit into the back. 'And I got the feeling that Matteo is as much a stickler for the rules as you are, Kate. You two would get on very well.'

'I'm not here on a man hunt. What's the matter? Don't you like him?'

Georgia shrugged. 'He's cute but there are a lot of fish in this particular sea and today is not the day to be casting my net.'

Kate snorted. She knew Georgia quite well enough to know that she wasn't the least bit serious about finding a casual sexual partner just for fun. This was just bravado, that was all. Was she trying to prove to the world that she was over the last disaster and more than ready to move on?

Pausing for a moment, before climbing into the driver's seat, Kate turned her head to look at the car parked a little further up the road. She lifted her hand in greeting and, by the instant response as he raised his, she knew that Luke had been watching her.

A weird frisson of something she couldn't identify rippled through her belly. Was it a little disturbing to have someone from her past suddenly appear in her life like this? As if Luke was some kind of ghost?

Or was it just nice to have reconnected with an old and very dear friend?

Yeah…that had to be it. Because the feeling was too pleasant to be a warning.

'Look…they're coming out of the house.'

Luke found himself hunkering down in his seat a little. It was pure coincidence that they were the next team for this particular scenario but, oddly, it felt like he was pushing himself back into Kate's life or something. Stalking her, even? Was she as pleased to see him as he'd been to see her?

Maybe not. It had been Georgia who'd spotted them and waved. Kate had seemed intent on putting her gear back into the car and checking her watch. Of course she would be making sure she was going to be on time for the next task—that was so like Kate. Responsible and reliable. And she was taking this contest seriously, as she did everything she became involved with.

It looked as though she was going to get in the car and simply drive off, but then she paused and looked straight at him and there was a smile to go with her wave.

Luke let out a breath he hadn't realised he'd been holding as he raised his hand in response. A sigh of something like relief as something clicked back into place. The connection of their friendship, perhaps, where he didn't have to worry about how his actions might be interpreted. A place he could relax in and simply be himself.

'Be nice to have an idea of what we're heading into,' he said. 'They weren't giving away any clues, were they?'

'And neither should they,' Matteo said sternly. 'That would be dishonest.'

'Not exactly.' Matteo liked to have his English improved. 'Dishonesty is when you fail to tell the truth. Breaking the rules of the competition to give someone else an advantage would be dishonourable rather than dishonest.'

'Hmm…' Matteo absorbed the correction. 'They are both unacceptable.'

'Too right they are,' Luke agreed.

The first scenario was initially confusing but, as soon as they discovered that the party was a red herring, the two men worked well on their paediatric resuscitation. In the next task, they found a man who'd summoned an ambulance because of sudden back pain and nausea. Diagnosing a case of kidney stones was easy but there was a twist in the case because the man had an anaphylactic allergic reaction to the morphine they administered for pain relief.

The twist was unexpected but Matteo spotted the first symptoms within seconds and they both reacted swiftly, attaching a bag of fluids to the IV line already in place and drawing up and administering drugs to counteract the reaction. Then they had to answer questions from one of the judges about which of the available hospitals they would be transferring their patient to.

'Hospital A,' Luke told them. 'They have an internal medicine department and an intensive care unit and they are the closest.'

'And what is the most important information to pass on about your patient?'

'That he has a previously undiscovered allergy to

morphine. We will write it on his notes and make sure the information is received by everyone we speak to. We will also advise the patient that it would be a good idea to wear a medic alert bracelet from now on.'

'That was good.' Matteo slapped Luke on the back as they left the house. 'I might not have thought of recommending the bracelet.'

'I was too slow to spot the change in our patient's condition. Well done, you.'

Matteo grinned at him. 'We make a good team.'

'We've got a break now, haven't we? About an hour?'

'We should use it to do the driving test.'

'Okay.' The driving test was something they could do at any point of the day. A gravelled area beside the river that ran through this village had been cordoned off. A line of orange road cones marked the test area. They could see an ambulance completing the test as they arrived, clouds of dust billowing as it snaked around the cones at high speed and then came to a sudden halt between the cones marking the end of the course.

Another car was waiting for its turn.

The car with the Scottish flags.

'Cute.' Matteo grinned. 'I didn't notice that before.'

Luke raised his eyebrows. 'You mean Georgia? Or Kate?' He wasn't sure he liked the idea of Matteo being attracted to Kate. Then he shook the reaction off. Why not? Matteo was a great guy and the best friend he'd had since Kate had vanished from his life. He'd make some lucky woman an ideal husband and father for her children and, if Kate felt the same way, he should do his best to make it happen.

But Matteo was laughing. 'Oh, the girls are both cute but that wasn't what I was looking at. Have you seen what is tied to the front of their car?'

No. Because Luke had been looking at Kate who was standing beside the car, talking to Georgia who was in the driver's seat. He glanced at the stuffed toy bear that was wearing a kilt and holding a set of bagpipes.

Matteo rolled down his window and pointed to the toy. 'He is going to get dirty, I think.'

'All part of the fun,' Georgia called back. 'Which one of you is going to do the driving? You're only allowed one person in the vehicle.'

Georgia was clearly the one doing the test for their team. Luke glanced at Matteo and unclipped his seat belt.

'You do it,' he said. 'You've got far more experience with emergency driving skills than I have. I'll wait with Kate.'

'Cool.' Matteo was already focussed on what Georgia was doing to see what his turn would involve.

Luke walked over to where Kate was standing, well away from where the dust clouds would drift.

'How's it all going?' he asked.

'Great.' Kate's expression was animated and she opened her mouth again as if she couldn't wait to tell him about something but then it snapped shut and the excitement faded into disappointment. 'But we can't talk about it yet.'

'No.' It was a moment longer before Luke turned away from watching her face. Did she have any idea how much of what she was thinking was revealed in how quickly her expressions could change? He'd forgotten that about conversations with Kate. Forgotten how entertaining it was.

They both watched Georgia as she careened through the serpentine, knocking over a couple of cones.

'She's a bit wild.'

'Enthusiastic,' Kate conceded. 'But she'll get another go. The team before us had three goes.'

So they had a few minutes, then. And nothing to talk about?

'Where did you say that you're working in Glasgow? At the Western?'

'No. The Eastern. We're a specialised maternity and paediatric hospital. Best PICU in Scotland.'

Luke nodded. 'Yes…some of our surgical cases have been transferred there. Are you based in PICU?'

'No. I'm on the wards as a senior paediatric registrar. I do the occasional shift in Emergency as well.'

'Are you happy?'

Kate's eyes widened. 'With the job? Of course. I've always loved working with kids.'

Luke wanted to know what that flicker in her eyes suggested. That she wasn't happy with her life away from work?

'I remember,' was all he said. 'You had a rapport with small people right from the start. How come you haven't got some of your own now? You never said last night…'

'Huh? Some of my own what?'

'Kids.'

'No.' Kate's gaze slid away from his to watch Georgia's second attempt at the course. 'I will, though. One day. It's certainly still part of the grand plan.'

There was a wistful note in her voice. A flick of a

glance that made him wonder if she was hearing the echoes of that champagne-doused conversation. Remembering his plan to have a stellar career and find the woman of his dreams to share the glory with?

His breath came out in a soft snort. Ah, well…he was well on the way to the career he'd dreamed of, at least. He flicked a glance back at Kate.

'So you've got a potential father lined up?'

Kate shaded her eyes against the sun. 'That's better, Georgia, but you're too slow now…'

'A partner?' Luke persisted. 'A boyfriend? Any kind of significant other?'

Kate sighed, sounding a little exasperated. 'No.'

Luke was silent for a moment, digesting the information, as Georgia circled back to where the officials were standing. They seemed to be having a discussion about whether she would have another attempt.

So Kate was single.

This was good, he decided. It meant that there were no barriers to them spending some time together and he didn't have to find someone so that they could double date.

This was more than good. It was excellent.

'And you're thirty-five…' Oh, help. Had he said that aloud?

Judging by Kate's dismissive snort, she had heard the impulsive statement.

'I can't believe you even remember that, given how drunk you were at the time.'

Kate had been just as enthusiastic about opening that second bottle of champagne. And *she* obviously remembered the pact…

'Anyway, it's null and void now. You got married.'

'Hey... I made a mistake.' Luke kept his tone light. 'You don't need to rub my nose in it.'

'Sorry.' Kate offered him a smile. 'Good thing you didn't have kids, I guess. Or did you?'

'No. Thank goodness. It was a clean—and complete—breakup.'

There was a moment's silence. Georgia was lining up to have what would probably be her last attempt at the driving test. Matteo was leaning out of his window, watching carefully.

Kate was also watching carefully but Luke couldn't resist the opportunity to tease her a little.

'The pact didn't have any sub-clauses that I remember,' he said. 'Didn't we solemnly declare that if we were both still single when we were thirty five, we would marry each other?'

The glance Kate gave him over her shoulder was dismissive. 'Thanks, but I intend to give it a bit more time. I haven't given up on true love yet. My soul mate is out there somewhere—I just haven't found him yet.'

Luke had to groan. 'You don't really believe in that, do you? Finding 'the one'?'

He could see her shoulders stiffen. And her voice was cool. 'Maybe I want what you and Nadia had.'

'No.' The word came out with unexpected vehemence. 'You don't.'

'It was great when it started, though, wasn't it? I'd never seen you so happy.'

There was that wistful note again and Luke's brain broke the rules and dredged up a memory of what it had been like to be so in love. How magic it had been. He shut down the memory instantly. He didn't need that kind of magic in his life now because that was all it was. A spell. One that could be reversed with no more than a click of someone's fingers to leave devastation in its wake.

Kate broke the silence. Maybe she realised she'd stirred up something unpleasant for him because her tone was gentle.

'You just found it with the wrong person,' she said.

'And you think you can find the right one?'

'I hope so.'

'How will you know?' Luke was genuinely curious.

'I don't know exactly,' Kate admitted. 'I guess I'll have to trust my instincts.'

'Good luck with that.' Luke was more than happy to leave this conversation. He was relieved to see that Georgia was driving back towards them, passing Matteo who went to take his position at the start. 'I really hope you'll find him,' he added. 'And that you'll live happily ever after.'

Kate smiled at him. 'So you agree that the pact is null and void, then?'

Luke shrugged. 'I'm over the whole marriage thing, anyway. Been there, got the T-shirt. Friendship's better.' He smiled back at Kate. 'Seems to last a lot longer, too.'

He could see sympathy in Kate's eyes. And something more. Something warm.

'You're right. True friendship is the most important thing in the world.' Her breath came out in a sigh as she smiled again. 'It's really good to see you again, Luke.'

'Likewise. We'll have to make sure we don't lose touch when we get back home. I'm still a fish out of water in Scotland. I haven't had time to meet anybody, apart from the people I work with, yet. I haven't been anywhere or seen anything, either.'

'I haven't done much sightseeing myself,' Kate told him, as Georgia joined them. 'I'm sure there are some great places to go in Scotland.'

'Are you kidding?' Georgia sounded offended. 'It's the most beautiful country in the world. We've got the most gorgeous lakes and forests and more castles than could ever wish for.' She grinned. 'The weather can be a bit grey and wet, of course, but it's summer now. You'll get at least three days of sunshine.'

'It's a plan, then,' Kate said. 'The first day we both have off, we'll go and find something to see.'

'Even if it's not one of the three sunny days?'

Kate laughed. 'I don't mind rain. You get to find a lovely old pub with a roaring open fire and have a long lunch.'

The sun was shining on them right now and Luke was feeling good. That unpleasant reminder of failure in his personal life was well buried again and the future was suddenly looking a lot brighter.

He had the promise of expanding his horizons. Of a new country to explore and company that he knew would make it a lot more fun. Waving Kate and Georgia off as they headed for their next task, he found himself smiling.

He was even hoping that it would rain on that day off. He was looking forward to one of those long lunches.

# CHAPTER THREE

THE STEW AND potato dumplings on offer for lunch were rapidly becoming unappetisingly familiar.

Not that Georgia was bothered.

'I'm starving,' she told Kate as they handed over their vouchers and found a place to sit in the dining area. 'I feel like I've been on a full shift already and we're only a third of our way through the competition. At least we get a break after this. I'm going to try and catch a nap.'

Kate wasn't that bothered either. She was barely tasting her food, in fact.

After they'd eaten, they wandered outside and found a grassy patch to lie on under a shady tree. Georgia promptly closed her eyes and gave every appearance of having fallen asleep but Kate found herself staring up at the play of light on leaves dancing in a soft breeze.

The pact had been dismissed.

It had been a relief not to have to argue any more about any lingering validity to that vow they'd made but, oddly, there was a feeling curiously like disappointment in the wake of that relief.

Why?

She'd made such a determined effort to get past that

crush when she'd first met Luke. To get over the heart-break of watching him get attracted to other women. She'd only ever been one of his close circle of friends and, in the end, she'd embraced that position in his life because it was a whole lot better than not having him in *her* life.

He'd never seen her as anything more than a friend, she knew that for sure. Such a good friend that those around them at medical school had commented more than once that they were perfect for each other and that they should make it official, but both Kate and Luke had laughed off the suggestions. Because Kate would never forget the first time it had happened—the look of shock in Luke's eyes as they'd caught each other's gazes. The embarrassment that the idea of having sex with a friend had generated.

It had been the final push to give up any remnants of that crush and she'd done it so successfully that the next time someone said something, she'd actually felt that same embarrassment herself.

But the pact had been a product of how much they'd cared about each other and, looking back now, Kate remembered that it had been almost an insurance policy and actually a comfort on more than one occasion when a relationship had hit the wall.

Only until Luke had married Nadia, of course. After that, she'd had to cope without the comfort of reminding herself that *someone* would still want her when she'd been on the shelf so long that her use-by date had expired.

And now she *was* that age and it was only the pact that had expired. Despite both Luke and Georgia's dis-enchantment with the whole business, she really did believe in love. In finding her soul mate. Someone that she would fall totally in love with and who would feel the same way about her. She knew what that felt like because she'd come close enough to touch it in the early stages of a past romance or two and she'd recognised the moment that the elusive goal had slipped from her fingers. The moment when it had become obvious that they weren't right for each other. The moment when the flicker had sputtered and died...

There was no such thing as a use-by date, she told herself. She had all the time in the world. She just had to silence that malevolent little voice in the back of her head that was not in agreement. The one that whispered in a taunting tone.

*You know there's a use-by date on some dreams, Kate. Just how long do you think you've got to keep looking? Until you're forty-five and too old to hope for that baby to hold in your arms?*

Was that what the disappointment was about? That, subconsciously, she had welcomed the idea that the insurance policy had been reinstated and that, even if she didn't find the love of her life, she could still have the family she'd always dreamed of?

How ridiculous.

Yes, she loved Luke but it was still only a friendship. She'd worked hard to make that a reality for both of them and, honestly, she'd been barely more than a teenager when she'd hoped for something more. She was grown up now and so was Luke. They were different people in many ways.

And the idea of having sex with him was still too embarrassing to even think about. It would be as bad as confessing the crush he'd been so oblivious to.

* * *

*This* was more like it.

The scene that Luke and Matteo entered that afternoon as their ninth task was exactly the kind of scenario that they'd expected from such a famous, international competition.

It was set in a huge park and it was a multi-casualty incident of a mini-bus crash. As the two men approached the cordoned-off area that had many spectators surrounding it, they took in the bus crumpled against a huge tree and a person lying motionless nearby. They could see people wandering aimlessly around, including a woman holding a blood-stained cloth to her head, and they could hear cries coming from inside the bus.

'Wow…'

Not only must it have been a mammoth undertaking to set this scenario up, Luke could see that it had been duplicated on the other side of the park so that more than one team at a time could compete.

Matteo was leading this scene.

'I think this is a triage exercise,' he told Luke, quietly. 'We don't stop to treat anything unless it's immediately life-threatening.' He pulled some brightly coloured labels from the kit as he raised his voice. 'Anyone who can walk, please come here.'

People began moving. A man climbed out of the bus. They all looked visibly shaken and some had minor injuries like scrapes and bruises. The man who had come out of the bus was holding his arm as if it hurt to move it.

'The driver,' one of them said. 'He's bad…'

'There's a woman still on the bus…' another person told them. 'She has a little boy…'

'Stay here,' Luke ordered the small group. 'We'll be back.'

Matteo was already beside the man lying on the ground. Their first patient was conscious and Luke could hear him as he got closer.

'It hurts,' he groaned. 'It hurts so much…'

He could talk, so his airway wasn't a problem. There was no obvious haemorrhage that needed to be stopped but he was clearly in severe pain, possibly with internal injuries, so he was tagged with a green label as status two—needing urgent treatment but no immediate life-saving measures.

'We'll be right back,' Luke promised. 'As soon as we check to see who else needs help.'

The woman with the head injury was confused and trying to wander away from the scene and she was rubbing at her neck as if it hurt. Matteo put the rubber band of another green label around her wrist and then called to one of the men in the uninjured group and gave him the task of looking after her.

'Get her to sit down and try to keep her head still so she doesn't move her neck. Don't let her go anywhere. We'll be back.'

Then they climbed into the bus. The driver was slumped over the steering wheel. A judge was seated near the front of the bus.

Luke lifted the man's head to open his airway. He felt for a carotid pulse in the man's neck.

'There is no pulse,' the judge told him.

Luke and Matteo shared a glance. Had the bus crashed because the driver had had a cardiac arrest? This was not the time to start a resuscitation that would take all their attention and stop them treating people that were more likely to be saved. This patient got a white label to indicate that he was deceased—a status zero.

There was a woman towards the back of the bus who had a small boy cuddled beside her. He looked to be about six years old and was taking his acting job very seriously.

'You have to help my mother,' he told his rescuers. 'She keeps going to sleep.'

'We will,' Luke promised. 'Are *you* hurt anywhere?'

Matteo was leaning over the back of the seat, talking to the woman.

'My leg is trapped,' she whispered. 'I can't get out. Help me…'

'We will,' he promised.

'I have a sore foot, too,' the boy told Luke.

'My leg hurts so much,' the woman groaned. 'Please…help me…'

Matteo was taking her pulse.

'The heart rate is one hundred and twenty,' the judge told him.

'Colour?'

'As you see her. She's very pale and sweaty.'

Matteo leaned further over the seat. 'I see blood on the floor. Is this a significant loss?'

'Yes.'

'Take the boy out to the others,' Matteo directed Luke. 'I need to control the bleeding.'

Luke scooped the boy into his arms and he obligingly wrapped his arms around Luke's neck.

'Do a secondary survey on the green-tag people,' Matteo added. 'And decide which hospital we need to transport them to. Get a cervical collar on the woman with the sore neck.' He already had a dressing in his hand and was applying pressure to the wound on the woman's leg but he was looking at the judge now. 'I need radio contact with the communication centre. Is there a helicopter available?'

Luke carried the little boy to the door and carefully down the steps.

'What's your name?' he asked.

'Ivan.'

'Are you having fun today, Ivan?'

'Yes.' The child's grin was impish and Luke had to smile back.

'Me, too,' he confessed.

Kate hadn't expected to have to walk so far carrying her heavy pack but this scenario was well off the road, in a park setting. As they came out of the woodland path, she could see what they were heading for and it took her breath away.

'Oh, my God...a *bus* crash?'

'It'll be a triage exercise,' Georgia told her. 'We'll have to check everybody and decide who needs the most urgent treatment. We'll only have to do something if it's immediately life-threatening, like a compromised airway or severe bleeding. They'll want us to decide what backup we need and which hospitals we are going to send patients to. And whether we call for air rescue backup.'

'Okay...' Georgia was focused on the area they were heading towards but Kate turned her head for a moment. Through the trees on one side, she could see that the scene had been duplicated. A team was already working there and she knew she shouldn't be trying to see what was going on but that single glance had given her a picture that froze in her head.

For a moment, all she got was the impression of a tall man wearing a high-vis vest and a helmet. A very good-looking man. It was a shock, in the next moment, to realise that it was Luke. She'd never seen him in a uniform like this before—was that what had made him look so different for a heartbeat?

He was walking away from the bus and he had a small boy in his arms. The child had his arms wrapped around Luke's neck but he didn't look as if he was supposed to be badly injured. He was smiling, in fact. And Luke was smiling back at him as if they were sharing a joke.

And, just for another instant, before she could bury the image and focus on what she knew was going to be a full-on task, Kate found her own lips curving into a smile. Something warm blossomed somewhere in her chest. Or maybe in her belly. The kind of melting sensation that she had sometimes when she saw the fathers of some of her tiny patients being so gentle and caring with their precious children.

Luke had sounded more than relieved when he'd confirmed that he and Nadia hadn't had a baby but surely he wanted to be a father one day?

He'd be the *best* father… Kind and funny and clever and so very, very caring…

Had Nadia had any idea of what she'd thrown away?

How could she have been so *stupid*?

Mist clung to the mountains and shrouded the trees as dawn broke the next day and the two friends made their way home after the series of night tasks.

They'd dealt with a young man having an acute stroke as a side effect of an incorrect drug dosage for hypertension, followed by a cardiac-arrest scenario in someone's house where the manikin available for CPR was linked to a computer that gave a printout of how effective their compressions and ventilation efforts had been. As if that hadn't been enough, they'd finished up with a mass shooting incident at a teenager's birthday party where they seemed to be working with teams of police officers who were having a scene management competition of their own.

'I haven't been this tired since those night shifts in my first hospital job when I'd already worked the day and had to keep going through the next day.'

'I know.' Georgia was looking pale with fatigue herself. 'Let's get some breakfast and then we'll have a few hours to sleep before the debrief.'

'I'm too tired to feel hungry.'

'Me, too. Let's just go to bed.'

The car door felt ridiculously heavy as Kate pushed it open when they'd parked near the accommodation block. Climbing the stairs felt like a mountain challenge and even having a shower was going to require too much effort. Kate lay down on the single bed opposite Georgia's and let her breath out in a sigh that was close to a groan.

Her body was telling her that this had been the craziest idea ever.

Her heart had something else to say, however. She was very glad that she had come. Not only had it been an experience that had deepened her friendship with Georgia and one that she would remember for the rest of her life, it felt like its effects could quite possibly change her world for the better in the near future.

That image of Luke with the little boy in his arms floated back into her mind and she fell asleep with a smile on her face.

Maybe that was why Kate felt so much better when their alarm went off four hours later.

And why she put a little extra effort into getting ready for the debrief session, where the judges were going to go over every scenario and tell them how they would have gained the highest scores. A lot of competitors would probably give the session a miss in favour of some more sleep before the social events of the prize-giving, convoy drive and the big party tonight but Kate knew that Luke would be going. He'd want to know exactly how well he'd done and—if he'd missed an expected diagnosis or intervention along the way—Kate could be quite sure that he'd be taking some notes so that it would never happen again.

When she entered the large room to see him sitting near the back with a notebook already open on his lap, she hid her smile.

He hadn't changed a bit, had he?

Except he did look older. Maybe because he had to be as tired as she was. Or maybe it was a sense of maturity that only came with age and the accrued wisdom of bitter experience.

He'd been through some tough times, hadn't he?

He glanced up, as if he was suddenly aware of the sympathy coming in his direction. His face was blank until he focussed on Kate and then his expression changed instantly. He wasn't smiling but the deepen-

ing of the crinkles around his eyes created enough
warmth for Kate to feel it all the way down to her toes.

The same kind of warmth she'd felt when she'd seen
him with that small child in his arms yesterday.

She slipped into the seat beside him.

'Where's Matteo?'

'Sleeping. I told him I'd take notes and tell him what
we did wrong over lunch.'

Kate laughed. 'He and Georgia have a lot in common. She just groaned and rolled over when our alarm
went off.'

'We might regret getting up when we fall asleep at
the party tonight.'

Kate was still smiling as she held his gaze for a
moment longer. Not likely. She and Luke had a lot in
common, too, and one thing they'd always shared was
a determination to learn from every experience and use
that knowledge to make them better at the profession
they both had a passion for.

Overall, it seemed like she and Georgia had done
well in all the scenarios. Luke was looking pleased
with his team's performance, too.

'Did you activate the air rescue service for the guy
with internal injuries at the bus crash?'

'Yes. Did you?'

'Yes. But we missed the clue that that teacher at the
school had vodka in her juice bottle.'

'The hypoglycaemic emergency?' Luke grinned. 'I
would have needed vodka too, I reckon, with that mob
of naughty children. We had one climbing out of the
window while we were trying to get a blood glucose
and get an IV line in the patient.'

'Georgia had them under control in no time flat.

And she got the school caretaker to take them away before we started any treatment.' Kate's spirits lifted. Control of that disruption had been one of the scoring points in that scenario. Maybe they'd done better than the other teams and would place at the prize-giving.

'You looking forward to the convoy? Did you hear the rumour that the local vet has to go around all the villages and give the horses a sedative so they don't freak out with the noise of all the sirens?'

'Really?' Kate frowned. 'And the owners are happy about that?'

'I guess so. They'll be out with everyone else, I reckon, watching us all drive by. It's a big event around here. Hey… Matteo suggested that you girls might like to come with us in our car. That way you can enjoy the view without having to drive.'

'I'll check with Georgia but it sounds like fun. She'll want to fly the Scottish flag, though.'

'That's fine by me. I'm kind of Scottish myself now.'

'That's right—you are…' The reminder that she and Luke were practically going to be neighbours as soon as they got home added to Kate's rising spirits. Any remaining fatigue was evaporating. The remaining time at this competition held the promise of being great fun.

It was a promise that delivered a lot more than Kate had anticipated. Georgia was more than happy to be a passenger in a shared vehicle and the two teams joined the others gathering in the town square for the prize-giving ceremony. It was a generous and good-natured crowd and the congratulatory cheers got louder as each award was bestowed. There were prizes for the doctor-only teams, the medical students, and the paramedics.

She and Georgia shared a delighted glance when the team from New Zealand came second in their category.

'Special category P2,' the master of ceremonies announced eventually. 'One physician plus a maximum of two paramedics.'

Kate held her breath. She knew there'd been other teams in this category that had a doctor and two paramedics. Surely they would have done better than teams like hers and Luke's where there was only one paramedic?

'And the winner is…'

Kate turned her head to find Luke looking at her instead of the master of ceremonies.

*'Scotland…'*

Kate's jaw dropped and her head jerked sideways as Georgia let out a squeal of delight. The two women threw their arms around each other for a brief, fierce hug before making their way to the stage to receive their trophy. She looked back for a moment, however, before they began threading their way through the clapping crowd.

Yes… Matteo might be looking a bit disappointed but there was genuine delight written all over Luke's face.

He was proud of her.

'Champagne's on us tonight,' he called after her. His grin stretched. 'Just like the old days, isn't it?'

Kate nodded, knowing her grin was just as wide as his.

She looked for him again as she stood on the stage beside Georgia, holding one side of the plaque commemorating their success, as a photo was taken.

He was wrong, she decided as her heart skipped a

beat when her gaze had found what she'd been searching for.

It wasn't like the old days at all.

There was something very different now.

Something new.

Rather exciting, even?

She knew what it was, too.

She didn't feel invisible any more.

'Pull your head in, Kate!'

Matteo was slowing their vehicle, tooting the horn in greeting as they got closer to another group of people standing by the roadside, excited children in front of the adults with their hands held out expectantly.

'But they can't reach...' Kate had to shout over the noise. They were nose-to-tail in a procession of dozens of emergency vehicles that all had their sirens blaring and their warning lights flashing. She was leaning right out of the window, her hands full of the small gifts they'd obviously stocked up on before leaving Scotland. Thistle badges, key rings with kilted Highlanders holding bagpipes, bars of Highland toffee and boiled sweets in the colours of the Scottish flag.

Georgia was hanging onto Kate's shirt, trying to make sure she didn't actually fall out of the car as Matteo accelerated again, but she was laughing. The excitement of this whole experience had clearly gone to her head as well. Luke swivelled in the front seat in time to see Kate sit down again with a thump. She was laughing, too.

'Your turn next, Georgie. Look—there's lots of people on your side of the road coming up. Give some stuff to Luke.'

'I'm not about to lean out and risk getting my head bumped.' But Luke had to grin. 'I can't believe I'm seeing you break the rules like this, Kate.'

'Yeah...' Georgia elbowed her friend. 'You heard them. No alcohol, no speeding and no leaning out of vehicles.'

Kate just pushed wind-blown hair out of her eyes and beamed back at them.

'But it's fun,' she said.

Luke had to admit that this was, indeed, great fun. But he wasn't sure what he was enjoying more. This extraordinary convoy or seeing Kate let her hair down and embrace the atmosphere so enthusiastically?

Maybe he was still feeling happy for her that she'd won the trophy. Or simply because they'd reconnected and there was no reason that Kate couldn't continue to be part of his life after this event was over. There wasn't even the obstacle of her having a boyfriend, which had been a huge—and, he had to admit, not an unpleasant surprise.

Perhaps friendship lacked the kind of excitement that falling in love might provide but it was even better. Because it was safer. He could relax with Kate and simply be himself with no danger of losing his head—or his heart. He'd been reminded of what it had been like to fall in love when Kate had been starry-eyed over what it had been like for him and Nadia in the beginning, but he was older and wiser now. As he'd told her, he'd been there and got the T-shirt.

Only that didn't really sum it up, did it?

You could throw away a T-shirt and its pithy message, like 'Marriage Sucks', but you couldn't get rid of the message he'd been left with. The words might be invisible but they'd been branded into his skin as a permanent reminder. Perhaps it was just as well that Kate had dismissed any idea that their 'pact' might still be valid.

Georgia was behaving just as badly as her best friend, leaning out of her window to distribute their small gifts as the children ran alongside the car, but Luke threw his into the waiting hands and returned the delighted grins when a catch was successful. In the wing mirror, he could see them scrambling to collect items that had landed on the grassy verge and then jumping to their feet as they awaited the vehicles still to pass.

The smile never left his face. He loved kids. The highlight of all the scenarios in this competition for him had been when he'd shared that moment with Ivan—the little boy who had been one of the actors in the bus-crash scenario. That moment of connection, when they'd both admitted their secret enjoyment of what was supposed to be a serious matter, had been priceless.

The pang that made his smile finally fade came from nowhere. How much stronger would a connection like that be if it was with a child of your own? He might have given up on the fairy-tale of marrying the love of your life that Kate still believed in but he wasn't ready to give up on the idea of having a family of his own. Lots of people settled for something far less than a passionate love story to achieve that, didn't they? They found someone they could respect and care about deeply and they learned to build a life together that was strong enough to protect the children they chose to bring into the world.

A glance into the rear-view mirror gave him a glimpse of Kate's profile, her blonde hair streaming back from her face as she tilted her head out of the window to see what lay ahead. Her cheeks were flushed and her eyes as bright as that happy smile.

Wow…

How come he'd never noticed how gorgeous she was in the old days?

She'd been right there all the time but she'd just been one of the gang. Just another great mate.

Shifting his gaze to the windscreen, Luke could see another bunch of children waiting with their parents. A father had a small child on his shoulders and a mother had a well-wrapped baby in her arms.

Families…

He couldn't help another glance in the rear-view mirror.

From this new, slightly more considered point of view, the concept of that pact he and Kate had made wasn't really so silly after all.

The final gathering of competitors, team members, families and officials was the perfect end to a time that Kate was never going to forget.

The combination of an extended period of such intense competition, fatigue and—for some—the pride of achievement made for a party atmosphere like nothing she had ever encountered before. It began with that astonishing convoy when Kate hadn't hesitated to break the rules and it just kept going.

There was champagne to be found and delicious barbecued food and so many people who now had a lot in common and wanted to enjoy the company of new friends or renew and deepen friendships that had been made in previous years because this event was an annual highlight for the majority of the participants.

'So who thinks they'll do this again?' Luke and Matteo were sitting at an outside picnic table, opposite Kate and Georgia. They were hemmed in by people from New Zealand, Croatia and Germany, and there seemed to be some friendly rivalry going on as to which team could provide the most in the way of beverages.

'Me.' Georgia and Matteo spoke at the same time and then grinned at each other and raised their glasses in a toast.

'I'd love to,' Dave the New Zealander said. 'Shame it's such a long way to come, which makes it horrendously expensive.' He winked at Georgia. 'I'll just have to start saving up, won't I?'

'We come every year,' a Croatian paramedic put in. 'And it gets better every time.'

Luke was looking at Kate, his eyebrows raised.

'Ask me next week…' she smiled '…when I've had enough sleep to be able to think straight.'

Luke leaned closer. 'We could do it together,' he suggested. 'As a doctor team.'

'Hey…' Georgia was scowling. 'You're not stealing my doctor partner.' She hooked her arm over Kate's shoulders. 'If anyone's going to do it again with Katy, it'll be *me*…'

But Kate smiled at Luke. She liked that he could see them being partners. And she liked that he was already thinking of a future that included her.

'I'm not sure that I'd want to do it again,' she said, 'but I'm very, very glad I did it this time.'

Luke's smile widened. 'I'm very, very glad that you did it this time, too.'

The party kicked up a notch as night fell and the music started.

The DJ, who was on a stage in the dining room that had been emptied of most of its tables, had clearly tried to find every great dance tune in existence and it was Georgia who was first onto the dance floor, dragging Kate along with her. It took very little time for the area to become crowded and now it was dance partners who were being exchanged instead of conversation. Kate found herself being twirled by people who spoke in languages she couldn't even identify but it didn't matter in the least because the language of dance was universal.

Eventually, she had to take a break and joined the queue at the busy bar to get a glass of water. Then she stood and watched the dancers for a while, trying to see where Georgia was. If she could spot her friend, she was going to tell her that she'd had enough. Fatigue was catching up with her and they had a very long drive to get started on in the morning.

But Georgia was nowhere to be seen on the dance floor. Or at any of the tables in here where people had gathered to listen to the music and watch the more energetic partygoers. She went outside and wandered around for a while where small groups or couples were sitting, deep in conversation near an outside bar and off to one side where a brazier was providing both warmth and an invitation to linger.

Back inside, her gaze raked the dance floor again but she couldn't see anyone she recognised, apart from Luke, who was dancing in the middle of a circle of young women. Then she saw Matteo coming towards her through a door that led to the bathrooms and exit.

'You don't know where Georgie is, do you?'

'No. I have no idea. Do you want a drink? I'm going to have one.'

'No, thanks. I've had enough. If you see her, can you tell her I've gone to bed?'

'Sure.' But Matteo was already moving towards the bar. 'See you tomorrow, Kate. Sleep well.'

'I will. You too.'

Kate stared after Matteo. Oddly, it felt like she'd said something to offend him but she didn't have time to try and figure it out. Luke came up behind her.

'Help,' he said. 'Get me away from here before I fall over. I need a rest.'

'You're not the only one. I'm heading off.'

'Oh?' Luke sounded disappointed.

'It's been amazing but if I stay any longer it won't be fun any more. I don't think I've ever been this tired in my life.'

'I'll walk you home.'

'You don't need to do that.'

'I want to.'

It was only when they got far enough away from the party that Kate realised how noisy it had been in there. There was still the background thump of the music and an occasional shout and peals of laughter but she could feel the increasing quietness and space, which made her more and more aware of the man walking beside her.

Outside the building that housed their apartments, they both stopped for a moment, caught by the view towards the mountains where a full moon was rising above the jagged peaks.

With a sigh of pleasure, Kate finally turned away.

'See you tomorrow, Luke. Or, if we miss you, I'll see you back in Scotland.'

'I'll look forward to that.' Luke was smiling. 'Goodnight, Katy.'

It was only natural to hug such a good friend to say goodnight. But maybe it wasn't so natural for the hug to go on for quite so long. Or for Kate to be feeling an odd stirring of sensation deep in her belly that was something quite a lot more than merely friendship should be sparking.

Startled, she pulled back but Luke's arms didn't loosen their hold and so she found herself looking up at his face that was so close she could feel his breath on her skin.

Stopping any further effort to pull away might have been a mistake. Catching his gaze definitely was because she'd never seen Luke looking at her like that. As if he wanted nothing more than to *kiss* her?

Astonishment made her lips drift apart. It occurred to her in that heartbeat of time that that might be interpreted as an invitation but, just as instantly, she didn't care. She'd already thrown her normal caution to the wind and broken a rule or two today so why stop now, when exhaustion and possibly a little more champagne than had been wise was a perfectly good excuse?

She couldn't have said who actually initiated that kiss but she didn't care about that either. And it wasn't a passionate kiss. Just a gentle, if lingering, touch of their lips that had notes of both pleasure and total surprise.

Kate was still grappling with how surprising it had been when she finally crawled into her bed, with thoughts that were not coherent enough to be put into words rather than feelings.

The gentleness of the touch that made her remember how she'd felt when she'd seen him with that child in his arms. The background memories of a friendship she'd treasured. The resurfacing memories of how she'd felt whenever she'd been close to him in the early days of that friendship.

That flicker of attraction that had been so hard to douse.

And—so surprising that it was more than a little disturbing—the idea of having sex with Luke was no longer embarrassing at all.

The only thing that felt weird about it was that it hadn't happened a very long time ago.

It wasn't that she was about to have a teenage-style crush on him again. This felt far more real. As if it would be quite possible to actually fall in love with her old friend, she decided, as sleep finally crept up to claim her.

Maybe she was more than halfway there already…

# CHAPTER FOUR

'I CAN'T BELIEVE we've been home for nearly a month.'

'I know…' Kate took the pan Georgia had finished washing and began to dry it. 'Time flies, doesn't it? And it was a bit of a struggle to get back into routine. It was almost like jet lag, the aftermath of that epic road trip.'

It shouldn't have been that hard to embrace her normal routine, however. Kate loved routine. Had the struggle been caused by an element of distraction? Because she had found her thoughts occupied by Luke so often? It had only taken a few days for the weariness of the long journeys and intense competition to wear off but even then, it was more than post-excitement fallout that had made Kate feel a little flat. She was too aware of what was missing from her life. She loved her job and she had great friends but there was a hole she'd been stepping around for years now.

And, more and more as the days went past, that hole was taking on a shape that looked as if it was custom made for Luke Anderson.

'I'm still tired,' Georgia groaned, scrubbing at the handful of cutlery she held. 'Or maybe I'm bored.' Her smile was mischievous. 'If I get a callout that isn't a challenge, I want to swap it for a new scenario. Like a bus crash or a shooting incident…'

'Don't say that. What if you're tempting fate? How bad would you feel if it happened tomorrow?'

'True. Guess I'd better be grateful for all the routine chest pains and stomach aches and overdoses.' With a sigh, she dumped the cutlery onto the draining tray. 'There you go. All done. Thanks for dinner, by the way. It was great.'

'My pleasure. Your turn tomorrow. Oh, no…you're on night shift, aren't you?'

'Yep.' Georgia dried her hands on the corner of the tea towel Kate was using. 'Hey, maybe you should go out for dinner. It's high time you and Luke got together.'

It was Kate's turn to sigh. 'We keep trying but it never works out that we've got the same time off. I can guarantee if I text him and suggest it, he'll be on call or something. We haven't been able to manage a coffee since we've been back, let alone a whole day's sightseeing.'

'Make it happen,' Georgia said. 'You never know— it could change your life.'

'You want to know something?'

'What?'

Kate felt her lips curl into a smile that felt hopeful. 'I think you might be right.'

'*Aha*… I knew it…' Georgia grinned back at her. 'You've been so quiet lately. You're really keen on him, aren't you?'

'We were such good friends, way back. I… I might have even had a bit of a crush on him.'

'No way…really?'

'It was short-lived. I got over it as soon as I realised he wasn't interested in me like that.' Kate bit her lip. Yes, she'd got over it fast enough but there had always been that remnant. That knowledge that this friendship had an element that made it unique. She let her breath out in a small sigh. 'I don't know if it could be anything more than what it always was but…'

'But you'd like it to be.'

It was a statement rather than a question and Kate found herself nodding slowly in agreement.

'So text him. Do it now.' Georgia followed Kate from the kitchen into the small sitting room of their house and watched as Kate pulled her phone from her bag.

'Oh… I've got a text.'

'From Luke?'

'Yes…' Kate could feel butterflies in her stomach as she opened the message. Good grief, she felt like a teenager who'd been waiting for *that* boy to call.

'What does it say?'

'That he's having a crazy week but has a day off on Saturday and maybe I'd like to go and find a ruined castle or look for the Loch Ness monster or something.'

Georgia laughed. 'Sounds like a perfect date.'

Kate made a face. 'Except I'm working on Saturday.' She shook her head. 'This is getting silly. Maybe it's not meant to happen.'

'Don't be ridiculous. What were the odds of you two meeting up again on a mountaintop in the Czech Republic? It was totally meant to happen.'

Kate had to smile. 'It was certainly unexpected.'

Maybe she should really make an effort this time. She could ask to swap her Saturday shift with one of her colleagues. More than one of them owed her the favour, in fact.

Her smile was getting wider. 'And it was you who had the mad idea of hooking up with someone while we were there. It was the last thing I was planning on doing.'

There was something about the way Georgia shrugged and turned away that raised Kate's suspicions. Her smile faded.

'I'm not the only one who's been a bit quiet since we got back. What aren't you talking about?'

'Nothing.'

Kate stared at her friend's back. 'You never did tell me where you disappeared to for so long during that party.'

The silence suddenly seemed charged.

'Oh, my God,' Kate breathed. 'You *did* hook up with somebody. And you never told me?'

'Wasn't much to tell.' Georgia's voice sounded tight. 'I'd rather forget about it.'

But Kate couldn't let it go like that. 'It can't have been Matteo,' she said, 'because I saw him and asked if he knew where you were and he said he had no idea.'

Georgia's expression suggested that Kate might have just beamed in from another planet. 'Why would it have been Matteo?'

'Oh, I don't know…' Kate's tone was teasing. 'Because he was gorgeous, maybe? Or because you two seemed to be getting on incredibly well?'

Georgia shrugged again. 'I guess some people aren't okay with casual sex. I don't think I am any more either. It wasn't my best idea, was it?' She reached for the television remote. 'Let's see if there's something worth watching, shall we?'

Clearly, it was time to change the subject but Kate was frowning. It wasn't like Georgia to keep things bottled up so the experience must have been more disturbing than she was letting on. She sat down on the couch beside Georgia and gave her a quick hug.

'It's in the past now,' she said. 'And yeah…it wasn't your best idea but you'll know not to do it again. Are you okay? Really?'

Georgia nodded, hugging her back. 'I'm fine. *Really.*'

One of their favourite dramas was on but Kate couldn't get involved with the new plot twists. She was still worried about her friend. Worried about herself, too, if she was honest. She was one of the people who weren't okay with the idea of casual sex herself. Not that it would be for her if she and Luke got together but, from his point of view, it would never be anything more than a friendship with benefits.

Was she setting herself up to be in a far worse position than Georgia had been left with after her ill-advised one-off encounter? Maybe calling in a favour to get the day off on Saturday wasn't such a good idea. Given this new spin, perhaps she needed some more time to think things through. Or to let her hormones settle down or something.

She still had her phone in her hand. She hit 'reply'.

Sorry, Luke. Working on Saturday. Let's try again next week.

Luke Anderson loved his job with a passion but there were occasional moments when he knew he desperately needed more in his life.

Like right now. Here he was, on a lovely Saturday

afternoon, when he could have been anywhere—doing any*thing*—that had nothing to do with the surgical management of injured children. But here he was, in his office near the paediatric intensive care unit, in Edinburgh's Royal Children's Hospital.

It was Kate's fault.

She hadn't suggested trying to swap her weekend shift with someone. She hadn't even offered a definite time that they could try again. 'Next week' felt vague enough to be a brush-off, albeit polite.

Perhaps she wasn't as keen to see him again as he was to see her?

After travelling back to Italy with Matteo and having a few days' holiday in Milan he had been later getting back to work than Kate but he'd made his first attempt to catch up three weeks ago now and it *still* hadn't happened.

With a sigh, Luke turned back to his computer screen. He had decided to prepare a case history to offer at the weekly lunch meeting next Friday, where interesting cases were presented for analysis and discussion. The little girl he'd operated on for a ruptured diaphragm and spleen was a good example of how dangerous a lap belt could be in even a relatively minor car accident and what early signs and symptoms were important to take notice of.

He'd only just set up his first slide to introduce the case when his office door burst open.

'Oh…you *are* here.' The anxious expression on the face of one of the senior nurses from PICU was morphing into relief. 'Someone said you might be.'

'What is it, Elise?'

'There's an incoming emergency. ETA about ten

minutes. Eighteen-month-old boy who was climbing a table and it flipped over onto him.'

Luke's brain engaged instantly. Where had the edge of what was probably a heavy piece of furniture landed? Did the toddler have abdominal injuries or was it his chest, neck or head that had been affected?

'How much information do we have so far?'

'The mother heard the crash. He was unconscious and having a seizure when the ambulance arrived.'

Elise was already leading Luke rapidly along the corridor towards the lifts. There was no question for either of them that he would take charge of this case, even if he wasn't officially on duty.

She pushed the button to summon the lift. 'He got to Glasgow's Eastern Infirmary thirty minutes later with a GCS of five and was intubated.'

The thought that the Eastern Infirmary was where Kate worked was only a flash of distraction. The low GCS score indicated a level of consciousness that suggested a severe injury.

'Investigations?'

'There were no obvious external injuries but they noted a mild upper body cyanosis and an ultrasound revealed a pericardial effusion.'

So it was a chest injury and there was fluid—probably blood—collecting around the child's heart. It was obvious that emergency surgery could well be needed.

The lift doors closed in front of them.

'Have we got a theatre available?'

'Yes. That was organised as soon as we got the call about the transfer. Apparently there wasn't anybody available in Glasgow for emergency chest surgery and we were going to page Colin but somebody said they'd

seen you here earlier so I checked your office first.'
Elise smiled up at Luke. 'If it was my kid, *I'd* want
you to be looking after him.'

The compliment regarding his abilities as a paediatric trauma surgeon had a bitter-sweet edge for Luke
as he recalled the moment of doubt he'd experienced
only minutes ago. He put everything into his work and
continued to strive towards being even better at his
job—but was it at the expense of so many other things
that life could offer?

The doors opened on the ground floor and they both
headed past a busy reception and waiting area, through
the emergency department and out through the automatic doors that led to the ambulance bay.

Only a minute later, they could hear the siren of an
approaching ambulance and then it came into view.
The siren was switched off but the beacons were still
flashing as it stopped and then swiftly reversed towards
the edge of the loading bay.

Luke could feel his adrenaline levels kick up several notches and he felt like he was the front line
again—the way he had been, working with Matteo at
the paramedic competition. Waiting right behind that
impression was a reminder of Kate but it was easy to
ignore. There was a potentially critically injured child
inside this ambulance and it was real this time. If it was
a blunt force injury to the little boy's heart, it would be
a miracle if he was still alive but, if he was, then Luke
was going to do everything in his power to save him.

The cabin of the ambulance was crowded. Luke
could see the tiny child, wearing only a nappy, lying
deathly still on the stretcher, surrounded by equipment
like the portable ventilator, a cardiac monitor and a

tangle of IV lines. A paramedic was removing oxygen tubing from the main supply to attach it to a portable cylinder. A distraught-looking woman who had to be the child's mother was holding her head in her hands and a woman dressed in scrubs had a stethoscope against the toddler's bare chest. She had her hair scraped back into a ponytail. Blonde hair.

Some tiny part of Luke's brain registered that this hair was the exact shade of Kate's hair and then the doctor straightened and turned, hooking the stethoscope back around her neck.

Of course the hair was the same shade as Kate's. It *was* Kate's.

The distraction was only the timespan of one heartbeat but Luke could feel it throughout his entire body.

Kate was here.

And it felt astonishingly *good*…

'We've got a systolic blood pressure of eighty.' The flash in Kate's eyes suggested that she was just as pleased to see Luke but she wasn't about to waste any time on personal greetings. 'He's in a sinus tachycardia of one hundred and eighty and the upper torso cyanosis is increasing.'

The ambulance crew wasn't wasting any time either. The crew member who had been driving had stepped through into the cabin and unhooked the stretcher restraints. Luke had to step to one side as they rolled the stretcher out, the wheels folding down and locking automatically as it emerged from the ambulance. He was intensely focussed now. This child was still alive…

'We're clear to bypass Emergency,' he told the crew. 'And an elevator's being held. We're heading straight for Theatre.'

The child's mother stumbled as she stepped down from the back of the ambulance in the wake of the stretcher and Luke caught her shoulder to steady her.

'Oh, my God…' she whispered, as she looked up to catch his gaze. *'Theatre?'*

'I'm Luke Anderson,' he told her. 'I'm a trauma surgeon here at the Royal and I specialise in chest injuries like this.'

They were moving now—straight through the emergency department towards the doors at the other end that led to the bank of elevators. Staff were moving obstacles like trolleys and wandering patients from their path.

'He's not going to die, is he?' the mother sobbed. 'This is all my fault… I should have been watching him more carefully…'

Kate turned her head, IV tubing in her hands as she protected a line. 'Jacob's in the best place he can be, Jennie. And with the best surgeon.'

The stretcher rattled as it went over the metal rim of the elevator and there was a moment's pause as the team manoeuvred everything to make room for people.

'Can I come with him?' Jennie begged.

'Of course you can.' Elise had been trailing the team but she stepped up now and put her hand on Jennie's arm. 'There's a place that you can wait and someone will be with you all the time. Come with me… We'll take the next lift. My name's Elise and I'm a nurse in the intensive care unit that Jacob will be going to after his surgery.'

Luke and Kate squeezed in alongside the stretcher. They were both trying to get as much information as possible by scanning readouts on the monitors and by what they could assess visually.

Luke caught Kate's glance and he could feel his mouth tighten into grim agreement. It might be just the strong lighting in this small space but they were both thinking that the bluish tinge to Jacob's skin looked worse. The ability of his heart to function was deteriorating rapidly.

The doors opened and it was another straight line, through two sets of double doors to the suite of operating theatres. A theatre team was waiting beside an empty bed covered with a white sheet. The transfer of the tiny child was swift and smooth and the ambulance crew gathered their equipment on top of the stretcher, preparing to leave.

Luke caught Kate's glance again as the bed was rolled towards the induction room where the anaesthetist was waiting. 'Are you going to stay?'

'Can I? You don't mind if I observe?'

'You're more than welcome. Someone will find you some gear. Or there's an observation deck if you want a better view from the close-up camera. I need to go and scrub in.' But Luke paused for a brief moment as he turned away. He didn't actually smile, but he could feel the corners of his mouth soften. 'It's good to see you, Katy.'

Maybe the view wasn't as good standing at the head of the operating table, out of the way of the surgical team, but Kate was happy. She wanted to be as close as possible to this small patient whose outcome she was already so invested in. And it meant she was also as close as possible to Luke.

She watched as he entered the theatre, gloved hands crossed in front of his body to prevent any accidental touch of something not sterile, a nurse still tying the strings of his gown behind him. With a hat covering his hair, a mask over his nose and face and protective eyewear on, it could have been any surgeon coming in but Kate's body told her exactly who it was.

The tingle of anticipation—or maybe it was more like attraction—was powerful enough to actually distract Kate from everything else going on around her. It felt like an electrical current touching every cell in her body and it was emanating from a knot of sensation deep in her belly.

Yep. That was attraction. She recognised the point of origin all too well. But had she ever felt it quite this fiercely?

For a nanosecond, Kate actually thought the alarm she could hear was something internal but, in the same instant, she tapped into the acceleration of tension around her.

'He's in VF.'

The nurse painting Jacob's chest with disinfectant stopped swabbing and her forceps froze in mid-air. Kate held her breath. Ventricular fibrillation meant that the small heart had given up trying to pump blood—probably because of the pressure of the fluid trapped around it. And, if that was the case, simply delivering an external shock would not be enough to keep this little boy alive.

It seemed like time had stopped and frozen this tableau but that impression lasted for only the time it took for Kate's heart to skip a beat. And then she watched as

Luke took complete control of everything with a calm confidence that took her breath away all over again.

'Scalpel, please,' he requested. 'And some blunt forceps. I'll need the saw in a second, too.'

Stepping closer to the table, he made a swift incision down the centre of their tiny patient's chest. Within a couple of minutes, the heart was visible. Using forceps, he lifted the tissue surrounding the heart in an enclosed bag and then made another incision.

'Suction, please…'

Luke was scooping clots of blood from around the small heart as his assistant angled the suction tubing.

'I can see where it's coming from,' Luke said a minute later. 'We've got a right atrial rupture here. Clamp, thanks…'

The bleeding from the heart was controlled within seconds but the heart was still not functioning.

Luke's hands were continuing to move with smooth confidence. Kate was biting her bottom lip so hard it was painful, as she watched him take hold of that tiny heart in his hand and start squeezing it with rapid compressions.

'Charge the internal defibrillators,' he ordered. 'But this may be enough…' He eased his hand out of the chest and Kate felt herself leaning forward, trying to see what the heart was doing. Was it still quivering ineffectively? Had it stopped completely? Or…?

The beep from the machine right beside her was a very different sound from the previous alarm. A single beep and then another one after a gap. And then the beeps got faster. Steadier…

'We're back in sinus rhythm,' Luke said. 'Thanks,

team. Let's get this damage repaired, shall we? Suture, thanks...'

Over an hour later, Kate was still watching Luke—this time in the PICU. Jacob had been transferred there for the intensive care he was going to need for some time and Luke was using transoesophageal echocardiography to examine Jacob's heart.

'I'm happy.' His words were directed at Jennie, who was sitting on the edge of her chair, one hand holding that of her son. Jacob's father was by her side now, too, and he was holding Jennie's other hand. 'There's no sign of any residual injuries and his heart is working perfectly.'

He removed the tubing that contained the transducer at its tip from Jacob's throat and then he stripped off his gloves.

'We'll keep Jacob in here for a day or two to keep a close eye on things but then we'll wake him up and move him to the cardiac ward.'

'Is he...will he...?' Jacob's father had to stop and clear his throat and then he couldn't continue.

'I'm happy,' Luke said again, and this time he was smiling. 'I think he's going to be running around again in no time—probably giving you all the normal worry that toddlers can create—but he's come through this crisis with flying colours.'

Jacob's parents were both smiling and crying at the same time and Kate felt the prickle of her own tears.

From the moment this child had arrived in her emergency department—hours ago now—she had had very little hope of an outcome as good as this.

And it was thanks to Luke. The parents didn't need

to know how close to a very different ending they had been up there in Theatre but Kate knew.

So did Luke.

His gaze met hers as Jacob's parents embraced each other.

He looked exhausted, which was hardly surprising. Kate felt like she'd just run a marathon herself and she'd only been watching, for heaven's sake.

At least he would get a break now. Jacob was under the care of an expert team who would only call Luke in if he was really needed and, the way things were looking at the moment, that was very unlikely.

They left the PICU together and walked in silence towards the elevator. Luke pushed the button and then tilted his head, one eyebrow raised as he caught Kate's glance.

'So this is what it takes to see you again? Full-on emergent cardiac surgery? Don't you think that's a bit high maintenance of you?'

Kate grinned. 'I have to say it was a very impressive performance but, no…it wasn't something I want to repeat in a hurry.'

'At least it broke the barrier.'

'Barrier?'

Luke waited for Kate to step into the lift ahead of him. 'I was beginning to think that you didn't really want to see me again.'

'Oh…' Kate could feel a flush of warmth in her cheeks, along with the flash of guilt that she had pretty much brushed Luke off in her last text. And then she looked up to see the way he was looking at her and the warmth suddenly went south.

There it was again.

That flash of a totally new kind of attraction.

'That's not true,' she said softly. 'I'm really happy to see you again.'

She couldn't look away. Neither, apparently, could Luke. They were locked in that eye contact until the elevator shuddered to a halt on the ground floor.

'How are you going to get home?' Luke asked as they walked through the reception area. 'Or do you need to go back to work?'

'I can go home. I was off duty a couple of hours ago. And I can call a taxi. My hospital will cover the cost because I came here as a medical escort.'

'Are you in a hurry?'

It only took a flash of that eye contact to set off that tingle again. No... Kate wasn't in any hurry to go anywhere away from Luke. Quite the opposite.

'Only I'm starving,' he continued. 'And I know a really nice Italian place not far from here, if you fancy having dinner with me.'

Saving a small life had been more than enough to make this a great day for Kate but, amazingly, it had just got a whole lot better.

Or maybe not.

'I can't go to a restaurant. I'm wearing scrubs.'

'This is a place that is a favourite with the staff. They're used to people wearing scrubs. Did you bring a coat with you?'

'No. We left in kind of a rush.'

'You can use mine. I'll get changed so I won't need it.' His eyebrows were raised enough to make his face a picture of persuasion. 'Deal?'

Kate didn't need much persuasion. She was, in fact, grinning.

'Deal.'

# CHAPTER FIVE

THE RESTAURANT COULD have been tucked away on a back alley somewhere in Florence or Rome.

Heavy beams on the ceiling had trailing vines coming from hanging baskets. The tables were rustic and covered with checked red cloth. Slim white candles had dribbled wax for a long time judging by how encrusted the old wine bottle in the centre of their small table was.

Kate had a glass of Prosecco in front of her but Luke was filling his glass from a carafe of water.

'Just in case I get called back,' he said. 'Even if I don't, I'll go and check on Jacob on my way home.'

'He's going to be fine.' Kate smiled. 'You did such an amazing job, Luke. He's one lucky little boy.'

She knew that her admiration of how Luke had handled such a critical case had to be written all over her face but she didn't care. He should be very proud of himself. *She* was proud of him.

'I only got to do what I did because you got him to the right place at the right time. If it had been anyone less competent receiving him in Emergency and not recognising what was going on, it would have been a very different story.'

Maybe it was the candlelight but Luke's gaze seemed just as admiring as Kate knew hers was. As if to remove any doubt, he lifted his glass to tap it gently against the edge of hers.

'Well done, you,' he said quietly.

'Well done, *us*,' Kate countered.

One side of Luke's mouth tilted upwards. 'We always were a great team, weren't we? Do you remember our first cardiac arrest?'

'How could I forget? Back in the days when you had to hold the paddles onto the chest to defibrillate and I was so scared my hands were shaking like I was holding a pair of castanets.'

She could smile about being a nervous medical student now but there was a far more lasting memory from that case. The way Luke had caught her frightened gaze as he'd paused his chest compressions to stand clear. That steady gaze had told her that she knew exactly what to do. That she could do this.

'How great was it when we got him back?'

'It was the best.' Kate took a long sip of her wine. 'And do you remember the kid that bit your finger?'

Luke laughed. 'I think I still have a scar.'

Kate was laughing, too. 'The look on your face! It was priceless.'

'It was a lesson I've never forgotten. I protect my fingers at all times now.'

'Didn't put you off working with kids, though.'

'Ah...but I keep them unconscious most of the time. I find it easier not to get bitten that way.'

Memories—and laughter—were easy to find as they shared an antipasti platter of calamari and olives and then deep dishes of the restaurant's signature lasagne that came with a fresh green salad and slices of crusty bread. It was only when they both sighed with pleasure over the first taste of the tiramisu they had both ordered for dessert that Kate realised something unusual.

'Do you know, this is the first time I've ever been to a restaurant when someone else has ordered exactly the same things I did.'

'That's bad, isn't it? It means you don't get the chance to taste something different.'

'No, no…it's good. I get terrible food envy.'

Luke grinned. 'You mean when you see what someone else has ordered and it suddenly looks so much better than what you chose?'

'Exactly.'

He was still smiling. 'We always did like the same things pretty much, didn't we? Same music, same movies.'

'Same friends, same careers…' Kate couldn't look away from that smile. The way his eyes crinkled at the sides. The warmth she could feel that came from knowing how intelligent this man was. How funny he could be. How caring she knew he was.

And then she remembered that kiss in the moonlight up in the mountains of the Czech Republic and the warmth twisted into something a heck of a lot more powerful.

Powerful enough to take her breath away.

Their friends had been right, all those years ago. She and Luke *were* perfect for each other. Why on earth hadn't Luke seen it before he'd met Nadia? Before it had been too late?

Luke had raised his glass again.

'To friendship,' he offered.

The toast was welcome because it gave Kate a much-needed gulp of her wine. Friendship wasn't what was making her blood sing right now. It couldn't account for the delicious knot of desire in her belly or the way her heart was being squeezed so hard it almost hurt.

This…

This was falling in love.

No. It was worse than that.

It wasn't falling. It was the moment when you hit the ground *having* fallen.

Maybe it had happened back at the competition. Or sometime over the last few weeks when she'd been thinking about Luke so often. Or maybe it had always been there and she'd just been trying to protect her heart by dismissing it as no more than a passing physical attraction. A silly crush…

Surely Luke could feel that something huge had just changed between them?

But he was busy scraping the last delicious morsels from his dessert plate. And then he glanced up and saw that Kate was watching.

'So much better than falling in love, isn't it?'

'Huh…?' For a heart-stopping moment, Kate thought he'd been reading her mind.

'Friendship.'

'Oh…' Kate blinked. She tried to smile. He hadn't noticed anything different, then.

Because he wasn't looking?

No. It was more likely because he'd never felt the same way. And never would.

'Especially this kind of friendship,' Luke continued. 'The kind that lasts for ever. It's what you'd hope you could have if you fell in love with the right person. After all the crazy stuff wears off.'

Kate swallowed hard. 'But what's wrong with the crazy stuff?'

She could feel a good dose of it herself right now, making her hyperaware of everything around her. The flicker of the candlelight, the rich smell of good food. Of how impossibly gorgeous Luke Anderson was. She couldn't take her eyes off him as he finished scraping the last of his dessert onto his spoon and lifted it to his lips. She could imagine those hands on her skin. Those lips on hers. The way he ran his tongue over his lips after the spoon had delivered its prize was the last straw. Desire was spiralling into something that felt out of control.

Feeling out of control was so alien to Kate she was sure she shouldn't be liking it at all. Not this much, anyway.

'It doesn't last.' Luke's clipped tone was like a splash of cold water. More than enough to halt that spiralling sensation. 'And you can't trust it, believe me.' His eyes narrowed. 'Are you going to eat the rest of your tiramisu?'

'Um…no.' Her appetite for the sweet treat had somehow vanished in the last few minutes. 'I've had enough. Here…' She pushed her plate towards him and the ease with which Luke accepted the gesture underlined everything they had between them. A closeness that could be tapped back into so easily. Like family…

But he was wrong. Okay, he'd been burned but so had she in the past, albeit that she'd never gone as far as marrying someone. You couldn't give up on something like being in love. If you found the right person, this feeling could last a very long time. Maybe for ever, if you were really lucky.

Kate believed in it. She trusted it. But she couldn't tell Luke that. And she certainly couldn't tell him that it was exactly the way she was feeling. If he even got a hint of it, that easy familiarity between them would vanish. He might convince himself that even friendship couldn't be trusted either and there would never be any more times like this. She might try and text him to set something up but he would always be unavailable. Working. Or simply wary.

'So…it's the sensible thing to do, isn't it?'

'Sorry?' Had she been on another planet while Luke was polishing off her dessert and had missed something he'd said?

Luke put his spoon down.

'To marry someone that you're already great friends with.'

'Oh, no…' Kate put her hands over her eyes. 'This is about that pact again, isn't it?'

'Is it such a crazy idea?'

Kate dropped her hands, her eyes widening. *'Yes.'*

'Why?'

'You can't just marry someone because they're a *friend*…' The concept was shocking. Why would anyone give up on the idea of finding true love that swept everything else into complete shade?

But Luke seemed to be taking this idea seriously. 'Why not? Seems like a pretty good place to start, if you ask me. You always hear people say "I married my best friend".'

Kate could feel furrow lines appearing on her forehead. 'Yes, but…'

'But what?'

'But they have more than that to begin with. You've got to have more than that.'

'Such as?'

Kate could feel colour creeping into her face now. 'Um…attraction?'

Luke leaned towards her. His eyes had a mischievous glint and his mouth had a cheeky curl on one side. 'You don't think I'm attractive? Are you saying I'm ugly?'

'No…' Her cheeks were on fire now. Her body was telling her just how woefully inadequate her embarrassed response was. Weirdly, it was also increasing its response to Luke. Maybe it was that glint in his eyes. Or that smile. He was not only incredibly attractive but he would probably be *fun* in bed, too.

Oh, help…there was that out-of-control sensation again. Sucking her in and hurling her into that spiral of desire.

'And you're gorgeous,' Luke said softly. 'No redblooded male wouldn't find you attractive.'

Kate's head was spinning now. He found her attractive? He *wanted* her…? With a desperate effort, she tried to find a sane corner of her brain.

'It's not just about looks. There's got to be…um… chemistry.'

'Ahh…' Luke sat back in his chair, nodding slowly. 'I get it. You mean the sexual compatibility thing.'

Kate had to close her eyes for a moment so that she could concentrate on breathing. There didn't seem to be enough air in here any more. Her cheeks still felt hot. Good grief, what if someone at a nearby table was listening in to this extraordinary conversation?

Her eyes snapped open. 'Can we go now?'

'Sure.' Luke still seemed perfectly relaxed as he signalled that he was ready for the bill.

'I'll wait outside for you. I could do with a bit of fresh air.'

The air was fresher than she'd expected and Kate pulled on Luke's heavy, wool-lined anorak she had grabbed from the peg on her way out. It was far too big for her but it was warm and…she wrapped her arms around herself and let her chin sink so that her nose was buried in the lining…it smelt like Luke. All macho and masculine and…totally delicious.

She was so lost in the moment that she didn't hear Luke coming up behind her. Wasn't aware of him until she heard the low growl of his voice right beside her ear.

'I think we'd be very compatible.'

Oh… Lord… She'd always thought that women in books going weak at the knees was verging on ridiculous but it *was* actually a thing.

Instinctively, she lifted her head to turn towards that compelling growl and Luke's fingers captured her chin. In slow motion, he tilted his head and closed the gap between them. Kate knew he was going to kiss her and now her brain felt just as weak as her knees. She couldn't have stopped this happening if her life depended on it.

Because she didn't *want* to stop it happening.

That gentle kiss under the moonlight weeks ago had been laced with pleasure and surprise.

This one was a revelation.

It ignited a level of desire that she'd never dreamed she was capable of feeling. She'd certainly never, ever felt anything like this before. But, then, she'd never fallen in love with someone that she already knew so well. Someone she had always loved as a friend…

The combination of that shared history and trust with this newly awoken—and astonishingly fierce—attraction was stunning.

It felt old and familiar as well as being totally new and unbelievably exciting. The softness and warmth of Luke's lips, the teasing touch of his tongue, the way he was holding her face as if it was made of something precious and fragile…

Her eyes remained closed as Luke finally lifted his head.

'See?' His voice sounded a little hoarse. 'That wasn't so bad, was it?'

Kate opened her eyes. She opened her mouth, too, but no words came out.

'But it *was* only a kiss,' Luke added.

Kate blinked. *Only* a kiss? That had been the most amazing kiss ever. Had anyone else in the world ever experienced a kiss quite like that?

'So…' Luke had that glint in his eyes again. 'All we need to find out is if the rest of it works.'

Kate's voice came out in a strangled sort of croak. 'The rest of it…?'

Luke wriggled his eyebrows. '*Sex*, Katy.'

How could a single word have an effect like being hit on that vulnerable point just behind your knees? It actually felt like she was stumbling even though she was standing perfectly still. Luke must have felt her lack of balance because his arm was around her now, holding her steady. He was smiling at her. Confidently—as though he'd found the perfect answer to a problem she was having.

And perhaps he had...

Kate sucked in a deep breath. 'And...um...when do you think we should investigate that?'

His smile widened. 'No time like the present. My apartment's only a couple of blocks from here.'

Kate had already discovered that going weak at the knees was a thing. Now it seemed that your eyes could grow stalks, too.

Luke's smile faded just enough to make him look, and sound, quite sincere.

'If we give ourselves too much time to think about it, we'll find all sorts of reasons why it might not be a good idea and then it'll just get harder.' He cleared his throat and a corner of his mouth quirked. 'No pun intended.'

Kate's breath came out in a huff of laughter. This was the friend she remembered. Incorrigible but, oh, so charming...

'This is a bit weird for me, too,' Luke said quietly. 'But I really think it makes sense. We're thirty-five. We both want more in our lives than just our jobs and we know we like each other, don't we?'

Kate could only nod. He made this sound so reasonable. Sensible, even. Or was desire sabotaging her brain and looking for any excuse to allow her to do what was rapidly becoming the thing she wanted more than anything else in the world?

'More than like,' Luke continued. 'I think we really care about each other. Trust each other. You do trust me, don't you, Katy?'

Kate swallowed hard. 'Yes.'

'Then trust me on this. It'll work.'

Of course it would work. After that kiss, Kate had no doubts whatsoever that sex with Luke would be the most amazing physical experience she would probably ever have. But what about afterwards? Would *that* work?

It might…

You couldn't really just decide to never fall in love again, could you? It either happened or it didn't—it wasn't something you could control.

Was it possible that Luke was already in love with her but he didn't recognise it yet? Possible that he would get the same kind of revelation that she had had?

That would make what they were planning to do a lot more than some kind of social experiment, wouldn't it? It would make it, well…necessary…

Luke found her hand and squeezed it. Still holding it, he turned and started walking.

And, without even a beat of hesitation, Kate followed him.

# CHAPTER SIX

ONE OF LUKE ANDERSON'S favourite things in life was technology—especially when it promised to help him do his job to the very best of his ability.

'It was mind-blowing, Matt. Unbelievable.'

His friend's face filled the screen of the laptop balanced against his knees as Luke lounged on his couch, a half-empty bottle of lager in one hand.

'Four-dimensional imaging? What is that?'

Matteo also had a bottle in his hand and Skype sessions like this were almost as good as the evenings they used to share in Milan. A few drinks, some good food and company that made you want to stay up half the night, talking about anything and everything.

'It's 4D magnetic resonance imaging. You can create a 3D model of, say, the heart, with data from MRI scans at different parts in the cardiac cycle. It's not just the anatomy—you can measure and visualise blood flow in individual arteries.'

'Wow. Sounds very cool.'

'More than cool. You could actually plan a surgical procedure and know how well it's going to work before you even pick up a scalpel.'

'No way…'

'It's true. I was in with our cardiology team today to get a sneak peak. You get the 3D model, plan the corrective procedure and then you can do a blood-flow simulation to see what difference it's going to make with post-operative performance. It won't be available for a while yet but, man, it'll be a game-changer when it is. Wish I could use it on a kid we're monitoring in ICU at the moment.'

'What wrong with the kid?'

'Chest injury from a car crash. We've drained a haemothorax and are managing the lung contusion but I'm starting to suspect that there could be some damage to the aorta.'

It had been Kate's idea, when he'd discussed his niggling concerns about the child's condition over their dinner earlier this evening.

'We've done a CT and transoesophageal echo but I'm thinking we'll run an arch aortogram tomorrow.'

'You mean today.'

'Yeah...' Luke's gaze flicked to the bottom of his screen. 'It *is* getting late. Sorry, mate. I've been talking shop for far too long. What's happening in your life?'

Matteo shrugged. 'Nothing exciting. Same old.'

'How did the date work out last week. With...um... what was her name again? That nurse?'

'Marcella. It was okay. I think she only wanted my body.'

Luke laughed. 'Lucky you.'

Matteo raised his bottle towards the camera in a toast. 'What about you? Still seeing Kate?'

'Yeah. She went home just before I called you, in fact.'

His sheets would still have the scent of her and, in a

short amount of time, he would be able to slide between them and revel in the memory of their time together. The incredible smoothness of Kate's skin. The warmth of her mouth. The taste of her—which was like nothing he'd ever tasted before. So delicious. So addictive. As for the way she responded to even the merest touch of his hands or his tongue. Well…he had no words to try and describe how that made him feel but it was the best feeling ever. As if *he* was the best lover ever…

Matteo shook his head. 'No wonder you're grinning like…what is it? A cheesed-off cat?'

'Cheshire cat. And I'm not.'

'It's getting serious, man. You're spending all your free time with her. And there I was thinking you were never even going to get round to seeing her again after you got home.'

'Fate threw us together.' Luke tried to wipe a new grin off his face, but failed.

He could understand Matteo's bewilderment when it wasn't that long ago that he'd been sharing the view that it wasn't going to happen. Why had they both made it so difficult to connect? All it had needed was a bit of effort on both sides to find time to text or talk on the phone, juggling rosters to make their days off coincide and taking any opportunity to snatch an evening to share a meal—and a few hours in bed…

'So what new adventures have you been on? Another ghost tour in those creepy, underground vaults?'

'No. One was enough.'

'Bike riding?'

'No.' But hiring bicycles to explore the network of disused railway lines running past canals and through forests and tunnels was an experience worth repeating.

'We did go to a bar last week that has a ceilidh every Friday night. That was fun.'

'A kay-what?'

'It's a Scottish thing. Dancing, with someone calling out the instructions. Very social.'

'Did Georgia go too? And her boyfriend? Are you double dating?'

'No.' Matteo's tone had been casual. Too casual? Was he fishing to try and find out whether Georgia was, in fact, single? 'I haven't seen Georgia since Kate and I have been together. We meet somewhere. Or Kate comes to my place.'

'Why don't you go to hers?'

'I don't know.' Luke frowned. 'I guess because she hasn't suggested it yet.'

'Maybe Georgia disapproves.'

'Why would she do that?'

'Dunno.' Matteo was shrugging again. 'She's got some funny ideas, that one.'

'I thought you liked her.' Luke was still frowning. He had the feeling that his friend was holding back about something and that wasn't like him. And it didn't sound at all as if his friend was interested in whether Kate's flatmate was single. Quite the opposite.

'I thought I did, too. Shows how wrong you can be about some people, I guess. Hey, man. I'd better go. Early shift tomorrow.'

'No worries. Let's do it again next week.'

Matteo's easy grin also dispelled the notion that he was holding back. 'We might be doing it for real before long. Don't forget you can't get married unless I'm your best man.'

Luke was still shaking his head as he ended the call.

Shutting the laptop, he lay back to rest his head on the arm of the couch.

A wedding wasn't on the cards. Sure, the 'pact' that he had resurrected was that he and Kate would marry each other if they were both still single at thirty-five but it didn't conjure up any images of a *wedding*. It was more like a general term to signify a committed relationship—the kind that you could build a future on that would be strong enough to raise a family in.

The last few weeks had been all about testing the friendship between them, hadn't it? To see if there was enough of a connection to build that future on.

Would a piece of paper make any difference to that? No.

And he was confident that Kate would feel the same way.

Except…she was a bit of a stickler for rules, wasn't she? Maybe she would want a committed relationship legitimised by something recognisable.

Okay. Why not? A quick trip to a registry office would be doable. As long as it didn't involve any of the hoopla that went with the usual celebration of true love and happy-ever-afters.

What really mattered were the things that would last the distance. A connection that was strong enough to provide a relationship glue that would hold people together through thick and thin. And it was becoming steadily clearer that he and Kate had an endless supply of that kind of glue.

Had he really suggested to Kate that sex would only 'work'?

Man… Talk about the understatement of the century…

If Luke had had any idea of what it could be like,

there was no way in the world that they would have remained simply friends back in med school.

Why on earth had he ever bought into the myth that you needed to fall in love with the person who was your perfect partner for life? That, somehow, that would make the sex better than ever?

*This* was the answer.

To take an established friendship to the next level. To be with someone you really liked, that you didn't have to treat like a piece of precious china that might break if you did something wrong. Someone you could be completely honest with, who knew you well enough to overlook any small wrongdoings and make them something to laugh about and learn from.

This wasn't a friendship with benefits.

This was…well…this was nothing short of perfect as far as Luke was concerned. And, best of all, Kate seemed to feel the same way. Maybe she hadn't invited him into her home yet but she'd been putting as much effort as he was into finding so much time to be together.

Matteo had called them 'adventures' and it was true that they'd been finding some very cool things to do on their days off. Like the ghost tour and the bike ride and the folk dancing. And what about that evening of pure luxury with the reclining sofas and full table service for a movie at the Dominion Theatre? That had been his idea of heaven after a full-on day.

Other couples had been holding hands or snuggling on the sofas but he and Kate didn't need that kind of mushy, romantic stuff. They were best mates when they were out and passionate lovers when they shared a bed. The absolute best of both worlds.

The ping of an incoming text message made him

reach for his phone. Had Matteo thought of something else to say? He was the only person who would text him this late at night. Even Kate kept their increasingly frequent communication to more civilised hours.

But maybe that was changing because this message was from her.

Thanks for dinner. Reckon it's about time you found out how bad my cooking is. G's on night shift Wednesday if you're free.

Had Kate been waiting until Georgia was absent before inviting him to her home? The unexpected twinge of anxiety was Matt's fault. Maybe her best friend *did* disapprove and could end up talking Kate out of making a commitment to a relationship that was based on something as unromantic as a pact.

Or…maybe Kate wanted the place to themselves so that dinner could naturally morph into the kind of sexual playground that was Luke's absolutely favourite place to be these days.

Yep…that was far more likely to be the reason, given how enthusiastic Kate was to play. Tilting the bottle to finish the last swallow of lager, Luke closed his eyes in a blissful moment.

It really didn't get any better than this.

'Whoa…wasn't expecting that.'

The spell of the lingering kiss was broken at the sound of Georgia's voice but, for a heartbeat, Kate's gaze was still locked with Luke's as they drew apart.

'Want me to go out and come in again?'

A huff of laughter from Luke tickled Kate's face.

'No. We're good. I'm just leaving.' Was it her imagination or was he having difficulty dragging his gaze away from hers? 'Sorry, Georgie. I thought I'd be gone before you got back from night shift.'

'No late jobs for a change and the traffic was light.' Georgia dropped her backpack on the floor beside the kitchen door. 'You are allowed to stay here, you know, Luke.' She grinned at him. 'I've known about you and Kate for weeks so it's not exactly a secret that you're sleeping together.'

Luke was grinning back at her. 'We're just good friends.'

Georgia laughed. 'Yeah, yeah...'

Kate was trying to smile. Trying to buy into this light-hearted dismissal that anything significant had been outed but it was difficult.

Almost...heartbreaking?

How ridiculous was that? She'd just had the perfect night, in a perfect setting. A cute little cottage to themselves, a candlelit dinner for two and her own bed to share with her lover.

And that, right there, was where the problem was, wasn't it?

Luke wasn't her *lover*. He was her friend that she just happened to be having sex with. Astonishingly wonderful, passionate, even tender sex and Luke might love her in the way that you loved your best friend but to be a lover, you had to be *in love*.

Luke was gone, with a friendly wave and a promise to text Kate later in the day.

'Any tea in that pot?'

'No. The coffee's hot, though.'

Georgia shook her head, sinking onto one of the

two chairs beside the tiny table tucked into the corner of the kitchen.

'I'm desperate to sleep. Coffee would keep me awake.'

'Really? You've always said it never made any difference after a night shift.'

Georgia yawned. 'Maybe I'm getting old. Or going off coffee or something.' She pulled the band off her ponytail and fluffed her hair with her fingers. 'I can make the tea. You must need to get to work, too.'

'No, I've got a later start. Long day.' Kate was filling the kettle at the kitchen sink but she was staring out of the window. Watching Luke's car as he got to the end of the driveway and turned onto the road.

Was he still thinking about her? About how perfect the night had been? Or was his mind firmly on the day ahead, perhaps going over the complex surgery he could be doing within the next hour or two on that child with a potentially damaged aorta?

The water flowing onto her hand over the top of the kettle made her realise how long she had been distracted.

'Oops…' She tipped half the contents of the kettle out.

'Not like you to be away with the fairies.' Georgia's eyebrows were raised. 'Short of sleep, huh?'

Kate shrugged. 'Maybe…'

'Ooh…do tell. I've almost forgotten what good sex is like.'

Kate was silent. She lit the gas under the kettle and then opened the cupboard to find the teabags and mugs.

'It *was* good, wasn't it? That was some kiss I interrupted…'

'Yeah…' With a sigh, Kate turned and leaned against

the bench as she waited for the kettle to boil. 'It was…
amazing. He's amazing. I'm…' It was disturbing how
intense her voice sounded. The way it broke before
trailing into silence.

Georgia's jaw dropped. 'Oh, my God… You're totally in love with him, aren't you?'

Kate closed her eyes. Her voice was no more than
a whisper. 'Yeah…'

'Does Luke know? Did he say it back? Is *that* what
that steamy kiss was about? Oh, help… I really did in-
terrupt something…'

Kate shook her head. 'No. And no and no.' She
opened her eyes to find her friend staring at her.

'That's a lot of "noes".'

Kate busied herself making the tea. 'I can't tell him.'

'Why not?'

'Because I'd lose him and…and I don't want to lose
him.'

Georgia was frowning now. 'That doesn't make
sense. From what I saw, he's totally into you.'

'As a friend.'

'Yeah…right…' The tone of disbelief echoed Georgia's reaction to Luke's claim that he and Kate were
'just good friends'. 'Who are you trying to kid?'

Kate put the mugs of tea on the table and sat down.
'There's something I've never told you. You know that
Luke and I were friends back in med school?'

'Of course. He was your best friend until he got
married and his wife couldn't cope with him having a
girl buddy.' Georgia grinned. 'Maybe she wasn't wrong
to think you might be a threat.'

'There was no attraction back then. Not on his side,
anyway. And not on mine after I got over that initial

crush. The idea of it would have been shocking. Like…
I don't know…incest, almost. He was like my brother.'

'So when did that change so dramatically?'

'At the rally. The night of the party. He…he kissed
me.'

'And now he's spending every spare minute he's got
with you and giving you the best sex ever and, I have
to say, he looks pretty happy about it.'

Kate nodded. 'He is. Because, as far as he's concerned, we're just friends. Because the "L" word is not
an issue. For him… We made a pact, Georgie. After
graduation, when we'd had too much champagne. We
agreed that if neither of us was married by the time we
were thirty-five—if neither of us had found "the one"
we'd marry each other.'

'No way… Are you trying to tell me you're engaged?'

The headshake was emphatic. 'We haven't actually
talked about that again. I tried to tell him that being
good friends wasn't enough. That there had to be a different kind of connection. I was talking about being
in love but he took it as meaning a sexual connection
and suggested that we gave it a try and…um…' Kate
bit her lip. 'I guess we're still trying that, as far as he's
concerned.'

'But surely he'd be delighted if he knew how you
felt. That you would be prepared to honour the pact.'

'But that's just it. He wants to reinstate the pact because we're not in love. He thinks that's the best foundation for a successful relationship. He fell in love with
Nadia, remember? The first woman he married? And
that was a disaster. If he knew I was in love with him,

or he felt like he might be falling in love with me, he'd run a mile. He'd know he couldn't trust it.'

'Hmm…' Georgia sipped her tea. She was silent for a long time but then her gaze met Kate's steadily. 'Maybe he's right.'

'What?'

Georgia shrugged. 'You're so sure that there are rules to follow and a proper order of doing stuff but what if something like this works better? Like an arranged marriage? He might not be *in* love with you but he cares about you, doesn't he?'

Kate nodded. 'Yes. He always has. As a friend.'

'And the sex is good, right?'

Kate could feel her cheeks warming. 'Oh…yeah… I never knew it could be this good.'

And it wasn't just the sex. Last night, for the first time, they had fallen asleep together. Or rather Luke had fallen asleep and Kate had been awake for a very long time, too aware of the solid presence of his body so close to hers that she could feel as well as hear every breath he took.

It had made her feel…safe?

Protected. It wasn't that she'd ever felt nervous about being in the house alone when Georgia was on a night shift, mind you. No, this feeling of protection was about something much bigger than that.

Protection from feeling alone, perhaps. Or from a future that was emptier than she would want?

Georgia's smile suggested that she could sense what Kate was thinking about. 'Does he want the same things as you? Like kids down the track?'

'Yes, I think so. He said he wants more to life than just his career.'

'And you share the same career. You could support each other and share the kid stuff. You know what?'

'What?'

'It sounds just about perfect to me.' Georgia yawned again. 'I need to sleep.' She got up and took her mug to the sink.

Maybe she was right, Kate thought. How many women would dream of having a gorgeous guy like Luke to care about them? To have fun with. To have mind-blowingly good sex with? To be their life partner and raise a family with? Being in love wore off, everybody knew that. Eventually, the lucky ones were left with…well, pretty much what she and Luke had now.

Georgia was still standing beside the sink. Staring into it, presumably at the dirty breakfast plates that probably had congealed egg fragments all over them.

'I'll do the dishes in a minute.'

But Georgia didn't seem to hear her. She had her hand pressed against her mouth and when she turned away from the sink, her face was pale. Very pale.

Shocked, Kate watched her run from the room. Their small, downstairs bathroom was right beside the kitchen so it was impossible not to hear her throwing up. Especially seeing as Kate followed her. A few minutes later, she was offering a damp facecloth as Georgia finally sat back on her heels and let go of the hair she had been holding back from her face.

'I'll never eat eggs again in my life,' she groaned.

'You didn't eat any in the first place. You just looked at the plates.'

'I know…' Georgia leaned back against the wall, the facecloth pressed against her eyes.

'Are you sick? Running a temperature?' Kate reached for her friend's wrist, to check her heart rate.

'I don't think so.'

'Did you eat something dodgy on night shift? Like a kebab?'

'No.'

Something was nagging at the back of Kate's brain as it collected all available information. Georgia had looked tired but not unwell when she'd arrived home. She hadn't wanted coffee because she said it might keep her awake. Or that she'd 'gone off it'. The nausea had been triggered by the sight of egg yolk.

'Oh, my God…' Kate could feel the colour of her own face fading. 'Are you pregnant. Georgie?'

Georgia didn't respond. She seemed, in fact, to have gone very, very still.

Kate sank onto the bathroom floor and shuffled around so that she was leaning against the same wall as Georgia. It was her sigh that broke the long silence.

'When were you going to tell me?'

'When it was too late to have an argument about whether or not it was a good idea to go through with it.'

Kate's breath came out in a shocked huff. 'Did you think I'd try and persuade you to have a termination?'

Georgia lowered the facecloth. Damp curls framed hazel eyes that seemed a lot bigger than usual. 'Why not? You've never approved of my plan for single parenthood. You told me the whole idea was hare-brained.'

'That doesn't mean I wouldn't support you in whatever you chose to do.' Kate could feel tears prickling at the back of her eyes. 'I can't believe you've kept this to yourself. How pregnant *are* you?'

'About ten weeks.'

Kate's brain had no trouble doing the maths. 'So it was the person you hooked up with at the rally. Who was it?'

'It doesn't matter.'

'Of course it matters. It's your child's father. You need to know about family genetics. You'll need financial support.'

Georgia's headshake was emphatic. 'That's precisely the reason I did it this way. I don't want to know about the father's family. I don't want financial support. I don't want anyone interfering in any way. This is *my* baby. And it's going to stay that way. Don't ask again, Kate, because I'm never going to tell you. I'm never going to tell anyone, *especially* the father. And I couldn't anyway because I don't have his address. I barely remember his name. And…oh, *God*… I'm going to be sick again…'

The vomiting almost seemed an appropriate finale to the impassioned speech. It was some time after that before the atmosphere in the small house felt calmer. Georgia tried another cup of tea and a piece of dry toast and declared herself to be over the bout of morning sickness.

'I'm going to sleep like a log.'

'Are you on another night shift?'

'Yes.'

'Should you even be working at the moment? Aren't there rules about being pregnant and on the road?'

Georgia sighed. 'Yes. And I'll sort that soon but I'm not looking forward to getting stuck behind a desk on light duties. I'm fine, honestly. I'm being careful about lifting and everything. It's not as if my body's not used to this stuff. It's only dangerous if you're doing different things—like riding a horse for the first time. The women that are used to it can ride safely pretty much until they give birth.'

'But there are rules. They're there for a reason.'

Georgia rolled her eyes. 'Cut it out, Kate. I'm a big girl. I get to make my own decisions.' She stood up. 'And right now I'm deciding that it's my bedtime. Have a great day.' She grinned at Kate. 'How could you not, after having such a great night?'

Shock waves were still ebbing around Kate as she drove to work an hour or two later.

Georgia had gone ahead with her crazy scheme not to miss out on being a mother and she was choosing to do it entirely on her own.

It was still beyond anything Kate could imagine doing and she had to admire her friend's courage and determination.

And no wonder Georgia thought that her relationship with Luke offered the perfect compromise. A partnership built on friendship and equality and trust. The idea of heartbreak or 'interference' seemed a million miles away.

On paper, Kate had to agree.

It sounded just about perfect.

So why didn't it *feel* perfect?

Maybe she needed to take a leaf out of Georgia's book. Absorb a bit of that courage and determination and let go of what her friend considered her ridiculous 'rose petal and bluebirds' mentality.

And then it really hit home.

Georgia was *pregnant*. She was going to have a baby

and be a mother. She was choosing to create her own family and give herself the future she wanted.

The kind of future that Kate wanted, too.

The kind that was within touching distance, even. With the added bonus of someone to share it with. Someone who would care about her and support her and…and be an amazing father.

Georgia was right.

*Luke* was right.

Friendship was what mattered.

And this was as perfect as it was ever likely to get.

# CHAPTER SEVEN

'I CAN'T SEE any monsters.'

'Neither can I.'

'It's beautiful…' Kate snuggled closer beneath the arm around her shoulders as she stared out at the glimmering expanse of Loch Ness. 'Bit cold, though.' She glanced up at a leaden sky. 'I think it's going to rain very soon.'

Luke didn't seem to hear her warning. He was shading his eyes with his free hand despite the lack of sunshine. 'Look…did you see *that*?'

'What?'

'There… No, *there*… I saw something.'

'Something long and smooth?' Kate's lips were curving upwards. 'Bit like a giant serpent, perhaps?'

'Exactly. You saw it, too?'

'No. And neither did you.' But the glint of mischief in Luke's eyes made her smile widen. Made her feel suddenly, inexplicably, enormously happy.

'Ah, Katy…' His sigh was theatrical. 'You know me too well.'

But Luke was smiling, too, holding her gaze, and Kate could feel something in the moment change. Maybe it came through the arm still slung over her shoulders. Or maybe it was simply the way he was looking at her. Was he about to kiss her? When the touch would be about something very different from sex?

She felt her heart skip a beat. If he did kiss her right now, it would give her hope that there could be more to this than a 'friends with benefits' thing. There was certainly something much deeper than amusement in that gaze. A familiarity laced with the sheer pleasure of each other's company perhaps. A connection that felt—in that moment—unbreakable.

Had Luke, at some subconscious level, recognised the shift in Kate's attitude to their relationship? That she was on board with the resurrection of their pact? That she realised now that what Luke could offer was actually better than the fairy-tale of being head over heels in love with someone who felt exactly the same way?

She couldn't hold the eye contact, however, in case he could see that this was a deliberate choice to hide how she really felt.

What she *really* wanted... So much that it sent a tiny shudder through her body.

'You're freezing.' Luke moved, taking Kate with him as he turned towards where they'd parked the car. 'Let's find a pub and feed you.'

The crackling fire they found to sit beside a short time later was such a change of scene that Kate found herself pausing before she dipped her spoon into her very welcome bowl of hot soup.

Here she was, warm and being cared for. Would she really rather still be standing beside a romantic, misty lake—being kissed senseless by someone who also hadn't noticed how cold it was?

She could almost feel Georgia poking her. No, of course she wouldn't. That was the stuff of idealistic, teenage girls. It wasn't real life.

'You don't feel like soup?' Luke had noticed her hesitation. 'Want to order something else?'

'No. Soup's great. I was just thinking.'

He grinned. 'Did it hurt?'

'Has anybody ever told you that sometimes you lack a certain maturity?'

His nod was solemn. 'Quite often. What were you thinking about?'

'Georgia.' The honest response slipped out.

'Oh…she was put out to find me in the house when she got home the other day, wasn't she?'

'Not at all. She's got more important things than my love-life to think about at the moment.'

'Like what?'

'She's…um…pregnant.'

'So she *does* have a boyfriend.'

'Not exactly.' Kate bit her lip. The pregnancy wasn't a secret given that everybody would know about it soon enough. But the intentional conception and the determination to keep the baby's father out of the picture was definitely a private matter and Kate would never betray her friend. Even to someone she trusted as much as Luke. 'What makes you think that?'

'Something Matt said. I guess she might have told him that there was someone else. I also think that he might have been a bit disappointed.' Luke's glance was quizzical. 'I got the impression they quite liked each other.'

'Mmm. Me, too.' Kate was concentrating on her soup now. Had the chosen target already been identified amongst the crowd of contenders at the competition when Georgia had told Matteo that there was someone else? It was just as well she *hadn't* chosen Luke's friend as her sperm donor. Imagine how complicated that could make things?

'Is she happy about it?'

'About what?'

She got a slightly bewildered glance this time. 'About being pregnant. Being a solo parent.'

'Ah…yes, I think she is. Her biological clock starting sounding an alarm a while back.'

Luke reached for another slice of the crusty bread in the basket. 'How's your clock?'

'Ticking. No alarms bells yet.'

'But you want kids?'

Kate nodded slowly. 'Yeah… I would certainly like to think of a family in my future.'

Luke caught her gaze. 'Me, too.' He smiled at her. 'How many?'

'At least two.'

'Girls or boys?'

'One of each?'

'Perfect.' Luke was smiling again. 'When do you want to get started?'

'Um… I hadn't thought quite that far ahead.' The next few months were enough to be dealing with. How things would pan out between herself and Luke. And now, watching Georgia go through each stage of this pregnancy until she was holding her newborn baby in her arms.

Kate caught her breath. Imagine that…

'The rate of complications goes up after you hit forty,' Luke said, matter-of-factly, dipping his bread into his soup. 'So does the ease of conception.'

'True.' Kate took another spoonful of her soup, marvelling at how they could be having a conversation like this and eating their lunch as if it was nothing out of the ordinary.

'So you probably want to have both of these well-planned babies before you hit the big Four-Oh, yes?'

'I guess.'

'And nobody gets pregnant on their first attempt.'

'I think Georgia did.'

'Do you know how rare that is? Some perfectly normal couples take a year to conceive.'

For the next few minutes they both ate in silence. Luke finished first, wiped his mouth with his paper napkin and sat back against the stuffed leather of the armchair.

'Right. I've done the maths.'

'Oh?'

'Two kids, with the apparently ideal gap of two years between them and preferably born before you hit the next decade. Allowing for a possible year for conception that brings us to…ooh, let's see…right about now.'

Kate's spoon settled into her almost empty bowl with a distinct clatter. She was doing her best to fully embrace the idea of committing to a long-term relationship with Luke even if he wasn't—and possibly would never be—in love with her, but this… This was a huge new step along that track.

'You want to try for a *baby*?'

'Why not?' Luke reached across the table and caught her hands. 'We've proved this can work, haven't we?

We like each other—a lot. The sex is…well, it's amazing for me.'

The skin contact of his hands on hers was enough to send tingles up Kate's arms to spread throughout her entire body. The extra squeeze only accentuated them.

'For me, too,' she murmured. Hopefully no one else in this quiet country pub was near enough to be overhearing this conversation.

'Do you remember what I told you the night we made that pact?'

'I have to admit that parts of it a bit blurry. It was a long time ago, Luke. And we'd both had a lot to drink.'

'Yeah…oddly, though, I remember a lot of it very clearly. I remember telling you that you were my best mate and I loved you to bits.' Luke's voice was also low. Intense, even. 'That doesn't seem to have changed. Right from when I saw you at the rally, it felt like things were just the way they always were between us. We both want the same things out of life. So…why *not*?'

'Um…' Oh, help. He'd said the 'L' word and, even though it had been delivered under the guise of friendship and was therefore perfectly acceptable, it was doing weird things to Kate. It was exactly what she'd dreamed of hearing but…but not like *this*…

For one horrible moment she thought she might cry.

Luke was watching her, a furrow between his brows. 'Is it because we're breaking rules, Katy? Your rules?'

Kate swallowed hard. 'We're talking about the rest of our lives, Luke. About…about a *family*…'

'Ah… I get it.' Luke nodded slowly. 'It's too much to think about having kids together if we're not married, right?' He smiled at her. 'It's okay. I know I said I'd been there and done that and I was over the whole marriage thing but I really only meant picking your partner by the crazy, totally unreliable, 'falling in love' business. I'm happy to marry you. It's just a visit to a registry office to sign some papers after all.'

Kate couldn't breathe. This had morphed into a *proposal*? One that was so far from being the romantic declaration she would have wished for herself, it triggered a sharp and totally unexpected pang in her chest. Was it actually physically possible for a little bit of your heart to break?

'You guys all done?' The cheerful voice of the waitress was a rude reminder that this wasn't the place for a conversation like this.

Except…maybe it was.

Like everything else about this relationship, it was based on common sense and openness and trust and there was nothing wrong with any of those things. Quite the opposite. Okay…maybe this wasn't the way that Kate had wanted it to happen but she was going to end up with exactly what she'd dreamed of, wasn't she? A future with someone she loved with all her heart.

A family. Maybe a lot sooner than she had expected.

Summoning a somewhat shaky smile, she nodded at the waitress.

'Thank you. Yes, I think we're all done.'

But when the plates had been cleared away and Kate caught Luke's gaze, ready to agree that a registry office wedding would be fine by her, she couldn't do it.

As friends, this idea of creating such a strong partnership that they could raise a family together was acceptable.

But marriage? A *wedding*?

That was too bound up in her head and her heart

with the concept of celebrating love in public. Of making pledges in front of others that were heartfelt and genuine. And…okay, maybe it was immature. Silly, even, but the traditions were significant, too. The white dress. The vows and the music and the party afterwards. An aisle to walk slowly down as you got closer and closer to the person who mattered more than anyone else in the world. Someone she was totally and absolutely in love with—who felt exactly the same way about *her*…

Perhaps it was a stretch to think of a 'quick visit to a registry office' as a wedding but it would be the only one she would ever have, wouldn't it? But if she was patient, maybe one day Luke might feel differently? Might see her as more than a friend or the potential mother of his children? That would be when she would want to consider a wedding—not now…

And…maybe knowing that a baby was a possibility would be a trigger for Luke to feel differently?

As he'd pointed out himself, it could take a long time to get pregnant so maybe giving up the protection they'd been using would be the first step to encourage Luke towards that change.

Her gaze slid away from his.

'We don't need a wedding, do we? Or a piece of paper to legitimise things?' Somehow, she even summoned a shrug. 'It's not as if we needed a written version of the pact to make it work.'

A quick glance showed how surprised Luke was looking. Impressed, even?

'That's true.' His smile had that cheeky edge she loved. 'Hey, if you're prepared to break the rules, count me in. But…'

'But?'

'I don't know… You might change your mind. It's a break with tradition that seems more like something I'd do than you would.'

'Maybe I'm getting older and wiser.'

'Hmm. And maybe you might change your mind. Why don't I see what's involved? How much paperwork it might take. Just in case.'

Another shrug was easy to find. 'Sure. But only if you want to. I'm not that bothered.'

'And the baby thing? You want to give that a go?'

Would it be totally irresponsible to take a risk like that? To break such big personal rules in the hope that the odds were in her favour and that it would take enough time for Luke to have some kind of epiphany when the possibility of becoming a father became increasingly real?

Kate was still riding the wave of that last shrug. 'Why not? It's not going to change anything anytime soon, is it? When—or if—it happens, I'm sure we'll be ready for it.'

'I'm late.'

'So am I. And there's no way I'm going to get these pants done up.' Georgia was struggling to get her buttonhole near the button but there was an obvious gap of a couple of inches. 'What am I going to do? I'm never late to work.'

'No. I mean I'm *late*…'

Georgia let go of her waistband, her eyes widening. 'You don't mean *late* late?'

Kate could only nod.

'How late?'

'A week.'

'That's nothing. Could be stress.'

'I'm as regular as clockwork. And it fits.'

'Fits with what?'

'When we decided not to bother with protection any more.'

Georgia's mouth was as wide as her eyes now. 'You *planned* this?'

'Not exactly. We both thought it would take ages. It never happens the first time.'

'It did with me.'

'I know.' Kate stared at Georgia's unfastened waistband. Would her belly be expanding inexorably like that in a few months' time?

With a *baby* growing inside her?

The thought was mind-blowing.

Confusing. Scary. But there were definitely tendrils of excitement trying to take hold.

'Okay.' Georgia's breath came out in a decisive huff. 'First of all, you need to find out. I've got a spare test kit or two in my room.' She grinned at Kate. 'I bought a bulk supply.'

'I could get a blood test at work.'

'Don't you want to know now?'

'I'm not sure.' Kate's gaze drifted back to Georgia's current problem. 'I reckon a safety pin would do the trick for now. Can you find a bigger pair at work?'

'Yes. But don't change the subject. Have you told Luke?'

'Not yet. I'm seeing him tonight.'

'Maybe you could do the test together?'

'Sounds like a fun evening.' Kate bit her lip.

Would Luke be as shocked as she was at the possibility of life changing so dramatically in the near future? She'd certainly know how committed he was to the idea of taking the pact to the ultimate conclusion, wouldn't she? Whether or not the test was positive, she'd see exactly how he really felt about it in a heartbeat. In the moment he raised his gaze to hers, having looked at that little window on the stick.

'But it's not a bad idea.' Kate smiled at Georgia. 'How 'bout you find the kit for me and I'll find you a safety pin?'

No way…

It couldn't be this easy, surely?

To have found the perfect partner and then to plan on starting a family and have it happen just like that?

He was going to be a *father*?

Luke didn't need the odd prickle behind his eyes to tell him how huge this was. The emotion was so overwhelming he couldn't think of a thing to say when he raised his gaze from the stick to look at Kate.

But maybe he didn't need to say anything. Kate was looking pretty misty herself. And…vulnerable?

Had she thought he might not be happy about this? Freaked out, even?

With the stick still in his hand, he gathered her into his arms and held her tightly. Then he pressed a kiss against her hair.

'I should have known.' He smiled. 'Set you a challenge and you have to exceed all expectations, don't you? Do better than anyone else.'

'I think we did this one together.' Kate tilted her head up. 'You're really happy about this, aren't you?'

'I'm thrilled. Aren't you?'

'I'm…a bit shocked, to be honest. I thought I had months to get used to the idea. To plan what to do about taking time off work and…and where we're going to live.' She pulled back from Luke. 'Where *are* we going to live? We work in different cities. This apartment's far too small and I can't ask Georgia to move out of our house—she's the one who took the lease. And she's already planning how it's going to work after *her* baby arrives.'

'How much do you love Glasgow?'

'I love my job.'

'Me, too. But I've always loved my job—it doesn't seem to matter where.'

'You mean you might want to shift?'

'I mean anything's possible. We could go anywhere, Katy. Anywhere in the world. We're going to be parents.' Luke blew his breath out in an astonished huff. 'How amazing is that? We could choose the best place on earth to bring up a family and make it happen.'

'Is there a best place?'

'I reckon. Somewhere that has a lot of sunshine, maybe. And beaches. Good schools and excellent hospitals. Australia?'

Kate's jaw dropped. 'You can't be serious.'

'No.' But Luke's lips were curving into a wide smile. Man, the possibilities suddenly opening up were exciting. 'I think New Zealand would be even better. I've got a friend who emigrated a few years back and he reckons it's the only place in the world he'd want to be raising his family.'

Kate shook her head. 'You're crazy.'

'*This* is crazy. But it's happening.' Luke pulled her back into his arms and spun them around with a few impromptu dance steps. 'We've chosen each other. We've chosen to start a family. Why not choose a whole new life? A new beginning for the rest of our lives?'

Excitement was morphing into an astonishing flash of happiness. This was so much better than anything he'd factored into his life plan. Because he could trust it? Kate was never going to break his heart. They had chosen to be together like sensible adults who knew that friendship was the only reliable base for a relationship. She felt exactly the same way he did about it and she was prepared to totally commit herself. The proof of that was in that little plastic stick he still had in his hand.

He let the stick drop as he brought the dance to a halt. He shifted his hands so that he was holding Kate's head between them and then he bent to kiss her. A long, slow kiss that she responded to the way she always did—as if she was melting into his arms.

He loved that. He loved it that you could be no more than the best of friends and that sex could be better than ever.

And he loved it that a whole new phase of life was taking shape around him—like ripples spreading out from a thrown pebble. He was that pebble.

No. He *and* Kate were. All these new possibilities were only there because they were together. A new home. Maybe in a new place. A real home, with a whole family of his own.

*This* was exactly why he'd had that epiphany that resurrecting their pact wasn't such a silly idea. When he'd realised just how much he loved kids, as he'd watched them scrambling for the sweets and gifts during that convoy at the end of the competition. After that moment he'd had with the little boy who'd been a part of that bus-crash scenario.

Everything was suddenly falling into place, far more easily than he would have believed possible.

Thanks to Kate.

He had to break the kiss. Before it spiralled into something that would make him forget anything else for quite some time.

'Thank you,' he whispered aloud.

Kate's eyes drifted open. She was blinking up at him as if it was difficult to focus.

'What for? Getting pregnant?'

Luke smiled down at her. 'For being you. For being my best friend. For not…' He wasn't sure exactly what he was trying to put into words now.

He could feel her body tensing as it came out of that melted state. Her eyes had darkened, too. They looked clear now. Piercing almost.

'For not falling in love with you?'

Luke closed his eyes, his breath coming out in a sigh of relief. 'Exactly. This isn't crazy stuff we can't trust. We both want this so we know it's going to work.'

'Mmm…' She was pulling away from him slowly. 'Well, it's in the fine print, isn't it?'

Luke frowned. There was something in her tone that he couldn't identify. Something that bothered him, even though Kate was smiling.

'The pact?' Kate stooped to pick up the pregnancy test stick that he'd dropped. 'We made it because we were friends. If that changed, it wouldn't work, would it?'

'Mmm.' Oddly, his tone was an exact echo of Kate's. A little off-key? Something was bothering her. But what?

He watched her drop the stick into the rubbish bin. 'Is it too early for me to have a craving for something, do you think?'

He couldn't see her face at the moment, but her voice sounded perfectly normal again. Light-hearted even.

'Depends what it is…' He knew what he wanted. To kiss her again and take her into his bed. To forget about everything else for the rest of the evening.

'Nachos.' Kate turned and grinned at him. 'That Mexican restaurant round the corner has the best nachos ever.'

'Takeout or eat in?'

'Takeout,' Kate said. 'That way you'll have your laptop handy. You can show me everything I don't know about New Zealand.'

'Wow…you'd really consider that?' Every time he thought he knew this woman so well, she had another surprise in store for him.

He loved that about her, too.

'Well… So far, you've persuaded me to buy into the pact and give up on my lifelong dream of being swept off my feet by a grand passion. Now we're actually going to have a *baby.*' There was a brightness in her eyes that suggested tears might not be far away but she was still smiling. 'I'd say the chances of talking me into starting a new life on the opposite side of the world are pretty good, wouldn't you?'

Was this what was bothering Kate at some level? How much of what was changing in their lives was about persuasion and how much was what Kate was really happy to be doing?

Had she brushed off the idea of getting married because she thought that was what he'd prefer? He had dismissed marriage along with the idea of ever falling in love again when they'd first reconnected but maybe it was more important to Kate than he realised. Especially with a baby on the way. Had she been hiding how she really felt?

'You know how I downloaded those forms about registering an intention of getting married?'

Kate was putting on her coat, ready to go out and get their dinner. 'Yeah. I had no idea you couldn't just rock up to a registry office and do the deed.'

Luke picked up his own coat. 'I think we should sign them. Just in case.'

'In case of what?'

'In case we…oh, I don't know…decide that it would be better for our kid to have married parents. Or if we decided to emigrate and suddenly find it's a whole lot easier to be legally a couple. It's not as if we have to set an actual date or anything yet. I'd leave that up to you. Whatever *you* want.'

A flash of something crossed Kate's face and Luke was certain that he was right. She had been hiding something and he was doing the right thing here, by giving her some options. Control even.

He couldn't be entirely sure but she looked a bit more relaxed.

'Okay. Thanks.' She was smiling again. '*Now* can we go and get some food?'

The lights were on in every corner of this paediatric ward of Glasgow's Eastern Infirmary, even though it was the middle of the morning.

Kate glanced through a blurred window at the heavy, grey sky.

'It's raining. Again.'

'That's Scotland for you.' Her registrar was leading the way to the next patient on their ward round.

'How long have you been here?'

'Two years. But I've applied for a job back home and I've got my fingers crossed. They're short of paediatricians in New Zealand at the moment.'

'So I hear…' Kate smiled at the young mother sitting cross-legged on the bed with a baby on her lap. 'Hi, Janet. Oh, my goodness…you're looking happy this morning, Muriel!'

It was such a grown-up name for the three-month-old and, along with the bright red curls on her head and the cutest button nose, it made her smile every time. Especially now, when Muriel had come through a terrifying battle with pneumonia but had now been out of Intensive Care for several days.

And she was such a smiler. Kate only had to touch the tiny nose or make a surprised face and the baby's mouth curved into a grin that seemed to go from ear to ear.

'She still sounds a wee bit wheezy. I'm going to have a good listen to her chest now. How's her feeding going?'

'She's still getting a bit tired so I have to do it little and often. I'm so happy to be breastfeeding again, though.'

'It's so much better for both of you.' Kate dangled the disc of her stethoscope so that Muriel could catch it in her hands. She smiled at the baby and got a big grin in response. For a moment she was completely distracted by the tiny fingers exploring the new toy.

Baby fingers were just *so* adorable…

These momentary distractions were becoming familiar now. She'd had nearly three weeks to get used to the idea of being pregnant herself. That, in the not-too-distant future, she would have one of these tiny people in her own life. Her own set of tiny little fingers and toes to marvel over. Her own smiles to make the world seem suddenly a much happier place.

Her own baby to hold and worry about and…and love…

She loved this baby growing inside her already. She couldn't give her such an adult-sounding name, though. Her favourites were the classics, like Emily or Amy for a girl and James for a boy. Of course, James sounded a bit too grown-up, too, but he could be Jamie to start with, couldn't he?'

'Sorry?' Kate covered up that she hadn't heard Janet's question clearly by making a show of gently extracting her stethoscope from small fists and placing it on the tiny chest.

'I'm just wondering what I can do to keep her safe when we get home. I'm so scared that she's going to catch something else and I'll end up watching her on that breathing machine…' Janet's voice hitched '…not knowing if I was ever going to get to hold her again.'

'The best thing you can do is to keep her away as best you can from anyone who has any symptoms of a respiratory illness—even a cold. Don't let them hold her or kiss her. Don't let anyone smoke anywhere near her. And she'll be old enough for her vaccines soon. That's the best protection. Make sure all her caregivers are up to date with things like the whooping cough booster and flu shots.'

Kate was silent for a minute as she moved her

stethoscope from one lung field to another. Muriel was staring up her with wide, blue eyes and one hand curled around the tubing of the stethoscope.

'That all sounds so much better... I think you're going to be able to go home very soon, sweetheart. Maybe tomorrow.'

Her next patient was a two-year-old boy who had suffered a serious leg fracture, requiring surgery, after an accident on a trampoline. Sean was a very different personality from the happy Muriel. Dark-haired and very shy, he was inclined to hide his face against his mother if spoken to directly by anyone he didn't know well. He'd been here long enough for Kate to become a familiar figure, though.

'Can you wiggle your toes for me, Sean? This little piggy goes to market...this little piggy stays home... Ooh... I saw that little piggy move. Yay!'

She shared a smile with Sean's mother. 'He's making great progress.'

'When can he go into a cast? And come home? My husband's about at the end of his tether with the older kids. My mum's great but she can't take much more time off work...'

'The surgeons are going to review him after his X-rays today. We should know something by this afternoon. I'll pop back and talk to you as soon as I can.'

Her registrar was shaking her head as they moved on. 'I don't know how some of these families cope. Did you know that Sean's the youngest of five and the oldest is only ten? How hard would that be?'

'I can't imagine.'

It was scary enough to think about being the caregiver for one tiny, defenceless baby and Kate was getting more worried about Georgia with every passing week. How would she cope on her own? Especially now that Luke was getting more excited about the possibility of a new life in New Zealand. He'd found several positions going, one in the biggest city of Auckland in the North Island and a couple in a much smaller town, at the top of the South Island, in a place called Nelson that seemed to have a hospital big enough to need specialist paediatric staff like both herself and Luke.

Last night, he'd shown her pictures of the kind of scenery they would have on their doorstep. Astonishingly beautiful beaches and forests and views of islands and it looked as if the sun shone all the time.

'Have you ever been to Nelson?' Kate asked her registrar.

'Only on holiday.'

'Was it sunny all the time?'

Her registrar laughed. 'Pretty much.'

'Would it be a good place to work?'

'It would be a dream. Great hospital with enough of a population base to keep things interesting. Not somewhere I can dream about until I get some impressive post-grad qualifications, though. It's competitive enough to give them the luxury of choosing the best.'

The comment came back to Kate as she finally finished her busy day and was struggling to open her umbrella as she emerged from the Eastern's front doors. She had arranged to meet Luke in a nearby pub across the main road for a quick meal before they went to an opening of a new art exhibition.

She would have to tell him about what she'd heard. That Nelson must be the place to pick if so many people wanted to live and work there. He wouldn't be fazed by hearing about how competitive it was to get a job. If anything, that would probably make him even keener. And he didn't need to worry, did he? Luke was the best in his field. And she had gathered some hard-won postgraduate qualifications herself. How good would it be if they could both get new job offers easily? A sign that it was the right thing to do?

Kate tilted her umbrella to try and stop it blowing inside out. She could feel her legs getting damp and cold as she hurried towards the controlled crossing at the intersection of these main roads and there was a knot in her stomach that she knew was caused by her worry about deserting Georgia. How could she be seriously considering emigrating?

Because this was the kind of weather she hated so much?

Because the dream of the perfect family deserved to have a perfect setting?

Maybe Georgia should consider the idea of emigrating herself? It wasn't as if she had family to help out here. How good would that be, to have her own baby growing up with her best friend's child as a kind of cousin? Georgia might actually like the idea. Not only would the father of her baby remain unknown, he could be half a world away and so much easier to forget.

Unless it had been one of the New Zealand paramedics that had been at the competition? That blond-headed guy they'd sat with at that first dinner maybe. What was his name...

Ken.

No... Dave.

He'd certainly been very friendly. He'd liked Georgia and he'd been a very long way from home. Why not throw a bit of casual sex into the enjoyment of a new experience?

Good grief…why hadn't that occurred to her before?

Slightly dazed, Kate realised that the lights had changed some time ago and most of the pedestrians waiting to cross were already more than halfway across the road.

And…wasn't that Luke standing on the corner outside the pub, waiting for her? She couldn't really tell from this distance but it seemed as if he was looking right at her, so she raised her hand in a wave. The unexpected pleasure of seeing him so soon prompted an automatic smile but it faded swiftly. Why wasn't he inside in the warmth? He didn't even have an umbrella, for heaven's sake…

The lights were flashing a warning now, but Kate made a run for it. Both she and Luke would only get a whole lot wetter if she waited for the next cycle of lights.

The rain was even heavier now and it distorted the headlights of the vehicles. Someone tooted and Kate turned her head for an instant, aware that she wasn't following the rules and probably deserved the reprimand.

That was why she didn't see the car in the next lane, hidden by the tooting SUV, taking off the instant the traffic lights changed.

She just saw the blur of headlights coming towards her.

And then…nothing…

# CHAPTER EIGHT

*No-o-o...*

For just a heartbeat, Luke was frozen the spot with disbelief.

He'd seen Kate waiting at the corner for the lights to change and he'd wondered why it had taken her so long to follow the other pedestrians. She'd clearly been lost in thought so the contrast, when she'd spotted him, had been revealing.

Even from this distance, he could see how happy she had been to see him. That smile...

It had made him feel so...special. To be able to give someone pleasure simply by existing. By waiting to give them your company. He might be getting rather wet by standing outside like this but he wasn't cold. How could he be when such an astonishing warmth was being created inside him? And he wasn't going to go inside either. Not until Kate was here.

He was actually smiling himself as he saw her start to run across the road. He could see that the signal was flashing, which meant that you weren't supposed to start crossing at that point. He'd have to tease her about breaking rules like this. Except that she was breaking those rules because she wanted to be with *him* and Luke couldn't think of anybody else who had ever done that.

He heard the SUV toot its warning. And he saw the moment the car in the next lane took off, so fast its wheels skidded slightly on the wet road. Kate was running and, for a split second, it seemed that she was going to make it. It would be a near miss that would probably give her nothing more than a fright.

Except she didn't quite make it. He saw her falling. Saw her umbrella float away from her in a graceful arc, tumbling over itself before it hit the ground. More vehicles were sounding their horns now because few people could see why the traffic had stalled in front of a green light. The cacophony of sound seemed an appropriate background to the sense of panic that kicked in after Luke's momentary freeze.

*Katy…*

People were getting out of their vehicles by the time he sprinted into the middle of the road. Horns were still blaring and people were shouting.

'What the hell happened?'

'Call an ambulance.'

'The hospital's just down the road.'

'Call the police.'

Someone picked up Kate's umbrella and moved to hold it over the crumpled figure on the tarmac.

'I'm a doctor… Let me through…' Luke had to push past the gathering huddle of strangers. He dropped to his knees beside Kate, oblivious to the puddle he was kneeling in or the cold rain trickling down his face.

The light was flickering, with the shapes of people moving in front of headlights and the traffic lights changing, but he could see that Kate's eyes were closed.

Was she breathing?

Luke cradled the top of her head with his hand, not simply because he needed to stop any movement in case she had injured her neck, but because he needed to touch her for way more than medical reasons. He put his other hand gently on her abdomen. He'd be able to feel the movements of breathing more easily than see them in this light.

'Kate? Can you hear me?'

Luke could feel the muscles beneath his hand lurch as a deep breath was dragged in. And then Kate's eyelids flickered.

'Stay still, hon… Don't move…'

He heard the blast of a nearby siren.

'Move out of the way,' someone yelled.

A police car edged its way through the traffic that had now stopped in both directions. And behind that were the flashing beacons of an ambulance that had probably already been in the queue of traffic leaving the hospital.

Kate was blinking up at Luke now and her mouth opened. The distressed sound was only quiet but Luke would have heard it no matter how loud the background was. It cut through him like a knife.

'It's okay, Katy… Everything's going to be okay…'

Was it?

How badly was she hurt?

Maybe nothing was going to be okay. For either of them…

The fear that kicked in then was crippling. Unprofessional. It didn't matter that he could see that Kate was conscious and therefore had an open airway and was breathing. He needed to check for any major injuries. Blood loss…

It was just as well the paramedics were here now. Luke simply had to hold Kate's head still and he could lean close enough to try and give her reassurance.

Give himself reassurance, too?

'It's okay,' he kept repeating. 'Everything's going to be okay.'

'Did anyone see exactly what happened?' the paramedics asked. 'How fast was the car going? Was she knocked out?

'Yes,' Luke told them. 'She was unconscious when I got here.'

'Let's get a collar on and scoop her. We need to get her off the road.'

'No…' Kate was trying to move. 'I'm all right.'

'I think she fell,' someone spoke up from the huddle of onlookers. 'I'm not sure that the car actually touched her but it was a bit of a blur what with the rain and everything. It all happened so fast.'

'Stay still, Katy,' Luke said. 'We'll get you into A and E so we can check you out properly.' Right now, it didn't make a difference whether she had fallen or been hit by a car. She had hit her head hard enough to knock her unconscious and that could well indicate a serious injury.

A cervical collar was strapped around Kate's neck and the scoop stretcher that separated into two pieces to be eased in from either side of her body meant that she could be moved without interfering with the alignment of her spine. There were warm blankets to cover her with and the heating in the ambulance was turned up high but the trip back to the hospital only a block away was slowed because of the traffic jam and both Kate and Luke were shivering by the time they were under the bright lights of the emergency department.

'You're soaked,' Kate said. 'I'm s-so sorry, Luke. This was m-my fault…'

'Shh…it doesn't matter. Is anything hurting?'

'Let's get her onto the bed.' A consultant was waiting to lead the team in the resuscitation area Kate's stretcher was wheeled into. 'On my count. One, two… three…' The doctor's eyes widened as he looked down at his patient. *'Kate?'*

'Car versus pedestrian,' the paramedic said. 'She was KO'd.'

'It was my fault,' Kate whispered. 'The lights were changing and I made a run for it.'

The scoop stretcher was being unclipped and removed. The consultant was keeping Kate's head still.

'Any trouble breathing?'

'No.'

'Any pain?'

People were removing Kate's clothing. Someone was sticking ECG electrodes to her skin.

'I… No, I don't think so. Maybe my head, a bit…'

Her hair was wet, dark against the white sheet on the bed. To his horror, Luke could see a faint pink stain appearing.

'She's bleeding,' he snapped. 'From a head injury.'

The consultant glanced up. 'And you are…?

'Luke Anderson. I'm Kate's…' The hesitation was involuntary. What could he say?

*I'm Kate's friend?*

*I'm the father of Kate's baby?*

He was much more than either of those things, though, wasn't he?

He was Kate's *person*.

The person who loved her enough to want to spend the rest of his life with her.

So much so that in that awful moment of standing there, frozen, on the side of the road, he'd known that he couldn't live without her.

He was…oh, God…he was *in love* with her, wasn't he?

And it felt like he always had been. The truth of it had just been hiding but something had shifted in the shock of seeing Kate hit by that car and now wave after wave of this extraordinary feeling was washing over him, threatening to knock him off his feet.

'Luke's a surgeon.' Kate was filling the gap his hesitation had left. 'Over at Edinburgh's Royal Children's Hospital. And he's…he's my fiancé.'

*Fiancé?*

But Kate had brushed off the idea of a registry office wedding as being unnecessary. Undesirable, even. On top of his stunning epiphany, the ground was still moving beneath his feet. What on earth was going on here?

'No way…' one of the nurses in the room gasped, looking up from her task of wrapping a blood-pressure cuff around an arm. 'You kept that quiet, Kate.'

'Let's celebrate the engagement later, shall we?' But the consultant was smiling. 'Right now, I want to see what damage you've done to yourself. What's the BP?'

'Ninety-five over sixty.'

'I'm usually on the low side.' Kate's voice sounded steadier now. 'Look… I can wiggle my fingers and toes. Nothing hurts.'

'We'll get an X-ray of your C-spine before we take that collar off. You hit your head hard enough to get knocked out, even if it wasn't for long. And I don't like the look of that bruise on your hip. Could have been where the car clipped you. We should check for a pelvic fracture, too.'

'No…no X-rays…'

Another tiny, surprised silence fell.

'I'm…' Kate's glance locked with Luke's, her eyes dark with something that looked like fear. 'I'm pregnant.'

The fear was contagious. Maybe he was less anxious about Kate now that he could see how alert she was and that she was claiming to feel all right, but there was someone else to worry about, too, wasn't there?

He took hold of her hand and squeezed it. Kate squeezed back but didn't release the pressure. She was clinging to his hand and that was fine by him. He didn't want her to let go. The pressure felt like an anchor, holding him steady in a space where he still felt like he was spinning out of control.

He had fallen in love with her. The one thing he had sworn never to do. The one thing that he couldn't trust. And Kate felt the same way. She'd said it herself only days ago. That she wasn't in love with him. That that was the only reason that the pact was working out so perfectly. He could hear very clear echoes of her voice.

*If that changed, it wouldn't work, would it?'*

*You've persuaded me to buy into the pact and give up on my lifelong dream of being swept off my feet by a grand passion…*

'Right.' The consultant had taken the new information in his stride. 'Let's do a thorough secondary survey, then. We'll hold off on the X-rays until we know what we're dealing with. Now…let's have a good look at your head. What day is it today, Kate?'

'Wednesday.'

'Time?'

'Um…it was after five when I left work. I was running late to meet Luke at the pub. Ow…!'

'Sore?'

'Bit tender.'

'You've got a good lump. And it's grazed a bit but I can't feel anything boggy. I don't think you've fractured your skull.'

'The bruising's superficial,' a registrar added. 'More consistent with hitting the road than contact with a vehicle. Abdo's soft. Pelvis is stable.'

'I think I tripped,' Kate said. 'I remember seeing the lights of the car really close and thinking that I had to get out of the way.'

The consultant undid the straps of the neck collar. 'Don't move yet.' He was palpating the back of her neck. 'Any pain?'

'No.'

'Try moving your neck very gently. Chin down… and up…'

'It's fine, honestly.'

'To the right…and left… No pain?'

'None. I've just got a bit of a headache. It's nothing that a paracetamol won't fix. Can I sit up now? Please?'

She was still holding Luke's hand as pillows were found and she was helped to sit up a short time later, when everyone was satisfied that she hadn't suffered a serious injury.

That was how he could feel her wince.

'What is it? What's hurting?'

'It's nothing.' But Kate's hand had gone to her abdomen. 'Just a bit of a cramp.'

She looked up in time to catch the swift glance between Luke and the consultant. 'What? It wasn't enough of a bump to have hurt the baby...' Her voice wobbled. 'Was it...?'

'Let's do an ultrasound. How many weeks are you, Kate?'

'We only found out a few weeks ago. Around seven weeks, I guess.'

'Try not to worry. Let's move you out of Resus to somewhere a bit quieter. We'll do the ultrasound. I want you to stay under observation for a bit, anyway, to make sure it's only a mild concussion.' He smiled at Kate as they prepared to move her bed. 'You've been lucky, haven't you?'

*Lucky?*

Kate didn't bother trying to wipe away the tears rolling down her face. She didn't open her eyes either.

'It could have been worse.' Luke's voice sounded raw. 'You could have been killed, Katy.'

She started to nod but it made her headache worse. Instead, she dragged her hand over her face, taking a deep breath that went in as a sniff and came out as a sigh.

'It's okay, Luke. You don't have to stay here all night.'

'I'm not going anywhere.'

With an effort, Kate opened her eyes. 'Don't be daft. Your clothes are still damp. My grandma would have said you'll catch your death if you sit around like that.'

'Urban myth. Like breakfast being the most important meal of the day.'

'Which is another thing. When did you last have something to eat?'

'I can't remember. Probably about the same time you did.'

The lopsided tilt of Luke's mouth showed his appreciation of her attempt to show concern for his well-being but was that really what she was trying to do?

Maybe she needed him to go away and leave her alone to deal with this.

Because it was huge.

Heartbreaking…

'I'm okay, Luke.' Kate swallowed hard. She needed him to believe that. Just like she needed him to believe that she wasn't in love with him. If he knew just how badly she needed him to hold her right now and keep telling her that everything would be okay—like he had when she'd been lying on that road—he might guess how she really felt.

How afraid she was of losing him, as well as their baby.

Was the perfect pact starting to unravel?

'It's not as if it was…*real*.' Kate had to squeeze her eyes shut. Her last word came out as no more than a whisper.

'What do you mean?' Luke sounded bewildered. 'Of course it was real.'

He was right. The baby had been very real. Knowing they were going to be parents had been very real. They'd been scouring the globe for the perfect place to raise a family, for heaven's sake.

She had loved this baby already…

Maybe what she was actually saying was that their partnership wasn't real? That there was something clinical about implementing that pact? That she didn't think that Luke could feel this loss as much as her because he wasn't as invested as she was in either the relationship or their future family?

But when the silence had continued long enough to make her open her eyes, what she could see in Luke's face was confusing. He looked so tired.

Sad…

As if he was hurting as much as she was?

It wasn't really fair to think she was the only one to feel devastated by this unexpected turn of events. He'd been delighted that she'd become pregnant so easily. As if it was confirmation that they were doing the right thing by basing their entire future on what was, as far as Luke was concerned, a kind of arranged marriage.

Or was it something else that was bothering him so much?

A flash of fear cut through her own grief. Was Luke realising that they couldn't control everything by being so pragmatic about how they made their choices? That maybe the pact wasn't worth the metaphorical paper it had been written on?

'I just meant that it was so early,' she said quietly. 'There's always a risk in the first trimester. And it happened so much faster than we expected, too. We'd hardly had time to get used to the idea, had we?'

'Mmm.' Luke didn't sound convinced. His gaze was searching. 'Are you sure you're okay, Katy?

With the biggest effort ever, Kate summoned a

smile. 'I will be. I've got a thumping headache and all I want to do is sleep for a bit.'

'You'll stay here until they're happy to let you go, though?'

'Yeah…'

'And you can't be at home by yourself. You'll need someone who can spot any signs of a change in the signs or symptoms of a head injury.'

'Georgie's more than capable. She's coming in later with some clean clothes for me and she said that she's juggled her shifts so that she can stay home tomorrow.'

Kate didn't add that it hadn't been a problem because Georgia had confessed her pregnancy at work and was restricted to lighter duties now. She didn't want to think about how obvious Georgia's bump had become in the last few weeks.

The kind of bump that Kate was no longer going to experience in the near future.

More tears were not far away. That she wanted Luke to stay so badly was a warning sign that things could unravel even more than they had already. If she wanted to keep at least their relationship intact, he needed to go. Now.

'Go home, Luke. I just want to go to sleep for a bit so there's no point in you sitting here.'

'But…' Luke had an odd expression on his face. As if he was debating whether or not to say something that she might not want to hear.

She could help him decide. Make it clear that she *didn't* want to hear it.

'Go. Please.' Kate closed her eyes again to signal an end to the conversation. 'I'll call you tomorrow.'

\* \* \*

'Are you sure you're up to this?'

Kate didn't pause in her progress up the steep hill. 'Stop trying to wrap me in cotton wool, Luke. I'm fine.'

'No headache today?'

'I haven't had a headache in more than a week. I'm fine. It was a mild concussion and it was nearly two weeks ago. I only needed a day or two off work and this is the first day off that we've both had since then.' Kate's smile was bright. 'Normal service has resumed. And I'm really looking forward to finally getting to see the inside of Edinburgh Castle.'

'Me, too.' But Luke could feel himself frowning as he stared straight ahead. It didn't feel as if 'normal service' had been resumed. There had been something different about Kate ever since the devastating news about the baby.

Something that seemed…off-key.

He'd tried to talk to her about it, more than once, but she'd brushed it off as being no big deal.

*It was all too easy and perfect anyway*, she'd said. *Fairy-tales don't happen in real life. We both know that.*

And that had been that, apparently. She had thrown herself back into work as soon as she'd been given the all-clear from her concussion and bruising and she seemed to be coping perfectly well.

Too well?

Like the way she'd agreed to this outing today, to visit Edinburgh Castle, as a fabulous idea—something she'd been intending to do for ages. Her smile had been bright when they'd met at the bottom of the hill and the quick hug and kiss on the cheek had told him how pleased she was to see him.

It was Kate who was keeping the conversation going, too, every time a silence fell.

Like it had in the last couple of minutes.

'Oh, look at that. Another specialist whisky shop.'

'It's a popular drop in these parts. There's a kilt-maker. Do you want to go and try one on?'

Kate laughed. 'No, thanks. Do you?'

Luke grinned. 'I'd be too worried about a windy day, wearing one of those.' He resisted another urge to take hold of her hand as they kept climbing towards the iconic castle on the top of the hill.

He hadn't held her hand since that awful night in the emergency department.

They hadn't made love since then either.

And it was killing him that Kate didn't seem bothered. That it felt as if she had taken a step back. Because the intimacy that had been created by knowing that they had a baby on the way had been extinguished?

He wanted to tell her that they could try again. That, this time, everything would be all right.

But he couldn't make promises like that, could he? She was right. Fairy-tales rarely happened in real life. Look at the mess his marriage to Nadia had turned into. Not believing in fairy-tales had been the very reason he'd decided that resurrecting 'the pact' had been such a brilliant idea and that it had a much better chance of working long term.

And it had worked.

Until the moment he'd realised that he was in love with Kate.

That should have been enough to make him back

off. To—figuratively—tear up that pact because it was
no longer valid.

He could never be simply her friend any more.

But the last thing Luke wanted to do was back off.
He couldn't, even if it meant he was headed for the
same kind of heartbreak that he'd experienced before.
He was too far gone.

He wanted the fairy-tale, dammit.

All the 'crazy stuff' as he'd called it back when he'd
had that conversation with Kate on their first dinner
date. When he'd set out to persuade her that friendship
was the way to go. That the pact had merit.

How ironic was that?

She'd accepted the invitation and now she was the
one who thought that it could only work if the ground
rules were respected. And *he* was the one who wanted
more. Who wanted the crazy stuff of not being able to
keep their hands off each other. Of drowning in eye
contact that felt like you'd discovered the meaning of
life. That kind of telepathy where you could say so
much through no more than a touch or a glance.

Could it happen one day? If they could stay together
and build on what they already had?

If it didn't, could he live with that? Being in love
with someone who didn't feel the same way about him?

He didn't really have a choice. Not if he didn't want
to risk losing her.

He'd lapsed into silence again and the quick glance
from Kate told him that it had gone on for a heartbeat
too long.

'I haven't even talked to you properly for a few
days,' she said. 'How's work been?'

'Busy. Had a hell of case yesterday. A ten-year-old

kid who had a DVD in his hand when the car crashed. It sliced his neck like a knife and nicked his carotid artery.'

'Good grief. He could have bled to death in no time at all.'

'I know. The ambulance crew did a brilliant job. Didn't Georgia tell you about it? She was on the crew.'

'I've barely seen her in the last couple of days. Sometimes our hours make us like ships passing in the night. I worked late last night so she was in bed by the time I got home and I slept in this morning, with it being my first day off for a while, so she was gone by the time I got up.' Kate raised her eyebrows. 'I thought she was on lighter duties now. What was she doing out on the road?'

'I asked her about that. She's been given one of those cars apparently. The ones that get sent out first—or as backup for a major incident? It means she can assess a scene for what's needed and give urgent treatment but has to call for backup for any lifting or transfer.'

'Oh, yeah.' Kate was smiling again. 'She told me that was in the pipeline a while back. I got the impression she had been whinging so much about the prospect of being stuck in an office and bored stiff, they bowed under pressure.'

The smile seemed to fade more quickly than it usually did. It had to be hard for Kate to be living with someone who was so far along in her pregnancy that it was the first thing everyone noticed about her. It had given Luke a jolt when he'd seen Georgia yesterday. Just for a split second, before he'd focused on the critically injured young boy being brought into his care, he'd felt the loss all over again.

The loss of their baby. *His* baby. The start of the family he wanted to have with Kate.

That wasn't what Kate wanted to talk about right now, though. And if he steered the conversation in that direction, this easy communication between them would dry up completely because Kate probably wouldn't make the effort to break that silence.

'She certainly got a good dose of excitement this time.' Luke abandoned any desire to change the direction of their conversation. 'She came back in the helicopter with the boy and got someone else to take her car back, I guess. Anyway, she was keeping pressure on the bleed and she wasn't going to let go of the padding until he was in Theatre, if necessary.'

'And was it?'

'He was in decompensating hypovolaemic shock. I wasn't going to risk her letting go and getting any further blood loss until we could stabilise him. We started fluid resuscitation in Emergency and then I put a clamp on the artery the instant Georgia let go, and we rushed him up to Theatre as fast as possible. All very dramatic—it was like we were in an episode of some TV medical show.'

Talking shop was the last thing Luke wanted to be doing right now but at least Kate seemed genuinely interested. More engaged than she had been, in fact, ever since the accident.

'Georgia wanted to watch so I let her gown up and come into Theatre with us.'

'She must have been thrilled. I'm sure I'll hear all about it when I get home tonight. If we're not too late with our dinner, that is.'

Luke's heart sank. Did that mean Kate had no intention of coming back to his apartment this evening?

No desire to share his bed, even for an hour or two?

He'd done his research. He knew that it was safe to have sex again as soon as you and your partner felt physically and emotionally ready but that it was best to wait until any miscarriage-related bleeding had stopped. That usually happened within two weeks.

Kate had said that 'normal service' had resumed but she wouldn't refer to making love in such pragmatic terms, would she?

His heart sank even further.

Why not?

It wasn't 'making love' as far as she was concerned, was it? It was just an unexpectedly good physical connection.

A friendship…with benefits.

Had he really believed he'd found the answer when he'd been so blown away by how amazing the sex had been with Kate? That a friendship with benefits was nothing short of perfect?

This didn't feel perfect any more.

It felt…wrong…

# CHAPTER NINE

IT WASN'T WORKING.

The amount of effort Kate was putting into making things feel the way they had before didn't seem to be making any real difference.

Here they were, on a day out to explore something interesting, and it was nothing like any time they had spent together in the last few months—like that day when they'd hired bicycles and gone down the disused railway lines or that memorable, misty day when they'd gone to hunt for the Loch Ness monster. That easy enjoyment of each other's company was missing.

This felt…awkward?

It should be enjoyable. Being inside the towering stone walls of the iconic castle she had admired for so long had been fascinating from the moment they'd walked beneath the massive portcullis gate with its spikes raised to allow visitors to enter. There'd been museums to visit, steep stairs to climb and cobbled streets to wander down. The ancient chapel of St Margaret's had been beautiful and the poignant dog's cemetery where soldiers had buried their beloved canine companions had almost brought her to tears. The silence between them at that point had gone on even longer than any of the previous ones and, embarrassingly, they'd both tried to break it at the same time, with some comment intended to break an increasingly tense atmosphere.

It should have been an opportunity to share a smile. To talk about what was creating this new distance between them and do something about fixing it.

But Kate had hesitated and the moment had been lost.

Because she was wondering if Luke might not actually want to fix it?

There'd been a brief period when Kate had thought they had been finding some old ground, when they'd been talking about the trauma case Luke and Georgia had been involved with yesterday, but as soon as the conversation had tailed off, she'd realised it was the sort of communication she would have with any of her medical colleagues.

It had lacked that extra dimension that talking to Luke usually had. The feeling that she could sense what he wasn't saying. He must have been deeply concerned to have a child presented to him with a life-threatening neck injury. Kate would have found the prospect terrifying but, thinking back on the conversation, she realised that Luke had sounded calm. Almost bored? As if he didn't really want to be talking about it but was making an effort to be polite.

'What does the guide say about these cannons?'

'Um…' Luke scanned the pamphlet he'd picked up in the visitor's centre. 'It's the Argyle Battery. They date back to the Napoleonic wars with France.'

'Wow…' Kate eyed the impressive weapons.

She was trying to be cheerful. To reassure Luke

that she was over the trauma of her accident and losing the baby. That she was still on board with their
plans for the future.

That 'the pact' was still valid.

But something had changed between them. Something that was big enough to be convincing her that
maybe Luke had changed his mind but he couldn't
think of a way to broach the subject yet.

Not all relationships ended with some kind of spectacular break-up, did they? Sometimes they just fizzled
out slowly as the distance between people got larger
and larger.

Kate didn't want that to happen to her and Luke.

The prospect of losing him was frightening. Life
would never be the same without the company of the
man she was so sure was her soul mate.

But doubts were creeping in now. This didn't feel
as if she was in the company of the one person she
couldn't imagine living without.

He hadn't even kissed her since the night of the accident. Not in any way that was on a level other than
mere friendship.

Wandering around the perimeter of the castle, with
its irregular outline, they came across an odd, three-
sided corner. A space that felt disconnected from the
traffic of other tourists. For a long time they both stared
out at the astonishing view, from what looked like most
of the city of Edinburgh and much further—to hills
and snow-capped mountains and the sea.

It was Luke who broke this silence, with a heartfelt sigh.

'Makes you think, doesn't it?' He turned his head
to catch Kate's gaze. 'I wonder how many people have

stood in this spot and looked out at that view and tried to figure out what life is all about. Or what *they* really want from it.'

Was that what Luke was thinking about?

Kate's heart skipped a beat. If she hesitated this time, she might not get another opportunity. Despite her determination, her voice sounded small and quiet against the backdrop of those limitless horizons.

'What do *you* want, Luke?'

He was silent for so long she thought he wasn't going to answer. When he did, he spoke slowly and his voice was almost sombre.

'I guess I want to grab life with both hands and make the most of it. To have someone to do that with. Someone who feels the same way about the important things…'

Kate's throat felt tight.

'We can do that.'

'What?' Luke's quick sideways glance was puzzled.

'Grab life. Together. A new life…'

His eyebrows rose further. 'You mean in New Zealand?'

'Why not? Have you applied for that job in Nelson yet?'

'No. I wouldn't do that without talking to you about it. And I wasn't sure you still wanted to.'

'Why not?' Kate's mouth felt dry now. She'd been right—he had been rethinking things. Making assumptions about how she felt?

'It had been all about raising a family. I thought you might have changed your mind after…after…'

'Losing the baby?' Kate didn't try and blink back the tears that pricked her eyes. 'You know what?'

'What?'

'I know I said that it wasn't real because it had been so early in the pregnancy but…it was *so* real for me. It was silly but I already loved that baby. I already *felt* like a mother. And I knew… I knew how much I wanted it to be real.'

'Oh, *Katy…*' Luke's arms were around her. Holding her tight. 'It *was* real. It was real from the moment we found out. I felt like a father. I told you I was thrilled. And I was.' She felt the shuddering breath he took in. 'When I left you in the hospital that night and went home, I cried.'

Kate kept her head buried against his shoulder, aware of his warmth and the faint thud of his heartbeat. She soaked in the smell of his worn, leather jacket. The smell of Luke…

She shouldn't have sent him home that night. It hadn't been only her who had lost something important, had it? They should have cried together. But she'd been so afraid of that kind of intimacy pushing him away because it might have revealed just how much in love with him she was.

Even now, in his arms like this, an alarm bell was sounding, snippets of an imaginary conversation flashing into her brain.

The horror in Luke's voice. *You're in love with me?*
*I'm sorry… I know I've broken the rules…*
*I'm sorry too, Kate. This has ruined everything…*

She took a deep breath, shutting out the unwanted voices.

'I thought you were crazy, you know?'

'Why?'

'Your idea that nothing more than friendship was

enough to make the kind of relationship that could last for ever. I believe you now, though.'

She could feel a sudden tension in the arms around her but Luke's words were steady. 'So you don't still believe that being in love is important?'

She couldn't look up at him. Not yet.

'What we have is better. The best. I… I wouldn't want anything else.'

As she felt the tension ebb, she could finally look up. Find a tentative smile, although that wobbled when she saw the way Luke was looking at her.

That *tenderness*…

She could believe that he loved her as much as it was possible to love someone. That he was *in love* with her, even if he didn't realise it.

And it was enough. Surely it would always be enough.

She found herself rising up on tiptoe. Lifting her face in an invitation to be kissed. An invitation that Luke didn't hesitate to accept.

The kiss was just as tender as that look had been. Enough to bring another prickle of tears to Kate's eyes, but these weren't sad tears.

They were tears of relief.

Everything was going to be all right.

This time, when they carried on their tour of the castle, they did it hand in hand.

'Do you really want me to apply for that job in Nelson?'

'If you want to. I'll start looking for something for me, too.'

'It's a long way away. It's the other side of the world,

you know. About as far away from here as it's possible to get.'

'I know.' But Luke would be there and that was all Kate would need.

'You'd be leaving your friends behind. Like Georgia.'

'Yeah… I was worried about that but then it occurred to me that she might want to emigrate too.'

'Really?'

'Don't let on that I've told you, but I've got the suspicion that the mystery father of her baby might be a Kiwi paramedic that she met. I know that she's determined to be a single parent but I don't really believe that she doesn't want more than that. And who knows? Maybe she would rethink things—especially if she was in the same country as her baby's father.'

'Interesting idea.' But Luke seemed distracted. 'Does it make it harder for you? Being around her at the moment? It made me think about things when I saw her yesterday.'

'The baby, you mean?' Kate nodded slowly. 'Yes. It's hard.'

'Do you want to try again? Or is it too soon?'

'I… Yes… I do want to try again. Maybe not just yet, though.'

Luke mirrored her nod. Their tour of the castle was almost done and the rift between them seemed to have narrowed to almost nothing. Maybe they would go and find a cosy restaurant soon. She could drink some wine again now and things would become even more relaxed.

They weren't that far from Luke's apartment.

If they went back there and made love, she'd know

that things were really back to normal. That she could trust they'd overcome the first, palpable obstacle in their relationship.

But as the castle walls towered higher behind them as they started walking down the hill again, Luke cleared his throat. 'There's something else…'

'Oh?' Kate's steps slowed.

'That night when you had the accident and we were in the emergency department and that consultant wanted to know who I was, you said I was your fiancé.'

Kate had stopped now. Or maybe it was Luke who had paused, waiting for her response. The traffic of other people flowed around them but there was only one person who mattered at the moment.

'It seemed like the easiest way to explain things.'

'I know. But… I liked it.'

'Oh…' Someone bumped Kate's shoulder but she barely noticed.

'I know you said we didn't need a wedding or the piece of paper but…you might think it's silly but I think I *do* want it.'

'It's not silly.' No more than feeling like parents when the reality was still a long way in the future.

'So you'd do that? Marry me?'

It might not be any more romantic than the first time he'd proposed to her and it was rather public but nobody else in this busy street had any idea of how private this conversation was. And she couldn't complain about the setting when it had the backdrop of this beautiful, ancient castle.

'When?'

'Soon. I knew there was a good reason to do that

paperwork. If I can find a registry office with a space, we could do it tomorrow.'

Kate's jaw dropped. 'You're kidding. I don't even have a *dress*.'

'Okay…next week, then?' Luke was grinning as he pulled her into his arms again. 'The clothes don't matter, Katy. It's what we do with the rest of our lives that matters and… I want to do it with you. I love you.'

'Are you free Thursday afternoon?'

'I'm not sure. Why?' Georgia had opened the fridge and was staring inside. 'I'm hungry but I have no idea what I want to eat.'

'Stay away from the eggs.'

'I'm over that now.' With a sigh, she pushed the door closed. 'But there's nothing in there that looks interesting. Let's go out for a curry.'

'Do you really think that's a good idea? Anyway, I'm making a great salad here.'

Georgia glanced at the chopping board in front of Kate and grimaced. 'I'm hungry. Salad isn't real food. And I'm bored. Let's go down Buchanan Street and do some late night shopping and then find something exciting to eat. What about nachos? You *love* nachos.'

'Mmm. I can't deny that.'

'And shopping is always fun. We haven't done that for ages.'

'I guess you do need some maternity clothes.' Kate paused in her task of slicing a capsicum and eyed her friend's midriff. 'You know, you look a lot bigger than I would have expected for not quite five months along.'

She turned to give Georgia her full attention. 'Is there something you're not telling me? Like, that you were already pregnant when we went off to that competition? Was it just a cover story that you were planning to hook up with someone you'd never have to see again?'

Georgia shook her head. 'But yeah…there is something I haven't told you.'

'Uh-oh…'

'It's not something bad. I didn't tell you to start with because I knew you'd worry more. And then, after your accident, I didn't want to make things worse…'

'How could it have made things any worse?'

Georgia closed her eyes. 'It's twins.'

The knife clattered onto the bench. Stunned, Kate walked to the table and sat down. Georgia followed her example.

'I'm sorry. It's like adding insult to injury, isn't it? I know you were excited about being pregnant, too.'

'It's not that.' Kate summoned a smile. 'I'm okay, really. Luke and I are going to try again as soon as we're ready.' She rubbed at her forehead with her fingers. 'It's… Oh, my God, Georgie…how are you going to cope with *two* babies on your own?'

'I'll cope.'

'But if Luke gets this job in New Zealand, I might be out of the country by the time the babies are born. You don't have any family to help.' She bit her bottom lip. 'I'll tell him I can't go until you're settled. Or… you'll just have to emigrate too.'

'I told you I don't want to move to New Zealand. I'm Scottish. This is my home. I'll come and visit, though. Hey…you're not going to *cry*, are you? I'm happy about this.'

'You are?'

'Of course. I'm getting an instant family. I won't have to go hunting for another father down the track so that my kid isn't an only child, like us.'

'But…' Kate's breath came out in a whoosh. 'You'll have to get two of everything. It'll be more expensive. Harder. You won't get any sleep. This makes everything so much *bigger*…'

'Including my waistline.' Georgia grinned but then sighed. 'This is why I didn't want to tell you, Kate. I knew you'd start worrying about everything and this is *my* business. *My* choice. I'll cope. One step at a time. And I don't want you to tell anybody. You have to promise not to say anything. Even to Luke.'

'Why?'

'Because I want to keep working as long as I can. You know how word gets around in medical circles. If other people react like you and just see the problems, I might find I don't even have light duties available any more. And then I won't be able to save enough money and things really will be harder.'

Kate was silent. Was that really what she was doing—only seeing the problems? Georgia was genuinely happy about this and she should be supporting her best friend.

'And I don't want you changing any of your plans because of me. I'll miss you like crazy, of course, but I think it's brilliant that you're going to go and have an exciting new life in New Zealand. You and Luke belong together. You're perfect for each other. Has he asked you to marry him yet?'

'Yes.'

Georgia gasped. 'And you didn't *tell* me? That's

*way* worse than me not telling you I've got two bairns on board.'

'I was about to tell you. That's why I asked whether you were free on Thursday afternoon. At two o'clock? I…um…need a bridesmaid.'

'And you're telling me this now? With…one, two…' Georgia was counting on her fingers. 'With *three* days to go?'

'I only just found out a couple of hours ago. We weren't planning on doing it this fast, but there was a cancellation at the registry office in Edinburgh and if we hadn't grabbed it, we might have had to wait for months. It's no big deal, Georgie.'

Georgia was shaking her head. 'I can't believe this. Me? I could imagine ducking into a registry office or running off to Gretna Green for a quickie marriage if I had the inclination to marry anybody, which I *don't*, but you? I always thought you'd go for the whole meringue dress and rose petal confetti and some mushy love song echoing around the church as you walked down the aisle.'

Kate shrugged. 'The window dressing isn't what's important.'

'It is to some people.'

'I love Luke. He loves me.'

'He actually said the "L" word?'

Kate nodded, a soft smile curving her lips. He *had* said it. And even if he'd only meant it in the spirit of deep friendship, that look in his eyes had told her everything she'd needed to know.

That this was real.

That it could last a lifetime.

It didn't matter that he wasn't *in* love with her. Or that this wedding was merely a formality.

It *didn't* matter. So why did it feel like her smile was fading into oblivion?

'Wow…'

'I know, right?'

'And you're happy?'

Kate's nod was firm. Was she trying to convince Georgia or herself? 'So happy.'

'That makes two of us, then.' Georgia was smiling now. 'But this lack of window dressing business, that doesn't apply to *you*, does it?'

'How do you mean?'

'You're going to wear a dress? Get your hair done? Carry some flowers?'

'Yeah…of course. I want it to be special.'

'So what are you going to wear?'

'I don't know. I haven't had time to think about it yet.

'It has to be new.'

'Does it?'

'Of course it does. This is the start of the rest of your life. And there'll be photographs. And…good grief… *I'm* going to be in those photographs. I've got to find a dress that doesn't make me look like a sack of potatoes.' Georgia grabbed the corner of the table to help her get to her feet. 'Come on. We're going shopping.'

'What do you think?'

Kate stared at her reflection as Georgia stood back, hair-straighteners still in her hand.

The soft, shiny curls of her blonde hair brushed her shoulders. Her make-up was better than anything she would have achieved herself. She was wearing the pretty dress they had found the other evening—a lace over silk number that was a shade of blue darker than her eye colour.

With the simple bunch of daisies waiting downstairs for her, her look would be complete—and perfect for an understated registry office wedding.

Their timing was perfect, too. They'd both managed to leave work in time to get ready at home and they still had almost thirty minutes to drive to Edinburgh and find a parking space in the central city. It was getting tight but, even if parking was difficult, they wouldn't be more than a few minutes late and that was traditional for brides, wasn't it?

This was it.

Her wedding day.

Kate met Georgia's gaze in the mirror.

'I can't do it.'

Georgia grinned. 'Uh-oh…pre-wedding nerves. I'll get you a glass of wine or something.'

The new curls tickled her neck as Kate shook her head slowly.

'No. Wine won't make any difference. This isn't nerves. I just can't do it.'

'What…you don't want to marry Luke any more?'

Kate shook her head again. 'It's not that either. I *do* want to marry Luke. More than anything. But I can't do it like this.'

'Like what? You mean the registry office thing?' Georgie pulled the plug from the wall but kept the hair-straighteners in her hand as she sank onto the side of Kate's bed. 'I was right. You want the meringue dress and rose petals.'

Kate was beginning to feel like a puppet, repeating her headshake yet again. Her limbs felt heavy as well—as if she wouldn't be able to move unless someone pulled the right strings.

'I can't marry someone I'm deceiving like this.'

Georgia glanced at her watch, biting her bottom lip. 'So…what do you want to do? Just not show up?'

And jilt the man she loved?

'No, of course not.'

'You want to text Luke and tell him you're not coming?'

'I can't do something like that in a text message.'

'Phone him?'

'I don't know.' Kate pressed a hand to her mouth. 'I don't know what to do, Georgie. I just know that this feels wrong.'

'Okay.' Georgia got to her feet with the kind of calm that only someone used to dealing with emergency situations could display. 'Here's what we'll do. We'll get in the car and drive to Edinburgh. You can talk to me on the way. If you still feel the same way when we get there, you can ring Luke. Or talk to him face to face.'

Face to face.

Yes…that would be the brave thing to do. The honest thing.

And Luke deserved her honesty at the very least.

It was good that Georgia was pulling her strings. Kate got to her feet and went downstairs. She walked past the bunch of daisies and headed for the car. She heard the door slam behind her and then Georgia got into the driver's seat. She handed Kate the bunch of daisies.

'Just in case,' she murmured. Once out of the driveway, she put her foot down.

'We haven't got a siren on,' Kate said. 'Take it easy.'

'Sorry…' Georgia slowed the car a little. 'It's the tension.'

'No… I'm sorry. I shouldn't have let it get to this. But I didn't know how important it would suddenly seem. I've been living a lie.' It was all becoming clear in her head as the words started tumbling out. 'It was so important to Luke that our relationship be based on that stupid pact. That we would both be very clear about exactly how we felt about each other because we wouldn't be blinded by being in love. And I've let him believe that I was in the same place. I pretty much promised him that I hadn't fallen in love with him.'

'Maybe he won't mind,' Georgia said. 'He *loves* you. He told you that he loves you.'

'Yes, but not like that. It's like when I tell you that I love *you*.'

'You haven't told me that in a long time.' Georgia turned her head to smile at Kate. 'Do you love me?'

'Of course I do. But I'm not *in* love with you.'

'Thank goodness for that. We've got enough complications.' But Georgia was still smiling as she negotiated a turn that would take them towards the registry office. 'I love you, too.'

They drove in silence after that. The traffic was heavy and it was taking longer than it should. They were going to be late.

'Oh, *look*…there's a parking space. Almost right outside the registry office. It's a miracle.'

A minute later and they were parked. The engine of the car had been turned off. And Georgia was waiting quietly.

'So, what now? Do you want to ring Luke? Or go and find him and talk to him?'

Kate's heart was hammering. Her phone was shaking in her hand. 'I can't ring. But if I go in there, he'll think I've come to marry him. Walking in there and saying I can't do it is almost as bad as not turning up at all.'

What if she walked in there and saw him waiting for her? Would he be looking impossibly gorgeous in a suit and tie, despite what he'd said about clothes being unimportant? He'd be smiling, wouldn't he? Maybe looking at her the way he had when he'd been holding her in his arms up there in the castle whose walls dominated the top of the road they were parked on.

In the face of that kind of tenderness, hope even, she might well lose the courage she was summoning to be honest.

Georgia looked at her watch. 'It's nearly a quarter past two. We have to do something.' She drummed her fingers on the steering wheel. 'How 'bout *I* go in? That way he'll have a warning that something's up. And I can tell him that you need to talk to him. And then I'll show him where we're parked and stay out of your way for a while.'

She didn't wait for Kate's response. She was already easing her expanding belly past the steering wheel and out of the car.

Kate watched her disappear up the steps that led into the building further up the street.

And then she waited.

She closed her eyes and tried not to think of the expression that might be on Luke's face when he came to get into the car and talk to her.

How disappointed he was going to be when she told him the truth.

But she was doing the right thing.

Luke trusted her enough to be prepared to make a public commitment to spend the rest of his life with her. Maybe—and this was a glimmer of hope she couldn't quite extinguish—Georgia was right and he wouldn't mind. He might even laugh off the idea that she'd fallen in love with him and tell her that she'd get over it one day. He might actually want to go through with the ceremony but he deserved the option of changing his mind.

Kate couldn't change hers. She would never get over being in love with him.

Minutes ticked past as her thoughts whirled and settled, getting a little more despondent with each circuit. She was holding the bunch of daisies in her hand so tightly they seemed to be wilting right before her eyes.

Like her dreams of the future…?

With her eyes downcast, focussed on the flowers, she didn't see the person approaching the car. The door being wrenched opened made her jump.

And then her heart sank like a stone.

'What happened? He…he doesn't even want to *talk* to me?'

Georgia shook her head. 'He's not there, Kate.'

'What? He didn't even wait for fifteen minutes…?'

Georgia shook her head again. 'It's not that.' She reached out to touch Kate's hand. 'I'm sorry…but apparently he didn't turn up at all.'

# CHAPTER TEN

'WHAT ARE YOU DOING?'

'Calling the hospital. I reckon he got caught up in some emergency. That'll be why his phone's going to voicemail.' Georgia held her phone to her ear. 'Hello. This is Georgia Bennett from the Outer Edinburgh Ambulance Service. Could you put me through to Dr Luke Anderson, please?'

The seconds ticked past. Kate could feel her heart thudding along with them. She leaned back against the headrest and closed her eyes. This turn of events was something she would never have expected and she wasn't at all sure how to deal with it.

She could hear the crackle of a voice coming back onto the other end of the line.

'Okay,' Georgia said, finally. 'Thank you. No, no message.'

She turned back to Kate who still had her eyes closed.

'The operator said he's unavailable for the rest of the day. On personal leave.'

Kate opened her eyes. She looked past the buildings around them. Up towards the walls of the castle.

'Where *is* he?' There was an angry edge to Georgia's voice now. 'How could he do something like this to you?'

A good question. Except that it was precisely what Kate had been about to do to him, wasn't it? She might not understand what was going on, but she couldn't put all the blame at Luke's feet. She blinked hard to keep tears at bay. Focussing on what she could see in the distance helped—that odd outline that created the kind of corners on the ramparts that she and Luke had discovered on their recent visit to Edinburgh castle.

Where they'd stood, looking out at that amazing view.

She could hear his words again, as clearly as if he was leaning forward from the back seat of this car to whisper them in her ear.

*I wonder how many people have stood in this spot and looked out at that view and tried to figure out what life is all about. Or what they really want from it.*

'I think I might know where he is,' she said quietly.

'Good. Let's go and find him.' Georgia was scowling now. 'Oh, boy... I knew you can't trust men. Any of them. I actually thought Luke was different but now I can't wait to give him a piece of my mind.'

Kate smiled. 'I don't think so. What you can do is give me a lift to the top of the hill, though. Close to the castle gates?'

'You think he's gone sightseeing?'

'I don't know. It's just a hunch. But even if I don't find him, I could do with some time to think about things anyway.'

'Not by yourself, you don't. You need a friend right now.' Georgia started the car. 'I'll wait somewhere close for a while, okay? I don't care how long it takes.

Text me when you need a ride home.' Her smile was sympathetic. 'I can buy chocolate and wine while I'm waiting.'

It helped to know that her best friend would be somewhere in the vicinity when Kate had purchased her ticket to tour the castle and went straight for the long flight of stairs that would take her up to the ramparts. If nothing else, she was going to get cold before too long. It might be a lovely, sunny day but there was enough of a breeze to ruffle the skirt of her dress and tease goose-bumps onto her bare arms.

Or maybe that was due to nerves.

She was running on instinct here, and it was quite possible she didn't know Luke as well as she thought she did. He could be miles away. Onto his third whisky in a bar somewhere perhaps. Feeling relieved that he'd dodged the bullet of committing himself to someone he couldn't really trust because she hadn't stuck to the premise of the pact?

He must have guessed somehow.

He had realised that she couldn't be trusted because she'd been hiding the truth.

Lying to him, even if it was only by omission.

This was a good thing, Kate told herself, rubbing at her arms as she kept walking. She would feel relieved to be able to be honest.

But…how devastating was it going to be to lose Luke?

She paused for a moment as the premonition of how much grief she was on the brink of became overwhelming.

Maybe she couldn't do this. It might be better to turn around and text Georgia to come back to the castle gates. To go and get that emergency supply of wine and chocolate and tissues and just go home and hide for a while.

And then she saw him.

Just a silhouette of a figure at this distance but she knew it was Luke. Not so much because it was obviously a tall, male shape but because it was in the exact spot that she had thought he might be. And because of how still he was standing, lost in the limitless view of those horizons that had made him ponder the meaning of life that most people had to deal with at some point. It was obviously his turn right now.

So Kate kept walking. It felt as though she was being pulled forward now, not pushing herself. As if she was within range of a magnetic force she couldn't resist. A force that became increasingly powerful with every step closing that distance between them.

And, as if he felt the same force, Luke turned away from the view by the time Kate was still metres away.

The colour seemed to drain from his face.

'*Katy*...'

He *was* wearing a suit and tie. He did look impossibly gorgeous. In a way, this was a comfort. Luke had obviously intended to go to the registry office. To marry her.

Whatever was going on, seeing her here was the last thing he'd expected, judging by how shocked he looked right now.

'Oh, my God... I only came here because I needed to think.' He wrenched at the sleeve of his jacket to expose his watch. 'I completely lost track of the time. We're so late...'

'Too late.' To her surprise, Kate's words sounded oddly calm. 'It's not going to happen now, Luke.'

He dropped his hands in slow motion and then his whole body seemed to freeze. Just a lock of that wavy brown hair got caught in the breeze and shifted on a furrowed forehead.

'You were waiting for me.' His voice cracked. 'You must have thought I'd changed my mind. That I wasn't coming...'

Kate shook her head. 'I couldn't go in,' she said, quietly. 'I couldn't do it.'

His face looked even paler now. His words came out in no more than a whisper. 'Why not?'

'Because I haven't been entirely honest with you. I broke the rules.' Kate wrapped her arms around herself as she shivered. 'I'm in love with you, Luke. I fell in love with you a long time ago.'

He didn't move a muscle. Even that stray lock of hair was completely still for a long, long moment.

But then one corner of his mouth moved, tilting upwards.

'That's okay,' he murmured. His whole body seemed to be waking up now. He was taking a step towards her.

It was Kate's turn to freeze. It was *okay*? He didn't mind that she had broken the most important rule? What was going on here?

'I broke that rule, too.' The warmth of Luke's hands on her bare arms was startling. Almost as astonishing as what she was hearing. 'I'm in love with you, too. Oh, Katy... I love you *so* much...'

His hands had moved to cradle her face and the touch was gentle. The touch of his lips on hers was gentle as well. Heartbreakingly tender.

And this kiss was different from any kiss they had shared before.

Because it was honest?

Because it was possible to let every ounce of the love she felt for this man rush through her body and be communicated through what was only a tiny patch of physical contact?

Maybe it was because she was receiving the exact same kind of message. She could sense the power of a love that matched her own and together they were fusing into something extraordinary.

Kate never wanted this kiss to end. It was only a lack of enough oxygen that finally forced her to pull back far enough to snatch a gasp of breath.

The breeze had picked up again. She could feel her skirt swirling around her legs and strands of her hair were blowing over her face to snag on moist lips. Luke smoothed them away, his gaze locked on hers.

Kate never wanted that eye contact to end either. How amazing was it that love could be felt as a physical force by the touch of a gaze as much as lips?

So powerful, it sent a shudder through her entire body.

'You're cold.' A furrow appeared between Luke's eyes. He shrugged off his suit jacket and draped it over Kate's shoulders. The smooth silk of the lining kissed her skin and the warmth that had come from Luke's body wrapped itself around her like an even more intimate caress.

For a moment, Kate was transported back to that memorable night when they had agreed to reinstate the pact. When she'd been engulfed by his oversized anorak and had caught the scent of Luke from its soft, woolly lining. She'd been under the erotic spell of those first waves of intense, physical desire for this man that night.

That spell had never worn off. If anything, it felt stronger now. A part of her life instead of just a temporary sprinkle of magic dust.

Luke took hold of her hand. 'Come on, let's find somewhere out of this wind.'

It didn't matter that there were tourists everywhere in the castle grounds. It felt as if she and Luke were the only people in the world. And when they went into the first sheltered building they could find, miraculously they *were* the only people in the space.

They tucked themselves into a corner of one of the few wooden pews in the ancient chapel of St Margaret's in front of its carved stone archway with the soft glow of the small, stained-glass window behind the altar on the other side of the archway.

It seemed entirely appropriate to celebrate the discovery of this new level of love by sharing another kiss.

And by speaking only in whispers.

'When?' Luke asked. 'When did *you* break the rules?'

'That first night we had dinner. At that Italian restaurant?' Kate had to smile. 'Just before you said how much better it was just to be friends and how you could never trust being in love. When you persuaded me to give the pact a go.'

Luke groaned softly. 'I did say that, didn't I? I actually believed it.'

'I couldn't tell you. Not after that. I was too scared you might disappear from my life. Because you couldn't trust me.'

'I could never *not* trust you, Katy. I'm trusting you with my heart for ever now. With my life…'

'But I was being untrustworthy. I was lying. Pretending that I felt the same way you did.'

Luke's smile was ironic. 'You did a good job, too. You were so good I believed you so well that I couldn't tell you how I really felt. In case *you* disappeared.'

'When did you know?'

'That night you got hit by the car. When I thought the worst for a few seconds and realised how much I didn't want to live without you. But you know what?'

'What?'

'I think I'd actually felt that way for ever. I just hadn't realised what had been hiding.'

Kate nodded. 'Do you want to know something else? When we first met, way back at med school, I…um… had a real crush on you.'

'What? *Really?* How come I never knew that?'

'I could see the way you looked at other girls. I felt kind of invisible in that way. I guess I got good at hiding it and then I convinced myself I was over it.'

'I must have been completely blind,' Luke groaned. 'Or maybe I just needed to grow up enough to see what was real and what wasn't.' He shook his head sadly. 'We've wasted a lot of time, haven't we?'

Kate mirrored the headshake. 'It wasn't wasted. If that's what was needed to get us to where we are right now, I'd do it again in a heartbeat.'

'I'm sorry about the registry office. It might be a long time before we can get a new appointment.'

'It doesn't matter.'

Luke kissed her before he spoke again. 'It *does* matter. And it doesn't seem enough any more. My first wedding was in a registry office. I think I want a *real* wedding this time.'

'With me in a meringue dress and people throwing rose petals?'

'Whatever spins your wheels.' Luke smiled. 'But, yes, I want it to be a bit over the top. With all our friends here to witness it. In a really special place.' He turned his head to gaze around them. 'Like this…'

'You probably have to book years in advance to get a wedding in this chapel.'

'We got lucky with the registry office. People cancel sometimes, you know.'

'Or they don't turn up.' Kate's smile was teasing. 'I wonder how often it happens that *both* people don't turn up to their own wedding?'

'That wouldn't work. We'd need at least a bit of time. So that you can buy the meringue.'

'I don't want a meringue. But… I *do* want a real wedding.' A bubble of excitement was layering itself onto the sheer joy of knowing that Luke loved her this much. That he was *in* love with her. The dreams of the future were within touching distance now. Maybe the dreams from the past could be indulged a little, too.

A sacred place. A white dress. Heartfelt pledges made in front of others. A slow walk down an aisle because every step would bring her closer to the man she loved.

Closer to the rest of her life with Luke.

'You know what?'

'What?'

'It wouldn't hurt to *ask*…'

The evening chill in the air wasn't entirely responsible for the shivery sensation that rippled down Kate's spine.

'What if he's not there?'

Georgie snorted. 'As if...'

She cast a critical eye over Kate's dress. The bead-encrusted lace bodice had a sweetheart neckline in the front and a deep V at the back. From just under the bust, a drape of pale, ivory silk fell far enough to touch the cobbles of this courtyard.

'Phew... I thought for sure you were going to get some marks on that skirt climbing those stairs.'

'I was being careful. What about my hair? There's enough of a breeze up here to have messed with it.'

'You look stunning.' Georgia's smile was misty. 'And I love that wreath. The flowers are so tiny.'

'You look pretty amazing yourself, Georgie.'

'For a bridesmaid the size of a small elephant, you mean?' Georgia ran her hands over her belly. 'Thank goodness for wraparound dress styles. I feel more elegant than I have for months.'

Kate drew in a shaky breath. 'This is really happening, isn't it?'

'It would seem so. I can't believe you're doing it here, though. At the *castle*.'

'I *know*. Who knew that some American couple was going to have a last-minute hitch with their visas? Or that we happened to make an enquiry on the only day ever that St Margaret's chapel didn't have a waiting list for cancellations?'

Everything had simply fallen into place after that. Finding the perfect dress in the first shop she and Georgia had gone into. Job interviews in New Zealand that fitted perfectly into the timeframe for an extended honeymoon.

'And you got the whole package. The party in that tower next door afterwards. Even the piper to serenade your walk up the aisle. Oh, look… I think that's him getting ready.' Georgia sighed happily. 'I do love a man in a kilt.'

Kate eyed the stone archway that was the entrance to the tiny chapel. She could see the soft light beyond that would be coming from the dozens of candles. The pews would be filled with the twenty or so close friends who had been chosen to witness this ceremony. Through the internal archway, in the space at the front beside the altar, would be where Luke was standing.

Waiting for her.

Some muffled squeaking sounds were coming from the direction of the lone piper as he got his bagpipes ready.

'Stand by…' Georgia said in a stage whisper.

'No…' The call came from behind them. *'Wait…'*

Both Georgia and Kate turned swiftly to see a figure running towards them. A tall, dark man in a dark suit, a black bow-tie against a snowy, white shirt.

For the briefest moment Kate thought it was Luke, arriving late to his own wedding. But then her face lit up with the widest smile.

'*Matteo*…you made it.'

'I didn't think I could. Not after the last delay with the fog.' Matteo was out of breath. 'But I couldn't let my best friend get married without me.' He put his hand to his chest as he tried to catch his breath. 'You look…*bellissima*, Kate. Luke is a very lucky man.'

'He certainly is,' Georgia put in. 'Hi, Matteo.' The glance she slid towards Kate was oddly accusatory. 'You didn't tell me Matteo was coming.'

'We really weren't sure that he could make it. Luke's going to be as surprised as you.'

But probably happier.

Was that why Kate hadn't mentioned the idea of flying in the only option for a best man? There'd been something between Georgia and Matteo back at the competition. Something that hadn't ended so well despite her friend's refusal to ever discuss it. Just how acrimonious had it been when Matteo had been discarded in favour of Dave the New Zealander—the man she still suspected might be the father of Georgia's babies?

She could see the shocked expression on Matteo's face as his gaze slid over Georgia's impressive bump.

He cleared his throat. 'Hello, Georgia. You're looking…um…well?'

'I'm very well, thank you.'

'I'd better get inside. Give me a minute to find my place, okay?' Matteo disappeared through the arched entrance just as the piper finished warming up and began to play.

'Here we go,' Georgia said. 'You good?'

Her smile was bright. If Matteo's presence wasn't something she wanted, she wasn't about to let it interfere with Kate's special day. She'd make sure she found time to talk to her closest friend later. To let her know how much she was loved and how much Kate appreciated everything she'd done to help her through the last few weeks.

'Never better.' She nodded. 'I feel like I've been waiting for this moment my whole life.'

'It was always going to happen. I knew you were fated to find your perfect person.'

'But I'd never have dreamed it would be Luke.'

'You can thank me, later.' Georgia touched Kate's arm and nodded towards the entrance. 'It's time, hon.'

But Kate hesitated a moment longer. 'It *was* down to you, wasn't it? It was your idea to go that competition. We might never have reconnected otherwise. I hope…well… I hope I can return the favour one day.'

Georgia shook her head, a stray curl escaping from the pins holding her hair in place.

'No, thanks. Just make sure *you* live happily ever after, okay?'

'I'll do my best.'

The sound of the bagpipes would have been over-powering in the small space of the chapel but, drifting in behind them, the haunting notes were beautiful.

Of course Luke was there. With Matteo on one side of him and the minister waiting on the other side. The pews were full but Luke was only looking at one person.

At *her*.

And that gaze was drawing her forward so compellingly it was hard to remember to walk slowly.

This was it. Her dream wedding. To the only person she could imagine wanting it to be with.

Luke was smiling at her as she got closer. A smile that was full of joy. Brimming with love…

Kate smiled back but she knew it was wobbly.

Her heart felt too full and her eyes were going to follow its example any moment. She could feel those tears of pure joy gathering.

Because she wasn't going to be alone in doing her best to live happily ever after, was she?

She had found her partner for life.

\* \* \* \* \*

# TWIN SURPRISE FOR THE ITALIAN DOC

BY
ALISON ROBERTS

MILLS & BOON

# PROLOGUE

'I THINK WE'RE LOST.'

Georgia Bennett had been enjoying the view of this pretty forest road as they wound their way through the Alps that bordered this part of the Czech Republic. It was her companion Kate's turn to drive and it was obvious she was a little out of her comfort zone, which was hardly surprising. Georgia was the crazy one in this friendship—the one that took risks and chased adventures.

And she had every intention of making this one of her most significant adventures ever.

'Whose bright idea was it to enter this international medical rescue competition?' Kate continued. 'Oh, yeah…*yours*…'

'It's an adventure.' Georgia threw a reassuring smile in Kate's direction but reached for the folder that had the maps so she could double check what the satellite navigation device was telling them. 'Admit it—you're loving it already.'

Kate still didn't sound happy. 'Road trips always sound more fun than they actually are. It's a hell of a long way from Scotland to the back of beyond in the

Czech Republic. I've never even heard of the town we're trying to find.'

'Rakovi. It's a ski resort. And this is the biggest competition of its kind in the world. I've been hearing about it for years—ever since I became a paramedic.'

Georgia had tried to get a whole team together from her colleagues and persuade the manager of her rescue base to let them take an ambulance on an epic road trip but, despite her best efforts, it hadn't panned out. Then she'd heard about the doctor/paramedic combinations that were allowed and that you could compete using a car. All she'd had to do was persuade Kate. Presenting the whole package as a birthday gift—along with a bottle of really good champagne—had done the trick.

'Well, I've never heard of it.'

'That's because you're a doctor and your lot aren't as adventurous.'

'Hmm…' It sounded like Kate had changed her mind. 'Have we even got out of Poland yet?'

'Ages ago.' Georgia made her tone as soothing as possible. 'It's not far now.'

'We don't want to be late for registration.'

'Don't stress. They've got a couple of hundred teams from about twenty different countries to process. If we're a bit late it'll just mean we don't have to queue for so long.'

Kate slowed again to cross a narrow bridge over a tumbling mountain stream. 'I can't believe we're competing in such a huge field.'

'It's broken up into categories, remember. There'll be paramedic teams with their ambulances from all over Europe. I can't wait till the end where everybody drives in convoy around all the local villages with their lights and sirens on. I've heard it's a memorable experience.' Georgia had come prepared. She had bags of sweets and Scottish-themed toys to throw from the windows for the children that would be lining the edges of the road. It would be such fun to see their faces light up…

Oh, boy…she had small humans on her mind far too much at the moment. She needed to focus.

'Then there are the doctors and medical student teams and other combinations,' she added quickly. 'I just hope there's enough like us to give us our own category, otherwise we'll be competing against teams that have up to four members.'

'I just hope I don't make an idiot of myself. I'm a paediatrician, Georgie. I work in a nice, safe hospital with any amount of resources and backup. You would have been better to pick an emergency specialist.'

'You do plenty of emergency work. And you've lived with me long enough to qualify as an honorary paramedic. You've even been out on the road with me a few times. You'll be brilliant and who cares if we don't win? We're here to have fun, remember? To have an adventure and meet lots of new people and…' Georgia's grin was decidedly mischievous now. 'We're both single and gorgeous. Have you thought about how many men there are going to be at this thing?'

Men who were presumably reasonably intelligent because they were doctors or medical students or paramedics. Successful enough to want to be competitive. Adventurous enough to take on this kind of challenge.

Just the kind of man she would choose to be the father of her child.

Best of all, they would be strangers. From foreign

countries. They would never have to know and they would never interfere with her life in the future.

'*Georgie...*' Kate sounded shocked. 'You never give up, do you? You've only just got over the last disaster and you're ready to do it again?'

The reminder of how gutting the last relationship mess had been was the last thing Georgia wanted to think about. Or maybe it was a good thing because she could feel her resolve strengthening. She was thirty-six now—a year older than Kate—and she didn't have the time or inclination to jump through any more messy relationship hoops.

She wanted a baby.

Not that she was about to confess her master plan, even to her very best friend who'd been her house-mate for years. Kate was too proper. She had set ideas about the way things should be in life and wasn't likely to approve of Georgia's intentions. A one-off, throw-away comment she had made a while back about a man only being essential for as long as it might take to conceive had been enough to tell her that. Kate had been appalled.

So she made her tone as offhand as she could. 'Oh, I have no intention of falling for someone.' And wasn't that the truth?

Inspiration struck. 'What's that saying? The best way to get over a man is to get under another one?'

At least she'd made Kate laugh. That wouldn't be the case if she'd guessed the truth.

'Casual sex has never appealed to me.'

'Yeah...you're so old school, Kate. An ultimate ro-mantic.' This was good. She could divert the attention to Kate's love life—or lack of it—instead of her own.

'You really believe that you're going to see 'the one' across a crowded room and it'll be love at first sight and a happy-ever-after with a few bluebirds fluttering over the carpet of rose petals and—'

'Oh, stop it...,' Kate growled. But she didn't sound cross. Her tone was more concerned than anything. 'Just be careful, hon. Okay?'

'Of course.' Georgia breathed a sigh of relief but that seemed to earn a sharp glance from Kate.

'You have given up on that hare-brained scheme you came up with after that bastard, Rick, walked out, haven't you?'

Uh-oh... 'I have no idea what you're talking about.'

'Oh, yes, you do. The one where you gave up on men completely and were going to have a baby all by yourself?'

Georgia pretended to be distracted by the map in her hands. She couldn't afford to allow Kate to get suspicious. She had the lid firmly in place over her own doubts about what she was planning and it would be too easy to get talked out of it if that lid got lifted.

She could almost feel that biological clock ticking more loudly than ever. Or was it her heart thumping? Excitement...or trepidation?

She cleared her throat. 'Well, obviously I haven't given up on men *completely*. And I'm over Rick. He's ancient history—like all the others.' Oh, man...she had to change the subject of conversation. Nerves were kicking in and the feeling was not pleasant.

She told herself to calm down. It was just an option—she didn't have to follow through with her plan if she wasn't sure. Maybe she wouldn't meet anyone suitable. And, even if she did, what were the odds of getting pregnant with a single encounter anyway? She wasn't even sure that it was the best time of the month, given that her cycle wasn't that regular.

There were other reasons to be here. Exciting reasons. And there was no need to continue with any hazardous chatting either. Georgia had seen the perfect distraction.

'Ooh, look…a signpost. We're only fifteen kilometres away.'

'Halleluiah. The end is in sight.'

'Nah…the *beginning* is in sight.' Georgia stretched her arms above her head and gave a whoop. 'Bring it on.'

# CHAPTER ONE

*YES...*

This was all shaping up to be even better than Georgia could have imagined.

While she was well aware that she was a part of the growing percentage of women succeeding in demanding careers like paramedicine, there were hundreds and hundreds of people here and it seemed like the majority of them were men.

The kind of men that had always stood out from the crowd for her. Intelligent, confident men who were caring enough to devote their working lives to caring for others. Born leaders who could wear a uniform like a second skin rather than an advertisement of achievement or authority.

One of them could be exactly the kind of man she would choose to be the father of her child.

The sense of unease that touched the back of her neck and rippled down her spine was becoming familiar but Georgia had come up with a way to shrug it off with what seemed a perfectly feasible argument in her defence. She wasn't the only woman who was prepared to embrace the decision to bring a child into the world without a partner.

She could have taken what was becoming an accepted route to parenthood by paying for the services of a sperm bank and the initial part of that process would be to peruse the profiles of available candidates. She would be making judgements based on physical attributes like height and colouring. Academic qualifications and profession could indicate levels of intelligence and determination and interests in things like sport or music could offer an insight into attitudes or talents.

She could well end up doing exactly that but what put her off that route to parenthood was the fact that it would be recorded. Traceable. The risk of that knowledge being used to interfere with her life was probably small enough to be insignificant but Georgia knew only too well how damaging that interference was capable of being. Why take the risk if it was possible to eliminate it completely?

She had convinced herself that all she was planning to do was to peruse profiles in a much less clinical fashion, by means of personal interaction.

The thornier issue of consent was more difficult to shrug off, of course, but there wasn't any point in facing that one unless she found a suitable candidate. Given her list of requirements, it was quite possible that even this best-case scenario of potentially great men wouldn't provide exactly what she was looking for.

What with getting through the registration protocol and transferring their luggage to their accommodation, the time since she and Kate had arrived at the rally had been a bit too busy to get more than a very general impression of their fellow competitors but that had just changed. Standing in a crowded dining hall, holding her dinner tray, Georgia found herself joining Kate's attempt to locate two empty spaces at a table. Except that it was the array of faces capturing her attention instead of any empty chairs. Surprisingly, many of those faces were looking back at them and they didn't seem to be simply curious glances that might be assessing competitors. There were smiles to be seen, along with raised eyebrows that suggested friendliness, if not interest.

Like that very tall guy, with a mop of sun-streaked blond curls and a cheeky grin. The tilt of his head was an unmistakeable invitation to claim the extra space at *his* table.

Georgia smiled back.

'There's some space on that table,' she told Kate, leading the way. She smiled again as they got closer. 'Do you mind if we join you guys?'

'Please do.' He looked delighted. 'I'm Dave. This is Ken and that's Sally, who's stuffing her face there.'

'You're from Australia, right?'

'No. New Zealand.' Dave sighed heavily. 'Everybody thinks our accent is the same but it really isn't.' He grinned at Georgia. 'No mistaking yours. You're Scottish.'

'I am.' Georgia took the empty seat right beside Dave.

New Zealand… It was a country that conjured up images of clean, green forests and pristine beaches—like advertisements for healthy lifestyles. Even better, it was a country on the opposite side of the globe. About as far from Scotland as possible. It was impossible not to register that that fact ticked one of the first boxes on the list of requirements she had drawn up on her potential master plan.

The plan that had suddenly become rather more than just a half-baked idea, in fact.

The dumplings on her plate were rather dense and speckled with something green that could be parsley. Dave appeared to be enjoying his meal and Georgia was never fussy with her food so she took a large bite and found that the dumplings were actually better than they looked, especially with a covering of the gravy they were swimming in.

She glanced sideways as she loaded her fork again. 'I like your uniforms. Are you paramedics?'

'Yeah…you guys?'

'I'm a paramedic. Kate's a doctor. Is this your first time here?'

'Sure is. Never seen anything like it.'

'Where are you based at home? City or country?'

'Auckland. Biggest city in the country. And up there in the top cities of the world to live in. You should come and visit sometime.'

'Oh? What's so great about Auckland?'

The attractions seemed to focus on fabulous beaches, a great night life and the best food and coffee the world had to offer. Sally and Ken were keen to tell her about what a great place it was to work in the ambulance service as well, but Auckland wasn't a likely destination to add to any future travel plans, as far as Georgia was concerned.

Especially if any more boxes on that mental list were going to get ticked and that was apparently happening without her even consciously thinking about it. Dave was tall, which made a good genetic balance for her own slightly below average stature. He was definitely good looking and there was a gleam in those blue eyes that suggested intelligence. As a bonus, his camaraderie with his teammates told her that he wasn't any kind of sociopath.

Dave seemed, on first impression, to be a very nice guy and Georgia experienced another pang of guilt that she could even be thinking along these lines. Was she really planning to cultivate a friendship enough to use someone for such a selfish purpose? Getting pregnant accidentally was common enough to be almost normal but it was more than a little disturbingly immoral to *plan* such an event.

She glanced at Kate, almost hoping that enough telepathy existed between them that her friend would sense the secret list-ticking and deliver a hint of shock with some raised eyebrows and then a frown, or perhaps a headshake, of total disapproval.

But Kate wasn't even looking in her direction. She seemed to be focussed on her meal and wasn't joining in with the conversation around her. Maybe she was more out of her comfort zone than Georgia had anticipated when she'd persuaded her to come to this competition. Kate was incredibly clever and hardworking and the best friend Georgia had ever had, but nobody could say she was overly adventurous. Or even spontaneous. If there was going to be a break in her normal routines, Kate liked to be able to plan how to cope with it. Making a plan that would turn her whole life upside down would be so unthinkable that Georgia had known instantly that it had been a mistake to even voice her idea of bypassing the search for a suitable partner and moving straight on to parenthood.

Or maybe Kate was thinking about the old friend from medical school she thought she'd spotted in the crowd at registration. The news that he was now married had been disappointing. Thanks to the latest disaster of being unceremoniously dumped by Rick, Georgia was completely over the idea of finding the love of her life but her flatmate was still a believer and, if anybody deserved the happy-ever-after of the full package, it was Kate.

Perhaps the vibe of wishing the best for her had transmitted itself to Kate because she finally looked up from her meal. She glanced from Georgia to Dave and back again, a subtle quirk of her eyebrow confirming what Georgia already knew—that Dave was interested and it would be very easy to turn this chance meeting into something more—but even that didn't provoke any hint of disapproval.

Kate started chatting to Sally and Ken then, clearly interested in hearing about what it was like to live and work in New Zealand. Seeing that she seemed more relaxed about being here allowed Georgia to release a small sigh of relief. Maybe Kate was making an effort to embrace this adventure and the next couple of days would be a lot of fun for both of them.

And maybe that was exactly what Georgia needed to do. To focus on this competition for what it was— an opportunity to demonstrate her skills to the best of her ability. Kate was smart enough to be right most of the time and the plan that had seemed like an epiphany a few weeks ago, however half-baked it had been, *was* a hare-brained scheme.

And wrong?

With a small, inward sigh, she joined in the conversation and avoided looking at Dave again until she had finished her meal. By the time they all filed out of the dining room on the way to the pre-competition briefing she had decided that Dave, despite how cute he might be, was safe. After only one candidate, she was done with her personal profile testing.

She didn't need Kate's disapproval because she had just tapped into plenty of her own.

Men who contributed to sperm banks were doing so with the full knowledge that they could be fathering children they would never know. Making an assumption that what someone didn't know couldn't hurt them was irresponsible and…and unacceptable.

All the men here were safe.

She was done with any list-ticking. The master plan had been scrapped.

'Between eleven-thirty and midnight tonight, you will all receive your list of events.'

Georgia felt her heart pick up its rate as a squiggle of excitement tickled her gut. This was really happening. She'd heard about this competition years ago, when she'd been training to become a paramedic, and it had always been a dream. *This* was why she was here and the crazy idea of hooking up with someone and possibly going home pregnant was no longer even remotely interesting.

'You will be given the GPS coordinates of the scenario and a start time,' the official continued. 'Please be there at least ten minutes before that time. If you are late, you will not be admitted and you will not be marked in that section of the competition.'

Georgia elbowed Kate, who was standing close beside her in this very crowded room. 'No chance of that happening,' she whispered. 'Not when I'm with you.'

The comment should have earned the kind of eye-roll that Kate bestowed automatically whenever she was reminded of her compulsion to obey rules but, instead, she received a quick grin. Maybe Kate was feeling as excited as she was now that this was actually beginning. Or would be in a few hours.

Starting at six a.m. tomorrow, there would be twelve tasks for each team to complete within twenty-four hours, with time allowed for rest and meal breaks along the way. A final warning about possible elimination from the competition if any teams were found to be sharing information about the tasks completed the briefing and a babble of conversation broke out amongst a shifting audience.

To Georgia's surprise, Kate immediately turned to the man standing on her other side.

'What section are you in?' she asked. 'All doctors? Doctors and med students?'

Her body language suggested the ease of an old friendship so Georgia realised that this man had to be the one Kate had told her about. Luke?

'Doctor/paramedic.' He put his arm over the shoulders of his companion. 'This is Matteo Martini. Italian paramedic extraordinaire.'

Georgia's gaze shifted. And then something a lot bigger shifted inside her chest.

This Italian paramedic had to be the most gorgeous man she had ever seen in her entire life. Well over six feet tall, his strong features were softened by a frame of soft waves of black hair and his eyes looked like the darkest, most luxurious chocolate you could imagine.

And that smile…just crooked enough to give a hint of playfulness. Mischief even?

Whatever. The net effect was drop-dead sexy.

'Ooh…' The sound was almost an approving hum and Georgia felt as if her body was shifting itself a bit closer, even though she knew she hadn't moved. And then her mouth opened without giving her time to think about whatever words she wanted to produce. What did emerge was vaguely appalling.

'A martini? Yes, please… Extra-dry—with an olive.'

She saw the flash of surprise in those chocolate-coloured eyes but then it vanished in the wave of laughter that Georgia managed to join in with, making her ridiculously flirtatious comment no more than a joke.

'This is Georgie,' Kate said. 'My paramedic partner.'

It seemed the most natural thing in the world to fall into step beside Matteo as Kate and Luke led the way to the bar where everyone was going to wait for the scenario list and start times to be handed out.

She felt small beside this solid male figure. And a bit embarrassed, to be honest, after her overly enthusiastic response to their introduction.

Matteo seemed perfectly at ease. He bent his head so that his voice was like a soft, teasing growl intended only for her ears.

'So…you and me, then?'

Oh, *help*… If her response to their introduction had been flirtatious, this was more like blatant seduction and the reaction of her body to both the sound of his voice and the implied invitation was like nothing Georgia had ever experienced. She'd met this man less than

a minute ago and already the attraction was so powerful she wanted…

An upward glance gave her direct contact with those
extraordinary eyes.

Oh, man…she wanted *everything*. The sheer force
of such an unexpected response to a stranger was actually alarming enough to make her break the eye contact within the space of a heartbeat.

And she didn't trust herself to say a single word.

Even more disturbingly, she could feel a faint fluttering sensation that she recognised only too well.

Hope…

That this was *it*. That perhaps she had found the person she had been searching for. *Her* person.

The mental stamp was forceful enough to squash
the flutter.

*How many times?* It wasn't even that long since her
heart had been broken for what she had sworn would
be the very last time. She was not going to be stupid
enough to take even a single step down that path. The
one that ended with someone waiting inside a pretty
church, bathed in all the promise of happily-ever-after.

No and no and *no*.

'The competition,' Matteo offered helpfully into the
short silence. 'We're in the same category. We both
have a doctor for a partner.'

'Oh…that's true.' There was a very different sensation dampening the flicker of desire now. Disappointment?

For heaven's sake, Georgia told herself firmly. Get
a grip…

Matteo paused by the entrance to the bar to allow
her to go in first. He smiled at her.

'I intend to win,' he said.

Georgia couldn't help herself. 'So do I,' she warned.

This time she didn't look away. Neither did Matteo. He was still smiling.

'Do you always get what you want, Georgie?'

The way his accent changed her name into something rather more exotic sent a shiver down her spine. The gleam in his eyes suggested amusement but there was a warmth there, too, that made her feel like he would be more than happy to help her get what she wanted, even if it meant sacrificing something he wanted himself.

She shook her head sadly.

'Not always.'

But she was smiling as well.

Maybe—this time—she would. The question was simply what she wanted more.

The first prize in this competition?

Or Matteo Martini?

# CHAPTER TWO

'WHAT'S THE TIME?'

'Five past eight.'

'We're early.' Matteo Martini sighed. Waiting had never been his forte.

It was an exercise in self-control. A tightrope to balance on between the need to follow rules and gather information and the desire to act. To help someone in trouble. To save a life perhaps...

This wasn't a real life situation, however, which made it impossible to gather any clues about what was to come from a radio conversation or updated pager messages. All they had was a minimal briefing sheet that had given them the GPS coordinates for the scene and that they would be assessing a thirty-five-year-old woman with abdominal pain.

Their tasks were listed as well and they had to assess the scene, examine and treat the patient, define a working diagnosis and means of transport if necessary, within a time limit of eleven minutes.

This was all about following rules. Waiting in their vehicle until it was their turn to enter what looked like a very ordinary village house to face their first scenario of this emergency response competition.

'Doesn't look like much.' Luke sounded disappointed. 'You sure we're in the right place?'

'*Sì. Assolutamente.*' Matteo pointed through the windscreen. 'That car parked over there is a competitor. It's got the numbers. And a light on the roof, like ours. And the flags are…'

'Scottish,' Luke murmured.

The tension of having to wait had just got a whole lot easier as Matteo felt himself being pulled back into the unexpected delight of meeting Georgia Bennett last night. What a stroke of luck it had been that her partner for this competition was an old friend of Luke's. He didn't even have to make an effort to get an introduction to a woman who would have caught his eye no matter how big a crowd she was in.

There was a glow of energy about Georgia that made him think of adventure. Fun. In combination with that tumble of dark blonde curly hair and those hazel-brown eyes that had rather fascinating flecks of gold, she was irresistible. Given their passion for a shared career, that easy conversation over a drink or two had been a bonus. And by the end of the evening, when they'd split up to study the lists of scenarios that had been handed out to the waiting teams, Matteo had been left with the conviction that the attraction he'd discovered was mutual.

Whether they would have the chance to explore that attraction any further was an enticing possibility but Matteo wasn't going to allow it to distract him for any longer than a delicious minute or two. He had, in fact, dismissed it from his mind completely well before their start time of eight-fifteen a.m.

Until he saw the two women emerge from the house,

that was. Until Georgia spotted them waiting in their vehicle and raised her hand to wave at him.

Until she smiled…

'Be nice to have an idea of what we're heading into,' Luke said. 'They weren't giving away any clues, were they?'

'And neither should they,' Matteo said sternly. 'That would be dishonest.'

'Not exactly.' Luke's tone was thoughtful. 'Dishonesty is when you fail to tell the truth. Breaking the rules of the competition to give someone else an advantage would be dishonourable rather than dishonest.'

'Hmm…' Matteo absorbed the correction. 'They are both unacceptable.'

Dishonesty was at the top of his list of despicable human traits. Right up there with cruelty and violence, particularly when children were involved.

'Too right they are,' Luke agreed.

Thrusting his arms through the straps of his pack of gear, Matteo had another moment of distraction.

Had he been a little *too* honest with Georgia during that conversation last night? He'd probably talked about his family with rather too much enthusiasm, hadn't he? If he had wanted to encourage any attraction on her part, he should have stuck to talking about the more exciting exploits of his career as a helicopter paramedic instead of how close he was to his mother and his sisters. Good grief, he'd had to blink tears from his eyes when he'd told her about how much of a thrill it had been to welcome his latest nephew into the world recently.

Weirdly, that slightly cringe-making moment of distraction became an advantage a very short time later, when the two men found themselves in a confusing scenario of a party going on in the house. If the memory of holding that newborn baby hadn't been still there in the back of his mind, would he have been so quick to run up the stairs when they'd heard there was a pregnant girl having stomach pains? And maybe he wouldn't have put quite the same amount of passion into resuscitating a baby who wasn't breathing if he hadn't been imagining that it could have been his sister as the terrified young mother.

In any case, there had been nods of satisfaction from the judges and both he and Luke felt far more confident when they arrived at their second scenario, which clearly had nothing to do with childbirth. Their patient was a middle-aged man who was curled up on a bed and groaning loudly as they entered the room. He was also holding a plastic bucket.

'He's been sick.' The woman who'd met them at the door had explained that she was his wife. 'He got this terrible back pain all of a sudden and then he started vomiting.'

'Could you get some baselines, please, Matt?' Luke was taking the lead on this scenario. 'I'll see what I can find out with the history.' He crouched down beside the bed.

'Show me where this pain is.'

The man put his hand on his side, under his ribs but then moved it towards his abdomen and into his groin.

'Is it the first time you've experienced it?'

'Yes.'

'How bad is it? On a scale of zero to ten, with zero being no pain at all and ten being the worst you can imagine?'

'Ten…' He groaned again. 'And I feel sick…'

'We'll give you something to help with that in just a minute.'

Matteo held a tympanic thermometer close to their patient's ear.

'Temperature's normal,' the nearest judge informed him as he continued taking baseline recordings. 'He's tachycardic at one-twenty, respirations are twenty-four and his blood pressure is one-thirty over ninety.'

Matteo caught Luke's glance. With a normal temperature, infection was less likely to be a cause of this pain so a diagnosis like appendicitis or diverticulitis could be ruled out for the moment. What was needed now was pain relief. He collected everything he needed to insert an IV line and put a tourniquet on the man's arm.

'The IV line is in.' The judge nodded.

'Have you had any trouble urinating?' Luke asked now. 'Is it painful or have you noticed anything different?'

'It hurts,' the man replied. 'And it's very dark.'

Luke glanced at Matteo, who nodded. The diagnosis and their management now appeared simple.

'We think you might have a kidney stone,' Luke said. 'And it's blocking your ureter and causing this pain. We'll give you something for the pain and then we'll take you to hospital. Are you allergic to anything that you know of?'

'No.'

Matteo was already going through the motions of drawing up the morphine.

'What dosage are you administering?' one of the judges asked.

'We'll start with five milligrams,' Luke replied. 'We

can top that up if the pain scale isn't reduced to less than five.'

The judge nodded. 'The drug has been administered.'

Matteo began tidying up and Luke was checking their briefing sheet that gave a list of available hospitals and means of transport. They needed to choose the most appropriate option, which ranged from leaving the patient where he was, transport by helicopter or ambulance to the nearest general hospital, a higher-level hospital or a specialised centre.

Matteo dropped the packages of IV gear back into his pack and turned to pick up the blood-pressure cuff.

To his horror, he could see that their patient now seemed to be having trouble breathing and he was clutching at his chest.

'Luke…' The word was a warning. He reached out to take the man's pulse. 'Do you have chest pain, sir?'

Their patient didn't respond. His head fell back against the pillow and he was gasping for breath.

Luke was still processing this unexpected twist in their scenario.

'Do we see any skin changes?'

'You see redness appearing,' a judge said. 'And hives.'

Nothing more than a glance between Luke and Matteo was needed.

'Anaphylaxis to morphine,' Matteo agreed quietly. 'I'll get a bag of fluids up. And we need some adrenaline, stat.'

They both worked swiftly to counter a potentially fatal situation, administering drugs, getting their patient on oxygen and a cardiac monitor. Within a couple of minutes the judges were nodding with satisfaction

and declared the scenario complete. They just wanted
to ask some questions.

'What is your hospital of choice for this patient?'

'Hospital A,' Luke told them. 'They have an internal medicine department and an intensive care unit
and they are the closest.'

'And what is the most important information to pass
on about your patient?'

'That he has a previously undiscovered allergy to
morphine. We will write it on his notes and make sure
the information is received by everyone we speak to.
We will also advise the patient that it would be a good
idea to wear a Medic-Alert bracelet from now on.'

'That was good.' Matteo slapped Luke on the back
as they left the house. 'I might not have thought of recommending the bracelet.'

'I was too slow to spot the change in our patient's
condition. Well done, you.'

Matteo grinned at his friend. 'We make a good
team.'

'We've got a break now, haven't we? About an hour?'

'We should use it to do the driving test.'

'Okay.' Matteo was looking forward to this test. He
might work on helicopters now but his early years as a
paramedic had been on the road and he loved the challenge of driving fast and doing it well.

A gravelled area beside the river that ran through
this village had been cordoned off for this part of the
competition and a line of orange road cones marked
the course. They could see an ambulance completing
the test as they arrived, clouds of dust billowing as it
snaked around the cones at high speed and then came
to a sudden halt between the cones marking the end
of the course.

Another car was waiting for its turn.

The car with the Scottish flags.

And there it was again...

Distraction. A delicious buzz of anticipation at the knowledge he would be seeing Georgia again.

It had always been a given that he would thoroughly enjoy coming to this competition again.

A smile took over his face as he spotted Georgia sitting in the driver's seat of the girls' vehicle. He just hadn't realised how much better it would be this time.

'Cute,' he murmured.

The swift glance from Luke held a note of surprise. Or maybe concern. Did he think that Matteo was here to chase women rather than focus on their performance? He thought fast, putting a casual smile on his face as he shifted his gaze from the woman in the driver's seat. 'I didn't notice that before.'

The look of surprise increased as Luke raised his eyebrows. 'You mean Georgia? Or Kate?'

Okay. Maybe his interpretation of that glance had been accurate.

He hoped his laugh was as casual as his smile.

'Oh, the girls are both cute but that wasn't what I was looking at. Have you seen what is tied to the front of their car?'

It was a stuffed toy bear that was wearing a kilt and holding a set of bagpipes.

Matteo rolled down his window and pointed to the toy, raising his voice so that Georgia could hear him. 'He is going to get dirty, I think.'

'All part of the fun.' Georgia was grinning at him as she called back. Holding his gaze.

*Mio Dio...* That smile. The sparkle in those eyes. It was enough to make Matteo's breath catch. For an odd warmth to ignite in his gut and then spread all the way through his body.

What was it about this woman that was so different? So compelling?

Could Georgia feel this same unusual level of attraction? Possibly not, by how focussed she clearly was on what she was about to do.

'Which one of you is going to do the driving? You're only allowed one person in the vehicle.'

There was a hint of something in her eyes. A challenge perhaps? Or did she want to watch him showing what he was capable of?

His lips twitched in a suppressed smile. He would be more than happy to demonstrate any skill she might be interested in—and he was apparently good at many things that women liked…

But did Luke want to do the driving?

No. His companion was already unclipping his safety belt.

'You do it,' he said to Matteo. 'You've got far more experience with emergency driving skills than I have. I'll wait with Kate.'

'Cool.' Matteo nodded as Luke got out of the car. He could focus now.

He needed to know exactly what was required to make sure he aced this particular test.

He needed to make sure he impressed Georgia…

'You're a bit quiet, Georgie. Not worried about the next task, are you?'

'Not at all. I was just thinking about that driving test. I could have done better.'

Georgia wished she'd done better. She might not

have been able to see his face but she'd *known* that Matteo was watching her and the effect had been to make her very uncharacteristically self-conscious. Clumsy even. She had felt his gaze on her like a physical touch of his hand on her skin and the hyperawareness it had created had messed with her concentration. How embarrassing had it been to send those road cones flying on her first attempt at the serpentine? It wasn't until she had been able to shut him out of her thoughts that she'd been able to demonstrate what she was capable of.

'You did great.' Kate's tone was reassuring.

'Not as great as Matteo,' Georgia muttered.

Kate grinned. 'He was something else, wasn't he? I've never seen anyone drive like that. *So* fast. And he didn't touch a single cone.'

Georgia scowled. 'Thanks for reminding me.'

Kate laughed. 'Let it go. I'll bet there are other things he's not as good at. He's a boy. And he's Italian. Maybe he had a Ferrari when he was a teenager.'

Oh, man, there was an image to play with. A younger version of Matteo Martini. With much longer hair perhaps, behind the wheel of a very fast car. With that easy grin on his face and only one hand on the wheel because his other arm would be over the shoulders of the girl in the passenger seat. Because there *would* be a girl, no doubt about that. Or maybe his hand would be resting on her leg, his thumb making lazy circles on that sensitive skin on her inner thigh. The girl would be smiling, too, of course. Georgia certainly would be…

It was ridiculous to experience a twinge of something so easily recognisable as envy.

No, it was even worse than envy. This felt like jealousy, thanks to the way Georgia's eyes were narrowing. She shook her head to stop it happening.

'What's the next task about?'

'It's called "School Bag". We're being called to a teacher who has tripped over a school bag and is lying on the floor, not moving. She's unconscious but breathing. Head injury, do you think?'

'I'm sure it won't be that simple. We'll have to make sure we rule out other causes of unconsciousness. Was the fall the cause or did she fall because of something else?'

'Like a cardiac event.'

'Yes. Or hypoglycaemia, drug overdose, a stroke, seizures, anaphylaxis, alcohol. It's a long list.'

'Let's hope there's someone around who can tell us exactly what happened. We need to know how she was acting immediately before she fell.'

The only other people in the classroom with the unconscious woman, however, apart from the silent judges, were a group of young children who were taking every advantage of their teacher being unable to control them. Some were having a race around the room, jumping from one desk top to another. One was ripping pages from a textbook. They were all shouting and laughing.

The teacher was lying face down near the blackboard. A school satchel was close to her feet, spilling its contents of an apple, drink bottle and box of pencils. Kate felt for a pulse on their patient's neck the moment they got close enough.

'Hello...can you hear me?'

'You have no response,' a judge informed her. 'The heart rate is one hundred and twenty.'

They rolled their patient carefully so that they could protect her airway. The noise in the classroom increased and Kate was hit on the head by a ball of screwed-up paper. Georgia's head swerved and caught the culprit—the boy who'd been ripping pages from the book. He grinned at Georgia.

An impish grin beneath a wild mop of curly hair. Such a cute kid, she had to stop herself grinning back. Instead, she jumped to her feet and tried to find her sternest expression. If they couldn't get this scene under control, it was going to make it impossible to do their job well.

'*Enough,*' she shouted. 'All of you kids come here. At *once.*'

A chair toppled with a crash in the sudden silence that followed. One by one, the children came closer. They were all acting so well, with their heads down to show that they knew they were in trouble. One little girl, with huge blue eyes and long plaits, was biting her lip and looking so scared that Georgia just wanted to give her a cuddle.

'It's okay,' she told them. 'But you have to stop being naughty. Your teacher is sick. Did anyone see what happened?'

'She fell over,' one of the children said.

'And before that?'

The children shook their heads. One boy turned away and pushed another one, who pushed back. Georgia caught a third boy who stepped past her, poised to start running again. From the corner of her eye, she could see Kate taking some baseline measurements, including blood glucose. Then she looked at one of the judges.

'Is there someone available who could look after these children?'

'There is a school caretaker outside the room.' A nod from the judge was the signal for the young actors to leave the scene. The boy who'd thrown the paper ball grinned at Georgia again as he left and this time she did return the smile. Along with a quick wink.

'Blood glucose too low to register,' Kate said behind her. 'Skin is cold and clammy and she's still tachycardic.'

'Cool. I'll set up for a glucose infusion.' Georgia turned back to the task as the door closed behind the last of the children. They could work in peace now but there was a part of her that was missing the energy that had been in the room a moment ago.

An energy that only children could provide. That wholehearted enthusiasm for being alive that adults learned to control too well sometimes. Taking advantage of an opportunity for adventure was a hallmark of a happy child and it always seemed to involve either laughter or tears—a pendulum that could swing unpredictably.

Georgia loved the unexpected.

And she loved kids. Even more than babies. She'd had always had dreams of having a whole bunch of them. A messy house and lots of noise with hopefully more laughter than tears. A frantic routine of cooking, cleaning, cuddles and school runs to deliver her little tribe to classrooms just like this one.

She had a job to do now that had nothing to do with small people and the fragment of that dream that the extras in this scenario had prompted was easy enough to push aside.

But it was a reminder that it was still there. Getting stronger with every passing week. If she was going to achieve even a part of that dream she was going to have to do it soon.

And having a kid you could take to school had to start in a very different place.

With having a baby.

And that brought her straight back to the plan she had just abandoned on moral grounds—of using this competition as an opportunity to start that journey to parenthood.

Georgia dismissed that line of thought easily as well as she taped the cannula to their patient's arm as evidence that an IV line had been established.

As they monitored the effects of their treatment, she tried to think of anything they might be missing that could be another twist in this scenario.

'She's not wearing a Medic-Alert bracelet, is she?'

'No.' Kate moved the collar of the shirt their patient was wearing. 'Or a necklace.'

'Can you check her bag? Or the drawer in her desk? It would be useful to know what medication she's on. Is she using insulin or medication to lower her blood sugar? She might have overdosed.'

Kate did find a packet of tablets in the teacher's bag but they weren't what they might have expected.

'These are antidepressants, aren't they?'

'Yes.'

The woman lying on the floor began to move and she groaned softly.

'Your patient's blood glucose level is returning to

normal,' one of the judges said. 'What is your plan for transport?'

Georgia thought fast. 'We will transport her to hospital. She has no one here to watch her and we don't know what her normal regime is for her diabetes control.'

'Which hospital do you choose?'

'Hospital B.'

'Why?'

'Because it's a higher-level hospital and there are psychiatric services available. The fact that she's taking antidepressants suggests that there are additional issues for this patient that might be affecting her control of her disease.'

The judges nod was pleased. So was Kate's.

'Good job,' she whispered, as they left the scene. 'I probably would have picked Hospital A because it was the closest. And I might not have thought to check her bag either.'

'You get patients delivered to you with a handover of any available information. I guess I'm just used to searching for clues.' Georgia shoved the bulky pack of gear into the back of the car. 'It's one of the things I love about my job—getting to play detective on scene along with being the medic.'

Matteo shared her passion for this job. He was probably as good at playing detective on scene as he was at emergency driving. They'd never run out of fascinating things to talk about, would they?

Oh, boy...this was getting worse. She was actually thinking in terms of for ever? Of growing old together and still not running out of conversation?

'You have to deal with all the distractions, too,'

Kate added. 'Those kids were doing my head in to start with.'

The bunch of children was being ushered back into the building now, probably to prepare for the next scenario. As Kate and Georgia drove away, they spotted a car they recognised heading towards the school.

'I think those boys are stalking us.'

Kate's lips twitched as if she was trying not to smile. 'Just coincidence.' But she turned her head to watch the car disappear. 'I wonder how they'll cope with finding a riot going on.'

Georgia lapsed into silence. Matteo would cope very well. He probably wouldn't even need to shout at the children to get their attention and gain control of the scene. He'd only need to smile at them and they would be eating out of his hand because they'd know how much he loved kids.

And he *did* love kids. A large part of the conversation they'd had over drinks last night, when Kate and Luke had been talking quietly, had been about his family. About how much he adored his sister's children and what a thrill the recent birth of a new nephew had been. It sounded as if the entire Martini clan had been at the hospital to welcome that new arrival and Georgia hadn't missed the way Matteo had spoken about his other sisters and his mother. She could have sworn he'd actually had tears in his eyes at one point. Family was clearly of the utmost importance in his life.

And wouldn't he make the best father? He would be totally devoted to his children and there would be a huge, extended family in the wings to make every milestone a glorious celebration.

If that was what Georgia was looking for, Matteo would be perfect.

A few years ago even, when she'd still had the dream that she could find her perfect partner and be totally confident that her own children would never face the kind of fear that had poisoned her own childhood, Matteo would have stood out as being exactly what she was searching for. Gorgeous and confident and super-smart. She'd been more than impressed to learn about his postgraduate qualifications in resuscitation and aeromedical transportation.

But the last remnants of that dream had come crashing down in the wake of the brutal ending of her last relationship. Her heart had been broken for the last time and she knew not to trust that tiny flutter of hope that had come from nowhere when she'd seen this gorgeous Italian for the first time.

His passion for his family was actually a massive negative in the grand scheme of things because if the worst happened, she would be facing an army of opponents if she wanted to protect her children. And she knew that fighting even one could be too many.

It was an automatic gesture to turn her arm a little whenever this memory surfaced. To see the jagged scar that remained from the arm that had been so badly broken when she was only five years old. To feel a shiver of that terror when her birth father had arrived to claim her and the struggle to drag her from her mother's arms had turned vicious.

Not that it had surfaced much in the last few years, because Georgia had believed she would choose a good man and could rewrite history, but her choices had proved untrustworthy. And, okay, maybe Rick had only been verbally vicious when he'd ended their relationship but that had been more than enough to stir the memories. Her 'father' had been just as quick to cause pain with words as anything physical.

And Italians had a reputation for having quick tempers, didn't they? Imagine having to face an entire family of angry Italians?

Kate's voice broke into her thoughts. 'Penny for them?'

'Huh?'

'You're miles away. What's up?'

'I'm just hungry,' Georgia said. 'It must be time for lunch, isn't it?'

Kate checked their schedule.

'Yep. We've got a break for over an hour.'

Finding a parking space near the main buildings of the ski resort, the two women handed over their vouchers to receive another meal featuring dumplings.

Georgia felt suddenly weary.

'I feel like I've been on a full shift already,' she told Kate. 'And we're only a third of our way through the competition. At least we get a break after this. I'm going to try and catch a nap.'

After they'd eaten, they went outside into the sunshine and found a grassy patch to lie on that was shaded by a huge tree. Georgia closed her eyes and hoped that Kate would think she had fallen asleep.

She just needed a little quiet time and maybe she could stop the unsettling thoughts that were only a distraction to why she was really here and then she could focus completely on winning this competition.

Childhood memories of the trauma of being forcibly taken from her mother, the intervention of child protection services and then being moved from one town to another until her father's death had finally freed them from the threat that had never gone away but were of no help to her concentration.

Stupid dreams of finding 'the one', like Kate still had, were just as useless.

The plan of launching her new future as a single parent by choosing her baby daddy at this competition were well and truly being laid to rest.

Because, if she had the choice, she wouldn't be able to choose anyone other than Matteo?

And he would end up finding out, wouldn't he? He was best friends with *her* best friend's friend and secrets had a nasty tendency to get revealed eventually.

Besides…she liked him.

She *really* liked him. Too much to consider the kind of deception that would end up haunting her for ever.

Her breath escaped in a small sigh as she turned her mind back to the tasks they had already completed today. The baby resuscitation. All those little scamps creating havoc in the schoolroom.

And thinking about those children produced an idea that Georgia hadn't ever considered before.

Perhaps she didn't actually need to have a baby herself. There were always children who needed adoption or fostering. Children who were having to live with the kind of trauma she knew about all too well.

She'd be good at that.

With another long, outward breath, Georgia relaxed into the companionable silence she was sharing with Kate.

Yes. That was an idea that merited a lot more thought in the near future. When this competition was over.

# CHAPTER THREE

IT WAS ALL over bar the shouting.

All tasks had been completed and the rest of the twenty-four-hour period after the lunch break had been jam packed with challenges and excitement.

The bus-crash scenario where they'd needed to triage so many injured people, including the woman who was trapped and losing a dangerous amount of blood. They'd dealt with a cardiac arrest and a young man having a stroke, whose acting had been superb. Even as Georgia had been asking her initial questions, his speech had become slurred and his face had started to droop on one side. The impressively set up scenario of a mass shooting incident in the last couple of hours had been responsible for finally using up any remaining ounce of her energy.

Skipping breakfast, she and Kate had gone to their room to grab a few hours' sleep but it hadn't been enough. When the alarm sounded to remind them it was time to go to the competition debrief, Georgia couldn't drag herself out of bed.

'You go,' she mumbled. 'Tell me all about it later.'

The extra sleep had been exactly what she'd needed. By the time the competitors gathered in the town square for the prize-giving ceremony, Georgia was refreshed and ready for anything. Standing in the crowd beside Matteo was adding considerably to the anticipation. More than once, she found her gaze caught by his as she glanced up and their eye contact was a conversation all in itself.

A reminder of a conversation anyway.

*'I intend to win.'*

*'So do I.'*

*'Do you always get what you want, Georgie?'*

*'Not always...'*

But her heart skipped a beat as the announcement became imminent for their section of the competition.

'And the winner is... *Scotland*...'

There was a split second as Georgia sucked in an astonished breath where she was still locked in a moment of that silent communication with Matteo and she saw something change in that gaze.

He was impressed with her.

More than that. He had to be disappointed that he and Luke hadn't won but she could swear he actually looked *proud* of her and, in that instant, that meant more than anything else could have.

She wanted to be the person that this man was proud of.

Because it made her feel as if she was a better person than she'd ever been before.

But then her lungs were full of air, and happiness laced with her own pride tipped into something that had to be let out, and Georgia emitted a rather unprofessional squeal of delight, threw her arms around Kate and squeezed her best friend as hard as she could.

Even then, in that moment of pure joy, she was

aware of a longing to feel Matteo's arms around her in a hug like this but there was no time for that. They had to weave their way through the sea of people and applause, to make their way to the stage and receive their trophy. The pace, and the excitement, didn't stop there either.

After the prize-giving came the convoy that was the highlight of this ceremony, where every ambulance and Jeep or makeshift emergency response vehicle put their lights and sirens on and drove through all the surrounding villages, throwing toys and sweets to the crowds of children lining the roads to enjoy the spectacle.

Georgia recognised the cute little boy from the schoolroom scenario and leaned further out of the window as they sped past to make sure her gifts landed as close as possible to his outstretched hands. When he caught the soft toy bear in a kilt that had been on the front of their car, amidst a shower of boiled sweets in the colours of the Scottish flag, she let out a whoop of satisfaction.

Matteo, who was driving, turned his head with a frown of disapproval at the danger she was putting herself in, but he was laughing at the same time.

He knew exactly how much pleasure she was getting by pushing both the limits of safety and the rules for this traditional convoy that, astonishingly, she'd just had to remind Kate of—no alcohol, no speeding and no leaning out of vehicles. It seemed that Kate was a little drunk on adventure, possibly for the first time in her life, but Georgia knew that Matteo was as addicted to this kind of adrenaline rush as she was.

Sharing that kind of personality trait would have given her an instant connection with anyone but there was more to it as far as Matteo was concerned. Not that she wanted to think about that right now. She just wanted to enjoy the delicious sound of his laughter. And his voice with that fabulous accent. And the fact that she could make the most of it all for the next few hours as all the competitors and their supporters, the officials and army of volunteers for this competition were treated to an evening of food and wine and dancing.

It was Matteo who brought a chilled bottle of champagne to the table that Georgia and Kate were sitting at, having loaded plates with offerings from one of the many barbecues being used. The long, rustic table was crowded with their new friends from places like New Zealand and Croatia and there was already a generous supply of drinks available, but that bottle of champagne instantly became the star.

Like Matteo…

He sat opposite Georgia and winked at her. 'I hadn't forgotten,' he said softly. 'You have a taste for champagne, yes?'

'Mmm…'

So this offering was a gift just for her, because he'd remembered what she liked?

Something inside Georgia was melting but she tried very hard to stop the process. Nobody was this perfect—it just wasn't humanly possible.

'So who thinks they'll do this again?' Luke asked after Matteo handed her a brimming plastic cup and filled one for himself.

'Me,' she responded instantly.

'Me,' Matteo said at exactly the same moment.

Grinning, they both raised their cups and touched

them together in a toast. Their gazes touched at the same time and that melting process suddenly accelerated.

The sense of connection that was there between them was mind-blowing. It was way more than a shared love of adventure. More than anything that could be encompassed by mere physical attraction. For a heartbeat, and then another, it seemed that she and Matteo were in a space that nobody but the two of them could ever inhabit.

A dangerous space. The kind of fantasy planet that came into being when you fell head over heels in love with someone. An orbit that could only last until it got annihilated by an inevitable meteorite of discovering how wrong you'd been.

But…maybe it was possible to *visit* that planet.

Just for a little while. A few hours?

The longing to do that was overpowering.

This had nothing to do with that crazy plan. This was simply the force of attraction for someone who had unexpectedly stepped into her life—and who would step out of it again very soon.

Someone with whom she felt a connection like nothing she had ever experienced before.

What would it be like to get even closer to this irresistible man?

Dave, the New Zealander, was saying something about how expensive it would be for them to come back to do the competition again but Georgia wasn't listening.

The prospect of getting *really* close to Matteo was both the most exhilarating thing ever and a bit scary. Georgia was playing with fire here, and she knew it.

At least the reminder that there were other people around them forced her to break the eye contact with Matteo but she knew the damage—if that's what it was—had already been done.

He was as aware of her as she was of him for the rest of that dinner and she knew he was watching her when she dragged Kate onto the dance floor when the lights dimmed and the live band launched into some rock and roll. It was a general invitation for everybody to start letting their hair down and enjoy themselves. It was also a private invitation for Matteo to cut in and claim her as a dance partner.

It took only a minute or two and there it was. An outstretched hand and a smile that melted her heart all over again.

The fact that they were surrounded by other people and the noise level was deafening only seemed to enhance the effect of his skin touching hers for the first time.

It was only his fingers catching hers, sending her into a twirl that took her away from Kate and towards a less densely populated part of the dance floor, but Georgia could feel the power of that touch sending a current into every cell of her body.

Circuits were being fried so that she couldn't seem to catch a coherent thought. Physical sensations, emotions, words—even the sounds, scents and colours around her were blurring into something that was too big to comprehend, let alone analyse. There were memories woven into whatever was happening, too. And desires.

Everything she had ever wanted, or could want, appeared to be within reach every time she was in contact with this man's skin. The bass notes of the music they were dancing to were a drumbeat, urging her towards…something.

Towards *this*… The look in Matteo's eyes when he tugged her off the dance floor and into a quieter corner past the doors.

As he bent his head to kiss her for the very first time…

If her brain was sending any warning that going any further could be risky, it was nothing more than a barely heard whisper amidst a roaring cacophony of desire. So easy to dismiss because it was insignificant. It didn't matter. Nothing else mattered.

Nothing else even existed…

Dancing with Georgia was like playing with light.

With fire…

The sparkle in her eyes and the shards of gold in her hair as those curls bounced and swung through shadows and into the gleam of the spotlights over the dance floor.

The way his skin burned whenever it touched hers.

He had never wanted a woman as much as he wanted Georgia Bennett right now.

He had to kiss her.

Nothing more, he warned himself as he led her away from the dance floor. This was too special to ruin by moving too fast. This was the beginning of something that made this first night together far too important to enjoy as nothing more than a casual sexual encounter.

But he had to kiss her. To find out whether the touch of her lips—the *taste* of her—could actually be as incredible as he believed it could be.

And, *Dio mio*, it was even more than he had believed was possible.

He had found the woman of his dreams. Gorgeous and clever enough to keep him on his toes. Someone with a passion for the same things in life. A body that was perfect, with just the right curves in all the right places. A combination that coalesced into a response to his own that was taking him somewhere he'd never been before.

In love…

Head-over-heels, crazily in love…

*'Ti desidero,'* he murmured, when he could finally lift his lips from hers enough to form any words. *'Così tanto.'*

It was safe to say how much he wanted her, wasn't it? She hadn't given any hint that she could understand his native language.

But maybe the language of love was universal and it was the tone that said it all, because Georgia's eyes were huge in this dark corner and they were telling him that she knew exactly what he was saying.

'Me, too,' she whispered.

He could feel the way she drew in a quick breath because his hands were still on her ribcage, his hands cradling the delicious weight of her breasts.

She used that breath to form some more words. 'My room or yours?'

For a heartbeat, Matteo froze, and that in itself was shocking. At any point in his life before this, he wouldn't have hesitated in accepting such an invitation from a beautiful woman. Sex was one of life's greatest pleasures after all.

But this was different.

Georgia was different.

And this…connection between them was so new. So beautiful but also fragile.

What if she thought he was only interested in the sex? That it meant nothing more than that?

Or what if he rejected the offer and she disappeared because she thought he *wasn't* interested?

He couldn't think straight. And then he saw the tip of Georgia's tongue appear and trace the outline of her bottom lip.

He could barely muster any words in Italian, let alone English.

'I haven't got… I mean it might not be…safe…'

He could feel the movement of her body between his hands as she pressed herself closer. She lifted her face, inviting him to kiss her again.

'It's safe,' she said softly, her eyelids lowering to shutter her gaze. 'I promise.'

A promise was a vow and Matteo let his eyes drift shut as he sank into the astonishing way her lips responded to his. The touch of her tongue sealed his fate. He trusted her.

How could he not trust the woman he knew he was destined to marry?

The grand, if half-baked, plan of finding someone suitable to father her child had not even been a consideration when Georgia had made that promise to Matteo that this was safe.

The fact that she'd lied to him by inferring that she was on the Pill or in a safe part of her cycle had also been dismissed as unimportant as she allowed herself to be swept away on this tidal wave of pure desire.

Okay, maybe that whisper of warning had returned to try and sneak past the breath-stealing anticipation as she led Matteo to her bedroom in the accommodation block but it had been a short walk and all it had needed to send any doubts into oblivion had been the look in Matteo's eyes and the touch of his fingers as he began to unbutton her shirt. Her knees almost buckled as he bent his head to kiss the curve of her breasts just before he undid the clasp of her bra and somehow tipping her head back in ecstasy had the same effect on the rest of her body and there they were—squashed onto the narrow confines of her single bed.

The size of that bed made it so much harder to shed the rest of their clothing but it didn't seem to matter. Any awkwardness dissolved under low peals of laughter, of pausing to share another passionate kiss. Of moving to make things easier that only brought new areas of their skin into contact. The only light came from the moon beyond an unshaded window but Georgia didn't need to use her eyes to discover that Matteo's body was as perfect as she had suspected. She only needed her fingers and her lips and sometimes her tongue to explore the planes of hard muscle, the soft fur of masculine hair and the exquisitely tender skin in secret places.

She only needed her own skin to experience the power in his hands but it was her heart that registered the astonishing gentleness with which that power was being harnessed.

Georgia had never been made love to like this. Carried to a place of such a mind-blowing release that it was inevitable that the roller-coaster would dip in its aftermath. Even so, it was a bit of a shock to find it so hard to swallow past a painful constriction in her throat as she lay in Matteo's arms, feeling the thump of his heartbeat finally returning to a normal level.

If she had been a crying type—which she certainly wasn't—she would have tears trickling down her face by now, wouldn't she?

It was a shock, too, to realise how hard it was going to be to walk away from this man.

She'd just given Matteo more than her body. Right now, her brain was fighting to retrieve her heart.

'I want to see you again,' Matteo murmured. 'Soon…'

Georgia turned her head so that she couldn't get undone by those eyes. She wanted to see him again soon as well. So much that it scared her.

'You live in Italy,' she reminded him. 'Scotland is a long way away.'

*'Nessun problema.'* He was smiling. 'I can find a way. I'm ready for new adventures. Scotland must be a very exciting place to work on rescue helicopters, yes? Lots of mountain work?'

Oh…*help*… How amazing would that be? To have Matteo living and working in Scotland? To be with him again, like *this*…

Again and again. To forge a relationship that could last the rest of their lives?

She'd done it again, hadn't she? Fallen in love at the drop of a hat and now she was dreaming of that little church and the house with a picket fence and a whole tribe of adorable children.

She couldn't do this.

She'd *promised* herself she would never be stupid enough to do this again. And she'd meant it.

The sliver of fear already in existence gathered force and shivered its way down her spine. There was a hint of anger there as well, that she'd allowed herself to let things go this far.

Not just the falling-in-love kind of far. She'd taken a huge risk in having unprotected sex.

Using Matteo as a sperm donor hadn't even crossed her mind when she had been swept away by this over-whelming chemistry. When she'd told him it was safe, it had been because she had somehow convinced her-self that she was in a safe part of her cycle.

She had to be, because she hadn't been able to fight a desire like nothing she'd ever experienced before.

However long the odds were, however, the possibil-ity was there. And if she hadn't won that spin of the pregnancy roulette wheel, there would be consequences she didn't want to have to think about.

What she could think about were the consequences of imagining that this initial head-rush of falling in love could last and become something permanent and trustworthy.

She knew how unlikely that was.

She knew how gutting it was when the dreams crashed and burned.

Georgia had just had one perfect night. The best thing she could do would be to keep it like that. Bottle it into a memory that would never get tarnished.

'I can't do that,' she heard herself whisper, her words strained with the effort of releasing them.

She felt the subtle shift of Matteo's body. The birth

of a tension that encompassed bewilderment and something else. Something darker.

'Why not? I… I thought we had something special here, *cara*.'

'We do.' There was a gap between them now but that couldn't entirely explain the chill she could feel. 'But that's just it. This is *here*. Anywhere else would be…impossible.'

She had to meet the intense gaze she could feel on her face. Even in this dim light she could see the expression in those dark eyes.

She was hurting him and she hated herself for that.

Enough that she could change her mind and break her vow? Take the risk that her heart was insisting would be worth it this time?

She actually parted her lips to tell him that but she didn't get the chance to speak.

Matteo was rolling away from her. Getting to his feet and starting to gather his clothes.

'So this was just a one-night stand for you?' He had dragged on his underwear and now his trousers.

The slip in his excellent English was poignant enough to make Georgia catch her bottom lip with her teeth. To generate the prickle that warned of tears she would never allow to fall.

Matteo didn't bother doing up his belt. He was pushing his arms through the sleeves of his shirt with jerky movements.

'There's someone else, isn't there?' He sounded angry now. 'Someone in Scotland? You're *cheating* on someone?'

Oh, how was it possible for one word to convey such ultimate disgust?

Georgia closed her eyes.

She remembered the conversation over drinks that first night. When Kate had been shocked to discover not only that Luke was no longer married but that his best friend had never known his ex-wife's name and only referred to her as 'the cheating cow'?

She could hear Matteo's words echoing in the back of her mind.

*'If someone cheated on me or lied to me like that, I would never let her name pass my lips again...'*

This was it. The easy way out. No further excuses would have to be found and Matteo's attitude to both cheating and lying would ensure that he didn't try to contact her again. He believed he'd been used for no more than a bit of fun. Worse, fun at someone else's expense. Someone who would possibly be devastated if they found out.

She knew that Matteo had been aware of the same level of connection she'd discovered with him so she couldn't blame him for being so angry. If the situation were reversed she would feel exactly the same way.

Getting her next word out was going to be the hardest thing she'd ever done.

She couldn't do it, in fact. All she could manage was a single nod of her head and that felt like an acknowledgement of how justified Matteo was to be reacting like this but, of course, it was interpreted as a confirmation of his accusation that she was cheating on a boyfriend back home.

And, maybe, the sane corner of Georgia's brain had intended it to be taken that way.

As she closed her eyes, she saw Matteo swoop on

his shoes and socks but she knew he hadn't bothered to put them on.

Because she heard the door of her room slam shut only seconds later.

# CHAPTER FOUR

IT WAS OFTEN the case that normal life could seem dull in the aftermath of an overseas holiday or a challenging adventure.

And Georgia Bennett had combined both of those into the few days of the Rally Rakovi international medical rescue competition. It had been the most extraordinary few days of her life and it was no surprise that she felt flat for a while after getting home.

But surely this heavy cloud of fatigue laced with waves of something that bordered on misery at frequent intervals should have worn off by now?

It had been *weeks*…

Enough time for the glory of arriving home as a winner and impressing all her colleagues at the Edinburgh Emergency Response Centre to have worn off.

Enough time to have had evidence that she been right to assume she had been in a safe part of her cycle when she'd slept with Matteo. That, even if she'd gone further down that unwise path of hoping to get pregnant by someone she would never have to see again, a one-off encounter would have been a disappointing failure.

And it was a huge relief. Of course it was.

She wasn't disappointed because she hadn't expected anything different. She had, in fact, been waiting for her period to start with an acute anticipation of the relief that it would bring.

It would be a line being drawn under that very brief chapter in her life. It would make it so much easier to put it all behind her, neatly packaged in a memory box that could be labelled 'The Rally'. Or, probably more accurately, 'Matteo'.

Georgia would, at last, be able to embrace life and the job she was so passionate about with all the enthusiasm and determination that was so much a part of who she was.

But there had been a note of, not disappointment, but sadness to be found amidst that wash of relief. She had taken a risk after all, and so there'd been that small chance that she could have conceived. Her brain might be telling her in no uncertain terms that it was a good thing she wasn't but her body—and her heart—were whispering a reminder of how much she wanted to become a mother. That, if it had happened, it would have been a genuine accident so she could have avoided the guilt of knowing she had done something she knew would have been so wrong.

As a final kicker, it almost felt as if someone or something in the cosmos was mocking the fact that she had stepped back, however briefly, into that fantasy planet of true love and happy-ever-afters. Of holding her own baby in her arms for the first time and feeling like her heart would burst from the joy of it.

She was putting a brave face on it, of course, and she was confident that nobody had guessed the internal struggle she was grappling with.

Certainly not her crew partner, Sean, whose face brightened with the priority call that was coming through on their pagers.

'*Yes*…a cardiac arrest. Finally—we get to save a life today. Come on, champ.'

It had been her new nickname on station ever since she had come back with the trophy that was now proudly on display in the staffroom. Every paramedic who worked here and even the doctors and other medical professionals she encountered during her working hours had wanted details about the competition. A description of how it all worked, of what the scenarios had involved and about the level of skill other competitors had displayed.

She'd told them everything they'd wanted to know. Encouraged them to think about entering themselves for a 'once in a lifetime' experience. The one thing she never mentioned, however, was what had left the most lasting personal impression.

Matteo Martini.

Georgia followed Sean at a run, slamming the passenger door of the ambulance and reaching for her safety belt as the garage doors came up and Sean put his foot down on the accelerator, flicking on the lights and siren the moment they exited the station gates.

Thank goodness the interest in the competition had finally worn off. She'd spent far more time than was healthy reliving every moment she had had with Matteo anyway. Every conversation, every glance, every touch. Being reminded of him every time she had talked about the rally to people who had no idea how much of an impact it had had on her had been a form of emotional torture.

It was still all bottled up inside her and she had no idea how to deal with it.

She couldn't even tell Kate about it, which had always been her go-to therapy for any emotional woes because Kate was more than a little starry-eyed about reconnecting with her friend from medical school and Luke was Matteo's best friend and it was all…complicated. Just a bit of mess, really.

Thrown into her seatbelt as Sean braked behind a slow car that seemed unaware of the noise of the siren and flashing lights was a helpful distraction. The blast he gave on the air horn to order the car to pull over and let them through the traffic was enough to tickle her adrenaline levels and she actually laughed as the ambulance swerved and even mounted the kerb briefly to get past the obstruction.

Sean sent a grin sideways.

Her favourite crew partner was enjoying this as much as she was. Relatively new to their station, Sean had become instantly popular. Tall, good looking and with a very cute Irish accent, he was particularly popular with his female colleagues and a month or two ago Georgia might have been interested herself, despite having sworn off the search for a long-term relationship in the wake of that crushing break-up with Rick.

But not now.

She liked him. And she loved working with him but as far as anything more was concerned, she couldn't summon even a flicker of interest.

Because he wasn't Matteo Martini?

Yeah… The bar had been reset at an impossibly high level, hadn't it? Which was a good thing, Georgia told herself, because she didn't want to go there. She didn't want to get lured back into a situation where the odds of it ending well, as in not ending at all, were sadly virtually non-existent in her experience. And she was at risk because she fell in love too easily.

Perhaps the most astonishing thing she'd learned about herself during those intense few days of the competition was that she was actually capable of falling in love at first sight…

'Next on the right,' she called. 'And then second on the left. ETA two minutes.'

'Roger. Hold onto your hat. And it's your turn to lead.'

With a nod, Georgia focussed on what lay immediately ahead. It would be a long shot, saving someone who had been found in cardiac arrest, given that it had been an unwitnessed collapse so they didn't know when it had happened, or whether effective bystander CPR was currently being performed, but she would give the effort everything she had.

Probably a little bit more, even, because this was her life and she wanted to love it again with the same passion she'd had before she'd gone to that damn competition.

The battle hadn't been won.

The resuscitation effort had been protracted, messy and, in the end, very sad. The victim had only been in his early fifties and his first grandchild was due to be born next week. His wife had been distraught and then his pregnant daughter had arrived at the house as they had been clearing away their gear and waiting for the doctor to come and sign the death certificate.

Georgia was not going to allow herself to dwell on

this case, however. If she did, she knew she would sink even further into a space she knew was there but didn't recognise.

A dark space where the hovering cloud of bone-deep fatigue with those shards of misery would come down and block out any remaining light in her life. Where she might start to feel so sorry for herself that it would become too hard to pick herself up and make things better.

It wasn't going to happen.

Georgia Bennett had faced worse things than this in her life and she had learned that she could not only beat them, she could become stronger.

Her share of the best things in life were just around the corner.

Maybe she couldn't see exactly where that corner was just yet but if she didn't stop moving forward, she would never find it.

So she put the distressing end to her shift firmly into the part of her brain reserved for work hours and made every effort to enjoy being home. She loved this little stone cottage that she shared with Kate, with its pretty garden and cosy kitchen and the steep, narrow staircase that led to their attic bedrooms.

She loved Kate's company, too. And her cooking. It was no hardship to tackle the dishes after eating the dinner that her flatmate had prepared tonight and their conversation offered an opportunity to think of someone other than herself for a while.

It was way past time that Kate and Luke got together—the way they had promised they would when they were both back in Scotland. How good would it be if she could look back on that competition and realise that it had been the catalyst for something amazing instead of the dark cloud that was making life so much less bright for herself? If something wonderful came from the interest she knew that Kate had in Luke?

'Make it happen,' she urged Kate. 'You never know—it could change your life.'

When they went into the sitting room to finish their evening by relaxing in front of the television and Kate discovered a text from Luke on her phone, Georgia was dismayed to find herself feeling…envious?

How would she feel if she found a text from Matteo on *her* phone?

It wasn't beyond the realms of possibility, was it? He could easily get access to her phone number by asking Luke to get it from Kate.

She could get *his* number by reversing the route.

And say what? Admit that there was no boyfriend that had been waiting for her back in Scotland so she hadn't been cheating on anyone?

By doing that, she would be admitting that she'd lied to him. Only by omission, but Georgia knew instinctively that a boundary like that would mean nothing to Matteo. Playing by the rules and, above all, being honest was an unshakeable foundation for the character that made him who he was.

Someone genuine. Trustworthy.

Luke was genuine, too, but Kate was shaking her head over a proposed date that wasn't going to fit with her hospital shifts. Saying that maybe it was never meant to happen.

'Don't be ridiculous.' Georgia was in danger of losing patience. 'What were the odds of you two meeting up again on a mountaintop in the Czech Republic? It was totally meant to happen.'

Kate's smile was endearingly shy. 'It was certainly unexpected.'

And then her smile widened. 'And it was you who had the mad idea of hooking up with someone while we were there. It was the last thing I was planning on doing.'

Oh… God…talking about that crazy plan she'd had for the competition was the last thing Georgia wanted to do. Trying to dismiss this conversational track, Georgia shrugged and turned away.

'I'm not the only one who's been a bit quiet since we got back. What aren't you talking about?'

'Nothing.' She thought she'd managed a tone light enough to squash any suspicions but it didn't seem to work. She could feel Kate staring at her back.

'You never did tell me where you disappeared to for so long during that party.'

Georgia froze.

'Oh, my God,' Kate said. 'You *did* hook up with somebody. And you never told me?'

'Wasn't much to tell.' Georgia's forced the words out. 'I'd rather forget about it.'

But Kate didn't take the hint. 'It can't have been Matteo,' she said, 'because I saw him and asked if he knew where you were and he said he had no idea.'

Oh, help… Kate must have seen him shortly after he'd slammed the door and stormed off after making love to her. Had Kate been aware of how angry he'd been? Had Matteo said anything to Luke that might make this whole mess even messier in the near future?

There was no point crossing that bridge until it became unavoidable but that meant that Georgia had to kill this conversation. Now. She glared at her friend.

'Why would it have been Matteo?'

'Oh, I don't know… Because he was gorgeous maybe? Or because you two seemed to be getting on incredibly well?'

Georgia put considerable effort into a dismissive shrug. 'I guess some people aren't okay with casual sex. I don't think I am any more either. It wasn't my best idea, was it?' She reached for the television remote. 'Let's see if there's something worth watching, shall we?'

The silence between them was odd. Georgia hated that she was deceiving Kate but she couldn't tell her the truth, could she?

If Kate had any inkling how she felt about Matteo, she would try and fix things, wouldn't she? Like Georgia had been trying to fix things between Kate and Luke by encouraging her to text him?

Kate might think she was doing the right thing by enlisting Luke's assistance. And then Matteo would find out and it would just make everything messier. Because he wouldn't want to know.

He wouldn't want her name to even pass his lips because she had lied to him.

Besides…she wanted to stop thinking about it. To stop the ongoing battle between her head and her heart about whether it could be worth taking the kind of risk that another relationship represented.

To move on from thinking that she'd made a mistake that could never be fixed.

And she was *so* tired…

Kate finally seemed to pick up the vibe. She sat on the couch beside Georgia and gave her a quick hug.

'It's in the past now,' she said. 'And, yeah…it wasn't your best idea but you'll know not to do it again.'

Wasn't that the truth?

She'd never have the chance to do it again.

'Are you okay? Really?'

Georgia nodded, hugging her back. 'I'm fine. *Really.*'

'Want a coffee?'

The wave of nausea the idea of coffee produced was weird. She must be a lot more tired than she'd realised.

'No.' Georgia shook her head, closing her eyes and swallowing hard in the hope that her stomach would settle quickly. 'Let's just chill out and watch some telly.'

After an adrenaline-filled day of big-city emergency response, there was nothing better than chilling with an old mate and an icy-cold beer.

And today had been one to remember. A huge pile-up on one of the motorways just outside Milan with critically injured people who'd needed to get to a major trauma facility in less time than any ambulance was capable of. They'd had to land their helicopter on the motorway, more than once, in a tight space that the police had managed to create in the middle of a traffic jam that would be making national headlines tomorrow.

Matteo Martini leaned back into the body-shaped dent on his favourite couch, his laptop on his knees, thoroughly enjoying one of his regular catch-ups via Skype with Luke. They'd just had a very interesting conversation about 4D magnetic resonance imaging

and the implications that such an advance in technology could give the world of medicine.

And then the conversation got more personal.

'What's happening in your life?' Luke asked.

Matteo shrugged. 'Nothing exciting. Same old.'

'How did the date work out last week? With…um…
what was her name again? That nurse?'

'Marcella.' Matteo wasn't proud of the fact that it
was an effort to remember. 'It was okay. I think she
only wanted my body.'

Luke laughed. 'Lucky you.'

Yeah… It had been a welcome release after several
weeks of abstinence.

But it had also been disappointing because that was
all it had been.

Because she hadn't been Georgia Bennett?

*No…* He wasn't going to think about her. He had
dismissed her from his life in the instant he'd learned
that she'd been cheating on someone to be with him.

He was still angry.

Still felt cheated on himself, in fact.

No. It was more than that.

He had given away a piece of his heart.

And he wanted it back, dammit.

He was only half listening to Luke telling him how
good things were between him and Kate now. About
the new adventures they were sharing. He was happy
for his friend, he really was. It was just unfortunate that
the new woman in his life was such close friends with
the woman Matteo was determined to forget.

A bubble of something he couldn't control put her
name on his lips. Maybe it was the mention of having
gone out dancing because it dragged him back to that

time on the dance floor in Rakovi. To the time when he'd been so sure that he'd found the only woman in the world who he wanted to spend the rest of his life with.

'Did Georgia go too?' He had to fight to keep any hint of bitterness from his tone. 'And her…her boy-friend? Are you double dating?'

Thinking about the man who was lucky enough to have Georgia in his life created a tightness in his chest that made it noticeably more difficult to suck in a new breath.

When some of that initial anger had burned off, he'd actually thought of trying to contact Georgia. Of get-ting her number from Luke, via Kate.

But then what?

Would he knowingly set out to break an existing relationship?

Would he want to be with a woman who would leave someone else for him?

Of course not. You'd spend the rest of your life with the suspicion that the person you were devoting your life to was capable of cheating on and abandoning you if a better prospect came along.

'No.' Luke was sounding a little puzzled. 'I haven't seen Georgia since Kate and I have been together. We meet somewhere. Or Kate comes to my place.'

'Why don't you go to hers?'

'I don't know.' Luke frowned. 'I guess because she hasn't suggested it yet.'

'Maybe Georgia disapproves.'

'Why would she do that?'

'Dunno.' Matteo shrugged again. 'She's got some funny ideas, that one.'

'I thought you liked her.' Luke was still frowning.

*Like...*

What an insipid word. It wasn't even on the same verbal planet as something that could begin to describe the feelings Georgia had evoked.

Even *love* didn't quite encompass the sense of promise and potential fulfilment that that connection had provided.

That connection that should never have happened because it had resulted in someone being cheated on.

'I thought I did, too,' he muttered. 'Shows how wrong you can be about some people, I guess.' He needed to stop talking about Georgia. It certainly wasn't helping his determined effort to stop even thinking about her. 'Hey, man. I'd better go. Early shift tomorrow.'

'No worries. Let's do it again next week.'

Matteo grinned back. 'We might be doing it for real before long. Don't forget you can't get married unless I'm your best man.'

He stared at a blank screen for a long moment when the call had ended.

Marriage...

Children. A family of his very own. He'd always known that was going to be the very best part of his future. It had been no more than a pleasant daydream all through his twenties because he'd known he had plenty of time to play. To do all the things that a devoted father and family man would never dream of doing.

Besides, he'd needed to play the field to make sure he found the perfect woman to share his life with. Because there would only ever be one woman he would marry and she wasn't just going to be his wife. She was going to be the mother of his children.

How had all those years slipped past so quickly? He'd begun to feel the clock ticking as he'd hit his early thirties and he *had* begun to take his relationships more seriously—when his hectic work hours had allowed, that was. He'd known that his dream of being a father instead of merely an uncle wasn't going to happen all by itself. He had to make it happen.

And he had truly believed, just for the tiny blink of time that that competition had provided, that he had found the person he could make it happen *with*.

But now that dream seemed further away than it had ever been and the reality check was laced with doubts. Sadness even. Maybe it wouldn't even be as good as he'd believed it would be.

Because the woman he married was not going to be Georgia Bennett.

'It's just a bug or something, Sean. I'm fine. Unlock the door and let's get back to station. I want to go home.'

'Nope.' Georgia's partner leaned against the back of the ambulance. 'I'm not going anywhere until you go and get checked out. You've been off colour for way too long. You're tired all the time and you turned your nose up at one of Nico's kebabs today. You have to be sick not to want the best kebab ever.'

'I wasn't hungry, that's all.'

'You're off colour. You've been off colour for weeks. Get back into ED and find a nice doctor. It's quiet. Get a blood test or something.'

'That would take ages. We're off duty. It's time to go home.'

'Exactly. We've got all the time in the world. I'm going to let them know we'll be delayed getting the truck back to station and then I'm going to get coffee and chat up some nurses. Page me when you're done.'

And Sean walked off, the keys to the ambulance still in his pocket.

Fifteen minutes later and Georgia was sitting in the office of Kathryn—one of the emergency department consultants who'd been only too happy to talk to her.

'The bloods won't be back for a few minutes yet, Georgie.' Her gaze was thoughtful. 'Are you sure there's no possibility of you being pregnant?'

'I'm sure.' But Georgia bit her lip. 'I mean, *theoretically* there is. I did have unprotected sex a while back but I haven't missed a period.'

'And your periods have been normal?'

The overwhelming memory was the anticipated relief at the first sign of that period, with that disturbing aftertaste of sadness, but what had the next day been like? Georgia thought harder.

'Lighter than normal, I guess. Especially the last one.'

Kathryn nodded. 'I think we might go and borrow the portable ultrasound while we're waiting for those bloods.'

Georgia couldn't identify the emotion that seemed to be gathering somewhere deep inside her gut.

Horror…or hope?

'You've heard of decidual bleeding, haven't you?' The consultant was leading her into a cubicle and whisking the curtain shut behind them. She carried on speaking as Georgia got onto the bed and unbuttoned her uniform trousers. 'Twenty to thirty percent of women will have some type of bleeding in the first trimester. It's not uncommon for spotting or light bleeding to carry on into the second or even third trimesters.'

'Yeah… I've heard of it.' The gel was cold against the skin of her abdomen.

'It's due to hormones being a bit out of whack. More common in the early days, before the lining of the uterus has completely attached to the placenta. In most cases, it's not thought to be a threat to the baby.' Kathryn was staring at the screen of the ultrasound machine as she angled the probe.

There was silence for a long moment. Too long for Georgia to keep holding her breath.

'Oh, my God…' she whispered. 'You can see something, can't you? I *am* pregnant?'

The sideways glance she received was cautious. 'How would you feel about that?'

'Um…'

Unidentifiable emotions were roiling now. Fear and excitement. Memories of how strong that desire to have a baby had been. Strong enough to have made her come up with the plan that the international competition was the perfect place to find the father of her longed-for baby.

An intense flashback to how it had felt being with Matteo. Being touched by his hands and lips.

That twist of sadness that fate hadn't stepped in to override her decision that she couldn't possibly go through with the plan.

'I think… I think I would be very happy about that.'

'Hmm…' Kathryn angled the screen so that Georgia could see the image. Not that she could recognise the blobs amongst the grainy black and white shapes but she could see something moving rhythmically. The beat of a tiny heart…

No…wait…

Time seemed to be standing still as her startled gaze caught the doctor's steady one.

'So…' Kathryn's question was somewhat tentative. 'You're going to be twice as happy to know that you're pregnant with twins?'

# CHAPTER FIVE

IT COULDN'T REMAIN a secret.

If it was a singleton pregnancy, she could probably have kept her situation private for months and passed off any new roundness in her belly and breasts as a bit of weight gain due to being slack with her healthy eating or exercise regime. But she had two babies growing inside her belly.

*Two…*

In a very short space of time—weeks at the most—Georgia knew that the changes in her body were going to be blindingly obvious to the whole world.

So she might as well spill the beans now, yes?

No.

One look at the puzzled frown on Sean's face as she re-joined her colleague, who had been waiting patiently for more than an hour, was enough to change her mind. The news would be like throwing a large stone into a pond. There were going to be big ripples that would affect other people as well. She could be taken off the road sooner rather than later and probably given some boring tasks that involved a lot of paperwork or time in storerooms. She would lose the joy of working with Sean on the road and the distraction that the variety and challenges of every job could provide. Being consigned to light duties would give her far too much time to think. About the future.

About the father of her babies...

This was a multiple pregnancy that carried higher risks for complications, she reminded herself, and she wasn't even that close to the end of her first trimester. It might be unwise to throw that rock before it was absolutely necessary.

'What is it?' Sean demanded.

'Nothing,' Georgia told him airily. 'I'm fine. Let's go home.'

Sean started the ambulance a minute or two later but his sideways glance was suspicious.

'I don't believe you.'

'I'm not sick, Sean.' It was easy to sound convincing. Pregnancy wasn't an illness. It was a perfectly normal state for a woman's body to be in.

'You look...different.'

'Do I?'

'Yeah...' It took another couple of searching glances before Sean could identify what was puzzling him. 'You look... I dunno...like you thought you had a terminal illness and you've been given the all-clear. Like you've won the lottery or something.'

Georgia's response was a bubble of laughter.

'You're right. I'd started wondering if I had some horrible disease but I haven't. I'm just...'

*Pregnant.*

'Just a bit rundown. I'm going to live to be a hundred years old and I'm happy.' She beamed at her partner. 'You should be happy, too. We'll be working together until we're old and grey.'

Sean laughed as well. 'I'll be grey by the time I'm thirty, working with you, champ. Don't scare me like that again.'

It was fortunate that Kate was staying with Luke tonight, Georgia decided when she arrived home. She had never needed a bit of quiet time more than she did right now.

Snatches of her conversation with Sean were still running through her mind. She had told him that she wasn't sick and it was the truth because pregnancy *was* a completely normal state for a woman's body to deal with.

Except it wasn't normal for *her*, was it?

It was… It was…

*Incredible…*

She was going to have a *baby*. No…*two* babies…

In a matter of months she wouldn't be simply a single mother with a baby. She'd be a mother with an entire little family.

A smile was trying to break out but there was a prickle behind her eyes that was so unfamiliar it took a moment for Georgia to recognise the imminent threat of tears.

Tears? She had learned how useless tears were when she'd been five years old and she'd only cried once since then—at her mother's funeral. Or, rather, well after the funeral, where there was nobody around to witness the evidence of weakness.

Maybe that was the reason for this current threat. If there was one person she'd want to talk to about how she was feeling right now, it would be her mother.

Closely followed by Kate, of course, but throwing

her rock in that direction would be more like aiming for a minefield than a pond.

Kate would be horrified at her flagrant disregard of how to achieve what she wanted within the rules of normal social behaviour. Wanting a family was no problem, but you were supposed to at least try to do it the right way. To be careful about contraception until you believed you had found a partner in life. Preferably until after you had married that partner.

There would be endless discussions. It was more than likely that Kate could home in on fears for the future that Georgia didn't want to think about yet. Things like where she was going to live and how she would be able to cope financially. She would probably only be being a responsible friend if she pointed out that Georgia still had options at this very early stage of her pregnancy.

Even as she was still reeling at the news that Kathryn had delivered, Georgia knew that the idea of not going ahead with this pregnancy was completely unthinkable but she did need time to get used to this... this rather overwhelmingly unexpected miracle.

And it *was* a miracle.

In the end, she hadn't planned for this to happen. She hadn't set out to seduce a potentially acceptable sperm donor on the off-chance of hitting the jackpot. She had been hugely relieved that an accidental pregnancy had been avoided.

Because she'd known how complicated it could become if Kate knew the truth.

For the first time since the shocking moment when she'd seen that tiny heart beating on the ultrasound screen, Georgia felt a flash of fear.

Kate couldn't know the truth. Not about who had fathered these babies anyway. The truth about the pregnancy would have to come out, of course. But not yet. Hopefully not until she'd had time to get all her ducks in a row and would have a convincing argument to counter any objections that Kate could come up with.

It was the eggs that did it.

Ruined any plans that Georgia was still formulating about the quiet conversation she was planning to have with Kate when she was ready.

Something about the sight of that congealed egg yolk on the white plates stacked in the sink ready to be washed, combined with the weariness of having just completed a busy night shift, and the vague nausea Georgia had been aware of for some time suddenly tipped into something far more violent. She ran towards the bathroom in the hope that she would make it as far as the toilet before her stomach turned itself inside out.

She didn't even notice that Kate had followed her until she felt the welcome touch of a damp facecloth as she finally let go of the cold, ceramic bowl of the toilet and sat back on her heels.

'I'll never eat eggs again in my life,' she groaned.

'You didn't eat any in the first place. You just looked at the plates.'

'I know…' Georgia leaned back against the wall, the facecloth pressed against her eyes. Had she really reassured Sean that she wasn't sick a couple of weeks ago? She had never felt this unwell in her life.

'Are you sick? Running a temperature?' Kate went into doctor mode, taking hold of her wrist to feel for her pulse.

'I don't think so.'

'Did you eat something dodgy on night shift? Like a kebab?'

'No.'

'Oh, my God...' After a short silence in which the sound of pennies dropping was almost audible, Kate sounded horrified. 'Are you pregnant. Georgie?'

So much for picking her own moment to share this news.

Kate's heavy sigh as she shifted to lean against the wall beside Georgia was exactly how she was feeling herself.

'When were you going to tell me?'

'When it was too late to have an argument about whether or not it was a good idea to go through with it.'

Kate's breath came out in a shocked huff. 'Did you think I'd try and persuade you to have a termination?'

Georgia took the facecloth away from her eyes. If the truth was coming out, it may as well be the whole truth. Well...not *quite* the whole truth, of course...

'Why not? You've never approved of my plan for single parenthood. You told me the whole idea was hare-brained.'

'That doesn't mean I wouldn't support you in whatever you chose to do.' There was a wobble in Kate's voice that broke Georgia's heart. It had felt so wrong keeping this a secret from her best friend and this was her punishment.

She had hurt Kate.

'I can't believe you've kept this to yourself. How pregnant *are* you?'

'About ten weeks.'

The silence was short. And shocked.

'So you did hook up with someone at the rally. I *knew* there was something you weren't telling me. Who was it?'

'It doesn't matter.'

'Of course it matters. It's your child's father. You need to know about family genetics. You'll need financial support.'

Georgia shook her head sharply enough to make her stomach try to roll again but she wasn't about to be sick. The rush of adrenaline that fear produced was enough to buy her some time.

'That's precisely the reason I did it this way. I don't want to know about the father's family. I don't want financial support. I don't want anyone interfering in any way. This is *my* baby. And it's going to stay that way.'

It *had* to stay that way.

From a dark, buried space in the back of her mind, Georgia could hear a small voice.

The small voice of a terrified child.

*'Don't let them take me, Mummy. I don't want to go...'*

*'You're coming with us. You're my daughter. You're going to get brought up in a decent, Godly household, not dragged up by your slut of a mother. Get in the car now and stay there...'*

There was pain mixed in with the terror as the car door slammed shut on the arm still reaching out in a desperate plea to the woman this man was shoving back with his other arm. She could see her mother fall to the footpath, could see the blood on the strange shape of her arm as she tumbled and then curled up on the back seat of the vehicle that was taking her away from everything she knew and loved.

Georgia squeezed her eyes shut against the agonising memory. Kate didn't know about her childhood. Nobody did. If people asked her about that scar on her arm, she told them she'd fallen off her pony one day, when she'd been out jumping every log she could find on the hills behind her country village. She'd covered the horrible reality with a fantasy of a perfect childhood so often she almost believed it herself. The only other person who'd known the real truth and could understand the fear that had poisoned so many years of her life had been her mother and she'd lost that rock in her life a long time ago.

She couldn't begin to try and explain any of this, even to her best friend. Because it was too big and she'd walled those memories off and tried to bury them for a very good reason—she didn't *want* to remember any of it.

It was inevitable that knowing she was bringing her own children into the world had prompted a backward glance at what was behind those mental walls but that was only as far as Georgia was prepared to go.

So she couldn't tell Kate why but she could make her understand that Georgia wasn't going to change her mind. She knew she was pushing her closest friend away with her vehement tone but this was self-protection.

No. It was even more important than that. She was protecting her babies.

It was a blessing that she'd stopped herself telling Kate how she felt about Matteo due to the link she had to him via Luke. Somehow, instinct had protected her babies even before she had known they existed.

It was infinitely more important that Kate never

know this part of the truth because Matteo would never let his children be brought up by someone he despised.

Maybe he wouldn't be as violent as her father had been but he would be just as persistent, even if he didn't believe that he had a vengeful God on his side.

Okay, she knew that Matteo would never condone violence. That he would probably be as reasonable as any co-parent could be and he would allow her access to her babies—perhaps even shared living arrangements. But that wouldn't be enough. Life would be an endless emotional roller-coaster where the dips would consist of anxiety and loneliness and probably something as nasty as jealousy.

What if…what if Matteo found a woman he could adore instead of despise? If she became a part-time mother to *her* babies?

No. She couldn't handle that.

And she still had the power to make sure she never had to face that kind of painful disruption to her life.

'Don't ask again, Kate.' Her voice came out in a kind of hiss. 'Because I'm never going to tell you. I'm never going to tell anyone, *especially* the father. And I couldn't anyway because I don't have his address. I barely remember his name. And…oh, *God*… I'm going to be sick again…'

The morning sickness gave life an edge of misery that made the following weeks seem very long but then it began to wear off and life suddenly seemed much brighter.

On the work front, Georgia's fears of being demoted to a paper-pusher proved unfounded. Her 'light duties' were actually going to be an opportunity she'd quietly dreamed of being offered. There would be no more lifting patients or putting herself into dangerous rescue situations but she would still be able to use every skill she possessed as a paramedic. She would be challenged, in fact, because she was going to be working alone at times. Given a fully equipped SUV that had everything an ambulance had apart from any stretchers, she could be sent first to a scene to assess and start treatment. Or she could be dispatched as backup to provide the kind of interventions and drugs a less qualified crew could offer.

She was going to get all the excitement and satisfaction her job was capable of delivering, without any of the drudgery. No hard physical challenges and no long transport journeys taking perfectly stable patients to a hospital while radio traffic announced the dispatch of available crews to far more exciting-sounding calls.

Her new duties would have been more than enough to restore her zest for life as the misery of constant nausea receded but there was another bright spot that was getting steadily larger. Even before the morning sickness had kicked in, Kate and Luke had finally managed to connect and their relationship had deepened steadily. Now it seemed believable that her best friend had found exactly what she had been searching for. The One. Which was just as well because Kate had, shockingly, broken her own rules, had had unprotected sex with Luke and—astonishingly—become pregnant as easily as Georgia had herself.

Was it really only a few months ago that they were both passionate career women in their mid-thirties who'd been facing the prospect of futures that might not deliver the extra dimension of having a real family?

Okay, things weren't *perfect*…

Single parenthood was not really anybody's dream. For most people, it was something that you coped with when you had to. When the fairy-tale concept of family hadn't worked out for whatever reason.

But Georgia didn't see it that way.

The best times in her childhood and adolescence had been when she'd felt safe with her mother. When they'd found a new place to live and knew it could be months before her father tracked them down and made another attempt to separate them. When, at best, the police or social services would come knocking at their door and there would be court appearances or the like to deal with.

At worst, it had been when Georgia had had to start looking over her shoulder all the time in case she was being followed. Or walk home from school with the fear that she might not find her mother still alive when she got there.

Georgia knew she could do more than cope with single parenthood. Without the threat of interference, she could ensure that the lives of her children were full of joy. And love. And that they would always feel *safe*.

She also believed that everything would work out for Kate. That she and Luke had the foundations for a perfect life together.

Georgia was quite convinced about this. Until that grey, wet day when she received the dreadful news that Kate had had an accident. That she'd been hit by a car as she'd run across a busy road.

That, while she'd been lucky enough not to receive any injuries more than a concussion, she'd lost her baby.

It was one of the hardest things Georgia had ever had to do, walking into that hospital room to bring fresh clothes and take Kate home. It felt like a giant spotlight was aimed at her belly to advertise her continuing pregnancy and rub salt into what had to be the rawest wound ever.

'I'm so, so sorry, Katy.'

But Kate brushed off her sympathy.

'It's not that big a deal, you know? I'd barely had time to get used to the idea anyway.'

And that was apparently all that Kate wanted to say about the subject. At home for the next couple of days, all she wanted to do was sleep. Georgia took time off work to watch her friend and make sure there were no signs of a more severe head injury that had been missed. That first night, she actually lay on Kate's bed beside her, waking her every so often just to check her level of responsiveness and listening to the pattern of her breathing as she slept again.

It hurt that she was being shut out. She knew how she'd felt even in the midst of the initial shock of learning that she was pregnant. That it was a miracle. Little beings were forming inside her belly. Her babies. She'd barely had time to get used to the idea either, but she already loved them enough to fight to the death to protect them.

But Kate had apparently been practising hiding her real feelings about Luke for a while now. Did she think that if she gave in to the grief she had to be experiencing now, it might not stop there? That she would confess she'd broken the rules of that stupid 'pact' they'd made at medical school to marry each other if they were both still single when they were thirty-five? That she *had* fallen in love and that Luke would call the whole thing off? She was pushing Luke away right now as well and that felt so, so wrong. They had found something very special between them and they should be fighting to protect it. This crushing blow should be bringing them closer together, not pushing them apart.

Georgia desperately wanted to help but she couldn't interfere, could she?

There was a barrier here that she had created herself because she hadn't wanted Kate to interfere with her own life by trying to influence her decisions. Because she hadn't ever shared the trauma of her own childhood. She hadn't told Kate that Matteo was the father of her babies. She hadn't even told her yet that she was carrying twins.

She certainly couldn't tell her that now, in the wake of her own loss that had to be devastating, even if Kate didn't want to admit it.

That barrier had just become a whole lot more solid.

The mess had just got a whole lot messier.

Something her mother had once quoted came back to her in the quiet hours of that night.

*What a tangled web we weave, when first we practise to deceive...*

Georgia couldn't even offer advice to her best friend to hang onto the connection she had found with Luke because they both knew how rare it was to find something like that. It would be a case of 'do what I say, not what I do', because she had found a connection herself that was just as rare and precious. With Matteo. And she was prepared to sacrifice that.

Not because she wanted to.

Because she *had* to.

She had to let her head win any battles with her heart because the lessons she had learned in life were so deeply engraved.

You couldn't trust love to last.

And some fathers could destroy your life.

There was a crazy moment, in those long hours where the silence was only broken by the sound of Kate's breathing, when it seemed that her heart could win the battle. Georgia seriously considered getting hold of Matteo's contact details and admitting the truth. The *whole* truth. Her heart whispered encouragement. Maybe it was worth taking the risk. Maybe Matteo also knew how rare this kind of connection was and would be prepared to move heaven and earth to make it work.

But her head had plenty of ammunition left.

*Are you crazy? You're expecting that kind of commitment on the strength of a couple of days and 'one' night together?*

*Maybe you imagined that the connection was mutual.*

*And do you really want to open that can of worms right now—when your very best friend is utterly miserable? Would you want to make her feel like she has to support you to chase the improbable dream of a happy-ever-after family when she's grieving for the loss of her own?*

Kate's breath came out in a sigh that became a whimper of distress that was timed perfectly to underline just how wrong it would be to make this any worse than it had to be. Georgia smoothed a lock of blonde hair back from Kate's face and whispered reassuringly.

'It's okay… Everything's going to be okay.'

It had to be, that was all there was to it.

And, with that determination, another convincing victory got handed to her head. Georgia had chosen the path she needed to follow. Now she just needed to stick to it.

'Hey, man…' Matteo started speaking even before Luke's image came onto the screen of his laptop. The tone of the Skype call had interrupted the movie he was watching but it was a very welcome surprise. 'Where the hell have you been for the last few weeks?'

'It's been crazy.'

'You talking about your work or your love life?'

'Bit of both. Hey, before I get distracted, what are you doing on Friday?'

'Tomorrow or next week?' Matteo blinked. 'Not that it matters. I'm working on both Fridays. Why?'

'Do you reckon you could swap a shift? For next Friday? That gives you a whole week to sort it out.'

'I don't know.' Matteo peered at the screen but Luke didn't look as if he was in the midst of some personal crisis. He looked…very happy. 'It's never easy but I could try, I guess, if it was important enough. What's going on?'

'You remember what you said?'

'I say a lot of things.' Matteo grinned. 'What particular words of wisdom are you referring to?'

'That I can't get married unless you're my best man.' Luke was grinning back at him now.

'No *way*…' Matteo was stunned into silence for a long moment and then he shook his head. 'You are kidding, aren't you? You're getting married next week? What kind of notice is that?'

'I know, I'm sorry. We just got lucky in finding the perfect place. In an ancient chapel right in the middle of Edinburgh castle. You'd normally have to book a year or more in advance but we happened to ask on the same day an American couple had to cancel because they had some problem with their visas.'

Matteo was still trying to get his head around the news.

'You're getting *married*? Are you sure about this? I know we haven't talked for a while but this seems a bit sudden.'

'You haven't heard the half of it, mate. I told you things have been crazy—ever since Kate lost the baby...'

'*Whoa*...' Matteo sat up with a jerk that nearly sent his laptop flying. 'Kate was *pregnant*?'

'I know. It's a long story but it's okay now. We're going to try again. Made it harder on her that Georgia's pregnant as well but—'

'*Cosa?*' The knot in Matteo's gut made it feel like he'd just been kicked. 'Georgia's pregnant? *How* pregnant?' His heart skipped a beat as his mind flew in a totally crazy direction. She'd cheated on her boyfriend. Had she lied about it being a 'safe' time when he had taken her to bed himself?

'I don't know exactly...' Luke was blinking as if he was surprised at Matteo's interest. 'But I saw her a couple of days ago and I'd guess at least six months. She's got a pretty impressive bump.'

Matteo's brain was still processing information at the speed of light.

Six months? At *least*?

The competition had been about five months ago.

That would mean that Georgia had already been pregnant when she'd slept with him.

Had she *known*?

If she had, that made it far worse than simply cheating on someone.

'You can ask her yourself,' Luke said. 'She's going to be Kate's bridesmaid, of course.'

Matteo's jaw dropped. How could Luke actually be smiling at the prospect of him seeing Georgia again?

Because he didn't know, he reminded himself. Matteo had never told anyone what had happened that night.

Maybe Georgia had never told anyone either. If she had, surely it would have been her best friend and Kate was about to be married to *his* best friend and that meant they wouldn't have any secrets, didn't it?

He certainly wouldn't accept anything less than total honesty from someone he was about to promise to spend the rest of his life with.

But of course Georgia wouldn't have confessed. What if her boyfriend had found out?

He was probably more than that by now. He would have married her the moment he'd found out he was going to be a father, wouldn't he?

It was what he would do himself without a moment's hesitation. Family was sacred. Parents belonged with their children if it was at all possible and the bond had to be protected with everything you had.

Matteo didn't want to know if Georgia Bennett was already married.

He didn't want to see her again either. He'd believed he was completely over her now but this conversation had just flung open the mental door he'd thought he'd locked on that unfortunate blink of time in his life.

'So you'll come?' Luke's eyebrows rose hopefully. 'And be part of the best day of my life?'

This was his closest friend, asking him to do something he'd vowed he *would* do. He needed to get over himself, didn't he?

And maybe it would be a good thing to see Georgia with her husband. With a baby on the way. Maybe then he could finally forget about her. For ever…

'I can't make any promises,' Matteo said slowly. 'But I'll see what I can do.'

# CHAPTER SIX

IT WAS THE most perfect setting for a wedding.

The tiny stone chapel had an archway that Georgia and Kate would be making their entrance through any minute now. There was a soft glow of candlelight from within that warmed the surface of the ancient stones far more than the moonlight out here as the two women paused to wait for their signal.

The sound of bagpipes to accompany Kate on her walk down the aisle to meet the love of her life would also be perfect for this gorgeously Scottish wedding. Everything about this moment was making Georgia ridiculously happy—including the way that this soft, midnight-blue dress draped over the enormous bump of her belly and made her feel like a Madonna. Maybe not that beautiful but a perfect foil for how amazing Kate looked. Her dress had a fall of ivory silk that was brushing the cobblestones and an exquisitely bead-encrusted bodice with a sweetheart neckline in the front and a deep V at the back. The bunch of pale peonies she was holding, with the silk bow that matched her dress, was simple and as elegant as everything else was turning out to be, but it was the glow of sheer joy on her face that really made her look more beautiful

than Georgia had ever seen her look. She couldn't wait
to start this new life with Luke, could she?

Suddenly Georgia couldn't wait either. Where was
the piper who was due to start this ceremony?

'Oh, look…' There was a beat of excitement to add
to her happiness now. 'I think that's him getting ready.'
Her breath came out in a sigh. 'I do love a man in a kilt.'

She could hear the piper getting ready to play. Any
moment now and those muffled squeaks as he filled
the bag with air would burst into the full glory of her
favourite musical instrument.

'Stand by…' she whispered loudly, her lips curving into a grin.

'No…' the call came from behind them. *'Wait…'*

Oh…*no*…

Georgia knew that voice. That *accent*…

Good grief… It felt like her bones were actually
melting—possibly due to the weird explosion of every
cell her in body, which was creating a tingling sensation that was so strong it was almost painful.

Both women turned in unison, so fast that Georgia's
smile didn't have time to fade completely.

*'Matteo…'* Kate sounded overjoyed. 'You made it.'

'I didn't think I could. Not after the last delay with
the fog.' Matteo must have run up all the steps to reach
this part of the castle but he still looked immaculate
in his black, beautifully tailored suit and a bow-tie
nestled in the collar of a snowy, white shirt. With the
soft moonlight, against the backdrop of this wonderful castle, he looked like an advertisement for some
fashion house.

Just…impossibly gorgeous.

And it was having the same effect on her that it had

had when she'd seen him for the very first time, at that competition briefing in Rakovi.

She needed to get a grip on this. Fast…

Matteo was still speaking. 'But I couldn't let my best friend get married without me.' He put his hand to his chest as he tried to catch his breath. He hadn't taken his eyes off this bride-to-be yet. Hadn't even looked at Georgia.

That hurt.

'You look…*bellissima*, Kate. Luke is a very lucky man.'

'He certainly is.' Georgia had to say something. To force Matteo to acknowledge her? Her heart was doing strange things—missing beats and then racing so fast it was scary.

No. *This* was scary.

Dangerous.

But…*thrilling* at the same time.

Oh, help… Why did she have to have this personality flaw that made danger so exciting? It was that addiction to an adrenaline rush that made her job such a part of who she was.

A part of why she had found such a compelling connection to this man. And being able to harness that adrenaline rush was part of what made her so good at her job but it was not a good thing as part of a personal relationship.

Not that she had a personal relationship with this man.

Not that she ever *could*.

'Hi, Matteo.' It was a test to see if she could actually say his name without giving away any of the shock that still clutched at her heart. It was a relief to find that she could.

She couldn't hold eye contact for more than a split second, however. Just that tiny brush and she could still feel it.

That connection.

Those impossibly powerful feelings that only this man had ever aroused.

Georgia flicked her gaze towards Kate, her message silent but probably desperate.

*How could you not warn me?*

*How am I going to cope with this?*

She *had* to cope, she had no choice. She managed to find a smile that said this was no big deal. To keep her tone just as casual. 'You didn't tell me Matteo was coming.'

'We really weren't sure that he could make it. Luke's going to be as surprised as you.'

Georgia couldn't help another glance at Matteo. Maybe it was just that first eye contact that would be so difficult.

But he wasn't looking at her face any longer. He was staring at her belly and, even in the moonlight that was already bleaching colour from skin, she could swear he had gone paler.

But…he didn't seem surprised. He looked angry more than shocked.

Had he *known* that she was pregnant? Had he put two and two together and was now preparing to make discover the truth and then make some kind of a claim?

Okay…this level of adrenaline was too much. Any thrill was rapidly being buried under an avalanche of fear.

Matteo seemed to have lost his voice along with the colour. He opened his mouth and then closed it again. Then he cleared his throat.

'Hello, Georgia. You're looking…um…well?'

Fear was morphing into a determination that bordered on anger. How dared he turn up like this and threaten her?

Threaten her *babies*.

'I'm very well, thank you.'

She could see his chest move under the pristine white shirt. He was dragging in a deep breath.

'I'd better get inside.' Matteo was already moving away. 'Give me a minute to find my place, okay?'

Georgia watched him disappear through the archway just as the stirring first notes of the bagpipes filled the air around them.

Traditionally, the bagpipes were thought to have been a call to stir the passions of soldiers on the battlefield.

It certainly felt as if they were doing exactly that to Georgia.

She only had a few hours to fight to keep her secret safe somehow. She wasn't sure how she was going to do that but Georgia was quite sure she was going to win.

Because she had to.

She had lied to him before, even it if had only been the omission of correcting his assumption that she was cheating on someone. She could do it again. She was ready.

'Here we go,' Georgia said.

She pasted a bright smile onto her face. Not only did she have a private battle to fight, she was going to have to make sure it didn't lessen the joy of Kate's special day in any way.

*'To have and to hold, from this day forward, till death us do part...'*

The vows were traditional, but they were spoken by both Luke and Kate with a level of emotion that made them sound as if they had been written just for them. In the flicker of candlelight, within the ancient solidity of these historic walls, this ceremony was so beautiful it brought tears to Matteo's eyes.

He wanted this for himself, more than anything.

To promise himself to the woman he loved above any other. To know that he would never be alone. That he could begin the most important task he could ever achieve—to be a loving and devoted husband *and* father...

Even more than the desire to be standing where Luke was right now, holding the hands of the most beautiful bride ever, Matteo longed to be standing beside the woman who was shaped by the creation of his first child. Who had that superbly rounded belly and the glow of impending motherhood, exactly like Georgia did right now.

He'd never seen her look *so* beautiful...

Matteo stole a glance beyond Luke and Kate as they exchanged their rings and then found he couldn't take his gaze away from Georgia as she stood there, holding Kate's flowers, her eyes sparkling with what had to be unshed tears and a tiny tremor in her bottom lip that captured his heart and squeezed it like a vice.

He remembered exactly what it was like to feel that

lip beneath his own. To feel the passion that was so much a part of this woman.

*'With this ring, I thee wed... With my body I thee honour...'*

The words about worldly goods became a blur of sound as Matteo grappled with the desire to be doing that to Georgia Bennett.

Honouring her.

Touching that magnificent belly with his hands. With his lips...

*Dio mio...* He needed to control himself better than this. For heaven's sake, the father of her child was most likely sitting in one of the wooden pews behind them. He would have to meet him very soon. Congratulate the man and tell him how lucky he was.

His glance finally jerked away from Georgia.

Who was he?

Perhaps that man in the second row who was sitting alone.

He looked a good ten years older than Georgia, with grey hair streaking a neatly trimmed beard and moustache. He was focussed on the ceremony and looked... content? As if he knew he was the luckiest man in the world?

Except, if he was Georgia's partner, he *wasn't* that lucky, was he? He was with a woman who had cheated on him.

Yes. This line of thought was helping a lot. His body—and his heart—might be telling him one thing but his head knew better. He just needed to remember what was most important in life and the one thing that meant Georgia could never be the perfect woman for him and he would be able to get through the next few hours without doing or saying anything that could lessen the joy of this occasion for Luke.

And then he could escape.

Champagne and canapés were to be served to guests in the Argyle Tower after the ceremony but there were some formal photographs to be taken before the bridal party could join the rest of the intimate group of the close friends chosen to share this occasion.

'Come with me,' the photographer ordered, after some shots outside the chapel. 'You can't not have the background of the whole castle behind you—it's a classic. We need to be just outside the main entrance.'

At least she wasn't alone with Matteo, Georgia reminded herself as she followed Kate and Luke towards the stone staircase. And it wouldn't take very long and then she could make sure she was always in the company of someone else. Dougal McGregor, her boss as the director of Edinburgh's Emergency Response Centre, was here by himself and would probably appreciate an introduction to many of the doctors from two of the major hospitals in their area.

In the meantime, however, nerves were kicking in. She had been able to lose herself in the actual ceremony as Kate and Luke had exchanged their vows to join their lives. Their love for each other was powerful enough to have taken her breath away and bring tears to her eyes.

And, if she was honest, a part of that emotional reaction was tinged with regret that she would never find this for herself—a loving partnership that could make her world feel so full of promise. So *safe*…

It wasn't that she hadn't searched for it. A psycho-

analyst would probably say that she'd been searching
her whole life because even her beloved mother hadn't
been able to make her feel completely safe. How could
she, when she'd never felt safe herself? Georgia knew
that she had to take the blame for many of her own relationships foundering as well. The huge barrier of not
being able to trust a man had been formed, brick by
painful brick, as she'd grown up, and she'd never quite
managed to climb over it. She'd tried. She'd believed
she had been successful last time, with Rick, but that
had come crashing down in spectacular fashion—as
it inevitably did, time after time.

*It's just not going to work, Georgie.*

*I feel like I have to try too hard all the time and I
don't even know what it is I'm supposed to be proving.*

*I'm sorry...but I've met someone else...*

She needed love in her life, though. Who didn't?
And Georgia knew she had always been destined to
be a mother. That was the ultimately trustworthy love,
wasn't it? Unconditional and fulfilling.

It would be enough.

She would protect her children with everything she
had and, right now, there was a threat to them.

Their father.

It wasn't simply that he might know the truth and
be about to make a claim either. Georgia was aware of
a threat that came from within herself. This extraordinary pull that she felt towards Matteo was dangerous.
Being this close to him, as the small group followed
the photographer towards the staircase that led to the
main entrance of the castle, was enough to have her
whole body vibrating with awareness of him. Everything seemed more acute. She could feel every breath

she was drawing in. The pale moonlight felt bright enough to be a spotlight.

And then, as they reached the first steps, Matteo was suddenly right beside her and his hand circled her elbow.

'Take care,' he said quietly. 'These steps are old and they could be slippery.'

Oh…dear Lord… The touch of his fingers against her bare skin took her straight back to that night. To those stolen hours of lovemaking that she could never forget.

Her head was telling her to pull her arm free. To smile politely and tell him that she was fine. Every other part of her was simply on strike. Any words refused to emerge. She could actually feel herself leaning into him, letting him support her balance, allowing her sense of touch to soak in the delicious heat that was making her skin tingle.

It was Matteo that broke the physical contact, dropping her elbow as if it was too hot to handle the moment they reached the bottom of the long staircase.

'We'll do the bride and groom first,' the photographer told them. 'Down here, so we've got you framed by the entrance archway and the braziers.'

Georgia and Matteo were left standing to one side. Alone. Together.

'It's gorgeous, isn't it?' Georgia scanned the scene that would become the background of the image. There were spotlights on the turrets towering above them and the round sweep of the Half Moon Battery. Dramatic flames danced over the tall braziers that the bridal couple were positioned between. 'Perfect spot for a wedding, isn't it? Did you know that the chapel was built in the twelfth century?'

She could hear herself speaking too fast and would probably cringe when she remembered the artificially bright note in her voice.

'It's the oldest building in Edinburgh.' Her words slowed as she glanced sideways to catch the intent stare Matteo was giving her. 'Um… St Margaret's chapel, that is…'

'So, is he the man with the beard?' Matteo's tone was clipped.

'Sorry…what?'

'The man with the beard who was sitting in the second row.' He sounded impatient now. 'That's your husband?'

For a moment, Georgia was confused. If Matteo had known about her pregnancy, surely he would know that she didn't have a partner?

How much *did* he actually know?

Luke and Kate were kissing now. A tender moment that would make a fabulous photo to remind them of this occasion.

Georgia had to close her eyes in a long blink, however. Shame was pushing past confusion. Of course Matteo thought she had a partner. He believed she had been cheating on him when she'd gone to bed with *him*.

'That's Dougal McGregor,' she heard herself saying aloud. 'My boss.'

Matteo's breath came out in a silent whistle. 'The boss, huh? That's nice.'

Georgia's eyes snapped open. 'What's that supposed to mean?'

Matteo's gaze seemed to be fixed on Luke and Kate.

They looked like they were sharing a joke now and Kate's head was tipped back as she laughed. Luke was grinning down as he held her in his arms. Maybe this would be the photo they kept on display, rather than the kiss, because they looked like the happiest two people on the planet.

Georgia was not happy. Matteo must have felt the anger in her glare because he turned his head. One eyebrow rose.

'You'll be well looked after,' he murmured. 'Even if you're not married.'

'Oh?' The single syllable was a warning but Matteo merely shrugged.

'He's the father of your baby, isn't he? Of course he will look after you.'

Anger got washed away in a small tsunami of relief. He didn't know the truth.

This was it. A cloak of protection that she could wrap around herself and her babies.

Weirdly, there was disappointment to be found in finding safety so easily.

Man…she really was an adrenaline junkie, wasn't she? It was a personality trait that she really needed to squash, given that she was going to become a parent in the near future.

It wasn't going to be easy, though. The temptation to hint at the truth was irresistible.

'Dougal is not the father of my baby,' she told him, even as a part of her brain registered that Matteo had no idea that this was a twin pregnancy. 'And he's not the only person from my work who's here tonight so I'd appreciate it if you don't spread any unfounded rumours.'

Matteo was scowling at her, dark brows lowered

over eyes that looked black in this light. 'But he *is* here? The father?'

Oh…the crazy part of her wanted to say 'yes' and flirt with danger again. But what if Matteo talked to everybody in the room over the canapés and champagne and worked out who that person could be by a process of elimination?

She could outright lie and say 'no' and make safety even more assured but, despite what Matteo thought of her, it wasn't easy to tell a lie.

Her moment of hesitation provided an escape.

'Over here, you two,' the photographer called. 'We'll do the whole wedding party now, please.'

'What *is* this?'

Luke peered at the tiny sandwich Matteo had in his hand. 'I think that's the smoked salmon and horseradish crème fraîche. It's delicious.'

'Mmm…' Kate's head was leaning against her new husband's shoulder. 'We made some good choices, didn't we? Have you tried the Scottish beef and mustard mayonnaise ones? I've had three.'

'Oink-oink…' Luke dropped a kiss onto her hair.

Matteo put the sandwich into his mouth and let his gaze rake the room as he chewed it.

Where was she now?

It took only a split second to find Georgia, who was standing beside her boss. Had she been telling the truth when she'd denied that he was the father of her child? He could have sworn that when he'd asked whether that man was here, she'd been on the verge of confirming it. He could still feel an echo of the twist in his gut that was something bigger than jealousy. A betrayal almost. As if something that was rightfully his had been taken away.

It was crazy. He barely knew Georgia. They'd had only a matter of hours together.

So why was there a nagging conviction, he had never quite squashed, that she was the only woman in the world for him?

That he still loved her, despite the evidence that she had the worst fault a person could have as far as he was concerned.

*Dishonesty...*

He swallowed the mouthful of food that had suddenly become like cardboard.

'Who is it?' he surprised himself by asking aloud. 'The father of Georgia's baby?'

Kate's jaw dropped and Luke's eyebrows shot up.

'She won't say,' Luke offered into the slightly awkward silence. Then he glanced at Kate, who bit her lip.

'I have my suspicions,' she confessed. 'I think it might be a paramedic from New Zealand that she... um...had a brief thing with.'

'New Zealand?' Matteo had to focus on something and this was easier than the idea that the father of Georgia's baby might not be in the picture any longer. 'Had' made it sound like ancient history. As if she had a space in her life that was glaringly empty. A space that *he* could fill...?

Could he do that? Not just get past the glaring fault of Georgia's lack of honesty but be able to be a father to someone else's child?

*Sì...*his heart whispered. Because it would mean you could spend the rest of your life with the woman you love...

*No…* His head shot back. Don't even think about it. Change the subject. A country on the other side of the globe was a *great* subject.

'Isn't that where you two are going on honeymoon?'

'More than that,' Luke said. 'I haven't had the chance to tell you about it yet, but Katy and I are thinking of emigrating there. We've got some job interviews lined up for next week.'

'What?' Okay, this was an effective distraction. 'You're serious?' A pang of something like envy tightened his chest.

He was ready for something new.

An excitingly different challenge.

More people edged closer to congratulate Luke and Kate, which interrupted their conversation about how wonderful a country New Zealand was. Matteo drifted away—towards where Georgia was still standing with her boss. She must have seen him coming because she apparently spotted someone she was clearly keen to talk to and excused herself smoothly the moment he arrived by her side.

'It's Dougal, yes?'

The older man nodded. 'And you must be Matteo, the "paramedic extraordinaire" from Milan that Luke was telling me about.'

Matteo laughed. 'He trots that line out everywhere. I would take it with… How do you say it—a spoon of salt?'

Dougal grinned. 'A pinch. But he was very believable, I have to say. If you're ever in the market for a new job, come and have a chat. We have a position on our helicopter team coming up very soon that I'm keen to fill with someone extraordinary.'

'Oh?'

'We have a very international team. In the past, we've had guys from all over the world.' Dougal sighed. 'I guess the characteristics that make someone extraordinary include the desire for adventure and travel. Which is great, but it does mean that I have to go through this exercise of finding new people a lot more often than I'd like.'

Matteo nodded, but he wasn't feeling sympathy over Dougal's extra workload. His mind had stopped at the 'international' reference.

'Have you ever had someone from New Zealand working for you?'

Dougal blinked. 'As a matter of fact, we did. A while back now, though. Must be about six months since he left. It's *his* replacement that we're trying to find someone to fill right now. Why do you ask?'

'No reason.' Matteo didn't need to do the maths. It fitted. 'It just seems a popular part of the world at the moment.'

'Ah…because that's where Kate and Luke are planning to live?'

'Mmm.' Matteo's gaze was roving again and, of course, it settled on Georgia. Why was her boss here if it wasn't as her 'plus one'? Kate and Luke were both doctors and it seemed surprising that they would count the director of a rescue service as a close friend.

Dougal had followed the direction of his glance.

'You met Georgie, didn't you? At the rally in Rakovi?'

'Ah…yes.' Somehow, he managed to make it sound as if he had to try to remember. 'She was Kate's partner.'

Dougal nodded. 'She was the one who introduced

me to Kate. We had her come to do some training sessions on station about dealing with paediatric trauma and we've been friends ever since. Have to say I'm delighted to share her happiness this evening.'

Matteo mirrored his nod. And, slowly, the smile. So there was a reason for Georgia's boss to be here tonight that meant he could let go of his suspicions.

And the probable father of her child was already back on the other side of the world, oblivious to what he'd left behind.

He took a sip from his drink as he relaxed.

'Tell me more,' he invited Dougal, 'about this job you have available...?'

# CHAPTER SEVEN

It was over.

The wedding guests followed the bridal couple down to the castle's entrance where a taxi was waiting to whisk them off to the luxury hotel they had chosen to celebrate their first night together as husband and wife.

Matteo was apparently staying in Luke's apartment for the night before he flew back to Italy tomorrow.

Georgia was going to drive back to the cottage that would feel very empty without Kate.

Her final hug with Kate was a fiercely tight one. The house wouldn't just feel empty for the three weeks that her best friend was on honeymoon.

Kate would never live with her again. Even if they weren't planning to emigrate to New Zealand in the near future, she would be living with Luke for the rest of her life, hopefully with the addition of children to complete their family.

Georgia was happy for them, she really was.

It was completely selfish to feel sad at the same time, wasn't it?

'I'm going to miss you,' she said.

'Same.' Kate had tears in her eyes as she finally let go.

Georgia found a smile. 'No, you won't. You'll be too busy living happily ever after.'

'That's not true and you know it.'

'What's not true?' Luke was beside Kate now. Holding her hand and about to urge her into their taxi.

'Kate doesn't think she's going to live happily ever after.'

'Oh?' Luke's glance at his new wife was so full of love it took Georgia's breath away. 'We'll see about that.'

Kate gave Georgia a long-suffering look. 'You'll keep. We'll talk soon, okay?'

Another quick hug and then the taxi pulled away, the rattle of the traditional tin cans tied to the back of the car almost drowned out by the cheers of the guests.

And then there was a moment's silence before the murmur of people taking their leave.

'Where are you parked, Georgie?' Dougal McGregor asked. 'I'll walk you back to your car.'

'I can do that.' Matteo's voice came from behind them.

'I'm fine,' she said firmly. 'It's not far and there's plenty of people around. Thank you both, but I'm quite safe.'

Dougal smiled. 'See you at work tomorrow, then.'

'You will.' Georgia turned, intending to dismiss Matteo just as politely.

'Didn't Luke have a word with you?'

'Um…about what?'

'Giving me a lift to his apartment. He said it was on your way home.'

Georgia hadn't noticed the old leather satchel that

Matteo must have had with him when he'd arrived. He adjusted the strap on his shoulder.

'No matter. I can get a taxi.'

They both looked at the empty street in front of them. Georgia closed her eyes for a moment. She had been too aware all evening of how the air around her changed when Matteo was present and her coping mechanism had been to keep as much space as possible between them. They were outside right now and the awareness was stronger than ever. Could she cope with being shut inside a small car with him?

She had to. She didn't want Kate finding out that she had let them down on their wedding night. Or maybe she didn't want to have to answer any questions about why it had been a big deal.

'It's not a problem,' she told Matteo. 'My car's this way.'

It wouldn't be a problem. It would take a matter of minutes, that was all.

She could cope with that breathless sensation of having this large man apparently using too much of the available oxygen in her vehicle. Of actually being aware of the warmth coming from his body that was only inches away from her own. Of the scent that was more alluring than any commercial aftershave.

Man...if some company could bottle the essence of Matteo Martini, they would make an absolute fortune...

What Georgia couldn't cope with, however, was that Matteo didn't get out of the car when she pulled up at Luke's address. He just sat there, staring out of the windscreen until the silence became unbearable.

She flinched at the low rumble of his voice when Matteo broke the silence.

'I need you to tell me something.'

Oh, *no*... Georgia felt as if any safety barriers around her had just evaporated. She was standing on the edge of a cliff and the slightest wrong move would be catastrophic.

Matteo didn't wait for her to respond. He still wasn't even looking at her.

'Did you know,' he asked quietly, 'that you were already pregnant that night? Is that why you said it was safe?'

Here it was. An opportunity to ensure that Matteo would never know the truth. That she would be safe for ever from having the father of her children try to interfere with her life in any way.

All she had to do was say 'yes'.

But she couldn't do it.

If she said 'yes' she would be tarnishing the memory of the most perfect night of her life. Turning it into something that Matteo would dismiss as being even worse than cheating on someone.

Her breath came out in a sigh of surrender.

'No. I didn't know.'

'But you were.' She could actually hear Matteo's painful swallow. 'Already pregnant when we were together.'

A flash of memory engulfed Georgia. She was in his arms again. He was filling her and her name was a groan of ecstasy as Matteo joined her in paradise.

Any science behind the timing of the conception was irrelevant. As far as Georgia was concerned, *that* was the moment she had become pregnant.

'Yes,' she whispered.

She never cried. But she had to blink hard right now.

'And you're happy about it?'

Good grief… It sounded as if Matteo was on the verge of tears as well.

It was Georgia's turn to swallow hard. 'Yes. I've wanted a baby for a long time.'

'But you're not with the father.'

'No.'

'Have you got family that will help you?'

'No.'

Another long silence fell. It felt different this time. Not threatening at all. Almost sad, in fact.

How could anyone be facing a future like Georgia's when they didn't have the support of a loving family?

Even trying to imagine it was breaking Matteo's heart.

It was brave and he admired that courage very much but it wasn't the way things should be. Especially for Georgia. She needed to be adored.

The way *he* could adore her…

His mother and sisters would love her, too. And their children would be part of a tribe of cousins when they gathered to celebrate family occasions like birthdays or Christmas. Nobody would need to know that their first child wasn't his own because he would love it as if it were.

Because it would be part of Georgia and he'd never quite managed to stop loving her.

He took hold of Georgia's hand and broke the silence.

'I will help you,' he said. 'I could be a father to your baby, Georgia.'

She looked totally shocked. Her mouth started to open but no words came out. She was clearly too stunned to say anything. Or even move to pull her hand away when Matteo raised it to his lips and pressed a kiss to her knuckles.

*Dio mio,* but his heart was winning this time. Hanging onto that image of the future when his own family was a part of a joyous, Martini gathering. The only branch of the family tree that could carry on the name, in fact.

He would be so proud to do that.

And he wanted Georgia as his partner.

He hadn't intended to say his next words but somehow he had to convey just how genuine his offer to help was. How deeply he was prepared to commit to being with both Georgia and her unborn child.

'Marry me,' he said.

# CHAPTER EIGHT

So…

Here he was…

Doing the craziest thing he'd ever done in his life.

Matteo Martini paused as he reached the top of the spiral staircase that led from the enormous helicopter hangar to the offices and staff quarters above.

The bright red overalls of his new uniform felt a little stiff and he rubbed the side of his neck where the coarse material was irritating his skin. A glance through the wall of glass beside him made him pause for a moment.

Edinburgh's Emergency Response Centre was an impressive set-up. This hangar and the tarmac where the helicopters were parked were side by side with the land-based arm of the ambulance service. He could see the huge building that housed the control centre and quarters for the dozens of paramedics who worked here. There was an astonishing number of ambulances lined up outside the building and a row of the SUVs that were painted in the same colours, with beacons on the top. They had similar vehicles in Milan, where experienced paramedics could be sent as a first response or backup to ambulances.

He could see one of these cars heading out as the automatic gates slid open. As soon as it outside the gates, he could see that the driver activated the beacons and he could hear the faint wail of a siren.

Matteo took a very deep breath.

It could be Georgia. Luke had told him that she was currently employed in one of those cars.

He assumed that she didn't know that he had taken this job on the helicopter team. Why would she? The land and air services might work closely together but these bases were separate entities. It might, in fact, prove difficult to see much of Georgia.

Especially given that she wouldn't want to be seeing *him*.

Okay. Perhaps taking this new job in a strange city wasn't the craziest thing he'd ever done.

That prize had to go to proposing marriage to a woman he'd only spent one night with. A woman who'd made it very clear that night, a couple of weeks ago, that she didn't need a man to help her.

Didn't *want* one.

And yet here he was. Making himself available. Putting himself on the line in a way that would have been incomprehensible for any other woman he'd ever met.

*Why?*

Because he hadn't been able to talk himself out of it, that's why. It just felt…right. He'd convinced himself that, if nothing else, this could be a good career move. He could get experience in things that were hard to come by in a huge city like Milan. Mountain rescues perhaps. Or working in difficult conditions, like deep snow. It would be an adventure.

The fact that it was the only first step he could think

of on a journey that could lead to Georgia changing her mind about him was irrelevant.

It had to be. Matteo started moving again. Dougal had given him a comprehensive tour of this facility yesterday and he would be waiting to introduce him to the new team of his paramedic partner and their pilot. His first shift was about to begin.

The new pager clipped to his belt could sound at any moment.

Matteo felt his heart rate kick up a notch. This was one of the things he loved about this job. You never knew when something was going to happen. Or what challenges it could present.

He was ready.

For anything.

The crescendo beat of an approaching helicopter had never been so welcome.

Georgia known that something was wrong as soon as she'd arrived on scene and approached the huddle of people at the bottom of the hill in this mountain biking park on the outskirts of Edinburgh.

A ground-based ambulance crew was already here and, when she saw the look of relief on the young paramedics' faces when they noticed her arrival, it was obvious that this situation was well out of any comfort zone.

At first glance, she couldn't understand what was disturbing them so much. Automatically assessing the scene for safety and any clues about what kind of injury she might need to treat, Georgia had already noticed a bicycle with a very bent wheel amongst the undergrowth and the young boy who was lying on his side, apparently unconscious. A group of other pre-teen children were grouped well away, clutching the handlebars of their bikes, and there were adults with them who were wearing blue polo shirts with a logo that had a bike in mid-air as it cleared an obstacle. Was this a school trip to an adventure park perhaps?

More adults in the blue shirts and a couple in civvies were close to the injured boy and one of the paramedics was taking a blood pressure. That suggested that the child was still alive but the expressions on the faces she could see were telling a different story.

And the silence was unnerving.

There was no time to waste on friendly introductions to a junior crew she didn't recognise. Georgia slipped her arms from the backpack with all her gear and dropped to a crouch, realising belatedly that the size of her belly made this impractical so she ended up on her knees beside her patient.

'Fill me in,' she directed quietly, her fingers already on the boy's neck, feeling for a pulse.

'This is Toby,' one of the paramedics told her. She was holding the boy's shoulders. Preventing him from being moved? 'He's eleven years old. He's come off his bike at speed, going downhill.'

A head injury? Georgia glanced at the helmet the boy was still wearing. She couldn't see any evidence of damage.

The pulse she could feel beneath her fingers was light and rapid. A little uneven, which was a concern.

Was he bleeding out from a severed artery?

Another searching glance didn't show her any signs of blood loss and surely even the most junior crew would have external bleeding well under control by now.

'He hit this tree. And…'

The tiny hesitation in the paramedic's voice came at the same instant that Georgia saw what the problem was.

It had looked as if the small branch that had snapped from the tree was just a part of the organic debris of this crash scene.

But only one end of the branch was visible.

The other end was hidden beneath a fold in the material of this young boy's shirt. Very gently, Georgia moved the material and her heart sank.

Just how far had this stick penetrated? Were the irregular beats she had noticed due to its proximity to Toby's heart?

This was beyond serious. It was critical.

The people all looking to her for guidance were probably reassured by how calmly she spoke. It was a skill honed over a long career of facing difficult situations. She might be on the verge of panicking but nobody would ever guess.

'Can you get on the radio to Comms, please,' she said to the first paramedic. 'Request urgent helicopter backup and then organise a place for it to land.' She turned to the second crew member. 'I need padding so that we can stabilise this branch. Then I'll need my IV roll out of my pack and I want you to get some ECG electrodes in place. Very carefully.' She looked up at the bystanders. 'Can I get someone to come and hold Toby's shoulders, please? And someone else to keep a hand on his legs? We have to make sure we don't move him yet, even an inch.'

By the time she heard the approach of the helicopter, Toby had IV fluids running, oxygen on, and a monitor that was recording his heart rhythm and blood pressure. Georgia had her hands on the doughnut-shaped padding that was around the base of the stick. She didn't know how close it was to this boy's heart but she could feel the movement of its beating and knew that even a small movement of the impaled object could prove fatal.

She was so focussed on what she was doing, she didn't even look up until a flash of red filled her peripheral vision. The legs of one of the critical care paramedics from the helicopter crew. Her glance flicked up swiftly and—despite that skill of keeping a personal reaction hidden in the face of a difficult situation—it was a miracle that her hands remained rock steady when she saw the face beneath the helmet.

*Matteo?*

The flicker on his face told her that her shocked thought must have escaped in an audible gasp but he wasn't about to waste a split second on any explanation.

'Vital signs?'

'Blood pressure and oxygen saturation have dropped in the last five minutes and the blood pressure's widened. Respiratory rate increasing. He's in sinus rhythm but I'm worried about an increasing number of ectopic beats. I'm querying a cardiac tamponade?'

Matteo was unhooking a stethoscope from around his neck.

'I'm going to check his breathing and heart sounds. I'll work around you. Don't move.'

Of course she wasn't going to move. Even if the 'fight or flight' part of Georgia's brain had activated itself and was urging her to flee.

To get away from Matteo.

A man who had offered to marry her and help raise what he believed to be another man's child.

She'd known that Italian men had the reputation of being passionate and impulsive but that had been the craziest thing she'd ever heard. That the offer had actually been as alluring as it was appalling was what had made it so dangerous. Fear had prompted the rush of words she had finally found to respond to him. To tell him that she didn't want him, or *any* man, in her life. He'd finally got out of her car and left—as silently as he had that night after he'd left her bed. And that, she had been quite confident, was the end of it all.

But here he was.

And a traitorous part of her brain was registering something like…happiness?

No. It was probably simply relief that people even more qualified than she was were here to help manage this critical situation where a small boy's life was at stake.

'Thank goodness you're here.' A male bystander who might be Toby's teacher was watching Matteo as he moved the disc of the stethoscope over the boy's chest and he seemed to share Georgia's relief. 'You'll know what to do.'

A flick of a glance from Matteo told Georgia that she'd been doing exactly the right thing to keep Toby safe until she had the backup she needed.

'Can you pull it out?' One of the female bystanders, perhaps a parent helper, sounded terrified. 'It's going to kill him, isn't it?'

'Pulling it out would be the worst thing to do,' Georgia responded quietly. 'It might even be saving his life at the moment.'

'*What?*' The man was incredulous now. 'You've got to be kidding me.'

Matteo glanced up as he reached to open his pack. 'If a foreign object has penetrated something important, like a major blood vessel, it can be the pressure of the object that's stopping uncontrollable bleeding.' He turned back to meet Georgia's gaze.

'I need you to keep the stick really still while I do as best as I can with an ultrasound. I need to know if this is a cardiac tamponade or a haemothorax. We'll need to cope with either of those scenarios before we can move him.'

'We'll also need to shorten this before we can get him in the chopper.' Matteo's crew partner was examining the length of the branch. 'I'll check that we've got a saw on board.'

Matteo's eased the small transducer of the portable ultrasound amongst the shreds of fabric where Georgia had already cut Toby's clothing clear. He was very gentle as he edged around the gauze padding that Georgia was holding firmly in place around the entry point of the stick. His hands brushed hers and, at one point, the back of his hand pressed directly onto hers as he took a closer look at the image on the screen.

'Look at that. You can see that the ventricle wall is functioning. There's no blood loss with the contractions that's going into the pericardium.'

Georgia skirted the awareness of the touch of his skin against her own. Except that it was actually helping her own concentration on this emergency. Making her feel as if she wasn't alone in trying to save this young life. That, together, the chance of success had somehow more than doubled.

'So it's a haemothorax?'

'Haemopneumothorax, probably. Same effect. I can see that air movement has decreased on this side even in the time it took to do the ultrasound.'

'Are you going to do a needle decompression?'

'Yes. I'd rather put in a drain but getting him to Theatre is the priority. It's only ten minutes' flying time and a needle decompression should be enough.'

For the next few minutes, Georgia watched both members of the helicopter crew working but she could do nothing to help except keep her position and keep this stick as stable as possible, especially when Matteo's partner, Shane, was carefully sawing the branch to leave a length that would be manageable as they transported him.

Matteo was working remarkably swiftly. As soon as he noted that Toby was not unconscious enough to be feeling no pain from the vibration of the stick as it was carefully sawn through, he drew up drugs and administered them into the IV line Georgia had already established. When the needle inserted between the small ribs failed to release enough pressure to improve breathing, he and Shame worked as a team to perform the surgical procedure to insert a proper drain and remove some of the blood that was preventing a lung from functioning.

It was impressive.

And then they were ready for the delicate task of moving their young patient to the stretcher and into the helicopter.

'Can you come with us?' Matteo asked Georgia. 'I know we can trust you to keep that stick stable.'

She still hadn't let go of the padding around this

object and she didn't want to until she knew that Toby was safe.

'We can get your vehicle back to base,' one of the original paramedics on scene said.

Georgia nodded. But the next few seconds were anxious ones. She had to get up off her knees as they lifted the stretcher without moving her hands and changing the pressure that was keeping the stick steady. Normally that wouldn't have been a problem but she had a huge belly that was affecting her balance now and couldn't know whether it was going to be a problem.

Matteo's sharp glance as she began to move told her that he was thinking along the same lines. He jerked his head at one of the ambulance crew to take his place at the head of the stretcher to lift it and he stepped behind Georgia, putting his hands under her arms to grip her body and help her to her feet.

The strength in those hands and arms was astonishing.

It was entirely inappropriate to even notice that they were in contact with more than her ribs but her body overrode her focus for just a heartbeat. Later—probably in the middle of the night—it would remind her that her breasts remembered that fleeting touch. And that would remind her of so much more…

It was just as well that there were too many other things to focus on right now. It was Georgia's job to keep the foreign object stable as the others worked around her. To keep her gaze on the monitor at all times and warn of any changes to vital signs like heart rhythm, oxygen saturation and blood pressure.

And part of her was savouring every moment of this adrenaline-filled mission. Her peripheral vision showed the mountain park scene fall away beneath them as the helicopter took off, and Georgia knew this might be the last challenge like this that she would have for a very long time. She knew her baby bump could have interfered with her doing her job if Matteo and Shane hadn't been there.

She'd held onto her front-line job for as long as she could but it really was time to step down and spend the next few months in an environment that was safer for everybody. The patients, herself and her babies.

And, maybe, that would also keep her well away from Matteo's orbit. That was something else that would be haunting her later tonight when she had the head space to revisit the shock of his reappearance in her life.

Georgia had no idea how she was going to cope with it.

Or even if she could.

Well…that had been a memorable first day on a new job.

He'd been right that this position was going to give him new experiences and enhance his skills.

Matteo paced the floor in Luke's small apartment in central Edinburgh, heading for the fridge in the hope of finding a cold beer.

That job this morning, with the young boy impaled by the branch, had been exciting. Challenging. That they'd got him to the hospital and into Theatre with no major deterioration in his condition had been a triumph. He would contact the intensive care unit tomorrow and ask for an update. Have a chat with the specialist in charge of his case, hopefully.

Because having an update to share would give him an excuse to make contact with Georgia?

No. That wasn't his motivation. He needed to know how his patient was doing. Whether he'd done everything he should have done on scene.

The fact that he would have a reason to get in touch with Georgia to pass on the information was simply a bonus.

But Matteo sighed as he twisted the top off the small bottle.

He was facing a bigger battle than he'd expected.

That look of shock on her face in the instant when she'd recognised him today.

Horror, almost... Or perhaps even *fear*?

What was that about?

How could you find a connection with someone that was *this* powerful and then not want to explore it further?

How could you make love with someone like that and not be desperate to try it again? To see if it really was the most extraordinary experience in your life?

Unless she hadn't felt the same way.

No. Matteo didn't believe that. The lines of physical communication had been the clearest he'd ever experienced. It hadn't made any difference that they came from different countries. They had been speaking exactly the same language that night.

Okay... Maybe he'd scared her by that impulsive offer of marriage. He could understand that. He'd been carried away in the moment. If she'd said 'yes', he would have put his heart and soul into making it work, but he was quite prepared to take this more slowly and win her heart.

But he'd never come across a barrier quite like this.

He had been left with the impression that Georgia *was* actually afraid of him and that was deeply disturbing.

Had it been his anger when he'd thought she was cheating on someone else by being with him that night? It wasn't as if he'd threatened her in any way. He hadn't even raised his voice. He'd simply walked away and then ignored her from that point on.

Maybe the anger had been enough.

Had Georgia been abused at some point in her life by an angry man? A boyfriend, perhaps. Or…her father?

The thought made him sick.

Whatever the reason, however, he could feel proud of the courage Georgia was showing, being faced with a situation she had made very clear was something she didn't want.

She had done her job, working so closely with him, with professionalism and skill. After that initial shock, there hadn't been any hint that she was distracted by anything personal. Even when he'd held her body to help her to her feet. She hadn't flinched. He would have felt the slightest tremor beneath his hands and, if anything, she'd let him take more weight than strictly necessary.

As if she'd welcomed his assistance. Trusted him to deliver it.

But the fact that the assistance had been welcome bothered him as well. Why was she still working on the front line like this when she was at such an advanced stage of her pregnancy? Surely there was a cut-off point when it wasn't allowed to happen?

She needed protection, even if she didn't think she did. Matteo took a long swallow of his beer. He might have a chat to Dougal tomorrow and just ask. Carefully. He didn't want to antagonise Georgia. She'd been clearly taken aback by finding out that her friend hadn't warned her he was arriving.

It had been a rather disappointing conversation all round, actually, when they'd finally left Toby in the hands of the operating theatre's team.

'Why Scotland? Why *here*?' Georgia had demanded, keeping her gaze on the long corridor ahead of them.

'Why not? I was ready for a new adventure and I happened to be offered a job when I was here for the wedding.'

'And Luke knew you were coming?'

'Of course. He offered me his apartment to live in.'

'But they're coming back. Next week. You're planning to live with a newly wed couple?'

'No. But they'll only be here for a brief time. To pack everything up and go to their new life in New Zealand. Kate said it wouldn't be a problem. She knew a place I could use.'

'So Kate knew, too?' Georgia had looked wounded. 'She didn't tell *me*.'

'I asked them not to. I wanted it to be a surprise.'

'Oh…' She made a hollow sound that wasn't quite laughter. 'I'm surprised…'

'Kate thought it was a good idea.'

'What? You coming to work in Edinburgh?'

'That I would be here for you, *cara*. That you would have a friend.' Yes, he had seen a flash of alarm in her eyes. He couldn't risk pushing her. 'If you need one, that is.'

'We're not going to be friends, Matteo.'

'Why not?'

'Because...' She was avoiding his gaze. 'Just because...'

He didn't sigh audibly. But if he was prepared to try getting past the fact that she'd lied to him, surely Georgia could get past whatever it was that was making her keep him at arm's length? No, it was more than arm's length. She would prefer the length of a whole country.

'We *could* be.' He'd given her his most persuasive smile when they'd parted company at the elevators. He was heading for the helipad on the roof and Georgia was going to catch a ride back to base with the next available ambulance crew. 'It might even be nice.'

A few days later, Georgia was at the airport late in the evening to collect Kate and Luke as they returned from their honeymoon. The anticipation of how good it was going to be to see her best friend for the first time in weeks was lifting her spirits for the first time in what seemed ages.

The last few days had been tough.

Her heart wanted to fill her thoughts with memories of Matteo Martini but her head drowned them with worry about the implications of him having anything to do with her life. Of him somehow finding out the truth.

Of *wanting* him to know the truth?

Yes. That was part of it. It wasn't just that her body and heart kept reminding her of the connection she felt with Matteo. This was making her feel guilty.

Telling her that she'd done something very wrong. No. That she was *still* doing something very wrong and it didn't sit well at all. It had been far easier to bury the guilt when the father of her children had been in another country and the chance of seeing him again had been remote.

Her heart also wanted to grieve a little for stepping away from her work on the road and her head was determined to find something good about being given a desk job. The research task of a retrograde data collection to identify the most effective airway adjunct to use in a cardiac arrest could potentially change protocols. It should be exciting. It was certainly a lot better than doing some kind of massive stocktake, except that if her hands had been busy at the same time, perhaps her brain wouldn't stray quite so often.

Back to the unexpected bombshell in her life. At least she had anticipated the change of lowering her workload.

She had never expected Matteo to reappear in her life.

And she hadn't expected to see him now but that tall back beneath the electronic flight arrivals board was unmistakeable.

'For God's sake, Matteo,' she snapped, when she was right behind him, a little gratified that it made him jump. 'What are *you* doing here? Kate arranged for me to collect them before they even left.'

'And Luke texted me before they took off from Dubai.' A dark eyebrow rose. 'Perhaps they have a great deal of luggage?'

Georgia glanced at the board. The plane had landed on time so they should be coming through Customs any minute now.

'Or perhaps you missed a call about a change of arrangements,' Matteo suggested mildly. 'You don't seem to like answering your telephone.'

Georgia could feel a blush of colour creeping into her cheeks. She *had* deliberately ignored the call from Matteo the day after they'd worked together. She had actually deleted the voicemail before listening to it, because she hadn't wanted to listen to his voice. That sexy, deep rumble. That accent...

It was inexcusably rude, given that Matteo was Luke's best friend. And Luke was now *her* best friend's husband. It wasn't just that connection either. Matteo was now part of her own branch of the emergency services and it was a close-knit community.

One way and another, she was going to have to spend time with Matteo, at least in the near future.

She really needed to get a grip on how she was going to manage that.

An apology for her rudeness might be a good first step?

'Sorry,' she mumbled. 'I've been really busy. What was it that you wanted to talk about?'

'Just that case we shared on my first day. Toby. You remember him?'

'Of course. An impalement injury like that is a once-in-a-lifetime type of job.' Curiosity got the better of her. 'Did you follow up on him? How *is* he?'

'Probably ready to go home. He was one very lucky little boy. That stick had actually penetrated his left ventricle but because it wasn't removed until he was in Theatre, the bleeding was easily controlled and the damage repaired. Antibiotic treatment prevented an infection and he only needed a short time in Intensive Care for monitoring after the surgery.'

'Oh…that's fantastic news.' Georgia's smile was genuine. 'What a great job to have done on your first day. You handled it brilliantly.'

'*We* handled it brilliantly,' Matteo corrected.

The corner of his mouth tilted in a crooked grin and, for a moment, it was like the first time she'd ever spoken to him. When she was completely captured. Flustered enough, even, to say something pretty stupid.

'Hey… Good to see you two getting along so well.'

'*Luke…*' Georgia and Matteo both spoke at the same time as they turned away from each other.

'And *Katy,*' Georgia added, throwing her arms around her friend with relief, both to see her again but also to have her attention so thoroughly diverted from Matteo. 'Oh…it's *so* good to see you.'

'We're going to have lots of time to catch up in the next couple of weeks while I work out my notice. I can't wait to tell you about New Zealand. And show you photos. You won't believe how beautiful it is. You should think about emigrating, too, Georgie.'

Matteo was walking ahead of them beside Luke, who was pushing the luggage trolley.

'Maybe I will,' Georgia murmured. 'Hey, do you want to go home in my car? Matteo could take Luke, seeing as we've doubled up on chauffeurs.'

Kate's eyes widened with something that looked a lot like guilt.

'What?' Georgia demanded. 'What's going on?'

'Um… I told Matteo I'd found a place for him to stay while we were back in town. I was hoping you'd give him a lift.'

It was something to do with that hopeful little smile

on Kate's face that planted the seeds of a suspicion that rapidly grew into disbelief.

'You *didn't*…'

'It seemed logical. A place to stay and he can use my car until I sell it. And you two are getting on better now, aren't you? You might even like him, Georgie, if you gave him a chance. Luke's told me all about Matt and he's a *great* guy…'

Her friend was matchmaking.

Worse than that, this was like an intervention. Kate and Luke had come up with a plan that would force their best friends to spend a whole lot of time together.

To *live* together…

'*No.*' Georgia was struggling to find words. 'You can't do this, Kate. Matteo wouldn't want it any more than I do.'

Kate ducked her head. 'Sorry…' She offered a tentative smile. 'It doesn't have to be for the whole time but it's a bit late to find something else tonight and a bit rude to stick him in some hotel. He could sleep on our sofa, I guess.'

Luke was putting the bags into the boot of his car now. Matteo was pulling a bag from the back seat. He smiled at Georgia, eyebrows lifted.

The smile was an echo of the one they had shared so recently when they'd been talking about Toby. When, for a heartbeat, she'd forgotten the barrier between them.

'You don't mind, do you? Dropping me at my new place?'

So he didn't know he'd been offered Kate's old room in the cottage.

How would he react when he found out?

Oh…this was playing with fire if anything was.

And some wicked part of Georgia wanted to poke the embers. Like the first time she'd spoken to him, unexpected words that she could well regret later simply slid past her lips.

'No problem. It's not out of my way at all…'

# CHAPTER NINE

'I'M SORRY, GEORGIA. I had *no* idea.'

Matteo had looked surprised when Georgia opened the door of the cottage with her own keys. And then he'd looked stricken as the penny had dropped.

'I know.' She shrugged. 'I think Kate and Luke have got this idea that we could…that we might…'

Matteo pushed his fingers through his hair. 'Take me back to town. I can find a hotel.'

The fact that it was Matteo who didn't want to be here perversely made Georgia more inclined to let him stay.

It was a battle between her head and her heart that was being played out in real life instead of in her imagination. And right now her heart was winning.

'It's okay. As Kate said, it's logical. You need a place to stay for a little while. There's an empty room here. For tonight anyway.'

'I would never force myself on you like this. You know that, don't you?'

Oddly, Kate *did* know that. Instinctively, she knew that this man's moral code would prevent him from ever hurting anyone—especially a woman—with no consideration taken for any personal injury that could be the result.

This situation should have been making her more afraid than ever.

But, weirdly, it was making her feel safer.

This was her turf and she was in control. And it *was* an intervention in a way that Kate knew nothing about.

Georgia didn't want to live with unresolved guilt for the rest of her life. Being under the same roof as Matteo was going to force her to find the solution, wasn't it?

Not that she had any idea what that solution might be, mind you.

Emigrating to New Zealand was starting to seem like less of a crazy idea…

By the time Georgia got up the next morning, Matteo was already gone. There wasn't even a dirty cup in the sink to suggest that he'd been in the kitchen but she could sense that he had been.

It felt different…

As if the emptiness of her house over the last few weeks had been smudged around the edges.

How had he managed to be so tidy? And so quiet? Had Matteo actually slipped out of the house at some point during the night and gone off to find a hotel?

The notion should have been a relief but it was curiously alarming at the same time. So much so that Georgia climbed the stairs again, which was getting to be quite an effort, in order to peep around the partially open door of Kate's old room.

Matteo's leather satchel lay on floor in front of the wooden chair in the corner of the room. The clothes he'd been wearing last night were carelessly draped over the back of the chair.

Georgia's breath came out in a sigh that felt like relief.

He was coming back, then…

Her gaze drifted sideways to the bed. The patchwork quilt had been pulled up but it wasn't as smooth as Kate would have left it. She could almost see the indent of where Matteo's body had been.

Her breath got stuck. Maybe that was why she was feeling a bit weird. Dizzy even…

There was definitely an edge of confusion.

Her hours of work were far more relaxed now, so Georgia had time to sit in the sun with her cup of tea and toast. Time to explore what it was that was nagging at the back of her mind and causing her confusion.

She missed Kate. This was the best thing about having a bestie. You got to think aloud and the supportive audience could help pinpoint not only what the real issue was but what you wanted to do about it.

But she couldn't bat this around with Kate. She was on her own.

And it wasn't that hard to mentally tiptoe closer to what she was afraid to look at so closely.

All it took was to allow an image of Matteo Martini to fill her mind. Those dark eyes that could see too much. That layer of genuine interest and concern in combination with a smile that was undeniably sinful.

He just oozed charm, didn't he?

But he also made her feel safe.

*I would never force myself on you like this. You know that, don't you?*

Of course he wouldn't. He had a moral code that was

so iron clad, he would never dream of lying. Or cheating on someone. He would simply walk away from someone who didn't share those values.

But he'd come back…

Because of her? Because the significance of what they'd found with each other was enough to be making him reconsider those iron-clad rules?

Because he really did want to be her *friend*?

No. He wanted to be more than that. He'd offered to marry her, for heaven's sake. To be a father to her child.

And now he was here but he'd taken a huge step back. He was leaving it up to her to choose whether she closed the respectful gap he was keeping.

No wonder she was confused.

Matteo was nothing like any man she had ever known.

Certainly *nothing* like her father…

And there it was. The real issue.

What if her father had used charm instead of violence? If he'd simply been there in her life and let her make a choice of whether she wanted him closer or not? If a genuine concern for her welfare and happiness had been there in his eyes and he'd had a smile that suggested she was the only person in the world who mattered at that moment?

Life would have been very different, wouldn't it?

She could have lived her early life without the fear of that pain—both emotional and physical.

She could have been like the kids she'd envied so much. The ones who'd had a daddy at home to tease them sometimes but protect them always.

Oh, boy…this was huge. Georgia tried to stop the

thought that was coming at her as relentlessly as a tsunami but she couldn't.

Did she *really* want her children to grow up without a father?

It was almost as if she had Kate sitting here with her. Understanding at least part of her new dilemma. Asking her what she wanted to do about it.

Suggesting that the only the thing to do might be to tell Matteo the truth.

The shock of allowing that possibility any head room at all was enough to push Georgia to her feet.

She needed to get to work. To work so hard, in fact, that she could close the lid of this 'too hard' basket very firmly indeed.

'Oh, my God…what is that smell?'

'Lasagne. A secret recipe that's been handed down in my family for generations.'

'You can *cook*?'

'Anyone who bears the Martini name has to know how to make the perfect lasagne. Just ask any one of my sisters.'

'Oh…' Georgia let the bag full of the papers she had brought home slip from her hand.

She was late. Coming home to a house that had its lights twinkling in the darkness had been a lift all by itself. Entering a kitchen that was redolent with the most delicious smell she had ever encountered was actually overwhelming enough to make her feel unsteady on her feet.

Maybe that was because her feet were so swollen today. Or that she'd been pushing herself so hard at work for the last week or more that she was exhausted.

It had worked, though. Any issues that were bothering her hadn't been allowed any significant head space and Matteo had made it easier out of work hours, too, with the way he had been using her home as little more than a hotel, always gone so early and often back so late their paths had barely crossed.

Which made this scenario even more blindsiding.

'You've been working too hard,' Matteo told her. 'And I've been rude. I've hardly been here. I had a night out with the guys from work. With Luke. At the gym. Anyway… This is my way of saying thank you. Please…sit down. I thought it would be more comfortable for you on the couch. Can I get you something to drink?'

There was bottle of red wine open on the coffee table in the small sitting room, between a basket of freshly sliced baguette and a bowl of what looked like a very crispy green salad.

The wine was tempting but Georgia's hand went automatically to her belly, where it was rewarded with the bump of a kick from a tiny foot.

'A water would be great.'

'Sparkling or still?'

'Oh…sparkling, please. I could pretend it's champagne.'

'Which is exactly why I bought some.' Matteo's smile curled more widely. 'I hadn't forgotten your preference.'

He had brought a chilled bottle of champagne to the table at the end of the competition, hadn't he? For her. The first move in that dance that had led them to its memorably intimate conclusion.

Georgia sank onto the couch. The wave of emotion threatened to drown her but she was too tired to fight.

Maybe she could just float for a while, she decided, easing off shoes that had become far too tight.

Every mouthful of this unexpected dinner was delicious, possibly because of far more than the actual taste of the food. What was astonishingly powerful was this feeling of being cared for.

Of feeling…safe…

Oh, man… Georgia took a large gulp of her water. She hadn't been this close to crying since she'd first found out she was pregnant. Or when she'd been standing there in that ancient chapel, listening to Luke and Kate pledge their undying love for each other.

Thank goodness the chirp of Matteo's phone broke the atmosphere.

'Ah…' His face broke into a grin as he opened his text message. '*Bel bambino*… Look.' He held the screen for Georgia to see. 'That's Arlo, waving hello to his uncle while he's having his bath.'

A fat, adorable baby with soap bubbles adorning his curly, dark hair was beaming at the camera, his chubby arms held up as if he was asking for a cuddle.

'Arlo?'

'My youngest nephew. Siena's first baby. Adrianna's pregnant again now. She'll be having her third, after a bit of a gap after the twins. I'll bet that will make Allegra jealous so I expect there'll be a new addition to her family soon as well.'

'How many nephews and nieces have you got?'

Matteo squinted as he concentrated and Georgia lost count as Italian names tumbled from his lips. He was scrolling through the photos on his phone at the same time. He leaned back on the couch for a moment in silence and Georgia watched the expression on his face change. His grin faded into something far more poignant and then he actually sniffed and rubbed at his forehead as if fighting back tears.

'What?' Georgia asked quietly.

'It's a video. My nieces—Mita and Lia. It was their third birthday last year.'

He tapped the arrow on the centre of the screen as he tilted it towards her. The sound of giggles filled the room. Two identical small girls wearing frilly white dresses, with flowers in their hair, were climbing all over a man who was lying on the grass.

Matteo. He was laughing, too, as he scooped a child under each arm and sat up, kissing first one girl and then the other. One of the twins wriggled free and reached into the grass to pluck a daisy, which she triumphantly presented to her uncle.

*'Grazie mille, tesoro. Ti amo...'*

The words didn't need any translation. That expression on Matteo's face was tearing at a part of Georgia's heart.

'You really love kids, don't you?' she murmured, as the video ended.

'Of course. They are the most important thing in the world. I ask for nothing more than to have the gift of my own family one day.' Matteo's smile was still poignant. 'No. I want more than that. I want to live to be a grandfather so that I don't leave my family with the sadness that we have.'

'You lost your father?'

'Many years ago. But I miss him every day.'

'And your mother?'

'My mama—Teresa Martini—is the proudest grand-mother on the face of the earth. She welcomes every new baby as if it's the greatest gift possible. And she moves in with each of my sisters, every time. For at least a month after the birth.' Matteo's gaze was sombre. 'I'm sad that you don't have your mother to help you. It's a time when family comes together. Not just to celebrate but to make life easier.' He was frowning now. 'How will you manage, Georgie?'

She swallowed hard. 'I'll manage.'

'You must miss your mother so much.'

Georgia nodded slowly. As the birth of her babies drew closer she was missing that rock in her life more and more every day. She had to press her lips tightly together to cope with a stab of loss that was the biggest yet but she could still feel them tremble.

Only for a heartbeat, but Matteo must have seen her reaction because he lifted his hand and touched her lips with the pad of his thumb, his fingers cupping her cheek and jaw.

It was the most exquisitely tender gesture. In no way sexual but the response of her body and her heart had a kick that was far more powerful.

This…this felt like real love.

The kind that could last a lifetime?

'It's not long now, is it?'

'Um…no…' Her brain was too tired to try and do the maths that would keep her story straight but if she was a month more pregnant than she really was—as she'd allowed him to believe—that would mean she was due…

Oh, help…next week?

Was Matteo going to push her for an actual date?

No. He wasn't even looking at her. He was staring at her belly. Looking down, Georgia realised why. She was so used to the rippling sensations of her babies moving within her that she'd almost forgotten how extraordinary it was to *see* that movement as well as feel it.

She had long ago given up trying to wear anything like uniform pants. She had some comfortable maternity jeans on today, with the silky, stretch fabric of the insert a thin layer under the uniform polo shirt. A shirt that was visibly moving at the moment.

A look of something like reverence claimed Matteo's features and his gaze, when it captured hers, was the most intense she'd ever seen it.

'May I?' he asked softly.

It was impossible not to grant permission with the spell that that look was putting her under, but Georgia had to close her eyes as she felt the gentle weight of his hand outstretched on her belly.

Her skin was aware of the pressure on both sides. Her babies beneath and Matteo's hand on top.

Their father's hand.

It was too much. Too *wrong*…

He had to know the truth, didn't he?

She turned, tilting her head upwards to catch his gaze, her lips parting ready to release the words he had to hear.

But Matteo's head was closer than she'd realised. He had tears in his eyes as his gaze locked with hers.

And it took only the smallest movement for his lips to make contact with her own.

A brief, soft kiss. As tender as that touch of his fingers on her face had been.

She could feel his breath on her skin when they finally broke that kiss and his words were no more than a sigh.

*'Ti amo, tesoro mio.'*

Again, the words needed no translation. His eyes were telling her exactly what he'd whispered but maybe he hadn't intended her to understand them. Or even realise that they'd been audible.

How could she could tell him the truth now? If she said anything at all, it was more likely to be that she loved him as well.

And how could she say that when he didn't know the truth?

It was wrong, too.

Everything about this situation was so wrong. Perfect but twisted. And Georgia had no idea how to fix it.

Something of her dilemma must have shown on her face but Matteo didn't seem to be bothered. He was smiling at her.

'I excuse you the dishes,' he told her. 'Go to bed, *cara*. You're exhausted, yes?'

Georgia nodded. She swallowed hard.

'Thanks, Matteo.'

'For what? The food?' He waved a dismissive hand. 'It was nothing.'

'It wasn't nothing. It was…perfect.'

He was moving now. Collecting the empty plates as if this was just a part of a normal, everyday life.

'I'm glad you liked it. We'll do it again. We have plenty of time before I have to go back to Luke's apartment.'

Finally, Georgia could return the smile.

Plenty of time…

That was something else her mother used to say, too.

*There's plenty of time, love.*

*Give it time…it'll be okay.*

*Time heals everything…*

There was comfort to be found in those echoes of her mother's voice.

Hope, even.


Teresa Martini's lasagne had been a favourite for Matteo for as long as he could remember but it had just become even more significant in his life.

He'd taken a huge step towards his goal tonight.

He had been permitted to show Georgia a part of how he felt about her. The food he'd made for her hadn't been rejected. He'd been allowed to share the miracle of feeling the new life stirring within her.

He'd kissed her even. A kiss of nothing more than tenderness because anything else at this point in time was unthinkable.

And even though nothing had been said aloud, he was quite certain that she had felt the same as he had— the profound depth of the connection between them. That she was thinking exactly what he was.

That she was in love…

It was enough of a declaration for now. He wasn't going to scare her again by trying to force something on her that she wasn't ready for.

Like too much of his company.

Or too much touching.

Or something stupid like offering to marry her again.

It was hard. Possibly the hardest thing he'd ever done, but he could take this slowly.

He could wait.

Until Georgia showed him that she was ready for more.

# CHAPTER TEN

'THEY'LL BE THERE by now.'

'I know. Are you okay?'

'Why wouldn't I be?' Georgia picked up the pot Matteo had just put onto the draining board and started to dry it.

Matteo was scrubbing the next pot. 'There were a lot of tears at the airport yesterday. From Kate, anyway.' An eyebrow quirked in her direction. 'You are much tougher, I think.'

Georgia shrugged, her gaze sliding away from his. 'I just don't cry.'

'What…never? I have five sisters and a mother who cry all the time. *I* cry sometimes. It's nothing to be ashamed of.'

Yes. She could remember the times she had seen tears glinting in his eyes. Happy tears that were evoked by tapping into the enormous love he had for his family.

He had an infinite capacity for love, this man, didn't he?

When he'd had his hand on her belly that night, she could imagine that he was already feeling that love for a child that he still had no idea he had a close connection with.

There it was again.

That pressure.

The feeling that the account in the bank of time she'd believed she had was rapidly draining.

'Just because I don't cry on the outside doesn't mean I don't feel things. And Kate was upset that she couldn't be here to be my birth partner. She said that she'd tried to delay the start of her new job but just couldn't make it work when we can't be sure of an exact date.'

'It can't be far away.' Matteo's head turned again. 'Look how far back you have to stand from the bench.'

'I know. I won't be able to reach the steering wheel of my car soon because my arms won't be long enough. Just as well I'm allowed to work from home until I start my maternity leave officially.'

'That decides it, then.'

'Decides what?' Georgia could feel her eyes widening. Oh, help...the pressure had just kicked up another notch. How had she become so used to the luxury of thinking she had plenty of time to pick the right moment to tell Matteo what he had to know? Relaxing enough to find an excuse every time anything like an opportunity presented itself because she couldn't figure out a way of softening the shock by giving him some kind of a warning.

Opportunities like now, when they were sharing such a domestic task like washing dishes. When they were becoming so at ease with each other's company. Matteo had said he would never force himself on her and he'd proved that his word was his bond in the last couple of weeks. He'd been nothing more than a perfect flatmate.

A friend.

But that tone in his voice suggested something was about to change.

'I can't move back to Luke's apartment.'

'Oh?' It wasn't that Georgia wanted him to move out but the decisiveness of this statement was a little disturbing. What if he simply decided he had no intention of moving out of her life, full stop?

That was a battle she might not want to win. It could well be only wishful thinking but the idea of having Matteo in her life for ever had a glow of being as close to perfect as anything could get.

'Not yet, anyway. Not when you'll need someone to drive your car. To get groceries, for example.'

'I can order online. They deliver these days, you know.'

Matteo scowled at her. 'You might need to go to the hospital.'

A flutter of something like panic was trying to make itself felt. It wouldn't be perfect to have Matteo here for ever. Arguing with every decision she tried to make.

Taking control...

'I have a phone.' Her voice tightened. 'I could call you.'

'You might need to go in a hurry.'

Muscles in Georgia's jaw tightened. 'I can call an ambulance. I know a few people who work there and they'd get here pretty fast.'

'You *want* me to move out?'

If she said yes, would he pack his bag and leave instantly?

She wasn't ready for that. If he left, it would be even easier to avoid finding the right moment to tell him.

'Um…' Georgia bit her lip. This was getting onto dangerous territory. Her mind was spinning.

There was a soft chant as background to the conflicting thoughts.

*Tell him…tell him…tell him…*

'Ah…maybe not quite yet. There won't be much room when the…when the…'

'Baby arrives. I get it.'

But he didn't get it. Georgia had slammed on the mental brakes when the word 'bab*ies*' had been about to emerge. She'd sworn Kate to secrecy about that, on the grounds that she wanted to surprise everyone she knew. It was gratifying to know that she hadn't even told Luke. Or maybe she had. Maybe guys didn't pass on that sort of information because it wasn't interesting enough.

The moment he knew she was carrying twins, the game would be over. He'd know that she was bigger than expected for dates and that her pregnancy wasn't nearly as advanced as she'd let him assume. It would force the truth to come out.

'When is it due?'

'You never know with first babies.'

The response was evasive. Despite trying to make that chant go away by giving in to it, something was overriding her determination and making it impossible.

'They're rarely on time,' she added, a little desperately, 'and usually late.'

She hurriedly poked the last pot lid into the cupboard and then reached for the drainer to stand it upright at the end of the bench. But Matteo was reaching for it as well and his hand caught her wrist.

'I need to know,' he said quietly. 'My mother and

sisters are putting pressure on for me to go home for a few days. My work schedule will allow it in a couple of weeks but that could be just the wrong time. I want to be here for you.' He was making circles on her wrist with his thumb. 'I could be your birth partner instead of Kate if you like.'

The sensation of those circles on her skin was travelling up Georgia's arm like wildfire, obliterating every other thought that was still spinning. Up her arm, through her chest and straight down to an area low in her belly. It felt odd to experience a bolt of pure desire like this. Did pregnant woman still have sex when they were the size of a small elephant?

Would anyone other than the father of the baby even want to?

And, if he did, how exactly did they make it work?

She closed her eyes on a long blink as that thought pushed the others away. She might know a way...

Matteo's thumb stilled. 'What is this from?' he asked quietly. 'This scar? I've been wondering about it...'

Someone throwing a bucket of iced water into her face could have had a similar effect on dousing that desire. For a moment, Georgia froze.

She'd already sensed that this was an opportunity to tell Matteo the truth. Or to at least tell him when her due date was so that he could work it out for himself and force a stop to this horrible procrastination. More than that, she realised that a better opportunity would never present itself. She was actually being given a chance to offer the foundation of any excuses for her deception before she dropped the bombshell of Matteo's impending fatherhood.

But, yet again, she couldn't do it.

Memory was such a bizarre thing. A smell could evoke a feeling of being straight back in your childhood, for instance. A thumb touching a jagged scar could suddenly burn, as though she could feel the pain of her arm being jammed in that car door all over again. She could definitely feel the shudder of remembered fear that had rippled down her spine.

She had to snatch her arm away.

'Don't…' she whispered. 'Please… I don't want to talk about it. I…*can't*…'

He couldn't let this go.

Okay, he'd said he wasn't going to force himself on her and he'd had no intention of pushing her at a pace she wasn't comfortable with.

But this was important.

No…it was more than that. Matteo's instincts were finely honed for signs and symptoms in patients that could mean that their condition was becoming critical.

*This* felt critical.

He followed Georgia into the sitting room. Already, she had picked up a sheaf of papers from work and seemed to be focused on reading them.

Shutting him out.

He sat beside her on the couch. Silently, for a long moment, as he tried to think of what to say that wasn't going to make that barrier even more solid.

'If you want to watch television, that's fine.' Georgia's voice was tight. 'I can go and work in my room.'

'I don't want to watch television,' Matteo said quietly. 'I want to talk to you.'

She was silent.

'You don't have to tell me,' he added. 'But I'd really like you to. I care about you, *cara*—you know that. I get the feeling that that scar on your arm is more than just physical and… I want to know you better. To understand…'

It was that last word that seemed to find a chink in her armour. The papers drifted onto her lap as she closed her eyes.

'My arm got broken when I was five years old. A compound fracture. I've always told people that it happened when I fell off a pony but…it didn't. It came from having it slammed in a car door.'

*'Dio mio…'* Matteo's stomach churned at the thought of that pain. 'How did that happen?'

'My father did it.'

Now he felt sick. He'd been right, hadn't he, when he'd wondered if someone had abused Georgia to make her fearful of men in some way.

And that meant that the violence had been deliberate, not accidental.

'Right before he pushed my mother out of the way. So hard that she fell and hit her head on the pavement. She was still trying to get up as we drove away. I saw her out of the back window…'

Georgia Bennett never cried on the outside, but Matteo could hear the sobs of a terrified child behind her words.

He had to gather Georgia into his arms. To hold her. The papers slid from her lap onto the floor but she didn't seem to notice. She rested her head in the hollow beneath his shoulder and, slowly, started speaking again.

'He took me to a hospital, of course. The police

came and I got taken home to my mother eventually but it was the start of fear for both of us. My father had become very religious and he made it his life's mission to make amends for the shame of the one-night stand that had brought me into the world, even though he'd wanted nothing to do with me when I was born. We had to keep moving. Trying to hide…'

It was an effort to keep the anger from his voice. 'Where is he now—this monster who was no father to you?'

'He's dead. He was killed in a fight. Stabbed by someone who disagreed with his lay preaching on a street corner.' He could feel the movement of Georgia's chest as she let her breath out in a sigh. 'My mum said it was karma.'

'It was certainly a good thing. You were safe…'

'I was still afraid. My mother developed epilepsy. The doctors thought it could have had something to do with a head injury that was never investigated properly that day I broke my arm. It was a petit mal seizure that probably caused her to step out onto a road…in front of a bus. I had just started work on the road after graduating from university.'

'Oh, no…you didn't find out by arriving on scene, did you?' Matteo's heart was breaking. He couldn't bear the thought of this story getting even worse.

'No…' Georgia tilted her head to look up at him. A hint of a smile tugged at one corner of her mouth. 'You're right… I hadn't actually ever thought of that. It *could* have been worse…'

No, it couldn't. Matteo tightened his hold on Georgia as he pressed a kiss to the top of her head. He'd guessed that there was something important about that scar. That it represented much more than simply a physical injury.

But this…

This was so huge he couldn't even begin to imagine how deeply it could have shaped a young life.

He needed to process this.

Thank goodness his instincts told him to back off. To take things slowly. To let Georgia choose when—or if—to invite him further into her life.

Telling him this had opened a door onto a space that was totally new.

A space that instinct told him nobody else had ever been allowed access to.

'There's something else I should tell you.'

He could feel the tension in her body now. Could feel her struggle.

'You don't have to,' he whispered. 'Not right now.' He stroked her hair. 'We have all the time in the world, *cara*. I'm not going anywhere. Not yet. I love you.'

She still felt incredibly tense. Trembling, almost, as if she was still afraid.

So he kept holding her, until he could feel that tension ebbing.

And then, when she looked up to catch her gaze, he kissed her again.

'You need to go to bed, *tesoro*. You need to sleep.'

'I don't want you to stop holding me right now,' she whispered. 'I love you, too.'

'I don't have to stop holding you.' Matteo murmured, but his words were coming out without him giving them much thought at all.

Georgia had spoken so quietly he wondered whether he'd actually heard that last bit. Had she really just told him that she loved him? He wanted to ask if it was really true. If those barriers were truly vanquished. But that would make this moment more about him than Georgia, wouldn't it? If it was true, she would tell him again and he could be patient. Like his patience in getting closer to this woman he loved, it would be worth the wait.

'I could still hold you while you sleep, if you'd like that.'

And that would be all he would do. Just be there for her. Holding her. Willing her to believe that not all men were untrustworthy.

She was very, very still in his arms now.

And then she pushed herself up from the couch and stood there in front of him.

Her outstretched hand an invitation.

# CHAPTER ELEVEN

GEORGIA BENNETT HAD believed that the lovemaking she had shared with Matteo Martini on that moonlit night in the Czech Republic had been the best she'd ever experienced.

She had been wrong.

The, oh, so gentle, heartbreakingly tender physical connection they'd inevitably shared when she'd led him to her bed that night had been something so extraordinary she was still stunned a week later.

Maybe it was due to the cathartic effect of talking about her childhood trauma for the first time. Of reliving such painful memories and then to find herself being cradled in arms that made her feel so safe.

She had definitely been about to tell Matteo the truth about her pregnancy right then because she had felt too drained to think about the consequences. She had still had to summon her courage, however, and he must have sensed how difficult it had been because he'd tried to make her feel even safer. He'd told her that she didn't need to say anything else and she'd let herself believe him. Let herself fall into that safety net of his arms a little further.

Just for that one night, she'd promised herself.

She'd tell him tomorrow.

But tomorrow was always another day. Until today.

Georgia had known it was different from the moment she'd woken up at the sound of the front door of the cottage closing.

Something suddenly seemed urgent.

She was out of bed as fast as it was possible to be these days. Down the stairs faster than she should have, although she kept a firm hand on the bannister to keep her balance. She actually threw the door open, thinking she might have a chance to catch Matteo before he drove away, but she was too late.

'I'm too late,' she whispered aloud. 'What am I going to do?'

She paced the floor of the sitting room. It wasn't too late. She could tell him tonight. She would make dinner and tell Matteo how much she loved him.

And then she would tell him the truth about her pregnancy.

He was leaving to spend a few days with his family very soon and that might be a good thing because it could give him time to get used to the news.

With the decision definitively made, Georgia felt calmer. Not calm enough to crunch data and start writing up the first conclusions to do with her research project, however. She felt restless. Every time she sat down to try and work, she would think of something else that needed doing. Like putting the rubbish out and wiping down the kitchen bench and then—oddly—taking every single thing out of the fridge so she could simply clean the shelves and put it all back again.

She was nervous, she decided, when she was dusting the top of the bookshelf in the sitting room—a task that hadn't been done for so long it would have been easy to write her name in the film covering the wood. No. She was impatient. She was finally ready to do the thing she should have done a long time ago and the hours were passing too slowly.

She spent most of the afternoon out in the garage, which was used for storage rather than as shelter for cars. It had a few old pieces of furniture in there. And the chest freezer that there was no room for in the house. Over the last month or more, it had also been used as a place to hide the fact that she was collecting so much baby gear. Two bassinets. Two car seats. A small mountain of baby clothes and nappies.

It needed sorting. To see what else she was missing.

By evening, that big task was completed and the house had never been so clean and tidy. Maybe the smell in the kitchen wasn't on a par with Matteo's lasagne but it would be good enough by the time the steaks were sizzling and could add their aroma to the baked potatoes already in the oven.

Georgia's feet hurt after all the pacing about she had been doing all day.

Her back hurt, too, which was hardly surprising.

Not that it mattered. She forgot about any pain the moment she heard the tyres of Matteo's car crunching to a halt on the gravel driveway.

Until the moment that the handle of the door turned and he was stepping into the kitchen.

She couldn't think of anything *but* the pain then.

Because it had suddenly blossomed into a cramp that made her gasp aloud with its intensity. Made it imperative that she get hold of the back of that chair beside the little table so that she had some support and didn't crumple to the floor.

'*Georgie?*' She could hear the thump of Matteo's satchel hitting the floor. 'Oh...*no*...'

He must be able to see what she was feeling—the rush of fluid down her legs that warned her that her waters had just broken.

The pain was still blinding her and Matteo was making it worse by making her move. Half-carrying her into the sitting room and then easing her onto the floor.

'Don't move,' he told her.

Georgia covered her eyes with her hand. She couldn't move even if she wanted to. How could this be happening so fast, with so little warning?

The first contraction had barely begun to fade when another one started.

She heard Matteo's voice. Sharp, clipped instructions to the control room at the rescue base as he demanded an ambulance.

She *had* had warning, she realised, groaning aloud.

That restlessness hadn't been impatience to get her confession to Matteo over with. And that back pain hadn't been simply due to too much time on her feet.

Her doctor had even warned her last week, when she'd gone in for her antenatal check, that this could happen.

'*It's twins,*' he'd reminded her. '*They're very likely to come a bit early. Things are getting pretty crowded in there.*'

Matteo was crouching beside her now, a stack of the towels Georgia had refolded earlier today in his arms.

'The ambulance is on its way,' he told her. 'We'll probably hear the siren in no time at all.'

'I don't think it's going to get here on time.' Georgia was frightened now. 'I can feel something happening. Oh, my God… I have to *push*…'

'It's okay…we've got this…' She could feel Matteo's hands as she pulled her legs up. Ripping her clothing clear. Pushing *back*…?

Of course…he was trying to slow a precipitous birth to keep the baby safe.

Georgia tried to pant and slow things down herself but her body wasn't listening. Another contraction and another overwhelming urge to push so hard that she had red spots dancing on the back of her eyelids and a roaring sound in her ears.

It didn't drown out the sound of Matteo's calm voice, though.

'Almost there… You're doing great… That's *it*…'

And then another sound cut through the noise in her head.

The warbling cry of a newly born infant.

Georgia struggled to push herself up on her elbows.

'It's a little girl,' Matteo told her. 'And she's gorgeous. Look…'

He was holding her baby in his bare hands. A tiny, wrinkled red face was screwed up, ready to emit another cry.

'You've done it, Georgie…she's okay. Everything's okay…'

'No…' Georgia's head dropped back to the floor. 'It's not over… *Oh*…' It was her turn to cry aloud as a new contraction built. 'It's twins, Matteo…'

'*What?* How could you not have told me that?'

What she hadn't told Matteo was the least of her worries at this moment. This pain was unbelievably intense. Matteo's voice blurred into the sound of her firstborn crying. Her own cries. The faint background wail of an approaching siren…

Matteo had never been this afraid in his career.

He'd attended many births but this was so different, he felt like he had no idea of what he was doing.

He could see his hands doing all the things they needed to be doing but it was like watching hands that belonged to someone else.

His brain was detached.

Reeling…

*Twins?* How could Georgia have kept such important information a secret?

They'd become so close since she'd shared the terrible story behind that scar on her arm.

She'd wanted to tell him something else that night, hadn't she?

But he'd stopped her.

*Why?*

Because he'd known that whatever it was she had been about to say was difficult? That maybe she hadn't really wanted to tell him at all?

Again…*why*…?

Any baby was a miracle. Twins were something very special. He knew that. His sister had been doubly blessed with little Mita and Lia. It was something to celebrate, not hide…

Unless she had believed that, for some reason, it put her in jeopardy?

Somehow he kept his hands moving. The baby girl was small but looked fine. She was breathing well and nicely pink. He wrapped her in soft, clean towels to keep her warm and then turned his attention back to the arrival of her brother or sister. A breech delivery, this one, which kicked his focus sharply back into place. This one had to happen slowly. Gently.

He heard the sounds of the ambulance crew arriving, the bang of the door and the rattle of stretcher wheels behind him.

'Don't push,' he warned Georgia. 'It's very important.' He turned his head and spoke to the first paramedic to enter the room. 'Grab some cushions off the couch, please. I need to get her hips higher than her shoulders.'

'It's a breech?'

'Yep.'

'You're doing a great job, Georgie,' the second paramedic said, depositing an oxygen cylinder and pack of gear onto the floor. 'Couldn't wait for us, huh? Looks like we're only going to be a taxi to get you into hospital.'

Georgia wasn't listening. 'I have to push,' she groaned.

'Okay…we've got this…' Matteo cradled the tiny buttocks that were on the move. A boy this time… and…thank goodness, he was going to be all right. His tiny limbs were twitching as soon as his head was delivered, his chest heaving as he made the immense effort of sucking in his very first breath.

'I can't believe it's *twins*.' The paramedic who seemed to know Georgia very well had picked up the baby wrapped in towels. 'Good grief, champ, you're good at keeping secrets, aren't you?'

Matteo was lifting her son in his arms, ready to place

him skin to skin with his mother as the other paramedic clamped and cut the cord. His gaze snagged Georgia's.

Yes…she was good at keeping secrets all right…

'Are they full term?' the paramedic asked.

It felt as though Georgia was struggling to pull her gaze away from his but couldn't quite manage it.

'No,' she said quietly. 'They're nearly five weeks early.'

And there it was.

The ground seemed to be slipping away from beneath Matteo's feet as he found the answer to all those unanswered questions.

This was why Georgia hadn't told him.

Maybe it was also why he had shied away from allowing her to.

Because, even in the midst of the miracle of new life, it felt as if something important had just died.

The maternity ward of this old Edinburgh hospital was never really quiet.

Even in the earliest hours of this new day, there were sounds to be heard. The squeak of wheels or soft-soled shoes in the corridor, a phone ringing somewhere or a cry from a hungry baby.

That sound generated an odd tingling sensation in Georgia's breasts and took her straight back to the miracle of feeding her babies for the first time, less than an hour ago, up in the neonatal intensive care unit.

She wanted to be there now. Had asked that she be allowed to stay beside their incubators all night, but the staff had been kind but firm. She needed to rest. She could come back as soon as she'd had a few hours of sleep and, in the meantime, her babies would have the very best of care.

She didn't need to worry. Her babies were both healthy—just small enough to need their breathing monitored for a day or two. So she'd left them—those two tiny bundles, one with a soft, woolly blue hat and one with a pink one.

Not that there was any chance of sleeping just yet, despite an exhaustion like nothing she had ever experienced before. Propped up against her pillows, Georgia was floating on the sea of this huge new life, trying to catch and process everything that had happened in the last, tumultuous hours.

The fear that had come with that unexpectedly early and precipitous birth.

The fact that Matteo had delivered his own children.

The bombshell of him having to find that out in what was probably the worst possible way.

But all those things paled in comparison to the knowledge that she was now a mother. That her precious babies were healthy.

Her *babies*…

This room felt incredibly empty. The need to get up and go back to where they were was so strong that Georgia actually pushed the covers back on her bed and began to move, as she turned her head to look towards the light coming through the open door of her room.

Two things made her freeze.

One was the painful cramping in her belly.

The other was the silhouette of a silent figure standing in her doorway.

For a long, long moment, they simply stared at each

other. As her eyes adjusted to the contrast in light, Matteo's features became clearer and Georgia's heart sank like a stone as she saw how tight they were.

As frozen as her body felt right now.

He stepped closer. Just as far as the end of the bed. Into the gentle light from her bedside table.

And now she could see his eyes and that made it all so much worse because he looked absolutely...devastated.

His words, when he finally spoke, were quiet. Calm even. He was just announcing a fact.

'You lied to me.'

'Not directly...'

A soft snort from Matteo made her ashamed of even going there.

'You told me you were already pregnant the night that we were first together.'

Georgia swallowed hard. 'Technically, I was. At the end...'

'Stop this.' The flicker of real anger in his eyes sent a chill down Georgia's spine. 'I don't want to hear any more of your half-truths. You lied to me, even if it was just letting me believe something that wasn't right, and you know it. Unless...' He was closing his eyes as he spoke. 'Unless there was someone else at Rakovi? And you didn't know for sure who the father was? Is that what this cover-up was all about?'

'No.' That he could even think that was astonishingly painful. 'There was no one else, Matteo. It was only you. It could only have been you.'

And she wasn't only referring to the fathering of her

babies. Matteo was the only man she could ever feel like this about. *Love* this much…

His eyes snapped open. 'So these babies *are* mine, then.'

It had been painful enough when he'd been speaking with his eyes closed. This was way harder, being unable to look away from him and having to absorb his pain on top of her own.

'Yes, Matteo. They're yours.'

'You've been lying to me every minute of every day that I've been with you, then, haven't you?'

How could she even begin to try and explain why? Or to tell him that she'd just been waiting for the combination of the right moment and enough courage? That she loved him…

He wouldn't want to hear any of it. Not now.

It was too late.

'I'm…sorry,' she whispered.

Another huff of sound came from Matteo. The note of something like despair in it took her down to a new low.

'You've stolen something from me that I can never, ever get back.' There was a moment's silence where she could see that Matteo was fighting for control. 'The knowledge that my first baby was being born. My first *children*…' His control slipped and his voice cracked. 'I held those babies as they took their first breaths and…and I didn't know that…that they were *mine*…'

There was nothing that she could say. He was right. She *had* stolen something so huge it was unforgiveable. It made no difference at all now that she hadn't intended to. That even a few hours more would have changed everything.

The silence was unnerving.

'Have…have you been to see them?'

'Not yet. I had to come here first. To find out the truth.'

Not to find out how she was?

Did that mean he didn't care any more?

Had this revelation changed everything between them to that extent?

The emotion of everything that had happened today and what was happening now were becoming too much. A heavy weight that was pressing down on Georgia and making it hard to breathe. The fear that she was losing Matteo was the final straw and she had no resources left to fight the painful prickling behind her eyes.

She never cried.

But right now a huge, fat tear was slowly trickling down the side of her nose. *She* should be caring for those babies.

With Matteo by her side.

It was never going to happen, though, was it?

'I can't trust you.' The words were weighted with sadness. Disappointment. Heartache. 'You're the mother of my children and the woman I love but…but I can't trust you. You told me that you loved me… But maybe you lied about that, too.'

Georgia rolled her head from side to side, denying his assumption, but Matteo wasn't looking at her now. He was turning away.

And then she rewound the words she had just heard a little further. He could still say he loved her? A tiny flare of something like hope flickered in the darkness of her fear.

'Please don't go… Stay…'

Matteo shook his head. A single, sharp movement. 'I can't. I need time to think.' He stepped towards the door. 'And…I need to go and meet my children.'

Georgia nodded slowly. 'Of course.' She rubbed at the unfamiliar moisture on her face and started to slide off the bed. 'I'll come with you.'

She needed to be there when Matteo was with their babies. To share his first moment with them knowing he was their father.

Because it was huge. As big as their first moments in the world.

*'No.'* The single word was like a physical blow. 'I don't want you to come with me. I… I can't think straight when I'm near you. I need to do this on my own.'

She pulled in a shaky breath. 'Will you come back… later?'

The question seemed to surprise Matteo. He paused but didn't turn around as he reached the door.

'I don't know.'

The room had felt empty before, because her babies weren't with her.

It felt infinitely more empty after their father had left.

Another tear rolled down Georgia's face. And then another.

Maybe he would never come back…

She sank back onto her pillows, wrapping her arms around one of them because she really, really needed something to hold.

Exhaustion was bleeding into the darkness of this

empty room and softening the edges of the awful aching in her heart.

She could escape all of it, couldn't she? At least for a little while. She just needed to give in to this crippling tiredness. And maybe…when she woke up…she might even find it had all just been a nightmare.

They knew who Matteo was as soon as he arrived at the neonatal intensive care unit and introduced himself.

Somehow, that astonished him.

Georgia had been lying to him for so long and yet she'd announced the truth to the world by officially naming him as the father of these children? That she had was confirmed by the labels on the incubators he was led towards.

*Bennett/Martini: Twin One and Twin Two.*

Not that this public confession made any difference.

Not when she'd had a million opportunities to tell *him* and she had chosen not to. Matteo was still reeling. Trapped in the darkness of what felt like an ultimate betrayal.

'You can hold them,' the nurse told him. 'They're only in the incubators to make use of the apnoea alarms. Sit here and I'll take them out for you.'

Matteo sat in the comfortable armchair and the nurse lifted one tiny bundle and then the other, to place the twins in his arms.

'I'll leave you alone to get to know each other for a bit.' She smiled. 'But do you want me to take a photo first?'

'Not yet…'

He knew he wouldn't be able to smile. He might even have tears rolling down his face if the wash of emotion he was feeling right now was anything to go by.

This was…

Like nothing he could identify.

He could relate to it, of course. Like when he'd held Arlo shortly after his birth and had experienced that wave of love and pride for the new member of the Martini clan.

But this was so different.

These were *his* very own children.

He had just stepped into his long-held dream of being a father.

No. He hadn't stepped. He'd been pushed in such a dramatic fashion it felt like he'd been hit by a truck he hadn't seen coming.

But that didn't seem to be making any difference right now. He was here and…and it was…amazing…

He could feel the weight of each baby nestled in the crook of each arm. He could see their little button noses and wisps of dark hair from beneath the blue and pink hats. He could hear the adorable snuffling sounds and soft squeaks of tiny humans who were getting used to their new existence of living and breathing on their own.

They were only a couple of hours old.

And it didn't seem to matter so much now that he hadn't known he was their father as they'd entered the world. A lot of fathers missed the actual delivery of their children, especially when they arrived unexpectedly early. He could have known and then missed the moment by something as simple as being caught in a

traffic jam. Georgia hadn't stolen something irrevo-
cable from him because it wasn't making any difference to this bonding process. To this genesis of being
someone totally new.

A *father*…

The love he felt for these tiny beings was swamp-
ing him.

It was the most beautiful thing in the world but…
but there was a fear there as well.

The fear of something bad happening to them.

Matteo had always been protective of the people he
loved but this new determination to guarantee safety
was so fierce it was painful.

Did Georgia feel like this, too?

Of course she did.

She had probably felt like this from the moment
she'd known she was carrying these babies.

He'd seen the fear in her eyes that night, hadn't he?
When he'd surprised her by arriving to be Luke's best
man at his wedding.

She hadn't wanted him to know the truth because…

Because she'd lived her whole life being afraid of
her own father.

Would he break his own iron-clad rules of not being
dishonest if he thought it could be the guarantee that
would keep these precious babies safe?

Yes. In a heartbeat.

And Georgia had been right, hadn't she? Technically, she hadn't *told* a lie. She had done what he might
have done himself, if he'd believed he was protecting
these babies.

She had been prepared to walk away from the love

they had found for each other, if that had been what it took to keep her babies safe.

Did that mean he could forgive her?

Did he love her that much? As much as the love he was feeling for his first-born children?

An image of Georgia filled his mind. Sitting on that bed looking so pale and exhausted.

Looking as afraid as she'd been when he'd first arrived back in her life.

*Crying…*

She never cried. He should have taken her into his arms as soon as he'd seen that tear trickling down her face but, instead, he'd only been thinking of himself.

Of how hurt he was by the deception. How angry he was that he'd had the most important moment in his life stolen from him.

Matteo bent his head, to place the softest kiss ever on the forehead of his son. And another one for his daughter.

Nothing had been stolen from him. He had, in fact, received the biggest gift he could ever get.

He turned his head to catch the glance of the nurse.

He was ready to have that photograph taken now.

Then he was going to take the image back down to the maternity ward and show it to Georgia.

And he was going to tell her that he understood. That he had already forgiven her.

He just had to hope that she loved him enough to forgive him for his selfishness now. That there was a way they could get past it all and make this brand-new family what it could be.

*Perfect…*

They knew who he was on the maternity ward,

too, but the nurse who intercepted him wasn't about to make things easy.

'Georgia's finally asleep,' she told him. 'Please don't disturb her. It's really important that she gets some rest.'

'I won't disturb her,' he promised. 'Let me just sit in her room with her so I can be there when she wakes up.'

But the nurse shook her head. 'Go home. Get some rest yourself and come back in the morning. It's not that long to wait.'

It felt too long.

Matteo stood in the corridor of the ward, reluctant to leave by pushing his way through the swing doors. Not that he intended to go home. He would wait in the seating area near the elevators.

He still had his phone in his hand and it was a comfort to look at that image that had just been recorded of him holding those bundles that were his babies. His smile said all that needed to be said about how he felt. About how much love he had to give.

He could send the image to Georgia, couldn't he? Even if he wasn't here the moment she woke up, she could see that image and she would know that he was coming back.

Maybe she would even believe that he had already forgiven her.

But the text wouldn't send.

Oh…of course. He'd put his phone on airplane mode so that it couldn't interfere with any hospital equipment like IV pumps.

He flicked it back, but before he could try sending the image again he heard the sound of an incoming text. And a buzz that indicated a missed call.

Two missed calls…no, make that four…*five*?

What on earth was going on?

He went to voicemail and waited. Had his family somehow known what he hadn't known? That he'd become a father?

No. His sister's voice was anything but happy.

*'Matti? Where are you? Why aren't you answering your phone?'*

The stifled sob he could hear sent a chill down Matteo's spine.

*'You need to come home. Mama's in hospital…we think that she's had a heart attack…'*

It was easy to push those swing doors open now.

Not just to leave the maternity ward but to do so at a run.

# CHAPTER TWELVE

'YOU'RE GOING HOME? *Already?*' Kate sounded shocked on the other end of the line.

'The twins are doing really well. Everybody's happy that they're ready to go home. Sean's coming later this afternoon to collect us all.'

'But the house won't be ready.'

'It is. I ducked home for a while yesterday and took all the stuff out of the garage. And I've got the car seats and lots of clothes here. We're all set.'

'Where's Matteo?' Luke was on speakerphone with Kate. 'He'll be able to help.'

'In Italy.' Georgia had to squeeze her eyes tightly shut. Her hormones were all over the place now and it seemed that she was going to make up for all those years of never crying. 'His mother's in hospital, apparently. He sent a text message from the airport. A very brief one. I don't know what's wrong with his mother or anything.'

Luke was laughing. 'Yeah…he's always treated text messaging like a pager from work. Succinct information with no frills and nothing personal.'

'Yep.' The message was burned into Georgia's brain by now.

Heading to Italy. Mother in hospital. Back when I can. Need to talk.

'He's good with Skype, though. You could try that.'

No, she couldn't. She couldn't force a conversation on Matteo when he needed time to think.

When he couldn't think straight when he was near her.

That was one of the two things she was hanging onto at the moment—that he still had to have some fairly powerful feelings for her if it messed with his head that much. And that meant that there was still hope…

'Send more photos of those adorable babies,' Kate put in. 'And have you come up with some names yet?'

'Yes, I will,' Georgia promised. 'And, no, I can't think of names. My brain is mush.'

She had come up with a hundred names but couldn't make a decision. Because it wasn't just hers to make? And she couldn't send them the photo that had come with Matteo's text, of him with his babies. Not until they knew the truth and when they found that out wasn't up to her. It had to be Matteo's choice. Maybe if it had just been Kate she was talking to, she would have confessed everything but it seemed like Kate wasn't just Kate any more. She was part of Luke and Kate—an inseparable team. And Luke's first loyalties after Kate had to lie with his best friend.

The sooner Matteo told them the better, as far as Georgia was concerned.

She was over keeping secrets.

She didn't want to be the person that Matteo had been describing the other night. Dishonest. Untrustworthy…

Oh, man…another bout of tears was imminent.

'I'd better let you go,' she said quickly. 'It must be the middle of the night for you guys.'

'It is but it doesn't matter. Call anytime…and *good* luck.'

'I'll be fine.'

'Of course you will. Oh, but I do wish I was there to help…'

Less than two days later and Georgia was also wishing that Kate was there to help.

The home help for several hours a day that was part of her ongoing maternity care had left and she was, once again, alone in her house with the babies. There were still a dozen things she needed to do, like fold the overflowing basket of washing in the corner of the sitting room, put away the rest of the online grocery order that had been delivered moments after her home help had gone and check her neglected email and phone messages.

Georgia stood in the middle of the sitting room, pushing the twin pushchair both babies were lying in back and forth as she sang a lullaby. The singing was on autopilot because her brain was busy trying to prioritise her list. As soon as she could be sure they were really asleep she could do the first thing on that list, but after last night she knew she might have a lot less time than she needed so she had to make sure she tackled the most important task first. Maybe it was finding some food. She was *starving*…

And then one of the babies started crying.

Her daughter, who still didn't have a name.

Picking her up, she held her cradled against her

shoulder and tried to keep rocking the pushchair with her other hand.

Lucy? Katy?... Bella?

She liked Bella a lot.

But Bella Bennett? No, it didn't sound right.

Bella Martini sounded so much better.

And, just like that, her thoughts shot back to Matteo, along with a stabbing sensation in her chest that felt a lot like loss.

The baby was still crying, rubbing her face on her mother's shoulder, that tiny open mouth communicating as clearly as any words.

Georgia sat on the couch and offered her breast to the hungry baby, still trying to keep the pushchair rocking, first with her foot on the axle and then with a free hand once her daughter was latched on.

For a few moments at least, a blessed silence fell.

'He's coming back,' she whispered, her forefinger gently stroking the cheek of the baby she held. 'Your daddy. He would never abandon you. He loves you.'

She might be saying it simply to reassure herself but Georgia believed her words. Because of that photo. Because Matteo had looked so happy holding the babies. He looked like the proudest father ever. He might not trust her and he might even want to fight for custody of his children but, right now, that didn't scare Georgia the way she would have expected it to.

Because she had seen something else in that photo. That Matteo was experiencing that same kind of life-changing, all-encompassing love that she had been swamped with from the moment she had first held both of her babies.

Because she wanted him to be part of his children's lives.

She wanted him to be part of *her* life, in whatever way they could make it work.

How weird was that?

The complete opposite of what Kate had referred to as her 'hare-brained' scheme. The one where she gave up on men completely and was going to have a baby all by herself...

What would her mother have said about that?

Probably something like, *'Be careful what you wish for, love...'*

Tears gathered so easily these days. Maybe it was just hormones. Or maybe a dam had been breached that night she had told Matteo about the scar on her arm and she was going to have to release all the tears that had accumulated in the years of being banished.

If only she'd been brave enough to tell him the whole truth that night.

She was feeling a little bit sorry for herself at the moment, in all honesty.

She *had* given up on that scheme to find an unwitting sperm donor at the competition.

But look at her now...

Alone. With *two* babies. She'd been so happy to find out that she was pregnant. So confident that she would be able to cope. Still so determined that she didn't want their father having any influence on how she brought them up. Of being any kind of a threat.

But this was Matteo she was talking about.

And that was why everything had changed.

She loved him so much. And love like that had its roots very firmly buried in trust. Her heart knew that.

It was just that her head had decided to override it for far too long.

Rocking wasn't cutting it for her baby boy and within seconds whimpers from the pushchair became a heartbreaking wail.

She used her little finger to gently break the suction on her breast, feeling guilty as she did so. Her daughter's eyes were drifting shut and maybe she would sleep for long enough for her brother to be fed. But Georgia could feel how damp her nappy was as she laid the baby into the nest of cushions on the couch beside her and her eyes were open again. She might have fallen asleep on the breast but her damp bottom was obviously bothering her now. Or maybe she hadn't had enough milk yet?

She'd seen pictures of women breastfeeding twins at the same time but how on earth did they manage it? Surely the only way it could be possible would be to have someone else to help position them?

Both babies were crying now.

And so was Georgia.

She desperately needed help and she missed her mum so much it hurt.

She missed Kate, too.

But most of all she missed Matteo.

The noise level in this small house was so overpowering it was astonishing that Georgia could hear anything else—like the slamming of a car door. Maybe she noticed because it happened more than once.

Was it Sean, perhaps? Or some of her other friends from work?

Whoever it was, she wasn't going to be able to pretend that she was coping brilliantly but she could, at least, try. She pushed tangled tresses of her hair back from her face and then scrubbed at those tell-tale tear tracks.

She could hear voices outside now.

A firm, male voice, speaking in… *Italian*?

Georgia's heart leapt. Matteo was here.

He had come back…

But he wasn't alone. She caught a snatch of female voices, who seemed to be arguing with him.

Her heart dropped like a stone from the astonishing height it had just achieved.

This had been her worst fear, hadn't it? Having to face an entire family of angry Italians who were determined to claim their own.

Somehow, she managed to scoop both her babies into her arms and, as if they sensed the significance of what was happening, they both stopped crying as the door opened and their father walked in.

One look at the way Matteo was standing told her that he was as tense as he had been the last time she had seen him, when he'd come into her hospital room. And one look at his face told her that he had, indeed, come to claim his own.

The question that she couldn't begin to find an answer to, however, was whether *she* could possibly be included in that number.

'I need you to tell me something,' Matteo said quietly.

He had said that to her once before, hadn't he? In the car that night after Kate and Luke's wedding. When he'd been about to ask her if she'd already known she was pregnant the night they'd first made love.

And she had felt as if any safety barriers around

her had just evaporated. That she was standing on the edge of a cliff and the slightest wrong move would be catastrophic.

She was on that cliff edge again but this time the catastrophe would be if Matteo was going to vanish from her life, not insist on being a part of it.

'Were you telling the truth when you said you loved me?'

And here it was. An opportunity to tell Matteo the absolute truth and Georgia didn't hesitate for even a heartbeat.

'*Yes*. With all my heart, Matteo. From the moment I met you, I think. And for always…'

For a long, long moment he was silent, his gaze holding hers from across the room.

The corners of his mouth curved as if he was about to smile and, in that moment, Georgia knew that everything was going to be all right. Better than all right, judging by the way her heart was soaring again. She needed to learn to trust what she could feel and she wasn't going to let her head argue the toss about anything this time. Matteo still loved her. It looked as though he had even forgiven her.

But both babies chose that moment to start crying again and, at the same time, a sound from behind made him turn his head.

'I said to wait outside, Mama… That Georgie and I need to talk…'

'She can't wait,' another voice said, in heavily accented but perfect English. 'And neither can I.' A tall woman with a tumble of black, curly hair and a rounded belly of early pregnancy edged past Matteo and walked straight towards Georgia.

'I'm Adrianna,' she said, her smile lighting up her face. 'Matti's sister. It's so good to finally meet you, Georgia. He's told us so much about you.' Her gaze dropped to the bundles cradled protectively in Georgia's arms. 'Oh, Mama…you have to see. It's Mita and Lia all over again…'

'I have to find somewhere to put this lasagne. Matteo…where's the oven?'

'I'm sorry, Georgie,' he said. 'I tried to stop them. I said I had to talk to you first, and make sure you were okay with this…'

There were tears rolling down Adrianna's face now as she gazed at the twins. 'They're just *perfect*, aren't they?'

There weren't many people who could look at screaming babies who needed both feeding and changing and describe them as perfect, but the upward glance from Matteo's sister told Georgia that this woman knew exactly how she felt about her babies. And how stressful this was.

'Let me help,' she said softly. 'Please?'

'And me.' Teresa Martini was an older, smaller version of Adrianna. With the same smile that was brimming over with love. 'My heart was broken when I heard that you didn't have your mama to help. Don't blame Matteo. We couldn't let him come back without us.'

'But… I thought you were sick. That you were in hospital…'

'Pff…' Teresa flapped a hand. 'It was nothing. I'm fine.'

'They thought it was a heart attack.' Matteo had come close. 'And then that it might be angina. They kept her in to do all the tests but she *is* fine. It was something muscular, probably.' But he was looking worried. 'This is too much, isn't it? I knew it would be. I tried to tell them.'

Both women were reaching for the babies.

It should have been terrifying and Georgia knew that, if she wanted it, Matteo would tell his mother and sister to back off.

But it wasn't terrifying.

It felt like…family…

And if her babies were being held for a little while by a loving aunt and grandmother, then there would be nothing in the way of Matteo holding *her*…

'So… Isabella Kate, then? Bella for short?'

'*Sì*…'

They'd had to wait until they were alone together, after a taxi had been summoned to take Matteo's mother and sister to their hotel, to start talking about private things. Like how much they loved each other and how sorry they were that things hadn't been handled well and, of course, what they were going to name their precious babies.

It had taken too long but how could he complain when he could see how the first representatives of his family were taking Georgia and the twins into their hearts so willingly. Nurturing them with food and love and laughter and tears.

And Georgia hadn't been totally overwhelmed by this small invasion, even when they'd taken over completely and tidied the house by putting away groceries and folding washing while they waited for the lasagne that his mother had carried all the way from Italy to get thoroughly heated in the oven.

The meal could have been in a courtyard garden back home, with grapevines overhead and tired children sleeping in corners like puppies. A little bit of Italy in rural Scotland. The best of both his worlds because Italy was his homeland and Scotland was the homeland of the woman who was the centre of his world now.

Matteo blinked hard to prevent his vision being blurred by any tears. He stooped to place the softest kiss imaginable onto the swaddled bundle in the bassinet. '*Ciao*, Bella,' he murmured. 'Sleep tight.'

His arm tightened around Georgia's waist as he straightened. They both shifted their gaze to the neighbouring bassinet.

'And our son?'

'Bella was my choice. Maybe you should choose his name.'

'You've given Bella a name of your closest friend. Maybe he could be Luca? And Pietro after my father for his middle name.'

'Oh… I love it.' Georgia's sigh sounded like relief. She followed his example and bent to kiss their baby boy. '*Ciao*, Luca,' she whispered. 'You sleep tight, too. Please…?'

She was smiling as she turned back to Matteo.

'They're not going to believe it.'

'Who?'

'Kate and Luke. That we've named our babies after them.' Georgia's smile dimmed. 'They're not going to believe any of it. Kate's going to be so hurt that I never told her the truth.'

'She didn't know?' Matteo was astonished. According to his sisters, best female friends told each other absolutely anything.

'She knew I was having twins. She has no idea who the father is but I think she decided it was a New Zealand guy that we'd met the first night at the competition.'

'Yes…she told me something like that.' Matteo wrapped his arms around Georgia. 'Did she know about your father? The story about your scar?'

'No…' Georgia's response was quiet. 'You're the only person I've ever told about that.'

He just held her for a long moment after that. It made him feel honoured that she had trusted him enough to share something so huge. That he was the only person she had trusted this much.

'I don't really want to tell her now either.'

It made him feel even more protective, too.

'You don't have to. It's our secret now. Nobody has to know when, or how, I knew I'd become a father. Or that things were…difficult between us for a while. All they need to know is that everything is as it should be now. And the date for our wedding, of course.'

He felt Georgia go very still in his arms.

'You still want to marry me?'

He eased his hold so that he could capture her gaze.

'I knew that you were the woman I was destined to marry from the first moment I saw you.' His lips quirked. 'I didn't expect to have to fight so hard to win, mind you. I had to fight myself as well as you.'

Her face crinkled apologetically. 'I messed up, didn't I?'

'Sì…' But Matteo could feel his smile trying harder

to emerge. 'But I understand why. When I held our… when I held Bella and Luca for the first time, I understood how powerful love can be. How it can make you do things that you might never really *want* to do. How someone else's safety can be so much more important than your own.'

He tilted his head so that his forehead rested against Georgia's.

'That's how much I love you, too, *tesoro*… I want to keep you safe and love you. For always and for ever.' He swallowed hard. 'So…will you marry me?'

'Yes. A thousand times, yes. Or should I say *si*?' There was laughter in her eyes as she lifted her head. 'I'd already decided that Bella Martini sounded much better than Bella Bennett. I'm going to have to learn to speak Italian, aren't I?'

'You might even want to live in Italy. We have so many things to talk about but all I want to do right now is to lie down with you. And hold you. And never let you go.'

'You might have to let me go sooner than you think. You have no idea how much our babies love their food.'

'They're half-Italian. Of course they love their food. They'll be eating Mama's lasagne before we know it.'

'Mmm…' Georgia licked her lips. 'I might just go and eat a bit more of it myself.'

'I should call her. She will want to know the names of her newest grandchildren.'

'We should call Kate and Luke, too.'

They held each other's gaze. Matteo could see that Georgia was thinking the same thing he was.

That this was their time. A bubble that they would never have again. The first, amazing moments of believing that they could hold onto happiness like this for ever.

It was too special to share with anyone else.

They both spoke at the same time as they wrapped their arms around each other and sank into that closeness like no other.

'Tomorrow…'

\* \* \* \* \*

# MILLS & BOON

## Coming soon

### THE DOCTORS' BABY MIRACLE
Tina Beckett

"Tucker, are you okay?"

Kady's soft voice called him back from the depths. "I'm fine. Just didn't expect to have to hold her, that's all."

"I could tell." She linked her arm through his for a moment as they stood there on the curb, the noise of traffic and voices outside very different from the canned silence inside the hospital. "You were a good father to her. Don't ever forget that."

A sudden wash of emotion spurted from behind the wall, stabbing at the backs of his eyes and clogging his throat. Oh, hell. Not now.

He pulled his arm from hers, afraid if they stood there any longer, she would see.

"We did everything we could for her. So did her doctors." His cool businesslike tone had to be a slap in the face after what she'd just said. But it was all he could manage without the past pouring out in a very real way.

She gripped his arm again. "Hey, don't do that. Don't you *dare* do that."

"Do what?"

"Act like she was nothing more to you than one of your patients. She was our *daughter*, dammit."

"You think I don't know that? That I don't have to deal with what happened every single hour of every single day?" The dam broke and he turned, yanking her against him. "I remember the second she was born, the second she smiled. The second she . . ."

Then his lips were on hers, hand going to the back of her head and clutching her to him. Grief and want and need all melded together into a huge tangled ball that was impossible to unravel.

Kady seemed to understand exactly what he was feeling, arms wrapping around his neck, giving back every bit as good as she got.

And it *was* good—too good—the heat and pressure of her mouth changing the tone in an instant. He deepened the kiss, and a familiar stirring took place, reminding him that he could indeed do things. *Wanted* to do them.

With Kady and no one else.

Continue reading
THE DOCTORS' BABY MIRACLE
Tina Beckett

*Available next month*
www.millsandboon.co.uk

# LET'S TALK
## Romance

For exclusive extracts, competitions
and special offers, find us online:

f facebook.com/millsandboon

⊙ @millsandboonuk

🐦 @millsandboon

Or get in touch on 0844 844 1351*

For all the latest titles coming soon, visit
millsandboon.co.uk/nextmonth

# Want even more
# ROMANCE?

## Join our bookclub today!

'Mills & Boon books, the perfect way to escape for an hour or so.'

Miss W. Dyer

'Excellent service, promptly delivered and very good subscription choices.'

Miss A. Pearson

'You get fantastic special offer and the chance to get books before they hit the shops'

Mrs V Hall

**Visit millsandbook.co.uk/Bookclub
and save on brand new books.**

MILLS & BOON